Another Kind of Paradise

Another Kind of Paradise

SHORT STORIES FROM THE NEW ASIA-PACIFIC

Edited by Trevor Carolan

CHENG & TSUI COMPANY
Boston

16 15 14 13 12 11 10 09   1 2 3 4 5 6 7 8 9 10

Published by
Cheng & Tsui Company, Inc.
25 West Street
Boston, MA 02111-1213 USA
Fax (617) 426-3669
www.cheng-tsui.com
"Bringing Asia to the World"™

ISBN-13: 978-0-88727-684-2, paperback; ISBN-13: 978-0-88727-735-1, hardback.

Library of Congress Cataloging-in-Publication Data

Another kind of paradise : short stories from the new Asia-Pacific / edited by Trevor Carolan. — 1st ed.
    p. cm.
ISBN 978-0-88727-735-1 — ISBN 978-0-88727-684-2 (pbk.)
  1. Short stories—Translations into English. 2. Pacific Area—Literatures—Translations into English. I. Carolan, Trevor. II. Title.

PN6120.2.A56 2009
808.83'10895—dc22

2008048297

Printed in the United States of America

Credits

Cover image: Rudy Lechleiter, "Tiger Swallowtail on Fuschia" (1996).

Martin Aleida, "Dewangga's Pendant," copyright 2005. Originally published by Utan Kayu International Literary Biennale, Jakarta. Reprinted by permission of Martin Aleida, 2008.

Kong Bunchhoeun, "A Mysterious Passenger," copyright 2003. Originally published in *Mānoa* 16:1, 2004. Original translation by Christophe Macquet, 2003, in the feature "*Littératures d'Asie du Sud-est*"; and by Marie-Christine and Theo Garneau, 2004. Reprinted by permission of the author and translators.

Outhine Bounyavong, "Wrapped-Ash Delight," copyright 1990. Translation copyright by Bounheng Inversin and Daniel Duffy, 1999. Reprinted from *Mother's Beloved: Stories from Laos*. Reprinted by permission of University of Washington Press, 2008.

Mi-na Choi, "Third Meeting," copyright Mi-na Choi. Translation copyright 2003, by Trevor Carolan and Kwangshik Jane Kwon. Originally published by Kemongsa, Seoul. Reprinted by permission of T. Carolan and K. Kwon, 2008.

The credits are continued on page 244, which constitutes a continuation of the copyright page.

For Ivan and Evalina Kats, in memory
And for Robert Aitken, Roshi

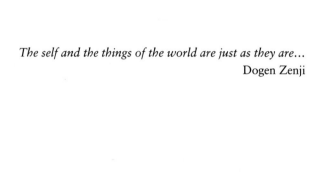

The self and the things of the world are just as they are...
Dogen Zenji

Contents

Acknowledgments

IN COMPILING A BOOK OF THIS NATURE, MUCH HELP WAS NEC-
essary and I am indebted to the authors, translators, and publishers of
the included works, and to the Research Office at the University of the
Fraser Valley which generously provided teaching release time for me to
complete this anthology. For their encouragement and valuable assistance
thanks are due to the late Ivan Kats, mentor and friend; Dr. Bruce Fulton,
University of British Columbia; Dr. David R. McCann, Korea Institute,
Harvard University; Prof. Michel Hockx, Head, and Prof. Justin Watkins,
School of Oriental and African Studies, London; Hanno Depner, Berlin
Literary Festival; Dr. Rosita Dellios and Dr. James Ferguson, Bond Univer-
sity, Queensland; Prof. Susan Kepner, University of California at Berkeley;
the ever-optimistic Frankie Sionil Jose, *Solidarity*, Manila; the late Sharon
Yamamoto, East-West Center, Honolulu; Dr. Jose Dalisay, Jr. and Dr.
Christina Pantoja Hidalgo, University of the Philippines, Manila; Anna
J. Allott, School of Oriental and African Studies, London; Kim Kadek,
Ubud Writers Festival, Bali; Nurzain Hae, Chair, Literary Committee,
Jakarta Arts Council; Dr. Farida Manaf, International Islamic University,
Kuala Lumpur; Sheila Leary, Director, University of Wisconsin Press;
Nola Accili, University of the Fraser Valley; Leza Lowitz, Tokyo; Adam
Williams, London; Jane Simon, Boston; Dafna Zur, University of British
Columbia; Mitsuyo Yoshimura, and Larry Li of North Vancouver; Dr.
Jan Walls, former Director, David See-Chai Lam Centre for International
Communication, Vancouver; Rebecca Bartlett, *Choice*; Ritu Menon,
Kali for Women, New Delhi; Esther Pacheco, University of the Philip-
pines Press; John McGlynn, Lontar Foundation, Jakarta; the librarians at
the University of British Columbia, Vancouver, University of Hawai'i at
Mānoa, University of the Fraser Valley, Simon Fraser University, and North
Vancouver District Public Library. Special thanks to Jill Cheng; my editor
Sue Warne; Prof. Paul Ropp of Clark University; the always encouraging
Prof. Frank Stewart and Pat Matsueda at Mānoa, Honolulu; Dr. Micheline
Soong of Hawai'i Pacific University, Honolulu; Frances Cabahug, research
assistant; Lach and Ann Loud for their hospitality during research visits to

New York; and for their patience and smiles, as ever to my wife Kwang-shik and our children Patrick Yung-Ho and Erin Yong-Ae. To all who contributed, many bows.

Aloha,

Trevor Carolan
University of the Fraser Valley
British Columbia, Canada

Foreword

NEARLY TWENTY YEARS HAVE PASSED SINCE TREVOR CAROLAN edited one of the first anthologies of new literature from Asia, *The Colors of Heaven*. Much has happened in the world, and in the world of books. What hasn't changed is the need—as important and urgent as ever—for books like *The Colors of Heaven* and *Another Kind of Paradise*.

In our work at *Mānoa Journal*, we have seen the results of literature's power to transform readers and societies. We have also seen its power to reach out to us, though appearing at first strange, exotic, or not relevant—bringing us all at once heart to heart and face to face with neighbors we had not recognized as our own kin.

Nevertheless, English language readers have yet to be given access to the rest of the world through the kinds of literary translating in *Another Kind of Paradise*—particularly from Asia, which we have neglected for too long, declining to join in the conversations taking place among four billion souls outside our linguistically gated communities, with all of whom we must learn to share this paradise or lose everything.

At a recent conference in Southeast Asia, American writer Barry Lopez noted the importance of what he called good conversations, especially conversations with people from other cultures and traditions. "Conversations are efforts toward good relations," he said. "They are an elementary form of reciprocity. They are the exercise of our love for each other, they are the enemies of our loneliness, our doubt, our anxiety, our tendencies to abdicate. To continue to be in good conversation over our emotions and terrifying problems is to be calling out to each other in the night. If we attend with imagination and devotion to our conversations, we will find what we need."

Like Lopez, the philosopher Kwame Anthony Appiah finds the word "conversation" a convenient term for the kind of reciprocity that can mark the beginning of understanding:

> Often enough, as Faust said, in the beginning is the deed: prac-
> tices and not principles are what enable us to live together in
> peace. Conversations across boundaries of identity—whether

national, religious, or something else—begin with the sort of imaginative engagement you get when you read a novel or watch a movie or attend to a work of art that speaks from some place other than your own. So I'm using the word "conversation" not only for literal talk but also as a metaphor for engagement with the experiences and ideas of others. And I stress the role of the imagination here because encounters, properly conducted, are valuable in themselves. Conversation doesn't have to lead to consensus about anything, especially not values; it's enough that it helps people get used to one another.

Such simple acts as getting used to each other may foster the kind of tolerance and acceptance that obviate the causes of communal conflicts: alienation and distrust. Conversations about stories, about narratives are a way of aligning our responses to the world with the responses of others, says Appiah. Because stories are often the repository of a society's values, good conversations about them may guide us toward an understanding of difficult community issues. Likewise, they may guide us to the reasoning behind the responses of strangers that otherwise would seem enigmatic to us.

What appears to be a simple story by a Vietnamese writer can be a staggering lesson in the clash between personal ethics and social mores. Reading such a story, we feel gratitude to the author for bringing us to the cliff's edge of morality and to the translator for enabling this moment of revelation. Through such stories, we are offered the chance to re-experience life, to exist among a different people without harm to them or their world. This is surely what we mean by world literature: writing that enables us to stay at home while traveling across temporal, cultural, and geographic boundaries. Reading this literature counters the ideas that the West is at the center of the universe and that its narratives of reality prevail over others. Reading world literature helps turns one into a world citizen.

And one further note about the importance of this book: over the past twenty years, we can be heartened that many more people in the West —including educators and publishers—have become aware that "world literature" has value; its definition has even come to include China, Japan, India, perhaps Korea, perhaps Vietnam, and one to two other countries; the best known of these nations have made efforts on their own to seek translators and publishers abroad. They are, however, but a few of the

Asian countries whose contemporary literary riches should be better known in the West. We at *Mānoa Journal*, who have been humble workers in the same vegetable patch of translation, salute Trevor Carolan for not only bringing many Asian authors together in this paradise of a book, but also—thanks to his intrepid travels, ravenous reading habits, and boundlessly inclusive soul (in league with the fine publishing house of Cheng & Tsui)—for managing in *Another Kind of Paradise* to present literature from nations seldom translated, such Burma, Thailand, Cambodia, Laos, Indonesia, Singapore, and Bangladesh. Truly these are keys to a mansion with many rooms.

An American poet once opined that poetry is what is lost in translation. But it might also be said that poetry is what is not lost in translation—that through the genius of particular writers and the skill of their translators, what is fundamental to our natures and transcendent of our limitations is saved. And this, of course, is as true of stories as it is of poetry.

The effort to write well, to be understood, to innovate, to celebrate, to comfort, and to protest—all are contained in this rich and transforming collection of voices from Asia. To read *Another Kind of Paradise* is—as Tu Fu said of being dazzled by the visual world and the world of literature—like living twice, though this is even better, because in these pages are many worlds within worlds, and we are each somewhere inside them pulling radishes.

Pat Matsueda
Frank Stewart
Editors, *Mānoa: A Pacific Journal of International Writing*
http://mānoajournal.hawaii.edu

Introduction

THROUGHOUT LONG HISTORY, THE ASIA-PACIFIC WORLD HAS produced a rich harvest of distinguished authors and literary traditions rivaling the canons from Western, Middle Eastern, or South Asian civilizations. Indeed, as the work of Thoreau, Pound, and Jack Kerouac, or the poetry of Anne Waldman and Allen Ginsberg reveals, the aesthetics of East and Southeast Asia's principal literary, humanist, and religious streams— Buddhist and Taoist especially—has been, and continues to be, a key influence upon North American arts and letters. Through such contemporary thinkers as Wendell Berry, Gary Snyder, Joanna Macy, and Fritjof Capra, this influence extends to our most critical environmental inquiries as well.

The diverse cultures of the Asia-Pacific are no longer unfamiliar to us. Through booming trans-Pacific migration, flourishing tourism, or media attention to East Asia's spectacular economic successes (and periodic implosions), most of us have heard at least some mention of the Confucian dimensions of Chinese, Korean, or Japanese society. Perhaps inevitably, the moral and ethical dilemmas that can arise from these Confucian underpinnings—which a generation ago might have seemed distant and exotic—are now comfortably recognized in the popular works of Maxine Hong Kingston and Amy Tan. Need we even point to the new significance of Islam within the societies of Indonesia, Malaysia, Brunei, and among key population groups in southern Thailand, the southern Philippines, western China, or the Pacific hub city of Sydney?

For all these reasons, the Asia-Pacific increasingly commands our attention: In the twenty-first century, we need to know more about it. In compiling a first major book of short stories in the 1990s from what North Americans commonly referred to as "the Pacific Rim," I noted that our very notion of "the West" arose as a symbol of differentiation from the cultures of Asia, and that the term *Asia* itself derives from a root meaning "alien." Times are changing.

With Asia's financial meltdown of the 1990s, the much heralded Pacific epoch seemed short-lived, giving way to the larger economic realities of globalization. The community of "Pacific Rim" nations now includes, among others, Peru, Chile, Mexico, Russia, Central America, Papua New

Guinea, Fiji, and a flurry of small Poly-, Micro-, and Melanesian nations in the South Pacific once heralded as Oceania and now often known amongst themselves as *Pasifika*. Understandably, a new term for the nations of East and Southeast Asia has also arisen, one that seems destined to stick: the *Asia-Pacific*.

As the stories you are about to encounter in *Another Kind of Paradise* confirm, things change quickly there. Few, though, could ever have predicted how swiftly the economic, social, and political recastings would tumble forth. From an educational perspective, we need new literary representations; hence this anthology.

As the stories in this collection reveal, social transformations are rarely wholesale. For reasons of stability and community accord, most often they appear as a kind of piecemeal shape-shifting. For example, the social roles of women progress and expand, but at different rates between city and country and among different generations and economic classes. Similarly, notions of marriage, divorce, and sexuality itself can vary in surprising degrees, even within what might ordinarily be regarded as conservative or authoritarian societies. And as the stories from Southeast Asia reveal, new economic opportunities afforded to rural dwellers may bring improved degrees of material comfort, permissiveness of speech, freedom of the person, and even rule of law, but not necessarily enhanced security or stability. Yet ideas of progress and modernity are still avidly pursued, even if the resulting conditions are seldom perfect. More often than not, however, and in a degree not previously witnessed in writing from the Asia-Pacific region, new social opportunities oblige authors to reflect upon the ties that bind the individual citizen to his or her family, community, and larger state.

Stories are perennial forms of entertainment and learning. In the Asia-Pacific they evolve out of village storytelling traditions; from professional tea-shop raconteurs, traveling actors, all-night puppet masques and shadow-plays; from native operas, epics, and myths; and from grandmother tongues. Still found widely in Asian newspapers, the short story has evolved as a variety of social commentary, one that thrives even under the omnipresent influence of imported consumer pop culture.

Well-crafted stories possess the ability to show us a country and its people up close, offering a poignant glimpse into the lives of characters at this time, and perhaps in an incalculable way for all time, in say, *uber*-urban Tokyo, sweltering Java, or somewhere in modernizing, hectic China. Good stories can shape a neighborhood or a moment in the life of a character who may appear uncannily like oneself. We can come to care about a character—about her or his fate—even within a society unlike our own. For as the strains of the Asia-Pacific's mature religious and wisdom paths profess, at the bottom of all collective individual experiences lies a deeper human interrelatedness, a basic existential interdependence that Vietnam's Buddhist variant calls *interbeing*. These stories reflect both everyday life and the changes taking place within it throughout the vast Asia-Pacific region. They are human stories we can give a damn about.

Perhaps the strongest element of this anthology is its reflection of how convincingly women writers have emerged throughout the Asia-Pacific. Traditionally, powerful women's writing excelled most notably during periods of Buddhist social and political influence, which women there still frequently regard as their golden ages, and names such as Lady Murasaki Shikibu of *The Tale of Genji* fame, Sei Shonagon of the celebrated *Pillow Book*, Sung dynasty poet Li Ching Chao, or early nineteenth century Vietnamese poet Ho Xuan Huong are of the highest distinction. Conditions for women of the Asia-Pacific world have varied enormously during local dynastic epochs, however. Since modern European contact with the Far East was established chiefly during climates of neo-Confucian sexual repression, Western images concerning the roles of Asian women have customarily, and not always correctly, tended to focus upon themes of subjugation. The educational and employment opportunities now available to urban women, along with national and international social mobility, has helped foster a generation of women authors who are determined to add to the body of international literature even as they work at refining the moral character and conscience of their own societies.

Given East Asia's remarkable economic successes of the past fifty years and the increased social expectations they have created, some of the material which follows may seem political, although this is not part of any overt editorial intent. Rather, these stories are an attempt to bring readers as accurate and engaging a portrayal of contemporary East, Southeast, and ancillary regional Asian life as can be deduced from a broad reading of many of its most gifted writers.

Readers will observe some notable differences in the literary approach of writers from the Asia-Pacific's different geographic areas. The rise and fall of writers and of literary trends throughout the Asia-Pacific reflects their national cultural sagas. Economics, education, politics, and an increased modern social engagement that is rooted in all three all play a role in this.

In nations where political struggle has been intense, national and artistic energies focus on the moral and ethical issues involved in cultural transition. In China, where writers have long been obliged to play safe politically and where the astounding pace of economic redevelopment is transforming the nature of urban society at breakneck speed, writers have begun to mirror these changes. As the selection by Hong Ying demonstrates, women authors in particular have been unabashed in rankling institutional political interests by following the lead of Japanese writers such as Amy Yamada and Banana Yoshimoto in addressing provocative issues of sexuality and gender roles. Other writers such as Yu Hua, whose work *To Live* has been transferred to the cinema screen by famed director Zhang Yimou, investigate questions of social mobility and the intoxication of China's young urban elites with western culture.

By contrast, writers in Korea have emerged from decades of bitterly concussive political turmoil and now feel secure in holding old injuries up for examination. For example, however tentative it may appear to western readers, Mi-na Choi's "Third Meeting" still strikes a disturbing note in Korean society. In helping to break down walls within the traditional Confucian concept of marriage that historically compelled women to live a kind of internal exile, its suggestion that a mother's emotional life can be more than that of subservient wife and child-bearer offers a soul-strengthening vision integral to feminist self-healing and genuine nation-building. Ironically, when material and social comfort is increasingly taken for granted by a generation spared the worst nightmares of previous military conflict, edgier psychological angles begin percolating into literary consciousness. Younger in flavor and inspired by novelists like Young-Ha Kim, for example, is a new kind of "bobo," or bourgeois-bohemian surrealism that floats beyond the political obsessions of earlier generations of writers. Yun Dae Nyeong's "The Silver Trout Fishing Network" is typical of this recent trend.

Japanese writers prosper through a healthy, well-established book industry, high national literacy, and literary craft traditions. But as critics there have often noted, the magnificent lineage of Sei Shonagon, Lady Murasaki, Basho, Issa, Kawabata, and Japan's other celebrated poets, diarists, and novelists has been cut off through the hybridization of a national literature that is periodically lamented as being no longer "purely Japanese." Perhaps the current renaissance of poetry in Japan has attracted many of the present generation's strongest writers, and there is evidence to support this, or other narrative techniques and voices have yet to evolve in Japan. Often interwoven from both indigenous and foreign influences, much recent fiction from Japan is self-consciously trendy and marked by a disingenuous pop cupidity, as if intentionally written for a presumed North American audience—a development that appears to be metastasizing among other younger Asian writers as well. Readers need not fear this from Seiko Tanabe's discomfiting portrait of relations between unmarried urban office workers in an uncertain economic climate. Similarly, in a breakout counter-movement to Japan's current literary cosmopolitanism, Shogo Oketani looks at Japan's recent past in searching for a coherent social grounding, one rooted in compassion for the "outsider" elements in society.

Whether through luck or sheer obduracy, writers from the Philippines have produced capable literary work for generations. Regrettably, as elsewhere throughout Southeast Asia, literature is still as much a commodity as an art form. Publishing remains a costly endeavor with a premium placed on producing saleable entertainment, thereby making it difficult for less commercial material to compete with imported mass market paperbacks. With the historic "writer as social conscience" beacon of late nineteenth century Filipino literary martyr José Rizal, though, Filipino literature continues to produce works of burning creativity in abundance, as the selections by Gilda Cordero-Fernando and Marianne Villanueva reveal here. With one of Asia's most avid cohorts of younger literary talent, the works of many others such as Lakambini Sitoy are equally deserving of attention.

In Indo-China and rural Southeast Asia, sketchy literacy conditions contribute to a publishing environment that is only now beginning to establish itself. Many governments throughout the region have routinely harassed authors of works deemed politically troublesome. Pressure has been exerted through direct threat or such indirect means as depriving controversial authors of state employment, notably in school teaching. As a consequence, for decades Southeast Asia suffered a chronic dearth of well-developed homegrown literature, but as the material that follows illustrates, this state of affairs is changing with encouraging effect.

What follows is a garland of discovery. Whether it be in the lack of posturing or the unconcern of these stories with fashionable pontification, what can be said of them is that as literature they are emblematic above all of writing from the heart.

"The Innocent" and "Storm Clouds over the Island of Paradise" address dilemmas of marriage and romantic entanglement. "Confinement" presents an uncommon view of family relations within Malaysia's Muslim society. "The Snuff Bottle" and "Pillow" are indicative of Asia's coming out of gay and lesbian writing, whereas "Bushouse" is a traumatic Filipino coming-of-age parable. In "Lizard" and "Nine Down Makes Ten," exacting portraits of feminist awakening emerge unexpectedly from Manila and Hanoi.

The phenomenon of recent large-scale Asian immigration to North America is examined through a single, awkward case in "Third Meeting," while "Arriving" emerges as an acute lens into colonial-era migration between India and Malaya. "The Python" by Nyi Pu Lay, an imprisoned writer from Burma, depicts new migration patterns—in this case the unspoken spread of criminal enterprise from a booming China into smaller, vulnerable client neighbors. In the late Thai activist author Samruan Singh's "The Necklace," a slice of life from Asia's indigenous hill peoples serves as a metaphor for the retreat of traditional ways throughout the Asia-Pacific world.

If perhaps one example is worth noting for exploring issues of raw *otherness*, surely it is Niaz Zaman's hauntingly beautiful "The Dance." Depicting an extraordinary and archaic fertility custom practiced when all else fails within Muslim society in Bangladesh, it reminds us that like neighboring India and Sri Lanka, this region normally visualized as "South Asia" increasingly commands our attention too, with an intriguing new geopolitical designation to embrace it—"the Indo-Pacific."

Throughout all these stories are illustrations of the joys and hardships visited upon daily Asian life as it adapts to new globalizing, cross-cultural influences. What is unmistakable are the elements of nativism that blow like spring winds through these works. This is the Asia-Pacific seen from the ineluctable perspective of its authors, inspired by life's small magic and injustices, by the breath of heaven, and simply put, by the music of what happens. The divisions, as they have been historically laid out, are between the Confucian cultures of Northeast Asia—Japan, Korea, China, Taiwan—and the warmer Buddhist and Malay cultures of the Southeast. Stories from the former are typically more psychological complex, probing, and structured upon family conflicts and love relationships. From Southeast Asia runs another current, easily mistaken for sentimentalism, but that more accurately is rooted in the region's historic spiritual concern with compassion for the hardships of peasant and lower working class life.

Within this anthology are also seeds of what the future may bring to writing in Asia. A new politically charged metaphoric style emerges in Xu Xi's "Until The Next Century," as the sensitive subject of Hong Kong's arm's-length relationship with China's administrative patriarchy hovers over the story. Other observers incorporate overlays from imported television, cinema, and pop videos. But whether looking forward or harkening back to colonial-era experiences, at the root of this anthology is the simple tradition of storytelling, the fundamental organizing ritual at the core of communal, agricultural life. It is in this that the writers of the Asia-Pacific plainly excel, and that elevates their works from quotidian documentary to meaningful discourse addressing both the individual's and their societies' moral and ethical dilemmas within the ongoing global crisis of spirit and meaning. As readers will discover, there is enlightenment here for the having.

Another Kind of Paradise

Seiko Tanabe ❋ *Japan*

Seiko Tanabe was born in 1928. She has enjoyed a long, distinguished career as an essayist and author of fiction. Widely known for her abridged version of the Japanese epic *Tale of Genji*, she received the prestigious Akutagawa Award for Fiction in 1963, and the Yomiuri Prize for Literature in criticism and biography in 1999 for *Dotonbori no ame ni wakarete irai nari (Since Parting in the Rain at Dotombori)*. Her story which follows, from a collection of the same title published by Kodansha, conveys the depth of her understanding of female roles within Japan's complex, shifting urban ecology.

The Innocent

Translated by Kate McCandless

"Hey!"

When Sachiko entered the lobby on the first floor of the building, Numata was sitting with his back to a wall mosaic. He spotted her immediately and called to her. Then he sprang to his feet. His dark face broke into a smile.

Since she had first met Numata, Sachiko had been unable to feel at all close to him. She wondered if it was because there was something lightweight about him. It wasn't physical agility or lightness of bearing, however. Perhaps it was more of a flippancy that made it hard to take him seriously.

That was it, seriousness. He didn't have the seriousness a man should have.

Somehow she found his flippancy strange and couldn't bring herself to like him. It's not that women don't like clowns and jokers, but not as objects for love and marriage, she thought. Her bad-mouth friends, Rie, Ryoko and that crowd, would have said worse yet if they could have seen Numata.

Sachiko was afraid it wasn't very nice of her, but she felt he was rather ludicrous and found it hard to feel any respect for him. The section chief at Sachiko's office had pushed her into meeting Numata, who had a university education and was now a high school Japanese language teacher. He also had a house his parents had given him. At thirty-five, he was a bit past the usual age for marriage, but he was healthy and came from a good family. It was amazing that such a man was still not married, according to the section chief, and it would be a shame for Sachiko, who was already twenty-seven, to miss this opportunity.

Right from the start Sachiko had only agreed to meet Numata to keep the section chief happy. But she was rather disappointed in him, and realized she may have had some expectations after all.

When she first met him, Numata looked like a slovenly old man. She didn't like that, to begin with. His small dark face wrinkled when he smiled. It was because of his health that he was a bit late marrying, his elderly aunt emphasized. To Sachiko he seemed like a man twenty years her senior and she remained unenthusiastic.

They had nothing in common to talk about. Numata talked only to her mother, explaining the Chinese poem hanging on the wall, and holding forth on various topics.

The night before, Sachiko had stayed up watching a late movie on TV to the very end, even to the last commercial, so she was terribly sleepy. She pretended she had to go to the ladies' room. There in front of the sink she gave a huge yawn. Looking in the mirror she was struck anew by the fact that she was a beautiful girl. She had to admit it to herself. That stupid section chief and his ridiculously stuck-up wife didn't understand how young she really was.

They were only judging her age by the usual standards of society. She actually looked no more than twenty-two or -three. She was small, but well-proportioned, and her heart-shaped, rosy face was as smooth and fresh as it had been when she was twenty.

Her slightly upturned nose and sweet, relaxed mouth gave her a seductive charm that put people at ease. When she was around twenty-four or -five Sachiko had quietly begun to make a particular effort to cultivate that expression. But deep within her was another Sachiko, of which even her old friends Rie and Ryoko were unaware.

Sachiko powdered her nose and returned to her seat. When Numata saw her, he raised himself slightly from his chair and put her drink, which had come in her absence, in front of her.

Even though he was of a suitable age for her, there was something unsettled in that insignificant gesture that was inconsistent with her impression that he was old and stuffy. It seemed unnatural. She had intended right from the beginning to turn him down, so she hadn't even taken a good look at him.

Numata was the one who had requested that they meet again. Her mother and the section chief seemed to assume their engagement was a foregone conclusion. Apparently the section chief was indebted to Numata's family in some way. Sachiko well understood that they were trying to conclude the negotiations tactfully without putting her off. She knew she couldn't turn Numata down point blank.

It was decided that they would meet for the second time alone, in the lobby of a building near Sachiko's office. It would be convenient because there were restaurants and a movie theater on the sixth floor. The section chief had arranged everything.

"I'm sorry I'm late. Were you waiting long?" Sachiko said as she pulled out her chair and sat down.

"No, no. You know the old saying, 'All things come to him who waits.' Ha ha ha."

Numata was clearly in a good mood. His entire face crinkled with smile lines.

How annoying! The conceited . . . thought Sachiko, but she smiled and looked out at the room, avoiding his face. She knew, though, that he was looking greedily at her. She also knew that the bright blue silk suit she wore showed off the gentle curves of her body, so she turned toward him.

"May I smoke?" he asked.

"Yes, go ahead."

He flicked on his lighter with one hand. "Would you like one?" he asked, holding out the pack in his bony hand.

"No, thank you."

"Really? There are so many women smoking these days. What makes a woman want to smoke, I wonder."

Sachiko did not reply.

"Besides curiosity, they must be trying to prove something."

"Yes, probably so."

"You know, the type that wants to show they're as good as a man and can do whatever a man can do."

"Are you a student of female psychology?"

"Well, I teach at a girls' school. That's all I know. But I do have a few romantic memories from when I was seventeen or eighteen. 'I once walked this road weeping. If I forget, no one else will know.' You must have such memories, too. The first love of your school years, for example?"

"I don't know what you're talking about. There were only girls at my school."

"Is that so? Such a pretty girl, didn't you have lots of men after you? You're particularly lovely today. 'Tonight everyone I see is beautiful.'" Numata was getting carried away with himself, and Sachiko thought his inserting lines of poetry in his conversation was nauseating. Maybe he was only trying to be funny, but she could hardly believe that such a pompous man could exist in this day and age.

"Last night I was reading a book of tips on dealing with women."

"Oh, really?"

"Would you like to look at it?"

"I don't like books much, anyway, but I really hate books that tell all about women."

"Oh. I thought if I was going to see you again, I'd better study up on female psychology. Better late than never, eh? You can't scold a student for cramming. Ha ha ha."

Sachiko was tired of being indoors so she said she wanted to go outside. Actually she meant to make her getaway before things went any further, but Numata said casually, "Shall we have a drink before dinner? Do you like beer?"

"Just one beer would be all right, wouldn't it?" he went on comfortably, peering into her eyes. "Come on, you can manage just a little, can't you? Just one beer."

"Okay."

"All right, we'll start with a beer."

He went on so about beer, beer, beer, as though it were something really special. But his persistence had the reverse effect on Sachiko. As her desire for a beer waned, her spirits sank, too.

Maybe this guy Numata had a strange talent for dampening people's spirits. He himself would be in a fine mood, talking away in raptures, completely unaware of the other person's feelings, while they became more and more depressed, forlorn and lonely.

"Two medium drafts," said Numata, after securing their seats in the beer hall. The place was starting to fill up, and the girl abruptly told him the price and held out her hand.

"What? Do I have to pay in advance?" Numata said angrily and reached into his pocket for his wallet, but he did it so slowly it looked as though he hated to kiss his money good-bye. This was even more disheartening to Sachiko.

"Oh, and we'd like something to eat..."

The girl ignored Numata's shouting and bustled off. Numata turned back to Sachiko self-consciously and said, "She wouldn't even listen to me. Cut me off, just like that!"

Sachiko smiled vaguely in his direction, thinking how enjoyable it would be to be there amidst the uproar of the beer hall, the bright lights and faces flushed with drink, if she were with her girlfriends, or Konno, or Kitazono, especially Kitazono.

The beer came at last.

"Okay, bottoms up, now. Drink up! Drink up!" said Numata.

He sounded to Sachiko like the magnanimous master of ceremonies at a lavish banquet.

"Drink up, now. Every last drop. I'll brook no refusal. 'The cherry trees blossom, but wind and rain scatter their petals, and we are loath to part.'"

Sachiko wished she could zip his mouth shut. She gulped down her beer and felt a clear passageway open in her throat. Her whole body was permeated with a golden coolness. Her parched throat was soothed and the flush disappeared from her cheeks.

Why am I brazenly drinking with this man, when I have no intention of marrying him, she wondered. It was strange. She had believed that she was doing it out of deference to her section chief, but maybe that was only a pretext. Perhaps she was really looking for security in a marriage to Numata out of an instinct for self-preservation. She was certainly paying attention to a man she wouldn't have looked twice at two or three years earlier.

Get hold of yourself, Sachi, she thought.

"Would you like some more?" Numata asked, a bit overawed at Sachiko's emptying her glass nearly in one go.

"Just a little."

Numata ordered another round.

"Oh, that's too much. I can't drink all that!" Sachiko protested.

"That's all right. Just have a little sip."

"Well then, if you insist."

Sachiko only meant to drink a third of the glass and stop, but she couldn't. The glass was so heavy she put it down halfway through, but she picked it right up again, saying, "I hate to leave this. Do you mind if I finish it?" and emptied the glass.

Numata handed her his own glass. "I don't believe this. You're really something, aren't you." He chuckled.

His tone was intimate. Perhaps he'd felt he'd seen a new side to Sachiko in the Osaka dialect that flowed so smoothly from her tongue. His countenance was ecstatic as he continued, "You don't have to worry. I'll see you home."

"Oh, I can't possibly drink this much. Please excuse me."

"No, I won't excuse you. You were hiding the fact that you're a good drinker, weren't you?"

"I wasn't hiding anything. You didn't ask."

"Ah, I do love Osaka dialect. Especially when a pretty woman speaks it."

"You've got to be kidding."

"I certainly am not."

"You'd say anything to flatter me."

"I like you when you're drunk. I'm a Tokyo man. But I think I'm getting to like Osaka more and more. If there are women like you here."

"Osaka's a filthy city. There's nothing good about it. And on days like this when the smog is bad, it's even worse. It blurs men's faces, so that they're all good-looking."

"Heh, heh, heh. You're in a bad mood, aren't you?"

"Don't touch me. It's catching."

Numata had reached for her arm trying to smooth things over, but she shook him off.

He was so annoying, she couldn't stand it any more.

"Have I made you drink too much? Are you all right?"

"Don't underestimate me. This much beer won't make me tipsy."

Sachiko was short, so she usually wore high heels, but a few beers were not enough to give her any trouble walking. She had a provocative way of swaying her hips slightly when she walked, anyway.

The words to the poem that stupid Numata had quoted when he was running off at the mouth before welled up in her like tears. "Tonight everyone I meet is beautiful." The ire was gone from her eyes as she looked through a slightly drunken haze at the busy street before her, as familiar as her own neighborhood, unexpectedly beautiful with its colors and lights blurred. She stood in front of a record store, pretending to be listening to a song and enjoying the autumn wind.

In the store, a record was playing, "Everything has changed now. Everyone has scattered." It played over and over. It seemed to be a popular song, and people passing in the street hummed along.

Sachiko wouldn't have stopped on a city street to feel the evening breeze two or three years earlier. Nor would she have stood quietly listening to a song. Now she felt as though she wanted to run after each disappearing moment and call it back. Her friend Ryoko had her work, Rie was married with a child, and even Kitazono was gone. And so were Konno and the other men she'd known casually.

Even as she stood there, Sachiko felt as though time and her youth were passing her by.

However, it wasn't a morbid sadness; it felt as though it was spreading slowly through her body. Perhaps it was her pleasant intoxication, but she savored the feeling leisurely.

Now she found her own behavior mean and disgusting, meeting a man she didn't even like, with marriage in mind, going out with him and coolly gauging his feelings so she could sell herself for the highest possible price.

She neither loved nor admired Numata. Perhaps she was only looking for a safe harbor for her uncertain voyage into the future.

I really am getting old, she thought.

She always used to think of herself as young, but now suddenly she was having such thoughts. In the old days, she had walked these busy streets joking and teasing with her friends, light-hearted and cocky, as though nothing but happiness awaited her in the future. These days, when she'd had a bit to drink, she became introspective, sad, and lonely for old friends.

Maybe she felt this way because of Numata.

He came noisily tagging along behind her. What was he going on about now?

"So, shall I take you home, now? I'd feel responsible, you know, if something happened to you."

"What could happen to me?"

"Oh, different things you're too innocent to know about."

Sachiko got in the cab, and Numata started to get in after her, but she said, "What are you doing?" and hit him on the head with her purse.

Whatever the cab driver may have thought, he pushed Numata out of the car with his white gloves, shut the door and drove off.

"You have to be careful. This town is crawling with wolves," he said as he drove. In the rearview mirror Sachiko saw a middle-aged man of forty-five or -six.

"Thank you," she said, feeling both relieved and anxious at the thought that her marriage negotiations with Numata were at an end.

Sachiko loved Osaka that night. She felt like going bar-hopping. The only person she felt like seeing was Kitazono. She had the cab drop her off in front of his apartment building and walked nearly two hundred meters around to the back to see if his light was on before going in.

He was there. He had set up a small folding table and was writing something. Surprised, he looked up.

"Do you want to go for a drink? My treat," Sachiko said.

He brightened. "No wonder your face is red," he replied, looking pleased and making no objection. "So, your treat, eh? OK, but I can't go wearing this." He went to change his shirt.

Sachiko looked around the familiar apartment: the bookcase, the small kitchen, the bare light bulb, the tattered cushions. The sight of his large awkward frame moving restlessly about the room made her feel like giggling. There was something poignant about his messy clumsiness.

"Oh, just wear anything. It's not like you're going out to seduce a beautiful woman."

"You *are* feeling good, aren't you?"

"I always feel good."

"I have some work I have to finish by tomorrow."

"Don't worry about it. You can do that any time. But I don't show up every night."

"Well, well," he said happily.

They went to a little place behind the train station where the two of them had always gone before.

"How's your work going?" asked Sachiko, warming her cup of sake in the palm of her hand. Beside her a glum, middle-aged woman grilled *kushi-katsu*. There was something apprehensive and insecure in the tentative way Sachiko held the cup in her small, delicate hands.

"Mm, good stuff." Kitazono emptied his cup in one gulp. It was sweet, intoxicating second-grade sake.

"Well, it's gradually improving."

"Really?"

Sachiko knew he was never one to brag or lie and felt a deep sense of relief. Her eyes grew brighter. She wondered if that was why he looked so cheerful before.

Kitazono used to work for the same company as Sachiko, in a different section. One cold night when she was working late and the heat was already turned off, she had taken a small flask of whiskey out of her brief-case and taken a swallow.

"Hey, good idea," someone passing by teased her.

"Have some?" Sachiko had to offer him some.

"You're not the kind of girl you appear to be, are you?" said the young man, straddling a chair and sitting beside Sachiko's desk.

That was Kitazono. From then on, they occasionally went drinking together. With him there was never any affectation or stiffness. They just drank and talked nonsense and went their separate ways. There wasn't the slightest sexual attraction between them.

Sachiko liked the simplicity of their relationship. She liked having a pleasant drink, then saying good night and parting without even a wave of the hand.

She had only found out that he'd left the company by hearsay, and if she hadn't run into him by chance in the subway one day they would have had nothing more to do with each other.

"How are you doing?" she asked.

"I've started up a company with three friends of mine."

"A company?"

"Well, sort of like an all-purpose advice service for businesses. I guess you'd call us management consultants. We trouble-shoot management problems for small to medium enterprises, and we do consultation and studies on opening a new store, or changing to a new line of business."

"Really ... does it look like you'll do well?"

The reason Sachiko asked so bluntly was that his appearance was so bedraggled compared to when he had worked at the office. But as she gradually questioned him further she discovered that at the same time he had quit the company, his brother had got married and he had taken that opportunity to move out of his parent's house.

Now he was living by himself in an apartment. Sometimes his mother would come clean up after him when it got too dirty.

"As for the business, well, we'll manage somehow or other," he had said.

Now Kitazono was enjoying his drink. There was a boxing match on the TV and all the customers were watching, so he was drawn in and looked up too. With his face as guileless as a child's he watched with pleasure as a Japanese boxer beat a foreign boxer.

Unlike Numata, there was nothing pretentious or preachy about Kitazono. He gave a decent answer to Sachiko's questions, and drained his sake cup to the last drop each time she filled it. He appeared to be thoroughly enjoying himself.

Sachiko felt more at ease with Kitazono than with any other man. She felt as though she would be quite content if he were to slip into the role of husband just as he was.

For a long time she had thought she wouldn't mind marrying Kitazono. He was about the only man she knew who wasn't unpleasant to be with. The feeling was somewhat like what she thought of as being in love, and somewhat different. But she didn't want some other woman to get him. Maybe it was love.

"Don't you want to get married?" she asked him.

"Huh?" His attention had been elsewhere. "I like drinking better." He laughed unselfconsciously.

"Women scare me. Not you, though. You don't lay on the femininity. It's a rare woman who makes a good drinking buddy."

"That's not much of a compliment to a woman."

"Yes, it is. A female drinking buddy has to be pretty. I couldn't drink with an ugly woman."

That exchange took place at the second bar they went to. It was an out-of-the-way drinking place. A young man in *geta*, wooden flip-flops, was making a long phone call at the cash register. The floor was concrete and from the mahjong parlor next door came the sounds of tiles clattering and chairs moving.

Sachiko felt her sense of self-esteem slipping lower and lower. She couldn't help feeling miserable. She didn't know what he'd meant saying she made a good drinking buddy, and a feeling of forlornness, like going around and around in circles, hanging in midair, made her wonder if her youth was passing her by. At that she felt a vague anxiety. She looked at the lights and colors along the shelf, the bottles filled with dark liquids, the shining metal fixtures on the counter, and her own image reflected in the mirror, and couldn't help feeling as though she had lost something somewhere.

Ryoko had worked hard to learn tailoring since she'd been in school and was now starting up classes here and there throughout the city. Her business was growing steadily.

Once Sachiko had hinted to Ryoko that she'd like to help with the business.

"So you're tired of being a secretary?" Ryoko turned to look at her through glasses that curved into points like a devil's ears.

"Yeah, I guess I am. I'm doing an about-face. This is my seventh year at it. I'll hit a slump soon."

"Well, sure you can help me but . . ." Ryoko thought aloud, her head to one side as though she were a bit at a loss. "To tell the truth, a former secretary isn't much good for anything else. Of course, I don't mean you, Sachiko," she laughed.

After that, Sachiko no longer spoke wistfully of making changes. Compared to her easy-going life as a secretary, even though that had its own hardships and pain, having to exchange ideas every day with a woman business partner would have been much harder. She couldn't have stood being a drag on Ryoko.

Maybe it would have been better if she had pursued a career like Ryoko or married young like Rie. But she had learned to like the taste of liquor, all too well. When a man tells you make a good drinking buddy, that means you've lost your looks and your youth, she thought, looking into the mirror.

"Shall we go? Want to have a drink at my house?" Kitazono asked.

"Okay," Sachiko replied. She took a few steps, wondering if she had drunk too much, but felt only a pleasant lightness. Her intoxication lay deep and stagnant inside her, but her head was completely clear.

After they had returned to Kitazono's house, Sachiko spoke as she took glasses out of the cupboard. "I went to a marriage interview today."

"Really?"

"It wasn't a very good feeling."

Kitazono was silent, looking sourly at the whiskey. When Sachiko tasted it, it was awful, not at all like before. It was the same whiskey, so it wasn't the quality. They must be getting tired, after all.

She wished Kitazono would do something decisive and put an end once and for all to this feeling of going around in circles.

If he was a man like Konno . . . she thought.

Konno was a heavy drinker and a playboy. He was the son of an electrical appliance store owner, but there was something magnetic about him. She always had the feeling she was being drawn in. She was afraid to see him. None of her friends or acquaintances knew about Konno. Both Ryoko and Rie were nosy, but neither gave any sign of knowing. Sachiko had carefully concealed his existence. She had no reason to think that anyone knew about him.

They had picked each other up like something you find dropped in the street. They went to a coffee shop. He looked tired. It was winter and he wore a red wool hat and a black ski jacket. He looked like a gangster, swaggering about with his cold, cruel eyes and rough skin.

He would come whenever she called him on the phone. It was like pushing a secret button and slipping into a secret room, a world no one else knew about. It was the kind of illicit relationship that is rarely discovered deep beneath the surface of the bustling city.

Looking at the city lights, Sachiko thought there must be countless relationships like theirs beneath the glitter. The words to the pop song she had heard earlier welled up in her. "Now everything has changed. Everyone has scattered." What she had had with Konno was not supposed to exist in this world. What she had thought happened only in novels and TV dramas had actually happened to her. What an innocent she had been. She didn't know what someone like Numata saw in her, but she felt like telling him, "I have many faces, you know."

When she was with Konno, she showed a side no one else had ever seen. She would cautiously ring the store. He'd say, "Come straight here. I don't want to go out to eat or anything."

"Yeah, we don't have to make up pretexts."

"Right," he retorted and hung up. He picked her up in a cab right on time, at the corner where she was waiting.

"There's something I want to talk to you about today."

"Uh oh, you've got me scared." Konno said, and immediately pressed his stomach with his hand and said, "You're pregnant?" Then he laughed uproariously. They often teased each other like that. They liked to pretend she was a young girl who had left home and been seduced.

"You never get enough, do you?" he would say in amazement and pat her buttocks. Sachiko was only half Konno's size, but her sexual capacity was much greater. She would perspire tiny beads of fragrant moisture.

One day, Konno said unexpectedly, "I'm thinking of getting married." Sachiko stopped in the middle of drying herself with a towel. Her skin was moist with perspiration.

"By New Year's," he continued.

"Who is she?"

"It's all been arranged. Are you mad? I shouldn't have mentioned it."

"I'm not mad. Go ahead and get married."

"Don't try and pretend you don't care."

At the sight of him sitting there smirking, Sachiko realized that she had been hoping to marry him eventually. It was so pitiful to contemplate that she turned away.

After that she didn't see Konno again. He was shameless and might come if she called even after he was married. A number of times when she was really lonely, her fingers would stray to the phone and she would start to dial the store, and stop halfway.

Now the whirring sound of the dial ran through her head along with the words to that song.

If only Kitazono were a man like Konno who would not hesitate to use force, she thought. He got up and opened a window for fresh air. Even though they had both been drinking heavily, they were unable to set aside their stubborn rational minds.

Sachiko flipped through one of his books without reading it and made no effort to leave.

Kitazono still stood facing the window, but suddenly he turned and said, "I've wanted to say this for a long time, but um . . . If you'd like, we could get married. No, that's no way to put it. I should say, please marry me. Before, my business hadn't come together yet. But now I think we could manage somehow or other."

Kitazono had returned to his seat and sat cross-legged looking down as he spoke.

"You don't have to think of it too seriously. Of course we'll have a ceremony and register the marriage. But I figure if you're going to get married, a woman you feel comfortable drinking with would be best. Isn't it more convenient to have a man and a woman under one roof? I'd do the man's work. You'd do the woman's work. And we'd spend the rest of our lives together. How would that be? Isn't that what marriage is all about?"

Kitazono was blushing right down his thick neck. He didn't have Konno's magnetic attractiveness, but there was a solid, reliable feeling about him. Sachiko was so happy her head felt funny.

"You're a smooth talker, aren't you?" she said with a giggle. She was starting to feel drunk.

"My business is talking to people. I'm used to it." Kitazono gave a wry smile.

"To tell the truth," he went on, "I've never been in love with you or felt like going around holding hands. But in the long run you're the only one for me. That's the truth. When my business got on its feet, I thought of you."

Sachiko stood up.

"Thank you. It's late, so I'd better be going. Do you mind if I think it over a little more?"

"Sure, that's fine."

When Sachiko got outside she wasn't sure if she could stand up. The streets were empty, so she set out walking, but she felt absolutely awful. She decided to go back to Kitazono's. He would look after her. But halfway back she could go no farther and squatted and vomited in the gutter. She clung to a telephone pole in solitary misery, her body contorted in pain.

What hurt her was Kitazono's saying he had never been in love with her. She wanted Kitazono to have the kind of desire for her that she had felt for Konno. At Konno's merest touch she had begun to tremble and tiny pink beads of perspiration had formed on her skin.

She had thought that's what love was. She and Kitazono hadn't even held hands. They'd both had plenty to drink and even then they couldn't touch each other and sat there soberly discussing marriage. She had been waiting for Kitazono to propose, but now that he had, she was left feeling bleak and disillusioned.

When she had finished vomiting, Sachiko realized she was crying, but whether it was from physical pain or mental anguish she did not know herself.

When Sachiko arrived at Ryoko's office, Rie had just got there. She was dressed from head to toe in an amber-colored ensemble and looked quite elegant.

"Sachiko, you're getting married at last?"

A student of Ryoko's brought in coffee for the three of them.

"Well, that's what I'd like to talk to you about."

Ryoko was in the middle of dealing in her brisk, efficient way with a constant stream of people coming in to ask her questions, but she paused and turned her chair towards them.

"Basically, Sachiko, you're too picky."

"No, that's not it. They just don't seem to take the bait."

"You're just not being sensible. You think you're going to be carried off in a jeweled palanquin. You keep holding out for the love of your life. If you don't hurry up and get married soon, it'll be too late."

"Well, thanks for the advice." Sachiko went straight to the closet as though she were well-acquainted with the room and came back with a bottle of brandy and three glasses. As she set them out she continued, "Ryoko, you have your work and Rie has her husband. I feel like you're determined to push me into this."

"Naturally! If you don't get married, you'll never understand life. And a woman's views on life change when she has children."

"I suppose so."

"It's no big deal." Rie spoke for the first time. She was the best-looking of the three. When she was in junior college she was always Miss this or that, but she got married right after graduating. Her speech, gestures and appearance were lovely and refined, but once in a while she'd make a remark that was quite shocking.

"Having babies is dirty!"

"Dirty?"

"Yes. Forget romance! When it comes right down to it, human beings are just like dogs and cats. Hmm, I guess your view of life does change." She spoke softly and slowly, holding the edge of her glass to her lips.

"Really!" said Sachiko, impressed.

"That can't be true. Doesn't having children give your life motivation? I'm going to get married, too, and have children," said Ryoko, lifting her glass. "After all, aren't a husband and children kind of like accessories? You can get along fine when you don't have them, but once you do, you'd be lonely without them," she asked Rie.

"Well, I don't know about the husband, but children are a good thing. When you consider I've never once wanted to stuff them back where they came from."

The other two burst out laughing.

"You mean you don't need a husband if you have children?"

"Well anyway, it's better then turning into a lush like Sachiko!" Rie slapped Sachiko's hand.

"You know, if you drink too much, and you have to have a Caesarean, the anesthetic won't work. Ugh..." Rie, who had had a Caesarean herself, spoke threateningly.

Sachiko laughed. "Don't worry. I won't let them try anything like that on me. I'll have a good, strong baby, naturally. I don't have hips like this just for show, you know."

"I can't listen to this. Please shut this girl up," Rie protested.

"Haven't you had about enough to drink?" said Ryoko, rather disgustedly.

Sachiko thought she might like to have a child. It would be Kitazono's child, too, of course, but at the same time she felt as though it would be hers alone. Perhaps having a child would wipe away the pain and misery of that night when she vomited in the street with the words to that song still running through her head. "Everything has changed now. Everyone has scattered."

The next day as she left work, her section chief called her over.

"Mr. Numata says he'd definitely like to proceed with the arrangements . . ."

"I have some reservations, so if you don't mind I'd like to let this drop for now," said Sachiko, lowering her voice. "I'm sorry to have put you to so much trouble."

"Hmm, is there some problem?"

"Well, you see, there is someone . . ."

"Oh, I see."

The section chief seemed awfully discouraged.

"You're such an innocent. I don't know whether I should say this, but you're not going to find another match like Mr. Numata."

"Yes, I realize that."

Sachiko looked down from the sixth-floor window at streams of traffic flowing smoothly and ceaselessly together without a sound.

She would probably accept Kitazono's proposal. But, she thought, she would have to be somewhat less innocent and more realistic. She tried to remember Konno's phone number, but suddenly it escaped her.

Shogo Oketani ✳ *Japan*

Shogo Oketani is a writer and translator living in Tokyo and Northern California. He is the recipient of the Japan–U.S. Friendship Commission Award for the Translation of Japanese Literature from the Donald Keene Center of Japanese Culture at Columbia University for his translation of *America and Other Poems* by Ayukawa Nobuo, published by Kaya Press. This story is from his collection of linked short stories, *J-Boys*, about growing up in Tokyo in the 1960s. A martial artist, he is married to the American poet and translator Leza Lowitz. They have one son and are the founders of Tokyo's highly successful Sun and Moon Yoga Studio.

A Day and a Half of Freedom

Translated by Ralph McCarthy

IT WASN'T RAINING TODAY, FOR THE FIRST TIME IN A WHILE. The clear, early November sunlight poured down on asphalt still dark in spots with drying puddles. Kazuo liked the feeling of the damp, warm air rising up from the street.

It rained a lot in autumn.

With each rain, the temperature dropped and the leaves changed color. Warm though it was here in the sunlight at the top of the hill, Kazuo could see scattered through the town below any number of trees that had begun to turn yellow or gold.

It was Saturday afternoon.

In mid-1960s Tokyo, kids went to school until noon on Saturday and most grownups worked at the office until two P.M. or so.

Saturday afternoon was Kazuo's favorite time.

Of course, everyone who worked or went to school loved Saturday afternoon—the start of a day-and-a-half of freedom. But what Kazuo especially liked was the atmosphere of the streets, the way time seemed suddenly to slow. Perhaps just the prospect of Sunday was enough to impart a collective sense of ease and luxury. The town, normally crowded

17

with people rushing about as if prodded by the second hand of some frantic clock, seemed to sit back and heave a great sigh, releasing all the tension and fatigue of the week. Kazuo often took walks by himself on Saturday afternoons, just to enjoy the feeling in the air and that sigh-like slowing of time.

Today, after a simple lunch of rice balls and miso soup prepared for him and his younger brother, Yasuo, by their mother (who'd finished her part-time job at the factory at noon), Kazuo had left the house alone, announcing only that he was "Going out to play!"

Now he was standing at the top of the hill of 4-Chome. The town, Ito-machi, comprised four fairly distinct sections: 1-Chome, the shopping district; 2-Chome, a residential area of old wooden apartment buildings and tiny houses huddled together; 3-Chome, with its small factories lining the muddy, polluted, and decidedly unlovely Tachiai River; and 4-Chome, the high ground, with its spacious homes and gardens.

Looking down from the hill, Kazuo felt like a bird hovering in the sky over his town. He wondered about the people living under all the little roofs that covered the level expanse below, and imagined what those he knew were doing. Back at home, Yasuo, having recovered from the disappointment of being left behind, might be playing at sumo with Father, who would be home from work by now. Mother was probably already starting to prepare dinner and looking forward to a leisurely evening with the family. Kazuo's best friend Nobuo, the local butcher's son, had perhaps been enlisted by his father to work in the shop. Or maybe he was somewhere else down there in the town, playing with other classmates. Everyone was enjoying Saturday afternoon in his or her own way.

Quite lost in his daydream, Kazuo turned his eyes from the sunlit roofs of the town to the foot of the hill below him. The reflected sunlight was at its brightest there. He heard the jingling of a bell and could make out, amid the glare, a figure beginning to move up the hill toward him. It was a man wearing a long-sleeved undershirt and a *hachimaki*—a thin hand-towel tied around his head. The undershirt was soiled and looked almost as old and battered as the man's knee-length work trousers. He was hauling a "rear-car"—a large, two-wheeled cart propelled by pushing on a handlebar in front—loaded with stacks of old newspapers. It looked like an awfully heavy load, and the cart was inching up the hill with all the speed of a snail.

Scrapman, thought Kazuo.

Scrapmen were familiar figures. They paid people a nominal price for old newspapers and magazines, beer and juice bottles, scrap metal, and the like. Whenever the weather permitted, you could find them slogging slowly through the streets, ringing the bells attached to the handles of their carts and calling out:

"Scrapman . . . Cash for scrap . . . Scrapman . . . Cash for scrap!"

It can't be easy, Kazuo thought, to bring a rear-car up a hill this steep—especially with load like that.

It must have felt to the man as if he were wearing leaden boots. For every step forward, the rear-car would drag him back half a step. If he eased up for even a moment, he might find himself back at the bottom of the hill.

Poor guy, Kazuo was thinking, when he noticed another figure behind the cart.

This figure was helping the man by pushing the cart from the rear. Judging by the size of him, he couldn't have been much more than Kazuo's age. Both of the boy's hands were on the back of the cart, his feet firmly planted on the asphalt. Kazuo hadn't seen him at first because of the stacks of newsprint, but with each laborious step the boy's head rose briefly into view. He was wearing a *hachimaki* just like the man's.

The kid seemed too intent on pushing even to look up. His white *hachimaki* bobbed up and down like a buoy floating on the waves. Even from up here, Kazuo could tell that he was giving it all he had, his body making a straight line from back foot to outstretched hands.

Ever so slowly the two ascended the hill until they reached the cross street halfway up. After parking the cart there, against a telephone pole, both the man and the boy removed their hand-towels and used them to wipe the sweat from their faces.

"Ah!"

As the boy leaned back and wiped his round face, Kazuo got a good look at him and gave a little cry of surprise. He felt as if he'd seen something he shouldn't and reflexively stepped into the shadow of the concrete-block wall beside him.

The boy was a classmate Kazuo had recently become good friends with. His name was Kaneda Minoru. Minoru, though born and raised in Japan, was of Korean descent.

He and Kazuo had become close after being placed in the same study group at school. The class had been divided into these groups by their teacher, Mr. Honda, who explained that the members of each group were to work together at various activities—performing science experiments, solving math problems, preparing current-event displays for the bulletin boards, and so on.

Minoru lived in 3-Chome, downriver from the factories, in a neighborhood of shacks with roofs of sheet iron. All his life, Kazuo had heard his parents and other adults refer to this district as "Little Korea." And he always noticed something strange about the tone of their voices when they did so. It was a tone that seemed to resonate with something like disdain, and something like fear.

But Kazuo had never had a clear idea of what sort of people the "Korean residents" were, or why so many lived in Japan, or even that Minoru was one of them, until a certain incident this past September.

That was when Minoru had got involved in a sumo-wrestling match with Takahashi Masato. Masato was a fifth-grader and the older brother of Takahashi Yukichi, the self-styled "boss" of Kazuo and Minoru's class.

Minoru was only an average student, but he was the biggest kid in third grade, and unbeatable at sumo. This must have bothered Yukichi no end. One day at lunchtime, he lured Minoru out to the sandbox in one corner of the playground, where his big brother Masato was waiting.

"Hey, Minoru," Masato said, glaring down at the younger boy. "I heard you said nobody could beat you at sumo."

"I never said that." Minoru lowered his head, looking ill at ease. "I just said I was good at it."

Early in the school year, Mr. Honda had taken time out to engage his new class in a discussion.

"As we study together in the year ahead," he'd said, "I hope to get to know all of you well. So, for starters, I'd like each of you to tell me what you do best. It doesn't have to be anything connected with schoolwork. Maybe you're good at drawing *manga*, for example, or you know everything there is to know about pro baseball players. Anything at all is fine. Everyone has a specialty, something that they can do better than anyone else. What's yours?"

It was then that Minoru had said he was good at sumo. (Kazuo, for his part, had admitted to knowing the day, time, and channel for every anime series on TV, which got him a big laugh.)

To Yukichi and Masato, apparently, that answer of Minoru's was reason enough to issue a challenge.

"Well, we'll see how good you are," Masato said. "Let's you and me have it out right here."

Masato moved to one corner of the sandbox and squatted down on his haunches, the way sumo wrestlers do before a bout.

This excited the curiosity of the other third-graders on the playground, who began to gather around.

Yukichi draped his arm over Minoru's shoulder in feigned camaraderie and gave him a sly smile. "Come on," he said. "Why don't you wrestle my brother, if you're so strong?" You could almost see what he was picturing: his brother flipping Minoru and planting his head in the sand.

"Well…just once, then," Minoru said. He still looked very uncomfortable, and his hesitant voice betrayed his lack of confidence.

Yukichi played the part of the referee.

"Square off!" he shouted, and the two contestants crouched, facing each other. When each of them touched both fists to the sand, the bout was on. Masato was the first to rise. With his right hand he grabbed hold of Minoru's belt, and immediately pivoted to throw him.

"Ah! Minoru's going down!"

Or so everyone thought. But in the next moment the balance shifted, and they saw Masato slowly falling backward. He ended up flat on his back in the sand. Minoru had used the fifth-grader's own move to push him off balance, then finished him with an over-arm throw. Masato jumped up, the back of his shirt covered with sand. He clucked his tongue and challenged Minoru again.

"I slipped, is all," he said. "One more time!"

The second time, Masato came forward with a flurry of hand-thrusts, in an attempt to keep Minoru from grabbing hold of him. But Minoru took the pushes and slaps without yielding any ground and finally got a grip on his opponent. Moments later, Masato was once again lying on his back in the sand.

Losing twice in a row to a third-grader was obviously frustrating for Masato. His face had turned bright red. "Once more!" he shouted and leapt at the younger boy. The result was no different. He was easily thrown once again.

All the kids in Kazuo's class, with the exception of Takahashi Yukichi and his sidekicks Ueki and Ozeki, applauded and cheered Minoru. Imagine beating a fifth-grader three times straight! But it was clearly unbearable for Masato.

He got up slowly, spat in the sand, and turned to Minoru. In a taunting voice, he said:

"Tsk! Who can wrestle with a Korean who stinks of garlic, anyway?"

At first, Kazuo didn't understand what Masato was trying to say. But the easygoing, always smiling Minoru transformed at these words. In the blink of an eye his round face narrowed into a fierce expression.

Everyone, surely, expected a fight.

Minoru was glaring at Masato, his mouth a tight, firm line, but little by little his features began to quiver. And then, standing there in the middle of the sandbox, he buried his face in the crook of his right arm. He was crying.

Relieved, perhaps, that Minoru wasn't going to attack, Masato jeered at the top of his voice:

"Korean creep! Korean creep!"

A little girl suddenly ran out from the circle of children and leapt at Masato, shouting:

"What's wrong with Koreans, you stupid Nip!"

It was Yanagi Hanae, a girl in Kazuo's class.

Just then a voice like a roar echoed over the playground.

"What are you kids doing over there?!"

Everyone turned to look. Mr. Honda was running toward them, his hair flying and a startlingly fearsome expression on his face

Mr. Honda was young and had only been teaching for about three years. He had a pale complexion and wore glasses and never seemed to get angry. Even when the boys in his class misbehaved, talking or making a disturbance during lessons, he never raised his voice. He would, rather, patiently and politely explain why it was inappropriate to cause trouble or disturb the class, looking into the eyes of each culprit as he did so. Though he never yelled at them or even used strong language, no one he looked at with those eyes of his could help but feel that what they'd done was wrong.

But right now, his face was truly scary. He looked almost demonic.

After sprinting to the circle of children, he stepped into the sandbox. Minoru was still crying, his arm across his face. Mr. Honda stood next to him protectively and faced Masato.

"What did you just say to Kaneda Minoru!" he shouted. No one could have imagined a voice like that coming from their always warm and gentle teacher.

"I called him a Korean creep," Masato said coolly. "He's Korean, isn't he? It's not my fault."

And now Kazuo witnessed something he could scarcely believe.

Mr. Honda's white hand flew up as if in slow motion—or so it seemed to Kazuo—and slapped Masato across the face.

Mild-mannered Mr. Honda had just struck a student, hard. Kazuo wasn't the only one who was shocked. A hush fell over the entire circle of students. Even Yukichi, the instigator of it all, stood gaping silently at Mr. Honda. And Minoru stopped crying and did the same.

"Aren't you ashamed of yourself, as a human being?" Mr. Honda continued shouting. "You're a fifth-grader, right? Where's the fun in picking on a boy two grades behind you? And don't you know how shameful it is to discriminate against others?"

Mr. Honda grabbed Masato by the arm and marched him off to the teachers' room. The remaining students maintained a stunned silence, as if they themselves had received the scolding. The same hushed mood prevailed even after lunchtime had ended and they were back in the classroom. No one moved or said a word as they sat there in their seats.

It was a while before Mr. Honda entered the classroom. His face seemed even paler than usual.

"First of all," he said, turning his gaze from student to student, "I must apologize to all of you. Today at lunchtime a fifth-grade student said something very hurtful to Kaneda Minoru. I lost my temper and struck him. There is no excuse for *ever* resorting to violence like that. It was the wrong thing to do, and I apologize."

He bowed deeply to the class.

"But I would like you to understand why I got so angry," he said and turned to write two Chinese characters on the blackboard.

"This is how you write *sabetsu*—discrimination. Discrimination is when you make fun of someone, or look down on them, because of the color of their skin, their nationality, their appearance, and so on. It's the worst and most shameful thing a human being can do. I was angry with that fifth-grader because he discriminated against Minoru, making fun of him because of his nationality. Minoru's country of origin is not officially Japan, but our neighbor North Korea. Or, more properly, the Democratic People's Republic of Korea. And he's not the only student in this school, and in this class, whose nationality is South Korean or North Korean."

Kazuo thought that Hanae must be one of these other students the teacher was referring to. When Minoru had started to cry, Hanae alone had leapt at Masato. A girl taking on a big fifth-grade boy all by herself—Kazuo couldn't help but be impressed.

"Now then," Mr. Honda said. "Why do you suppose there are so many people living in Japan whose nationality is South or North Korean?"

He went on to explain. Before the War, Korea was a colony of Japan. A colony, he said, was a country under the military and political control of a foreign power. The people of the colonized country were treated like servants and often weren't even allowed to use their native language or the names they were born with. During the War, all able-bodied adult Japanese men were drafted into the military, which made for a lack of workers in the coal mines and factories and so forth. Many men were brought from Korea and China and elsewhere, forced to work like slaves, and fed and treated poorly. Many died. Women from the colonized countries, meanwhile, were taken to the fronts and forced to ... (Mr. Honda paused at this point to search for the right words) ... to take care of the Japanese soldiers. Who were Japan's "Korean residents"? People who'd lost their homeland. People, or the sons and daughters of people, who were brought forcibly to Japan, or who had no choice but to seek work here.

As Kazuo listened to the teacher's explanation, he became aware of a very uncomfortable feeling. It wasn't, of course, that he objected to what Mr. Honda was saying. He had heard his parents talk about the War any number of times. About how difficult life was then, with almost daily air raids and scarcely anything to eat. Millions had died in the atomic bombing of Hiroshima and Nagasaki, they told him, and thousands in the air raids on Tokyo, including the son of the couple who ran the neighborhood tofu shop. Kazuo had come to think of war as a very bad thing, something that brought untold sorrow and suffering.

But according to what Mr. Honda was saying, the Japanese too had caused their share of suffering, virtually enslaving the parents and grandparents of people like Minoru and Hanae. So many Koreans and Chinese had died, or lost loved ones—just like the old couple who ran the tofu shop had. It was terrible, Kazuo thought, but the cause of all that misery wasn't just some abstract thing called war, which you couldn't see or touch directly. It was, in this case, the Japanese who had done the unforgivable. The Japanese—which meant Kazuo himself, his parents and grandparents, and everyone they knew, including the very Mr. Honda who had just told them about their nation's wartime aggression. That was what was making Kazuo uncomfortable.

It reminded him of the uneasy feeling he got when he'd done something bad and had no idea how to go about making up for it.

From that day on it had been Kazuo's intention to treat friends like Minoru and Hanae kindly. Why, then, had he reflexively hidden from Minoru just now, when he saw him helping his father push that rear-car up the hill? Though his view was blocked, Kazuo could sense Minoru and his father still there, resting midway up the hill, and he was aware of a heavy, sinking feeling inside himself. A feeling like guilt, or shame.

Maybe, Kazuo thought, part of him had instinctively guessed that it would be awkward for Minoru to meet up with him. If he were Minoru, he reasoned, and met up with a classmate under these circumstances—helping his father the scrapman push a rear-car and dressed in what no one could conceivably describe as nice clothes—he would probably be so embarrassed he'd want to crawl into a hole and disappear. Maybe he had hidden because, without even thinking about it, he had realized that Minoru would feel ashamed, as if his secret had been discovered.

So it wasn't, he thought, as if he'd done something wrong. He had simply empathized with Minoru, and that was why he'd instantly ducked for cover. But, if so, what was this heaviness that kept seeping ever deeper into his heart?

No sooner had he asked himself this than it occurred to Kazuo that maybe it had something to do with what Mr. Honda called discrimination. He had been afraid of embarrassing Minoru, yes—but wasn't that because he looked down on Minoru's father for being a scrapman? Until now, Kazuo had been sure that he'd never discriminated against anyone. But wasn't that exactly what he was doing by thinking of the job of scrapman as an embarrassment?

He heard Minoru and his father begin pushing the cart again after their brief rest. They seemed to be proceeding along the level street that crossed the middle of the slope. Minoru's father was ringing the little bell again—he had ceased to do so during the steep ascent—and calling out "*Cash for scrap!*"

What if Kazuo, from the top of the hill, had called down to Minoru as he rested, greeting him with the usual "Hey, Minoru! How's it going?"

Maybe Minoru would have waved back cheerfully, with the usual smile wrinkling that round face of his.

Kazuo couldn't help seeing himself just then as petty and foolish for not calling out to his friend.

The sound of the rear-car's bell, and the voice of Minoru's father calling *"Cash for scrap!"* moved slowly away through the quiet Saturday streets. To Kazuo, it seemed that something in that voice was reprimanding him for his failure to do the right thing.

He stood there in the shadow of the concrete block wall, listening closely as the sounds of bell and voice receded into the distance.

Pham Thi Hoai ✻ *Vietnam*

Schooled in Archival Studies in Germany and hailed as one of the brightest stars in contemporary Southeast Asian literature, Pham Thi Hoai was born in Hai Duong province in 1960. An essayist, children's writer, translator, and author of short stories, ironically, she no longer lives in the country she writes about. While her stories are set in Hanoi and depict daily life there during the 1990s— a time when communist Vietnam was feeling the dramatic impact of *Doi Moi* in opening up its markets to international trade and investment—she lives in Berlin with her husband and child. In 1988 her first novel *Thien Su (The Crystal Messenger)* was published. Translated into ten languages, it won the influential Frankfurt LiBeraturpreis in 1993. Part of the post–Vietnam War literary generation that includes Duong Thu Huong, Bao Ninh, and Nguyen Huy Thiep, Pham Thi Hoai has proven herself unafraid to criticize the institutional communist party and the country's endemic corruption. As a consequence, her books have been banned in Vietnam. In *Sunday Menu*, her latest collection of stories in translation, she continues to address the anxiety of a people disillusioned by socialism and confused by the capitalist future.

Nine Down Makes Ten

Translated by Peter Zinoman

THE FIRST MAN IN MY UNHAPPY LIFE WAS SLENDER AND GENTLE, with an honest face. His was an honesty easy to find at any time, especially in people who have lived continually and without interruption in a sheltered environment. From an ordinary and uneventful childhood, to a college life, really no more than an extension of high school, and on to years as a government-employed technician, he displayed diligence, trustworthiness, and benevolence. It seemed that his was a kind of innate goodness, God-given and protected. It seemed that he had always been righteous and good, but in a modest way, throughout a life untouched by self-doubt. I often thought of his goodness as a small thimble of fire, incapable of contributing much heat to the world, but occasionally heartwarming,

27

though only in a symbolic way. And everyone, especially me, would strain toward this warmth; this effort would eventually become a habit and, later on, a moral imperative. Actually, by his side I could perhaps have lived the most suitable kind of life for a woman, in an apartment somewhere with that small flame. I'd give birth to well-fathered children and sit nightly clutching a ball of colorful wool, knitting colorful clothes, oblivious to self-doubt. Moreover, I would never fear unfaithfulness from him, as he could barely conceptualize adultery. But then I was too young, and I saw him as a sort of precious chessman, fortunate to have been moved by some unseen hand toward the safe squares and away from the violent battles. It seemed he would remain like this until a natural death finally seized him—and of course he'd remain honest, even in death. At that time, I considered my own birth some kind of cruel prank. I underestimated the size of his thimble of fire and failed to realize that his conventional honesty was no less believable than any other thing in life. Lacking skepticism, how could he understand science, art, religion, and in short, how could he understand love, which I considered the most fundamental craving for such a person as myself? I grew dissatisfied because he was too respectable and secure within his own respectability.

The second man was frivolous and merry, an urban child who had yet to go through the period of spiritual crisis characteristic of civilized society. He was crazy about music, from Beethoven to the Beatles, and possessed a good singing voice, but couldn't bear to practice. He also loved soccer and had a decent kicking foot but no concentration for workouts. Generally speaking, he had no concentration for anything, not even love. It's difficult to trust such a man, since it's never clear where the vectors of his personality are going. He seemed on first impression someone tremendously frivolous, one who possessed rare and peculiar notions of life, often puzzling to those who met him. His face was so natural it provoked suspicion, and I believed that under that wonderful skin lay hidden an extraordinary nature. How else to explain the perfect harmony existing between him and his environment, a final symbol of his capacity to live so deeply and so freely? But after only three sentences had been uttered from his lovely smiling month, this first impression quickly evaporated. He was one of a countless number of fortunate young men who live an unexamined life, not because of some conscious principle, but simply owing to circumstance—frivolity as a habit, as a way of life. He was frivolous in all details, and only details concerned him. His frivolity manifested itself in the care he took in striking a relaxed pose, and in the attention he devoted to celebrations, to feasting and to appearing knowledgeable; this all in the context of a larger existence that was not at all frivolous, but serious and substantial. At a certain age, those as extroverted and unaffected as he sink into the cloudy chaos of life's problems. Nevertheless, he was a person who brought me many pleasant hours, almost my happiest ever. I learned several important things from him, namely the discovery that I have a body and that it has a voice, a voice initially timid, then passionate, sometimes daring and profane, and progressively harder to please. He was the first man to show me that I am a woman, and for a long while after, how long I'm not sure, I remained grateful to this ordinary man. Life would certainly be impoverished if it lacked such merry and superficial men. Furthermore, he loved good food, and that truly is a worthwhile quality.

Man number three was around for less than a week but made me the most miserable. He was extremely handsome, so handsome that expressions of envy clogged the throats of those who met him. I immediately forgot who I was and experienced my first near-death state. After that I remained struck by a sensation both dangerous and seductive. This feeling has stayed with me throughout the remainder of my life, flooding and overwhelming smaller emotions, causing them to shrink and shrivel up. Recovery would demand a very large dose of optimism and an ability to adjust to new extremes. I knew that he was an inarticulate dullard, useless except for the ability to please the eyes, over-reliant on his unusually gorgeous appearance and frightfully uninteresting. But in his presence I completely forgot and forgave everything, although he was genuinely uncouth, foul and cruel. After one week, I abandoned my urge not to indulge my self-pity and cried like a child whose toy has been stolen before she gets a chance to play with it. He would continue to be so gorgeous and useless for his entire life, and I, throughout my life, would flee from the desire to give myself to him, tormented by the absurdity of God and of myself even more. That affair was perhaps my only experience with true platonic love, especially the time I timidly ran my fingers through tufts of hair so beautiful they seemed not to belong to him and then abruptly jerked away as if stung by an electric shock.

After that I had an old man, experienced and worldly. He was born into a family whose members had participated for many generations in great historical events. They were thoughtfully educated, upwardly mobile, skilled at rubbing shoulders wherever they went, and never ruffled by callous twists and turns of fate. His handsomeness had a majestic air, and his every gesture suggested a profound awareness of his own value. I lived with him the longest, more than two years, and I grew much during this period. He knew how to answer all of my questions, whether about politics, love, religion or the psychological taboos of bygone eras. He knew the way to sit cross-legged, drinking and composing poetry with literary friends; he was dignified and serious with academic friends, simple and easygoing with old women and children in the neighborhood, and brutish and cocky with the scum of the street. Many women revered him as some sort of idol. Old people found him loving and affectionate: he never said anything to hurt them. I enjoyed his generosity until it gradually became like a solid gold chain clamped around my neck. "What right do you have to be so generous?" I protested. And his answer suggested, "Just carry on with your life, little girl. You are still so small." Perhaps his brand of perfection was like a perfectly baked earthenware vase, adorned with brightly colored and well-proportioned designs; but its basic components, earth and rocks, originally loose, dirty and unformed, would remain essentially unchanged forever. In describing him, it's important to emphasize that he seemed profoundly satisfied with himself. Due to his advanced age and precious experience, plus a certain humorlessness, he did not dare or perhaps was unable to reject any part of the status quo. He gave me many things, or he almost gave me many things: affection to a nearly affectionate extent, warmth to a degree almost heartwarming. The whole of his perfect existence symbolized the limitless limitations of mankind. Not only did he unconditionally accept these limitations, but he used them to justify his behavior. He adroitly maintained a cozy family life while simultaneously offering his generosity to me. He explained that people are truly small creatures, fettered by their environment at birth and by various obligations as an adult. Thus they can maneuver only in a limited way and within the confines of some predetermined grid. I hated those grids and harshly mocked the way he struggled with his limitations. Up until the final moments, he still offered me a generous smile, and it seemed that compared with other men, he cared about me the most. Countless times thereafter, I longed to abandon my high-pressure work and relationships and run back to him, hiding my face in his solid chest and conceding that he has always been right. But I clicked my tongue and decided against it. This flexible man was considered exemplary by the successful members of society, but who really cares what they think?

Man number five was an idealist. He belonged to that breed of man not born for woman, money, or pleasure, and this made me curious. My curiosity, however, did not last long, for contrary to my expectations, he was insipid and shallow. His ideal world—to be brought about by struggle either to reform educational science, protect the environment, or reestablish a tradition of sarong-wearing among the ethnic minorities (what a big deal!)—perhaps could really exist someday. I never doubted its attractiveness, and sometimes, in a highly inspired state, he could transmit a bit of his passion and emotion to nonbelievers. But in general his view of life suggested a narrow corridor that was periodically repainted but remained cramped and dreary. In a calculating way, I studied and applied tactics of love, and bearing the costs of lost time and more annoyance than happiness, I contrived to probe the bulwarks of his idealism, to test its endurance. This plunged him into an overwhelming spiritual crisis. Friends took him to an emergency room, where his deeply self-tortured soul was inflicted with tens of thousands of units of antibiotics, and just because he could not choose between his love and his ideals. He was the kind of person who possesses only enough internal strength to devote himself to one thing at a time. Leaving the hospital, he embarrassingly thanked me and disappeared down one of his mysterious corridors, this one concerned with the public reform of morning exercises for people too physically unfit to work. However, my calibrated burst of love had misfired, and his ideals gave him an easy way out. That was the only affair in which I actively played the role of the seductress from beginning to end, and after he was gone I was genuinely sad and regretful. After thinking a while, it became clear that he had chosen his dreary and narrow world over me. A lesson for simple curiosity. But I must admit he was the purest man I have ever met.

The sixth man was extremely complex, almost irrationally so, in the context of this most poor and backward society. When I met him, he had achieved an undeniable level of prestige in the diminutive intellectual world of Hanoi, a place where one can meet the most famous people without a prior appointment and use intimate terms of address within the first moments of striking up a conversation. I immediately surrendered before him—this human labyrinth, this infinitely dimensional zone cluttered with the disorder of contradictions, ideology, experience and ambition. But I couldn't help wondering: Do all these interesting and complicated things really exist, or are they only an expensive and ultimately meaningless drama that people feel compelled to stage in order to cope with their fellow men and themselves? Conventional geniuses never seem to have personalities; who would dare say that Shakespeare, for example, was melancholy, bitter, or sharp-tongued? Therefore I concluded that my sixth man was no genius. He had too much personality and was too worried about his originality. His complexity seemed the natural outgrowth of the uncontrolled interaction between two currents. On the one hand was the traditional educational system, in which the value of everything—romanticism, historical method, even the slipping of cushions under the bed before a night of lovemaking—is fixed according to a guaranteed standard of truth, goodness and beauty. And on the other hand was real life: vivid, crowded, subverting all conventions regarding of tradition, undermining all ideologies, and naturally overturning all values. Because he was sensitive, he found it hard to overlook clashes between the two, but because he was at the same time intelligent, he refused to take sides. Gradually he found that the best way out was to situate himself somewhere above the fray and contentedly gaze down. Consequently, people who participated in increasingly public discussions claimed that in fact he systematically rejected everything. They were wrong. He was too complicated and lost in his own complexity to reject everything. However, he did become a somewhat legendary and original figure, and as people stood anxious and sweaty in his presence, time passed and I grew tired. During the time I lived with him, I tended to dwell obsessively on my own sadness. I uttered strange and often contradictory phrases, ate and dressed on purpose in a slovenly manner, and lavished praise on only those books that no one understood. When we broke up, I felt the world to be shallow and its people superficial. It seemed that I never received from this famous man a soulful kiss, meaning one both natural and pure. Afterward, I heard that he had become a radical moralist, preaching about the nature of three distinct roads: the acceptance of, rejection of, and escape from conventional morality. Later on he became a kind of popular sage, a dialectician who approached society's intricate problems through dialectical methods and by applying extracts of oriental and occidental knowledge. In the end he became a recluse, and in an unrelated development, the intellectual life of Hanoi contracted, and no one spoke further of him.

The seventh man brought me much excitement but also my moments of greatest uneasiness. He was not unusually attractive: short, with thinning hair and a small forehead. Only his voice was exquisite, deep, melodious and full of unforeseen contingencies. Upon hearing his voice, difficult-to-please listeners, even those impressed only by outward appearance, would be riveted and believe that before them was, if not a genius in disguise, some sort of otherworldly species of man, a being who used this earth only as a temporary dwelling. Or perhaps they would feel that this small man must deeply understand the quintessence of life, as if his existence had spanned scores of generations and consequently could draw on the experience of both ghosts and men. It was said that he followed nihilistic principles, but I didn't understand what this meant. I speculated that it was a unique philosophical idea that could never be fully grasped, or perhaps the final foundation of all foundations, or a mode of behavior reserved especially for those without virtue, those both unhappy and very lonely. But this man refused to advertise his noble misery, the pain he felt for humanity, the loneliness in his blood, or the weariness with which he experienced the age. On the contrary, his expression suggested contentment and freedom from worry, the capacity to accept or reject circumstances with equal ease; and sometimes he was simply difficult to read. His one fascination was with the brevity of human existence, and the only being who provoked him to fits of anger and an enduring sensation of confusion and helplessness was God. He considered God to be his only worthwhile rival and lamented the fact that the great one so rarely showed himself. It was perhaps the complexity of his relationship with God that fundamentally distinguished him from the mass of nihilists in the movement. Their lazy activism was habitually insignificant, and they always seemed prepared to shout "I've found it!" after taking only a half step out the door. It was not easy to label him godless, immoral, or relativistic, and finally one could say that he had a great sense of humor, his genius lying with his comic gifts. Many women went out with him. This small Don Juan was thoughtful and considerate toward them, and because of his skill in the various stages of love affairs, he earned a sultry reputation. After studying with him, many miserable women left, and turning on him, denounced what they had learned. I also left him, after admitting to myself that I was to remain a weak woman and would spend my entire life searching for strength outside of myself. In my present state of panic I dare not enter into his zone, a zone wonderful for creating poetry and philosophy but inappropriate for comforting the hearts of women. I'm afraid that I will forever grieve over this unhappy Don Juan, and I can drive away my sadness only by shrugging my shoulders and saying, "He was really pitiable: no emotion, no passion, no faith; in short, he didn't know what to live for."

The eighth man had the hair of a poet, the face of a poet, and a soul especially given over to poetry. Such qualities are found only in people who have a lot of time and no concrete obligations toward life. When engrossed in the rising and falling of his watery waves, and once acquainted with his passionate love of writing—swiftly, without semicolons—I began to understand that the most worthwhile obsession is an obsession that is actually independent of the object of fixation. The object is only borrowed as a pretext, a means, an environment, through which or in which the obsessed person can project his own eternal and essential hunger, thus fulfilling the requirements of death—the dissolution of the ego for something, anything, that exists independently outside of one's self. Perhaps that obsession should be controlled. At some point the most mundane catalyst, a skirt or a fallen leaf, is enough to provoke a series of captivating chain reactions, while at another time much more important objects will inspire only an absurd indifference. I did not know whether I was worthwhile or mundane, but this was not really the issue. I was grateful to this man and enjoyed the taste of his affection, despite a small stubborn girl within me who refused to cooperate. She said: According to this particular mode of obsession all objects are equal, and therefore I am no different from a potato or an ant, but if people like to manufacture an obsession by constantly stoking their own engine, then by all means they should go ahead. Gradually I learned to repress that obstinate girl and ignore my uneasiness with the difference between artificially produced obsessions and primeval obsessions. Let Proust distinguish between the two, or the column "Mothers Advise Daughters" in some women's magazine; I am interested only in my own obsession and its consequences. The most ironic aspect of its unforeseen consequences was that both he and I became pitiful victims of the obsession. It forced him to wait by every street on which I might pass, to pull me away from all activities, no matter how fundamental to existence: eating, sleeping, seeking work; it interfered with all my relationships, with my family, colleagues, friends, and expanded into all areas and times that I liked to save to myself. I no longer had my own space, time or lifestyle; my environment was upset, my psychological state was upset, my language went out of my control. The obsession was like a third character in a love triangle leading him and poking me in the back; it followed its own dizzying trajectory and changed obstinate people into slaves, oblivious to their limited abilities. In short, it swallowed us without chewing: he failed his examinations, unable to resist the rush toward inertia, and I turned blind, like a Chinese lantern at a festival. In this situation, people can't help but grate on and annoy each other. The demands of individual liberation eventually transform society into a mass of "I"s, each one desiring to control the others. This naturally provokes conflict. Exhausted after such a time-consuming conflict, he abandoned the relationship for the call of religion, but this new obsession exacted an even higher price. I returned to my original form of a potato or maybe an ant, and heaved a sigh of relief. I felt sorry for God or Buddha, as this poet would certainly grate on them. But perhaps those two gentlemen understand the essence of life better than I and can look beyond him.

The ninth man was a man of actions, few words, forthrightness, and pragmatism. He was intelligent, decently educated, and sensitive enough to appreciate the real value of such nonmaterial activities as wordplay, pipe dreams, fortune-telling, or making love. However, the road he chose for himself satisfied a predilection for certitude and controlled vigilance. He believed in no one, entrusted himself to no one and struggled to force life itself to bend to his will. His profound desire to conquer life was impressive, vaguely like Don Quixote's, both desperate and dauntless. He had held down many jobs, for many different reasons, ranging from the desire to secure life's basic necessities to attempts to secure glory and power. But he was rarely satisfied, as work never quite met his expectations. The only measure he took seriously was that of practical advantage, immediate material gain being optimal and the forging of useful future connections merely acceptable. He was strict and prompt in the repayment of debts. While people found him useful, they were often cool toward him because he was completely lacking in false ethics, those gastric juices that allow for the digestion of the inedible components in the relations between people. He promised little, yet was so helpful with my unhappy life's most pressing problems (more so than all the other men combined), that during those moments of satisfaction and gratitude I confusedly asked myself if this really could be love. And could women like myself have lost such confidence in themselves and in this difficult-to-understand era that we need such a love as this? He did grant me three things: first, because he was always so busy, he did not have the time to undergo a period of spiritual crisis, something that I had already been blessed with enough times before; as relations with women never took up his whole life, I enjoyed a notable degree of freedom; and third, with him I suddenly felt a daily sensation of being deeply and snugly attached to my life, a sensation that I had thought about many times before but never actually experienced. I grew stronger and more contented, and began to seriously consider the prospect of marrying him. Life with such a thoroughly practical man would certainly promise a measure of success, like entering into a contract in which each side does not sap the other's vitality, as often happens with those claiming to be madly in love. There is certainly some advantage in avoiding excessive closeness and coolly carrying out contractual provisions. At our final meeting, he said, "In all areas including marriage, I am always faithful to a single measure of value: practical advantage." And on considering this measure, he determined that I was not the one to satisfy his requirements. Now he must bear the responsibility for his heartlessness.

Enough. He was the ninth man.

Ku Ling ❊ *Taiwan*

Ku Ling is the pen name of Wang Yuren. He was born in 1955 and graduated from Taiwan University. One of the noteworthy personalities in Taiwan's literary scene, his work caught on quickly with the popular media for its willingness to lampoon political culture. In a nation where politics have been torn between nationalist Chinese yearnings for the mainland and a growing Taiwanese nativist pulse, his use of political satire has proven a successful means of treading through difficult ideological terrain. In "Lord Beile," the frequent references to Manchu culture hark to the last imperial dynasty overthrown by the democracy movement spearheaded by Dr. Sun Yat-sen. Ku Ling has been a middle school teacher, literature editor, freelance writer, and perhaps unsurprisingly, television talk-show host. He has published over twenty books in various genres and has won prizes for fiction, prose, and poetry.

Lord Beile

Translated by John Balcom and Yingtsih Balcom

"GOOD FORTUNE, LORD BEILE."

"Get up, you little brats!"

"As you command—we are your cringing slaves."

The three of us burst into fits of laughter. Lord Beile laughed too, showing his two yellow front teeth.

"Off you go! But if you get caught, don't tell the drill instructor it was me who let you out."

We took off. From the open window of the chemistry laboratory, several pairs of eyes watched with envy as we left the school through the side gate. It was a bastion of iron, like a prison—but those aren't my words. Our teacher liked to say, "Go ahead and play hooky, I don't call roll. But I don't think you can escape from this school—just look at the high fence, the barbed wire, the guards and the police dogs, it's just like a ..."

"A prison!" we said in unison.

"You said it, not me!" Pleased with himself, he turned to the black-board and began to write. We'd already crouched down and sneaked out the back door of the classroom.

The main gate was impossible, of course—it would be easier for main-landers to escape from behind the Iron Curtain—but that's easier than it used to be. What I should say is, it was more difficult than for a main-lander to get to Taiwan. The side gate, however, was watched only by Old Wang, the janitor. Provided we took the time to buy some peanuts and dried bean curd and spent some time in his shack by the fence listening to his crap, there was hope that he would be merciful and "let the oxen out to graze."

"I'm pure Manchu nobility—Yellow-bordered Banner of the Bahrin Left Wing. You know the bannermen, don't you? They're the Manchus. If Dr. Sun Yat-sen hadn't overthrown the Manchus, I'd still be 'a Lord Beile.'"

We couldn't help laughing.

"What's wrong, you don't believe me? See!"

I was expecting him to be like the last emperor and show us some sort of palace treasure, but he didn't. He rolled up his trouser leg and showed us his sock which had a big hole in it.

"You see how the nail on my little toe is one unbroken piece? Now, check yours; they're split, aren't they?"

Not sure whether to believe him, we took off our shoes. The whole room was immediately filled with a stink like a salted fish stall. "Look! It's true, two pieces! We all have two pieces!"

"Of course! All Han Chinese have split nails. Only Manchus like me have unsplit nails."

Our biology teacher never mentioned this. He just went on and on about things we never understood, like DNA and RNA . . . . In order to obtain our freedom as early as possible, we put up with the saliva sprayed out through Old Wang's yellow front teeth.

"I hate the Cantonese. Damn them! If it hadn't been for Sun Yat-sen, you little brats wouldn't have the right to sit in front of me. You'd have to kneel and call yourselves despicable slaves."

"The Manchus were overthrown for the sake of democracy!" said Ruffian, who loved to argue. One time, he spent the entire class arguing with our Chinese literature teacher about whether "man is by nature good or bad" until our teacher choked with anger.

"Democracy?" Old Wang lifted his head and drained his cup of rice wine. "Where is this democracy?"

We didn't know where democracy was, but we knew quite well where the side gate was. We took advantage of Old Wang's—no, "Lord Beile's"— good mood and sneaked out one by one.

It's true that school was boring, but it wasn't any more interesting outside. When we skipped school, we usually went to see blue movies at the King Theatre. Every time I watched one of those movies, I'd drool. Ruffian would snore and C. C. would tear off to the restroom. We watched so many we finally lost interest in them. Sometimes we went to the amusement arcades to play the video fruit machines, but we never had enough money and were always afraid of being caught by the drill instructors. Sometimes we even thought that it would be better to sit in Lord Beile's shack listening to his crap while he drank his rice wine and we drank cola; both were good with peanuts. His shack was right across from the Dean of Students' office, but as they say, the most dangerous place is also the safest. So as the days passed, the place became our rendezvous.

Once, on a sudden whim, Ruffian got worked up talking about how he was going to join the air force one day, boasting how he would fly an F5E and launch a counter-attack on the mainland. Hearing this, our blood boiled with righteous ardor.

"Attack? Attack your ass! What are you going to attack with?" was Lord Beile's blunt reply.

We were silent. Deep in our hearts our doubts were the same as his. According to *Jane's Yearbook*, Communist China had two hundred submarines. We used to have two subs; rumor had it that one couldn't submerge and the other couldn't surface. We had two others which had been purchased recently from Holland. Though we had historical examples like Shao Kang's resurgence or Tian Dan's recovery of the motherland, did we really think we could overcome such heavy odds?

"Attack, shit! Even Rambo wouldn't stand a chance against ten guys, he'd be trampled to a pulp!" C. C. didn't talk much, but when he opened his mouth he made a lot of sense.

"Will ... will the two sides fight, then?" I stuttered, thinking of the TV show "Ninety Minutes," which showed all those dead Iranians, Lebanese, and Pakistanis.

"Of course not," said Lord Beile with curt finality. "Both sides will just muddle along! Why fight?"

We all agreed with him. Suddenly Ruffian sounded the alarm. "Here come the drill instructors, let's get out of here!"

The three of us fled helter-skelter. I hid between the little shack and the fence and heard two instructors talking loudly as they passed by. I also heard Lord Beile murmuring to himself.

"You've got nothing to be cocky about! If you're so tough, why don't you go fight the communists instead of strutting around in front of these kids!"

He wasn't a nobleman for nothing, what he said really did make a lot of sense. If he had been in the Imperial Court, all civil and military officials would have knelt and kowtowed, shouting, "Lord Beile, we bow to your wisdom!"

We came to know about another side of Lord Beile the day he started wearing a Pierre Cardin shirt. We had skipped assembly and gone to his "lodge" as usual. Assemblies were a waste of time anyway. All we did was read aloud rules for youth—junk like loyalty, courage, kindness, and justice. As for making suggestions and complaints to the school authorities, it was just as foolish a thing as C. C. throwing money away on video games. One time, Ruffian stood up and made a vigorous protest against the school bus carrying more than ninety students at a time. His blood boiling, he spoke sternly from a sense of justice. The whole class clapped in support of him, but the teacher was unmoved. "Then you can walk to school!" was all he said.

That day, after shooting the bull for a while in Lord Beile's shack, we noticed he was wearing the designer T-shirt.

"Wow! Did you strike it rich, Lord Beile?"

"Did you steal a snuff bottle from the palace and sell it?"

"It's a fake, NT$150 just like mine."

Surprisingly, he got upset. "Enough. How dare you!" He took a wrinkled receipt out of his pocket. Wow! NT$1,600. It was the real thing. This made us see him in a new light.

"You guys assume that I'm just one of the last of the nobility, but I'm also a representative in the National Assembly."

I fell off my small bench; C. C. was doubled over with laughter and kept slapping his thigh; Ruffian ended up blowing the instant noodles he was eating out of his nostrils like a couple of worms.

"Stop laughing! Let me ask you a question first. Do you know how National Assemblymen are elected?"

"They are elected every six years," replied C. C., the most literate among us.

"For additional members, yes, but how about the senior members?"

"You mean those old representatives? The *Progressive Weekly* said there hasn't been an election in nearly forty years." Ruffian was very pleased with his knowledge. "When the old ones die, they co-opt new people! Shit!"

"Right! By co-opting, you see ..." Lord Beile rummaged around in his drawers and found a yellowed newspaper clipping.

"Of the votes cast in Lindong district of Rehe province in the National Assembly elections, Zhao Baiqi received five hundred thousand three hundred ... Wang Jixiang one. Aren't you Wang Jixiang?"

It was a stupid question. Lord Beile snatched the clipping out of my hand.

"Don't look down on me because I only got one vote. When the candidates ahead of me die off one by one, I'll be co-opted, won't I?"

"How did you get the crazy idea of running for the National Assembly?"

"At the time, I was idling back home and couldn't stand the idea that only the rich and the powerful could run, so I went to register. In the end I received only one vote—my own. Even my mom and dad wouldn't vote for me."

"Weird! Imagine getting only one vote and still being a member of the National Assembly! That's a miracle."

We really got excited. "When will it be your turn to be co-opted?"

"Soon, there's only one man left ahead of me now. You see ..." Furtively, he took a small rag doll out from under his bed. A name was written on the doll.

"This is him." He took a rusty needle and plunged it repeatedly into the doll's heart. "This is a secret Lamaist method which was used in the palace. It's very effective. If I stab him for forty-nine days, he won't stand a chance."

Then he laughed. In the shadows his face looked quite hideous. I felt a sudden chill and excused myself under the pretext of attending military training. Not long afterwards, Ruffian and C. C. followed me out.

As final exams approached, we seldom visited Lord Beile. One reason was that that last experience had made us uncomfortable. Ruffian was always a vociferous critic of this or that. We used to think it was because he read too many opposition publications. But when we saw that our school janitor, an old deadbeat whom we knew so well, would one day be a great assemblyman, we felt uneasy. Another reason was if I didn't start working harder, I'd probably have to spend another year in high school, and that would mean forty or fifty thousand NT$ of my father's money down the drain—he'd skin me alive.

Though we rarely visited Lord Beile's "lodge," we heard a lot about him. First he refused to clean the toilets and had a big fight with the director of general affairs over it. Later he put in a request to be allocated staff quarters. School janitors usually live in illegally constructed shanties or in some space under the stairs. Naturally, our wise principal could not set such a bad precedent and this led to another big row. Finally he made a sign out of a board and hung it over his door. The sign, which was untidily written, read: "Office of Wang Jixiang, First National Assemblyman." The school administrators met and voted unanimously to fire him. He stood in his doorway shouting, defending his shack. He drew quite a crowd of students.

"Kick me out? Easier said than done! You ungrateful Taiwanese! If we hadn't brought those 900,000 taels of gold with us, would you be so well off today? Don't look down on me, you dogs, I'll be a National Assemblyman soon! I'll make eighty or ninety thousand a month, and for doing nothing, do you understand? When presidential elections come around, I'll get another two hundred thousand and I'll be given a house, do you understand? Kick me out? Damn it. When the time comes, I'll be back to make an inspection and you'll all be finished. Understand?" He went on and on, his voice growing slurred until one could only make out "Do you understand? Do you understand?" like a peeping bird.

Lord Beile was, after all, a blue-blooded nobleman with a powerful future ahead of him. In the end, the school couldn't fire him, nor did they give him any work. There were other janitors to take up the slack, so they ended up working an extra hour each day.

"It's human nature to be sympathetic. I feel sorry for him because he's old and alone. What does he mean by the National Assembly? Do you think I'm afraid of someone who has delusions about being a member of the National Assembly? He's just an old ..." Fortunately, before he could finish, the principal was stopped by a warning tug on his suit from the director of general affairs. In class, our teacher repeated what the principal had said. When he got to the point where the principal had stopped, in one voice we all added, "old thief." We were so loud that the drill instructor came running in. "What's wrong? What's wrong? Where's the thief?"

The flame trees bloomed and the blossoms fell. We finished our final exams. When the last bell rang, everyone pushed and shoved, jostling to be the first out of school. The three of us, who were always sneaking off campus, now for some reason were reluctant to leave. We strolled around the school. Ruffian didn't break all the windows on campus as he had vowed to do on the last day of school. Even the drill instructor whom we hated most had become friendly all of a sudden and came over to say hello.

"That's strange, didn't we swear we were going to get him?" said C. C. in a low voice.

"A smile melts all hatred ..." said Ruffian with a wave of his hand. He never liked to study, but he could spout such fine words. He must have picked them up from some martial arts novel.

I suddenly thought of him. "Hey, we haven't visited Lord Beile for a long time."

In high spirits, we ran to the snack shop, which was about to close, to buy peanuts, dry bean curd, dry shredded squid, rice wine and six beers— we were old enough to have a beer, now. We ran happily to Lord Beile's little shack. The National Assembly placard hung crookedly, and Lord Beile was sitting on a small bench outside without moving, staring blankly. His motionless profile was silhouetted against the setting sun, making him look just like the tarnished statue at the school gate.

We called to him several times, but he didn't answer, seeming not to recognize us. Ruffian waved his hand in front of Lord Beile's face, but he didn't even blink. "Don't bother him!" I softly placed the rice wine on the ground. C. C., who had gone inside the little shack, came out and dragged us away.

I turned back from a distance. Lord Beile still sat there without moving, biting his lower lip with his yellow teeth. He couldn't have looked worse if he were weeping. Suddenly I wondered if that was how the emperor Xuantong looked after he was forced to abdicate.

"Fuck! Do you suppose his sorcery backfired on him?" asked Ruffian, biting viciously into a piece of dried squid as if he had a score to settle with it.

"Nonsense! Look what I found in his room!" C. C. spread out a piece of wrinkled newspaper: "The last Assemblyman co-opted under the old regulations assumed office today. Old regulations to be officially discontinued."

"Ah—" Ruffian and I cried out at the same time. We suddenly realized it was already dark.

On the day of our graduation ceremony, the district police arrived at the school first thing in the morning. The drill instructors who followed on their heels seemed to have suddenly lost all sense of dignity and authority, and had a difficult time getting us lined up properly. It was utter chaos in front of the auditorium.

"Senior year, second class in the center. Dress by the center."

"All officials who have memorials to present, come forward now; if there is no business, we will retire ..."

The commands had suddenly changed; everyone burst into laughter. We looked up. Above the pale faces of the drill instructors, above the portrait of Dr. Sun Yat-sen and the words "The revolution is unfinished, comrades exert yourselves," was a man in a black robe, his messy hair in a small queue. He stood on high by the flagpole where we daily raised the national flag with its white sun in a blue sky on a red field. He was shouting in a husky voice.

"Lord Beile!" It was the old janitor, he must have gone mad.

The students were overcome with mirth. Everyone was so bent over with laughter that they couldn't stand up straight. Some got down on their hands and knees, shouting "Long live the Emperor!" Contrary to our expectations, Lord Beile actually raised his head and with a wave of his hand, said, "Ministers, you may all rise." This only provoked more pranks from the students. They rolled around on the ground, shouting: "Thank you, long live your majesty!" It was more chaotic than ever. No one seemed to notice the principal and the honored guests in suits standing in the doorway. Their faces were livid.

The drill instructors motioned to one another. One after another, they climbed onto the roof of the reviewing stand. Lord Beile made an effort to fend them off. Finding himself hemmed in, he retreated, screaming defiance. Finally, he leaped ...

More than one thousand heads looked up and more than one thousand mouths fell slack. "Ah—" All eyes saw Lord Beile fall stiffly to the stage with a thud in a splash of red and white. When I opened my eyes, I realized something entirely different had happened. Lord Beile had slid down the flagpole and actually landed on his feet on the reviewing stage. There was complete silence for a few seconds, then hearty applause erupted. For a moment he seemed stunned, then he smiled and raised his arms with a regal air to acknowledge the applause. But several drill instructors were on him in a flash, like an eagle seizing a baby chick. His thin frame struggled to resist as they dragged him away.

"Don't touch me! Martial law has been lifted. You soldiers ought to get out of here, do you understand?"

"I want to restore the monarchy! I'm a lord, I can have your heads for this, do you understand?"

"I am a legally empowered official. The country cannot survive without me in the Assembly. Do you understand? … Understand? … Do you …"

Lord Beile's sad cries grew fainter and fainter. After hotly debating the matter for a while, the students grew calm. As we filed into the auditorium in an orderly fashion, we heard our teacher murmur, "Why? Why cause such a commotion?"

I was suddenly overcome by a feeling of disgust for the teacher and no longer felt like attending the graduation ceremony. When he wasn't looking, I sneaked out. I went to Lord Beile's shack and saw that C. C. and Ruffian were already there.

Everyone was silent for a long time. "Where will they send him?" C. C. finally asked.

"To a mental hospital, maybe to Longfa Tang," said Ruffian in a dejected tone.

"Is he really a nobleman?"

"Nobleman, shit! He's neither a lord nor a member of the National Assembly. What's so noble about him?"

Seeing Ruffian so overwrought and C. C. so distressed, I recalled something they didn't know, something maybe no one knew. One afternoon, after I had done badly on a mock exam and turned it in early, I went to Lord Beile's shack alone. "Are you a real nobleman?" I asked.

"A nobleman?" He sipped rice wine. "You know in ancient times when an official presented himself in court he held a long, pointed tablet. Those tablets were usually made of jade. The side held away from him was white, the other side was used for writing notes so he wouldn't say the wrong thing to the emperor and end up losing his life. An official could avoid saying the wrong thing this way, but things like coughing and spitting just couldn't be helped. What did they do? They raised Pekingese dogs and carried them into court in their sleeves. If an official felt the need to spit, he'd spit in his sleeve and the little dog, which was well-trained, would open its mouth and swallow the spittle. That's the truth, no joke.

So spitting could be avoided, but what about farting? If an official ate the wrong thing for breakfast he might have the uncontrollable need to hoot while the emperor was talking. Since offending his majesty this way would mean execution for the whole family, what was a poor official to do? Of course there was a way: An official could shove a cork up his bottom before he went to court to prevent any unwanted sounds. He would be safe. Even if some sound did manage to squeeze through it would be . . . hard to hear. Of course if too much gas built up, it might be like when you open a bottle of champagne. The cork might shoot out."

I thought I was going to die laughing when I heard this, but he continued on in all seriousness: "Officials usually kept a number of these things on hand at home ready to use. Some were inlaid with gold or silver or decorated with carvings. They were more exquisite than snuff bottles. You know, they used to call these little toys 'bunghole stoppers.' Each time the foreigners invaded, the Empress Dowager Cixi would take refuge at her palace in Rehe province, escorted by hordes of civil and military officials. In the rush, many forgot to bring their 'bunghole stoppers,' but they still had to present themselves at court. What were they to do? Now that's business. My grandfather took to selling 'bunghole stoppers' at the palace entrance. Three for five dollars! Three for five dollars! Business was great!"

This was the real story of Lord Beile—I never breathed a word of it to another soul. After standing there dumbly wrapped up in my memories for what must have been a long time, I suddenly noticed the other two staring at me. I hurriedly changed the subject: "Well, what are you going to do now that you've graduated?"

"Pass the university entrance exam, study abroad, and later . . . we'll see." Even though he probably had a bright future ahead of him, C. C. looked very glum.

"I don't know yet, but I'm not going to be an F5E pilot, that's for sure," said Ruffian, in low spirits too.

"What about you?" they asked in unison.

"I . . ."

Originally, Lord Beile promised me that if he became a member of the National Assembly, he'd hire me as an assistant with a monthly salary of NT$15,000 for doing nothing. That promise now gone, I'd have to find some odd job or other until I went up for military service. I wondered if there was still a place where I could sell "bunghole stoppers."

Hong Ying ✸ *China*

Hong Ying, the pen name of Chen Hongying, was born in 1962 in Chongqing, Sichuan province. Her father was a boatman on the Yangtze River and her mother a factory worker. She began writing poetry in 1981, and fiction in 1988. A year later, she went to study at the Lu Xun Writers Academy in Beijing only months before the infamous June 4 Tiananmen Square massacre. As a result of her experiences, she published her novel *Summer of Betrayal*, which remains one of a rare few Chinese works to address that shameful tragedy. A graphic *cri de coeur* as notable for its expression of sexuality as for its depiction of political cruelty, the novel was followed by a memoir, *Daughter of the River* (trans. Howard Goldblatt). More recently, her erotic novel *K: The Art of Love*, based on letters and journals by the British poet Julian Bell, who taught in China and was killed in 1937 in the Spanish Civil War, became an international *cause célèbre*. In the novel, Bell has an affair with a poet named Lin, who teaches him the inner secrets of Taoist sexual technique. A legal dispute arose when a lawsuit was filed by a British citizen, claiming that Lin was based on her mother, the late writer Ling Shuhua. The Chinese government demanded an apology from Hong. Hong Ying refused to knuckle under. She continues to write and live in Beijing, tackling political and experimental themes, as well as gay and lesbian sexuality.

The Snuff Bottle

Translated by Jenny Putin

ON THE AFTERNOON WHEN THE BOY FAINTED, THE SUN WAS white hot. Each intake of breath felt like a puff of fire from a charcoal furnace. As his body began to sway, he held onto the telegraph pole for support, but it was too smooth and as everything in front of his eyes went black, he fell to the ground. After a few minutes, maybe less, he was aware of someone bending down and picking him up. He felt his feet knock against what seemed to be a door frame. They laid him down flat. Someone prized open his tightly clenched mouth and poured in a bitter liquid. After that his mind went fuzzy and he drifted off to sleep.

47

The door banged shut. The boy stirred. His limbs were weak and floppy and his throat was parched. He opened his eyes: On a windowsill was a stack of yellowing, string-bound books like broken bricks. A pungent smell of medicinal herbs permeated the room. The boy deduced immediately that he was in the old hermit's house down the flagstone slope. The old man knew how to take pulses and diagnose illnesses. Most of the people in the area went to him when they were ill. When they were well they never gave him a thought, but he never turned anyone away, stupid old fool.

The boy put one foot on the floor, then slipped on his sandals. The room was dark. Pieces of wallpaper, grubby and torn, were coming away from the wall. The few sticks of furniture—a bookcase, table, and bed—were old and the varnish had worn away except in the cracks, but everything was clean and neat. The boy had a good look around. Next to the bookcase were several large shelves fixed to the wall. At the very bottom were bundles of medicinal herbs. The second shelf was covered with large and small bottles, some empty, some full of what looked like grain seeds. His hand lighted upon a two-inch-high, mud-colored bottle. The boy polished it against his shirt. The dust left black marks on his clothes, at the same time exposing the shiny, rich smoothness of the bottle. He poked his finger into the neck of the bottle. It was such a tiny hole, only his little finger would fit. The stopper that had dropped down onto the bundles of herbs was like a small glass bullet, crystalline and translucent. The more he looked, the more he liked it. He pushed the stopper on, whistled under his breath, and then put the bottle into his trouser pocket. Tiptoe he pushed the door open gently. The kitchen was on the other side, with two long benches against the wall where the old man did his consulting. There was no one in the street. The sun was still burning fiercely overhead. Hitching his trousers, the boy set off in the direction of his home, keeping close to the walls under the eaves.

The boy had been counting on his fingers the days until Big Brother came home from the boat. School term was almost certainly about to begin. That day he had forgotten where he had counted up to, but his brother had appeared anyway. Hui was there too, helping him to sort out his sailcloth bag with his toothbrush, face flannel, clothes, and other things. Scattered in amongst these were some peanuts and red dates. Hui had had her plaits cut short. They just reached her shoulders. She was really good-looking, with her brows, eyes, and lips fine and expressive. In his heart, the boy called her Sister-in-Law.

After saying goodbye to Hui, Big Brother told their mother that she wasn't to do any more child-minding or laundry for other people.

But with only their father's pension and his wages, how were they to make ends meet? Mother was washing the dishes as she spoke. They would need the money if he was going to get married. She would manage okay. There was life in her yet.

Big Brother opened his mouth to speak but thought better of it. It would be a while before he could get married. Hui's father didn't approve of the romance between his daughter and her classmate. Stuck-up old git, lounging around all day drinking tea. He was no better than their father, who worked in a ship's engine room, but he thought his daughter pretty enough to marry above herself, too good to remain a worker all her life.

The usual meeting place was by the nursery school wall. There was a clump of bushes by the curve in the wall. In amongst the thickets of weeds was a profusion of smelly white flowers. The boy was late. He squatted down at the foot of the wall. The primary school was opposite the middle school, separated by a pond which was littered with rotting cabbage leaves and carrot tops.

Three shadows scuttled past; the tall one in front was Liu Yun. The boy stood up quickly and told him that his brother was back from work but that he was being closely watched and had been unable to get away.

To his surprise, Liu Yun did not shout at him. He was clutching a pile of books which he tossed down to the edge of the pond. The book at the top of the pile had a picture of a big bearded foreigner. The boy had been coveting this for a long time, but he concealed his eagerness: Liu Yun didn't like songs. Though he looked like an innocent, pale-faced schoolboy, he was behind all the local mischief, added to which he was quite a fighter— and books, he just liked to steal them. And he liked girls too.

Liu Yun was three years older than the boy. He had failed to finish school but he was hanging around the streets all day, smoking, drinking, and singing dirty, and he liked to side with the underdog. He had made quite a name for himself on the streets. Suddenly the cicadas began to whir as if they had just realized the people were there. The boy went to swat a long-legged mosquito that landed on his arm. He missed. Liu Yun dragged him over to the street lamp. The boy saw that Liu Yun had curled his hair into two waves and his shirt was clean and neat, not like the boy and his mates who went about bare-chested when it was hot. It wasn't Liu Yun himself who had broken in through the library window; he was always some distance away, giving orders.

"Who's that visitor at your house?" Liu Yun asked.

"My sister-in-law," the boy replied.

"Shameless! Not even married, and already he's got into her knockers, eh? Any more juicy morsels where she came from?"

Liu Yun's tone was playful, but his expression was perturbing. He had had a string of girlfriends, barely finishing with one before he was on to the next. The boy was worried. He wanted to be off, but his hand reached into his trouser pocket for the bottle. He fingered it. He looked at Liu Yun, gritted his teeth, and handed it over.

Liu Yun took it nonchalantly. At first glance, under the dull yellow street lamp, the bottle was nothing special.

"Shine your torch on it. Look there, two fish!" said the boy.

Liu Yun didn't need the torch, he had already seen them. The bottle gleamed exquisitely. He gave it a good once-over.

"I'll have it."

"Only if you promise not to go after my sister-in-law." The boy's words were muffled, but his meaning was clear enough: Leave Hui alone!

Liu Yun was the local heartthrob, all the girls fancied him. He could pull whoever he chose.

"What are you getting at? I'll stay well away from her, ok?" Then Liu Yun switched on the torch. The beam shone onto the bottle. "Those can't be fish. It's a couple snogging. They've got old-fashioned haircuts, and there are trees, mountains, and a river."

"They're completely starkers!" Liu Yun whooped while showing it to the boy. But the boy was shy, and Liu Yun shouting at him made him even more embarrassed. Liu Yun pointed to the scatter of books at the edge of the pond. "All yours, sonny boy."

In the holidays, Big Brother did odd jobs on a building site. His evenings were spent canoodling with Hui. No matter how the boy itched to get out, he had to pretend to be good. His mother, under orders from Big Brother to rest, busied herself with the cooking and housework. With more time on her hands, it was as if she had grown extra pairs of eyes. She went about supervising the boy's homework, what time he went to bed and got up, his meals and going to the toilet. He was like a caged monkey.

That day the boy had been sent out to buy soya sauce. As he emerged from the shop, he caught sight of the old hermit heading up towards the crossroads. His clothes were even scruffier than usual and he kept looking from side to side, obviously fretting about something. A woman who was buying vegetables grabbed hold of her fat lolly-sucking daughter and intercepted the old man. She told her daughter to stick out her tongue for the old man to examine.

He waved them aside and carried on walking.

The woman jumped forward, hurling a mouthful of abuse at the old man over the vegetable stall. Her language was colorful.

"Take yourself off to the hospital. Go on!" the old man retorted coolly, staggering off up the steps.

The woman shut her mouth in astonishment. People on the street were taken aback: the old man never had a good word to say about hospitals and was always such a softie. What was going on?

The boy's face went pale, then red. He hadn't stolen it exactly, the little bottle, and besides, the old man had so many. Surely it wasn't because of that. Nevertheless, he slipped off into a doorway and waited until the old man had gone past.

"Look at me, boy." His mother put a bowl of fried bean sprouts on the table. There was not a drop of oil in the bowl. She wiped her hands on her apron. "What have you been up to?"

"Nothing." His voice was feeble.

"You're lying. How dare you lie to me!" Mother was onto something.

The boy buried his face in his book. Mother grabbed the soya sauce. "Just you wait till your brother gets home. He'll have a few things to say to you."

"What things?" The boy wasn't frightened of his mother, but he was really scared of his big brother, just as he had been of his dad. When his dad was off-work he used to take Big Brother and him fishing in the stream or the pool. When his dad was in a good mood he used to laugh and joke. Big Brother was just like him, strong, dark and full of spirit. The boy was fine and delicate. Even though he ran around in the sun all day he never went brown, just pink. Because of this, he felt a bit of a wimp.

"The police were here earlier. Cases of cigarettes have gone missing from the cigarette factory again. Some workers on the nightshirt saw the culprits, a bunch of young boys apparently." Mother was mixing the dressing for the cold noodles. "If they own up, they'll be let off lightly, otherwise they'll end up inside!"

The boy breathed out slowly. He put the book down and beamed. He went over to his mother and fanned her gently. He swore that he hadn't had anything to do with this. He was all charm and sweetness. His mother couldn't make head nor tail of it, but the boy knew who was behind it—Liu Yun.

After dinner, everyone in the neighborhood brought their chairs, mats, and bamboo beds outside to cool down. They would wait until the temperature had dropped before going back into the house to sleep.

A neighbor called over to his mother: "They've caught the hooligans who stole the cigarettes."

"They have?"

The neighbor had a long, thin neck. She was wearing a pair of wooden-soled slippers. She nodded. "They took whatever they could lay their hands on, not just the cigarettes. They've got them though."

The boy, who was sprinkling cool water onto the bamboo recliner, glanced at his mother. As he lowered his eyes he seemed to say: "See, it wasn't me!" She smiled. Liu Yun had got his just deserts. The boy was sad about the bottle. The clouds and countryside on the bottle moved in front of his eyes. He regretted giving it away. Water from the basin splashed over his feet.

Big Brother came in followed by Hui. The boy poured them each a cup of cool water. Then someone called his name.

He looked out of the window. His heart gave a start. Liu Yun was standing at the side of the street. He wasn't behind the cigarette job after all.

Liu Yun marched in uninvited, saying he wanted to borrow a book from the boy. Liu Yun never read books. The boy said he would fetch it. Hui offered him a seat. Big Brother was in the kitchen filling a basin with water to wash his face. Hui asked Liu Yun what books he liked.

Liu Yun said he liked reading stories. His face was deadly earnest.

Hui giggled. The boy thought he detected a change in her voice. Liu Yun looked very mature, much older than seventeen.

The boy grabbed two books and pointedly went to stand outside. "The books are here."

Liu Yun said goodbye to Hui politely. Big Brother came back into the room carrying the basin. He brushed shoulders with Liu Yun as he went past.

Liu Yun walked ahead quickly. The boy followed closely behind. When they got to the edge of the pond, the boy had still not spoken when Liu Yun swung round and gave the boy a shove. He fell backwards, sitting down in a puddle. Water seeped in, soaking his vest and underpants. The books he was carrying fell into the mud.

Liu Yun said, "You're very shifty and unwelcoming. I only came to borrow some shitty books."

"You lying bastard." The boy got up and headbutted Liu Yun. He caught him off guard, and Liu Yun staggered, almost falling face down into the pond. "Give me back my bottle!" the boy shouted.

"Give you your what?" Liu Yun, who had recovered his balance, exploded. "You can't give someone something then ask for it back!" And he started to lay into the boy. "And don't ever speak to your elder and better like that again, or you'll be drinking out of that sewer."

Liu Yun had not gone all the way, holding back his fists. The boy hated him all the more.

When his mother saw his bloody face she panicked, worrying that the neighbor had seen him. She reached out and pulled the boy into the house, shutting the door tightly behind him.

The boy didn't say anything except that it was only a nosebleed. He just kept moaning. From the other side of the table Big Brother asked, "Who did this to you?"

The boy didn't flicker as if he hadn't heard his brother's question. His mother stuffed cotton buds up his nostrils and wiped the blood from his face, and then told him to look up. "Wicked business, my boy. What on earth have you been doing to get into this state?" The boy couldn't bear to see his mother cry.

Actually, he ached all over and stank of sewage. But his mother and brother couldn't see the real cause of his pain.

His mother opened the chest of drawers to find some clean clothes. Then it came to her: "It wasn't that Liu Yun who called round for our boy this evening, was it?"

The boy neither shook nor nodded his head. It was enough that Mother had said it: Now Big Brother would be after Liu Yun for sure. He would never forgive him.

His mother cleaned the boy up and rubbed alcohol and gentian violet into his bruises. He lay on his mother's folding bamboo chair while she fanned him gently.

The stars, large and small, were like flying insects darting into view then out again, as if playing hide and seek with the clouds. The wind had cooled. The streets were deserted and peaceful. The boy and his mother went back into the house.

"Where's your brother?" His mother peered out into the moonlight.

The boy sat up on the bed ready to go off and look for his brother. His mother put her hand on him to restrain him.

That night the boy had a nightmare. He woke up shouting. It was already morning. He couldn't remember what time Big Brother had come home the night before or what had happened. There was no one at home. Mother had probably gone to the market to buy the vegetables fresh in from the suburbs, and Big Brother of course had gone to work.

The boy scooped a ladle of water out of the pot, drank two mouthfuls, then spat the rest out. He noticed a half sheet of paper on the windowsill weighted down with a broken brick.

He picked it up. The writing was clumsy and crooked. It was Liu Yun's. It was all sorted, he had written, and he wouldn't be coming over to the boy's house again provided that the boy didn't come after him for the bottle. The boy hadn't expected this. This was not at all like the proud Liu Yun he knew. Big Brother must have given him a real good hiding.

"Strange," the boy muttered. The aches in his limbs had disappeared. He rolled the paper up into a ball and threw it out of the window. Deep down inside he forgave Liu Yun. He should be even prouder than Liu Yun.

He gulped down a bowl of rice porridge, hesitated, then walked out of the house. He wouldn't have an opportunity to get away once his mother was home.

Where should he go to play? With no particular destination in mind, he jumped on the spot three times at the crossroads, then ran off down the hill.

Passengers who had just disembarked from the ferry walked in dribs and drabs up the old abandoned cable car tracks. They were a long way off and not clearly visible. The boy stood facing the backwater. The gently sloping beach was bigger than the school playing field. There were no strange stones or submerged rocks, the water was calm and warm, and the sand soft and fine. Twice in every three days an evil drowned spirit floated down into the backwater where it would linger whirling around. The boy didn't care. Drowning river water was no different from ordinary river water. He dog paddled for a while, then turned over onto his back, his fourteen-year-old frame supported by the murky river water. The sun had not reached its full intensity. Some young boys about the same age as the boy were having a water fight. It was true, there were not many swimmers this early in the morning. From then on he would make sure he always came down at this time. He narrowed his eyes. The cloudless sky dipped down to within an arm's length of his face. It was heavy and he couldn't push it away. His ears picked up the rhythm of the waves lapping against the bank. If Dad hadn't gone back four years earlier to save the others from the fire, he could have jumped into the river and swum across in one breath. The boy made his way over to the bank. He berthed himself on the spongy, soft beach, his face nestling into the sand. The warm river water lapped around him. He was like a fish.

A hand grabbed hold of the back of his neck and squeezed lightly. The boy screamed.

The hand let go. The boy turned over and looked up. It was the old hermit. The boy trembled.

All the way back to the old man's house, the boy did his best to get away, but the old man held on to him tightly. His beard was grey, but he was still very strong.

The old man lifted the lid on his teacup and blew the tea leaves to one side. "Give me back my bottle."

The boy shook his head as if he hadn't understood what the old man was saying. It was like being summoned to the teacher's office. His arms hung straight down by his sides and his head was bowed. He was used to being kept behind by the teacher.

"You've got some cheek for one so young!" the old man went on, saying that he had been looking for the boy for several days. He'd taken him in after he had fainted and looked after him, and in return for his trouble all the boy could do was steal from him.

"That's not true. I'm not a thief!" The boy curled his lip and leaned back, perching his bottom on the edge of the table. He pointed at the bottles sitting on the shelf. "They're only medicine bottles anyway!"

"Those are. But the one you stole is different."

"I haven't got it on me," The boy blurted out carelessly. He wanted to carry on but his tongue got tied in a knot: "You . . . stupid old fart."

The old man stood up and paced up and down the room. He picked up the teacup and put it to his lips, then of a sudden smashed it on the floor. Tea and shards of porcelain shot across the floor.

The boy watched the old man, his mouth agape. The old man's anger subsided and he seemed calmer.

"Imagine a city moat and a cloudless sky, the capital city stretching out beneath the intense blue firmament, the Forbidden City resplendent like an enchanted palace. Once upon a time, there was a foreigner with a delicate nose who possessed a very special trinket. To restore his breathing, he would pour a drop of potion from the trinket, inhale gently and sneeze. The potion in the trinket could cure all manner of ailments. The foreigner adored opera. He fell in love with one of the opera female impersonators. He became a regular opera goer and an amateur performer. The broken-hearted hero longed for love, his tears flowed like rain as the melancholy refrains rang out. Vainly he searched for a beautiful soul among the blossom sprays. The fairy maidens performed the dance of Chu. River Wu overflowed with regret. When the foreigner came to leave, he gave the trinket to his 'lady.'

"The opera singer pined for him day and night, making himself ill. He saw a host of doctors but none could cure him. Then a young doctor who had come to the capital to visit relatives prescribed a concoction of herbs that saved the singer's life.

"The doctor took the place of the foreigner. Imperceptibly time went by, to the start of the Republic when the warlords took up the battle. The doctor had to return to the south, where his wife and elderly mother awaited him.

"'Endless wanderings over mountains and rivers, farewells come easily but meetings are hard.' This poem by the Dethroned Emperor Li is inscribed on the inside of the bottle. The calligraphy is the work of the great Master Ma, as the signature and seal testify, to complement the intrinsic pattern of the clouds, the rolling landscape, and the embracing couple, a union of heaven and earth! A pair of eyes that would drive many a mortal to suicide."

The old man went on. "After the singer and doctor separated, the fighting intensified. Their letters never arrived, and after a year without news the singer disappeared. Some people said that he committed suicide or was killed in the war."

The boy was completely bewildered.

"Hurry up and give me back the bottle you stole!" The old man snapped out of his reverie and fixed his eyes on the boy. "Ill-gotten precious things are unlucky. You're too young to understand these things."

The old man rambled on incoherently. "The bottle is a most exquisite light honey color. Your imagination could roam forever around the lines of the natural grain. The person who traced those lines was exceptional indeed. It's a rare work of art handed down from generation to generation. The hollow at the base of the bottle complements the undulating line and movement of the two bodies. Don't think of it as a work of art labored over for many years, commissioned by the foreigner. The beauty is in the grain and essence of the jade, a genuine precious stone."

The boy heard the last sentence loud and clear. What was he saying? That the pretty medicine bottle was a precious stone? He must be joking! The old man was skint, all he had was that broken brick pile of yellowing books. He's having me on!

"Please bring it back," the old man pleaded.

"I didn't take it." The boy decided to deny everything.

The old man broke into a long laugh. It was a couple of minutes before he regained his composure.

The boy was petrified. The old man patted his shoulder solicitously. "You go home and think it over. Take your time. When you've thought it through, come back and tell me."

Hui had not called round for ages, but Big Brother didn't seem bothered. He never mentioned the evening when he had gone out to revenge his brother. It must have been ugly. Liu Yun was a head shorter than Big Brother and must have taken quite a beating. Even though Liu Yun was no mean puncher and kicker, he wasn't a seasoned street fighter like Big Brother. Otherwise, why would Liu Yun have kept his promise? In fact, there had been no sign of him for some time.

The boy needed to consult the calendar. Only one more week before Big Brother had to return to the boat.

"Are you still going to the building site?" he asked his brother.

"No. Do you want to go fishing?"

The boy nodded. "Shall we tell Hui?" He felt stupid. Why did he have to go and ask?

"No. She's busy." The boy hadn't expected this answer. His brother didn't seem keen to talk about Hui—or so the boy thought. If there was a problem with Hui, it must be Hui's father didn't approve of them getting married—the same old story. What was to be done about it? The boy was worried.

The two brothers set off, one behind the other, fishing rods in hand, bait, little bugs, and earthworms in a small plastic bag. The hot spell had passed and the temperature was much cooler. Flecks of sunlight pushed through the branches of the trees, searing the patches of ground where they landed. The shaded areas were cool and dark. Neither spoke as they followed the stone path up the hill. Rear Mountain Reservoir offered a good vantage point. As you fished you could watch hundreds of boats in full sail going by. Images of days they spent with their father reappeared behind his gaze. The boy felt happy and began to hum a tune though the words were unintelligible. Suddenly he stopped in his tracks: On a slope under some trees sat the old man cross-legged in close-fitting cotton trousers, as if purposefully. His completely white hair was neatly combed and shining as if smoothed with honey locust oil. The boy could not help walking over to the old man.

"Oi, boy!" Big Brother called gently yet forcefully. He seemed upset.

The boy turned around and walked silently over to his brother's side.

"What's your interest in him? He's got a bad name," Big Brother scolded.

"He's a healer," the boy explained.

"He's under surveillance, an evil element from the old society."

The boy picked up his fishing rod and whipped at the tree. The leaves shook and began to drop one by one.

When they climbed up the hill, they came to a wide steep road, in one direction the cigarette factory, the other the textile factory. They crossed the road to the textile factory taking a small path through fields. His brother told him there were all sorts of stories about the old man. Curious, the boy pestered Big Brother to tell him.

His brother didn't really know. He remembered the grown-ups talking about the old man when he was little, but the stories were not considered suitable for children's ears.

"He was from the lower Yangtze region. Before Liberation, sometime around 1949, his wife left him, apparently taking the children with her. She couldn't stand him. Then he was taken very ill. When he recovered, he announced to everyone that he could cure the sick, and people believed him. It's best to keep away from people like him, the farther the better." Big Brother warned him not to go getting involved.

But I am involved, the boy thought. The old hermit had given medical advice to so many people. He never turned anyone away, even when he was woken up in the night. Big mouths and dossers, they all preferred the convenience of consulting him to queuing up in the hospital and forking out for medicines. And he didn't even require a thank you. Dodging the nightsoil collector and holding his nose against the stink of shit, the boy cursed the lot of them.

The pool was run by the production brigade. There were new rules: twenty cents per fisherman. That was forty cents for the boy and his brother. It was only five cents to see the film, *The Guerrillas on Lake Hong*. With forty cents you could see it four times. Mother couldn't bear to part with so much money, but the boy had been to the cinema with his father.

Big Brother paid and they were admitted into the bamboo enclosure around the pool. There were quite a few people fishing while a bunch of nondescript boys were sitting and squatting beside the pool whiling away the hours. Two little girls sitting under the locust tree with their picture books stood out particularly.

The boy filled a plastic bag with water and put it in a stone hollow. He sat down next to his brother. All the places where you could watch the boats sail by were occupied. Disappointed, the boy stretched out his legs and dangled them over the edge of the pool.

Several hours later when they set off down the hill, the boy carried the plastic bag cradled in the frame of the fishing net. In the bag were three silver carp just bigger than the palm of his hand, swishing around in the water, their mouths gaping and closing as they gasped for breath. "Those peasants from the production brigade must have taken all the big fish," the boy grumbled to himself, then swore out loud.

Big Brother handed him the two fishing rods. "I've just got to see to something. You go on ahead." The boy saw that they were not far from home. They were almost at the crossroads.

Big Brother disappeared off round the corner where there were two wooden walls. The boy was happy. The fishing had been as exhilarating as ever. At least it had revived his brother's spirits. He was off to look for Hui at last.

His mother descaled and gutted the three fish, put them in a bowl, sprinkled them with salt, ginger and garlic and drizzled a few drops of oil on them. She stood the bowl in the pan to steam. The boy pursed his mouth.

"Oil is rationed, and it's expensive."

His mother rolled her eyes. "Oh, here's Hui." His mother's voice softened.

"Big Brother's gone to look for you. You two must have missed each other."

"Why would he go looking for me?" Hui's shoulders twitched and she began to cry. The boy and his mother were both dumbstruck. His mother gave Hui a dump cloth, and when she'd stopped crying she wiped her face. She said that Big Brother had been avoiding her for the last two weeks and when ever they'd spoken he'd been very cool. Mother said that it couldn't be the case, he was devoted to her. But Hui was not putting it on. The boy was angry. He didn't know whether to stand up or sit down. He wanted to say something to comfort Hui but was afraid he'd say the wrong thing. He simply strode out of the house.

The boy wandered aimlessly along the street. The shadows at the foot of the walls were dark, the houses tumble-down. In the street, women were calling their children home to dinner. There was a smell of oil and chilies, and sounds of coughing sputtered through the narrow windows. He hated all this. The wall posters had been washed away by the rain, leaving only a single corner of paper. The boy tore it off gently and threw it onto the ground. That's it. He would go and find Liu Yun to see if the bottle was real jade, though he in fact could not tell real jade from imitation. Nonetheless, he found himself halfway down Flagstone Slope.

The door to Liu Yun's house was locked. The boy asked a neighbor to tell Liu Yun he had called by.

The neighbor promised to pass on the message. She looked the boy up and down and glared. The boy glared back at the skinny woman. A duck puffed out its chest and nuzzled her toes. She gave it a kick. The duck squawked and flew off. She gave it an angry stare and swore. The boy had never heard such a shameless curse. But he was used to insults and just lowered his head and walked off, the strange rude words going round and round in his mind.

The following afternoon, Liu Yun bowled into the boy's house, his face glowing.

Although Hui was not there and the boy had picked up the piece of paper bearing Liu Yun's promise and kept it, seeing Liu Yun made him agitated. It hadn't been very smart of him to give that serpent an excuse to come round to their house.

Big Brother came in and they greeted each other with martial arts salutes. He and Liu Yun seemed to have patched up their differences, there was no sign of a grudge, and within a couple of minutes they were calling each other "brother." The boy's fears had been groundless.

After leaving the house, they found a quiet spot. The boy asked if he could have a look at the bottle.

"I haven't got it on me," Liu Yun replied. There was a new brightness and sparkle in his eyes. He seemed a different person.

The boy felt the hairs stand up like bristles on the back of his neck, as if the old hermit were shadowing him in pursuit of his debt. "I stole the bottle

from the old man and now he wants it back. He says it's a snuff bottle."
The boy didn't risk telling Liu Yun that it was made of precious stone.

"You quite finished?" Liu Yun was twitching to go.

"The old man wants it back!" The boy could see that Liu Yun was uncomfortable and his voice began to tremble.

"Hardly a matter of life and death, is it!" said Liu Yun in a slightly mocking tone.

Was it really so serious? Would it kill him if he didn't return a snuff bottle? The boy sensed trouble from Liu Yun's words. Otherwise, why was he so nervous?

His mother had collected pig bristles from the workshop and had brought them back to the house for sorting, black with black and white with white. The boy gave his mother a hand, but he was too hasty and mixed up the black and white. Everything around him seemed strange.

The day before Big Brother was due to return to the boat, he and Liu Yun were caught red-handed in Liu Yun's house by Public Security officers. The evidence was confirmed, they were handcuffed and led away. Everyone said that it was Hui's father who had reported them. The boy ran with the neighbor all the way to the road. As the police car pulled away, the boy heard his brother shouting. "Look after Mum, Boy."

The boy had barely taken stock of what had happened, when everyone, adults and children alike, began shouting at him. They seemed to be repeating what Big Brother had said and laughing loudly. Someone said that Liu Yun had confessed to having been seduced.

It rained lightly during the night. All the houses were quiet.

The boy climbed out of the window and made his way to Liu Yun's room. The snuff bottle was in the secret place in the brick wall where Liu Yun hid things. Only the boy knew where to look. He tucked the snuff bottle inside his shirt. Liu Yun was not a bad sort, but whenever the boy thought of him, for some unknown reason, he felt uncomfortable inside. He had walked quite a way along the road when, unable to resist a temptation any longer, he took the bottle out and looked at it under the street lamp.

"Don't look at it!" An elderly voice reverberated behind his back and a hand grabbed the bottle. "There's already been a seduction, yet you go looking for another one. There's already been a mistake and you want to go off and make another one?" The old man gave a long sigh.

The boy dashed up to the old man and grabbed for the bottle. He could clearly see the white beard and long white hair. The old man's grip wasn't tight enough and the bottle slipped away into the bushes as he fell to the ground. Ignoring the old man, the boy dived into the bushes to retrieve the bottle.

On the day of the trial, it was cold even when wearing padded clothes. Mother kept close to the boy. She was in a daze. If the boy took one step away from her side, she called hysterically: Sonny! Sonny! The announcement was posted on the east-facing wall at the cross-roads. It said that Big Brother was the principal culprit and that he had committed a grave, despicable crime. His crime was made more serious as he had driven an unnamed girl to attempted suicide. The People could not deal with him leniently, and therefore, in accordance with the judgment of the court, the death sentence had been passed. Beside his brother's name was the word "Sodomist," and over his name was a large red cross. As Liu Yun was the younger one, he was considered an accessory to the crime and was sentenced to a labor reform camp in the Extreme West.

The boy and his mother sat motionless with their tweezers in their hands. Some of the pig bristles smelled of urine and rotten fish. The boy stared at the small hillock of pig bristles on the table. He thought that one of the tufts looked like his brother's hair. The image of his brother with a shaved head was unfamiliar, particularly surrounded by all those people. A single bullet pierced his brother's chest. His brother swayed a little, then stood still. The second bullet hit him in the head. His brother fell to the ground. His bearing was unlike the other executed prisoners, but the boy couldn't say why exactly.

When a story is passed around it changes dramatically. The boy did not want to hear a word of it, nor did he challenge any of the versions. The neighbor thought it was odd that the boy never cried for his brother. Mother was angry but held her palm in mid-air without letting it come to rest on the boy's narrow, thin face. By now, not only did the boy not cry, he began to smile.

Time passed by like water through sand. The boy met Hui only once in the street. She was no longer the sort to kill herself by drinking pesticide. She'd married a worker from another province. She was fatter and seemed unfamiliar. When she called out to the boy, he stuck fast and didn't budge. She talked on and on, her breath pungent with garlic. When she noticed one of her friends, she abandoned the boy and engaged the friend in conversation. Further down the street her voice was still audible.

The boy donned a red armband. He was the first in his school to adopt the revolutionary cause and join the Red Guards. He kept it from his mother. He didn't want to go home, so he banded together with his classmates to catch a train to Beijing to see the Great Leader. He risked his life in the crush, pushing and shoving. In the end, he alone managed to squeeze his way onto the train, while his friends were thrown back into the sea of people on the platform.

People were everywhere, in the corridors, on the luggage racks and the window-sills, underneath the seats, and even in the toilets. In the middle of the night, the boy curled up and went to sleep.

He was walking and walking. Eventually, he reached the old man's house. The old man was lying in bed already half paralyzed. Why should he care about this man? The dunce's hat in his hands required a head. Whose? The boy threw a stone at the window, glass splintered and flew everywhere. All he heard was the sound of the glass breaking, no one came out to investigate. He pretended he didn't know Hui's parents. He was simply watching others smashing the house of some counter-revolution-aries who had slipped through the net. Hui's father was beaten to a pulp. The boy sat on the window-sill throughout. He didn't lift a finger. He just gave the orders. They were running short of dunce's hats. They would have to make a new batch. Perhaps they could use the slogan posters.

The boy tossed and turned then woke up. The train trundled on, *kacha, kacha*. It felt as if it were running over his body. The dream and reality converged in a mush. He pushed the person sleeping against him off, and stretched out his aching legs.

Having rearranged himself, he reached into his purse for the little piece of jade. Excitement pulsed through his body. He felt very lucky to be experiencing such a thrilling revolution. The train was speeding across a starless plain. In the expansive darkness, only the dim lights of the carriage glowed. They outlined the contours of other pale faces just like the boy's: grass-green uniforms, burning red hearts, and gently swaying bodies.

Yu Hua ❀ *China*

Yu Hua was born in Hangzhou in 1960 and grew up in the coastal town of Haiyan near Shanghai. After a five-year career in dentistry he became a full-time writer while still in his twenties, publishing his first fiction in 1984. His early work is known for its jolting episodes of random violence. However, unlike Chinese literature written under Maoist patriarchy, Yu Hua's output became associated with a new experimental thrust reflecting China's national turn from socialist orthodoxy toward an authoritarian, more market-influenced economic system. The author of six collections of stories and four novels, Yu Hua has had his work translated into many languages. *Huozhe (To Live)*, his second novel, was made into a motion picture by China's renowned director Zhang Yimou, and *Xiongdi (Brothers)*, his most recent book, was a bestseller in China. Yu Hua lives in Beijing. "Their Son" offers a provocative glimpse into China's rapidly emerging new generation. Its focus on consumer comfort marks a dramatic contrast with the pro-democracy ambitions of urban Chinese youth during the late 1980s.

Their Son

Translated by Allan H. Barr

AT FIVE O'CLOCK ON SATURDAY AFTERNOON, OVER THREE hundred workers crowded around the main entrance to the machine factory, waiting for the bell to sound that would mark the end of their shift. The metal gate, still tightly shut, clanged as the people in front banged against it, while a buzz of conversation rose up from the people behind, punctuated by shouts here and there. As they awaited release, the workers were like livestock trapped behind bars, idly clustered in the dimming light of dusk, crowded together in the howling winter wind. The large windows in the factory behind them were already shrouded in darkness, and the desolate scene was enlivened only by the clouds of dust that swirled around the workshops.

Shi Zhikang, a man of fifty-one, stood in the front row in his military overcoat, directly facing the crack between the two leaves of the steel gate. The icy wind blew in through the narrow gap and onto his face, making him feel as though his nose were shrinking.

Next to Shi Zhikang stood the old gatekeeper, his bald head flushed by the chilly wind. Over a thick padded jacket he wore a faded boiler suit; the end of a large key projected from his chest pocket. People were yelling at him to open the gate, but he might as well have been deaf. He looked from side to side; whenever someone directed a comment his way, he would turn his face and look the other way. Only when the bell rang did the old man finally take the key from his pocket. The people in the front row took a step back to give him room. He moved forward, at the same time thrusting his elbows behind him; he put the key in the hole only after making sure that his arms met no resistance.

Shi Zhikang was the first to make it out the gate. He set off rapidly along the road to his right, planning to walk to the stop before the factory and catch the trolleybus there, to avoid the scrum outside the factory gate. At least forty workers would try to push and shove their way on to the trolleybus, although it would already be full of passengers by the time it got there.

As he walked, Shi Zhikang thought about those forty workmates. He did not need to look back to imagine how they would cluster around the bus stop, just as they had crammed in front of the gate. There would be a dozen hefty young men, and at least a dozen women, three of whom had started work the same year as him. All three had medical conditions now: One had a ropy heart, and the other two had kidney problems.

As he was thinking about that, the bus stop came into view, and at the same time he saw a trolleybus heading down the road, so he took his hands out of his pockets and ran, arriving at the stop just as the bus pulled in. People were already waiting there in three clusters, and as the bus slowed down, the clusters moved to position themselves in line with the bus's three doors. When the bus stopped, the clusters became stationary. The doors opened and passengers squeezed out in a tight, solid stream, like toothpaste from a tube, and then, in a dense mass of limbs, people piled on.

By the time the trolley approached the entrance to Shi Zhikang's factory, he had already pushed his way into the middle of the bus, and his arms were wedged vertically into the gaps left by bodies pressed up against him. The bus didn't stop outside the factory but drove right on past. Of the forty workers that had been waiting at the stop, only five or six were left, along with seven or eight people he didn't recognize; before his bus, at least one or two others must have come by. The three women had evidently been unable to cram aboard, for they still were waiting at the stop, the one with the bad heart in the middle, the two with kidney disease on either side. They stood in a tight clump in their dumpy padded coats, each with a black woolen scarf around her neck. The cold wind blew their hair every which way, and the deepening darkness blurred their features, as though their faces had been charred by fire. As his trolley passed them, Shi Zhikang noticed how their heads turned to follow it. They watched as the bus he was on sailed away from them.

After nine stops, Shi Zhikang got off the trolleybus and walked back thirty yards to another stop, where he would board a public transport bus. By this time the sky was completely dark; the street lamps cast only a feeble glow, and it was more the bright lights of the stores on either side of the street that illuminated the sidewalk and the area around the bus stop. Many people were already waiting, and those closest to the front were practically standing in the middle of the street. As Shi Zhikang made his way into the crowd, a minibus came along, and when the door opened, a young man with a canvas satchel hanging from his neck poked his head out and yelled: "Two yuan, two yuan...."

Two men and a woman boarded the minibus, as the conductor continued to shout, "Two yuan ..."

At this point a public transport bus turned a corner away in the distance and came into view. Seeing it, the guy on the minibus quickly ducked back inside and the minibus drove away from the waiting throng, as the bus rumbled towards them.

Shi Zhikang swiftly pushed his way to the front, and then spread his arms a little, pressing backwards as the bus approached, pushing the people behind him back onto the sidewalk. As the front door of the bus slipped past, he monitored the bus's speed and calculated that he should be perfectly in line for the middle door. But what happened was that the bus came to an abrupt stop, leaving him a yard or two away from his target door. He'd lost his position in the front row, and now he found himself on the outer edge of the crowd.

When the door opened, only three people got off. Shi Zhikang took a couple of steps into the crowd, and thrust his arms into a slight gap left by the people in front. As he pushed his way forward, he made good use of the upper body strength that a fitter like him naturally had at his disposal. He steadily widened the gap, then squeezed into the space created, and continued to force open a gap between people yet further forward.

With the utmost effort, Shi Zhikang knocked a hole between the people ahead of him, and then, exploiting the impetus of the people behind shoving him forward, he launched himself into the space by the door. Just as he placed his feet on the step of the bus, someone grabbed the collar of his overcoat and dragged him backward. His bottom landed heavily on the ground and his head collided with someone's leg. The leg in turn gave his head a knock, and when he looked up, he found that the leg belonged to a young woman. She fixed him with a glare, then looked away.

By the time Shi Zhikang was back on his feet, the doors had closed and the bus was beginning to move off. A woman's handbag was trapped in the door, leaving a corner of the bag and part of the strap sticking outside, so that it swayed back and forth with the motion of the bus. He turned around, determined to find out who had pulled him back. Two youths about the same age as his son were watching him with a cold glint in their eyes. He looked at them and at the others who had failed to squeeze onto the bus. Some were looking at him, and some were not. He was tempted to let off a swear word or two, but thought better of it.

Later, two buses arrived at the same time, and Shi Zhikang boarded the second. Today he did not get off at the stop closest to his home, but got off two stops earlier. There was a man there with a flatbed cart who at three or four in the afternoon would sell bean curd that tasted better than what you could buy elsewhere. Shi Zhikang's wife, who worked in a textile factory, had asked him to pick up a couple of pounds on his way home from work, because today was Saturday, and their son, a junior in college, was coming home for the weekend.

After buying the bean curd, Shi Zhikang did not try to catch another bus but simply walked the rest of the way home. When he arrived, it was almost seven o'clock, but there was no sign of his wife. This upset him. His wife should have got off work at four-thirty, and she did not have such a long commute. Normally, his wife would just about have dinner ready by this time, but today he had no choice but to set to work on an empty stomach, washing vegetables and slicing meat.

When his wife Li Xiulan returned, she was carrying a couple of fish. As soon as she saw her husband slicing meat, she asked, "Have you washed your hands?"

Shi Zhikang was not in a good mood, so he answered curtly. "Can't you see my hands are wet?"

"Did you use soap?" Li Xiulan asked. "There's flu going around, and pneumonia too. You need to wash your hands with soap as soon as you get home."

Shi Zhikang snorted dismissively. "Then shouldn't you come home sooner?"

Li Xiulan dumped the two fish in the sink. She told Shi Zhikang that they cost her only three yuan: "They were the last two. He wanted five yuan, but I wouldn't go higher than three."

"Does it take so long to buy a couple of dead fish?"

"They haven't been dead long." She showed him the gills: "See, the cheeks are still red."

"It's you I'm talking about." He pointed at his watch and raised his voice: "You don't come home till after seven!"

Li Xiulan's tone also went up a register: "So what? What's the big deal about me coming home late? Every day you get back later than I do—do I complain?"

"Do I finish work before you do? Is my factory closer to home than yours?"

"I fell," said Li Xiulan.

She flung the fish down and stamped into the living room. "I fell off the bus," she said, "and it was ages before I could stand up again. I had to sit there on the side of the road for thirty or forty minutes. I practically froze to death."

Shi Zhikang set down the cleaver he'd been using to slice the meat, and walked over to her: "You fell? So did I—someone tugged my collar."

He didn't finish the story, for now that Li Xiulan had rolled up her trouser leg, he could see there was a bruise as big as an egg on her knee. He bent down to touch it. "How did it happen?"

"When I was getting off the bus, there were too many people behind me. They pushed so hard I lost my balance."

Just then their son arrived home. He was wearing a red down jacket, and as soon as he saw his mother's injury, he bent down just like his father and asked with concern: "Did you trip?"

As he took off his jacket, he went on: "You should take a calcium supplement. It's not only babies who need calcium, older people need to have it too. Every day your bones lose significant quantities of calcium, and that's why you're prone to bone fractures . . . If I was pushed off a bus, there's no way I would end up with such a large bruise."

Their son turned on the television and plumped himself down on the sofa. He put on the earphones of his Walkman, and began to listen to the FM music station.

"Are you watching TV?" Shi Zhikang asked. "Or are you listening to the radio?"

His son turned to look at him, but seemed not to have understood, and turned away again. Then his mother asked, "Have you washed your hands?"

He turned, and removed an earphone from one of his ears: "What did you say?"

"Go and wash your hands," Li Xiulan said. "There's flu going around now, and it's easy to pick up germs on the bus. Go wash your hands, and be sure to use soap."

"I don't need to wash my hands." Their son replaced the earphone. "I took a cab."

Shi Zhikang couldn't get to sleep that night. For five months now, his wife had been bringing home only a little over a hundred yuan. He was in a better position—four hundred yuan—but still their combined monthly income was less than six hundred. The cost of rice had now risen to one yuan thirty a pound, and pork was twelve yuan a pound—even chili peppers were three yuan a pound. They still gave their son three hundred yuan a month for living expenses all the same, leaving a bit over two hundred for themselves. But this hadn't stopped their son from taking a taxi when he came home on Saturday.

Li Xiulan had not fallen asleep either. Seeing her husband tossing and turning, she said: "You can't sleep?"

"No."

She turned to him. "How much did our son pay to take a taxi home?"

"I don't know. I've never taken a taxi. I think it would have cost at least thirty yuan."

"Thirty yuan?" Li Xiulan moaned.

"We sweated blood for this money," he sighed.

They said nothing more. Before long Shi Zhikang fell asleep, and she soon followed.

The following morning, their son again put on his earphones and watched TV as he listened to music. Shi Zhikang and Li Xiulan decided to have a good talk with him, so she sat down by his side, while her husband brought a chair over and sat in front of them. "Your mother and I would like to have a chat with you," Shi Zhikang said.

"What about?" Because he was wearing earphones, their son said this very loudly.

"Family matters."

"Go on." Their son was practically shouting.

Shi Zhikang leaned over and removed his son's right earphone. "These past few months, we've had a few problems. We didn't want to tell you, for fear of distracting you from your studies…"

"What's happened?" Their son removed the other earphone.

"Nothing much," Shi Zhikang said. "Beginning this month, there'll be no more night shift in our factory, and of the three hundred in the workforce, half will be laid off. As far as I'm concerned, it's no big deal—I have skills, the factory still needs me.… It's more what's happening with your mom. Currently she is just bringing home a bit over one hundred yuan a month. She's due to retire in four years, and if she were to take early retirement, she could get three hundred yuan a month, and that would carry on for three years…"

"You get paid more if you take early retirement?"

They nodded. "In that case, why don't you retire?" their son asked.

"Your mother and I are thinking that too," Shi Zhikang said.

"Yeah, retire." Saying this, their son prepared to put his earphones back on. Shi Zhikang threw Li Xiulan a glance.

"Son," she said, "our family finances aren't what they used to be, and in the future they may be in even poorer shape…"

Their son, one earphone in place, asked, "What did you say?"

"Your mom was saying that the family finances aren't what they used to be…" Shi Zhikang said.

"Never mind about that." Their son waved his hand. "State finances are not what they used to be either."

His parents exchanged glances. "Tell me this," said Shi Zhikang, "why did you come home in a taxi yesterday?"

Their son looked at them, perplexed. "Why didn't you take a bus?" Shi Zhikang asked.

"The bus is too crowded."

"Too crowded?"

Shi Zhikang pointed at Li Xiulan. "Your mom and I cram ourselves onto buses every day of the week. How can a young guy like you be afraid of crowded buses?"

"It's not the pushing that's the problem, it's the smell."

With a frown, their son went on, "I really hate smelling other people's body odor. In buses, everybody's jostling you, forcing you to smell their stink. In those conditions, even perfume smells bad. Plus there are people letting off farts as well . . .

"I feel like throwing up every time I get on a bus," he concluded.

"Throwing up?"

Li Xiulan was shocked. "Son, are you ill?"

"No, of course not."

She looked at Shi Zhikang. "Could it be stomach trouble?"

Her husband nodded. "Have you got a bellyache?" he asked.

"There's nothing wrong with me." Their son was getting impatient.

"How much are you eating these days?" Li Xiulan asked.

"I don't have any stomach trouble!" their son yelled.

"Do you sleep all right?" Shi Zhikang asked. He turned to Li Xiulan: "If you don't get enough sleep, it'll make you feel nauseous."

Their son stretched out all ten fingers: "I sleep ten hours a day."

Li Xiulan was still anxious: "Son, you'd better go to the hospital for a checkup."

"I told you, there's nothing wrong with me." Their son jumped to his feet. "This is all about me having taken a taxi for once, isn't it?" he cried. "Well, I won't take a taxi again . . ."

"Son, we're not bothered about the taxi fare," said Shi Zhikang, "we're thinking of you. You'll be starting a job soon, and when you rely on your own salary you'll understand that money doesn't come easily, and you have to budget accordingly . . ."

"That's right." Li Xiulan went on, "We never said you couldn't take a cab."

"In the future I definitely will not be taking cabs." Their son sat back down on the sofa. "In the future I will drive my own car," he added. He put the earphones over his ears. "Many of my classmates regularly take cabs."

"His classmates regularly take cabs," Li Xiulan repeated, looking at her husband.

Seeing him nod, she went on, "If other people's sons can take cabs, why shouldn't ours?"

"I never said he couldn't," said Shi Zhikang.

Their son now was maybe listening to one of his favorite songs, for he was rocking his head back and forth and mouthing some lyrics. They looked at each other and smiled as they studied his contented air. Maybe the future would bring more and more difficulties, but this did not distress them unduly, for they could see that their son was now his own man.

Yun Dae Nyeong ✱ *Korea*

Yun Dae Nyeong was born in 1962 in Yesan, Chungchongnam-do. He graduated from Tanguk University with a major in French literature. A series of short
stories, "The Silver Trout Fishing Network," "Miari, 9 January 1993 Network,"
and "Once in a While, a Cow Visits a Motel," established his reputation as a
writer who captured the ethos and sensibilities of the Korean people in the 1990s.
The curious parallels in the tale that follows, and the title of the story itself, must
inevitably put readers in mind of the late Richard Brautigan's pathbreaking story
collection *Trout Fishing in America*.

The Silver Trout Fishing Network

Translated by Young-Jun Lee

THE DAY I WAS BORN, JULY 12, 1964, MY FATHER HAD GONE
*silver trout fishing at the Wangp'i River in Ulchin. He went freshwater
fishing every summer, sometimes at the Wangp'i, and other times at the
Kagok River in Hosan, or even the Namdae River in Yangyang. So my
mother ended up giving birth to me one sweltering July day, sweating
alone in labor.*

*My father had luck in the waters that day, returning home with a buck-
etful of silver trout.*

*"I'll take him trout fishing when he's old enough," he said, gazing
down at me swaddled in a blanket.*

I awoke and began to cry at these words.

*I grew big like a "forced" vegetable and soon began to tag along with
my father on fishing trips. The silver trout rose to the bait we cast out on
the water when we went fly-fishing, or when we trolled, using live trout
as decoys. We'd fish all the way up to the month of September, when the
silver trout would head downstream to spawn by the river's mouth.*

*Just as the silver trout would return from the ocean each spring and
swim upstream, I, too, would go back upriver every summer.*

✱

The first time I received their bulletin was late one Wednesday night. It had been placed in my apartment mailbox. That rainy autumn evening I had just come back from Lawson's, a 24-hour convenience store. I was carrying some quick-fix food items—bread, V8, cans of beer, coffee filters, things of that sort. In the faint glow from the streetlight, I cast a long and rather lonely shadow. Stepping over my own shadow as I entered the foyer of my apartment building, I found a sky-blue envelope tucked into my orange mailbox.

In the left corner was "The Silver Trout Fishing Network." The sender's name, address, or telephone number were nowhere to be found. I thought for a second it had been delivered to the wrong place but my name and address were printed on the bottom right in the same font.

I stood at the entrance to the building wondering where the envelope had come from while the security guard, taking a break from the nine o'clock news, shot a sullen glance at me through his window.

I threw my wet clothes into the washer, ate dinner, and took a shower. Then I turned on Billie Holiday and sipped a beer alone on the sofa in the dim living room, which seemed to cry out for a visitor. Billie Holiday had been unable to escape the depressing cycle of alcohol and drugs. She had crooned melancholy lyrics right up to her death at the age of forty-four in 1958. On lonesome and gloomy evenings I often drank beer and listened to her sad words. Why would someone with such a great gift take her own life? I listened to the lonely voice of a black singer who had died before I was even born, and shuddered at the realization that I had somehow arrived at the loneliest place in the world.

The phone suddenly rang, rattling the dead air in the room. I glanced over at the darkness gathering beyond the windowsill, and waited for five rings before picking up. It was rare for someone to call me so late at night.

I said hello, but for a while there was no answer. I almost hung up thinking it was a wrong number, but then I heard a faint, faraway voice, "Um ..." I felt something wasn't right and brought the phone closer to my ear, waiting for the caller to say something. After about ten seconds, a thin, unfamiliar female voice spoke.

"You are listening to Billie Holiday."

"!..."

I felt as if someone had pricked my nerves with a sharp needle. As if someone had somehow snuck into my locked room. I held my breath tightly. When faced with unexpected encounters I usually try to relax and proceed calmly. I never just charge ahead because there have been times when I made myself vulnerable to counterattack that way.

"You must be surprised by my calling so late. I am phoning because…"

Now her voice was really raspy.

"…I was wondering if you'd received the invitation from our Silver Trout Fishing Network?"

"Silver Trout Fishing Network?"

She didn't respond to my question, as if waiting for my reaction. Was she about my age? She sounded single. She must have been calling alone, talking to me from an empty room. I was old enough to sense things like this. I grabbed the unopened sky-blue envelope and asked her.

"If you hadn't called, I would never have thought to look inside. What is it anyway?"

"It's an invitation from the Silver Trout Fishing Network."

I glanced at the clock on the wall. A call from a fishing club at 11 P.M. and it wasn't even fishing season. What's more, I'd long since quit fishing, and had never been a member of a fishing club.

"Do you recall writing a newspaper article about silver trout fishing last summer? Our club read it, and we followed your advice and went to the Puk River in Kansong and the Wangp'i River in Ulchin for some mountain stream fishing. Anyway, we want to invite you to join our club."

"Sure, I'll read the invitation then."

"You'll find the time and location written on it. We'd really love for you to come. I have to hang up now, but I think side A on your record is done."

She hung up the phone before I had a chance to respond, like a postman who quickly vanishes after delivering the mail. I disliked such late night calls. They disrupted the fragile emotional rhythm and balance I was just barely maintaining. I decided to let this one go though. She knew Billie Holiday. That was a good enough reason for me to put up with it.

I calmly cut the edge of the envelope with scissors from the desk, and took out the contents.

Inside was a postcard with a xeroxed picture. It was, to my surprise, a piece by the American frontier photographer Edward Curtis called *Hopi Indians*. I couldn't imagine where they found this image. I was both

delighted and shocked at the same time. I had once owned a collection of
Curtis photographs called *The North American Indian*, but after I lost it I
never imagined I'd run into a photograph of his again.

"Something is about to happen…this doesn't feel like a normal invite,"
I muttered to myself, sitting back on the sofa.

I sat bolt upright. Reading the machine-engraved letters on the back of
the postcard, I started to feel increasingly tense. Finally, I felt as if I were
being seized against my will by some police force.

The Silver Trout Fishing Network 930911
*After reading the article on silver trout fishing you published last
summer, we decided to have you present at our club meeting. You might
recall meeting and parting with a woman several years ago. We cannot
reveal to you who this is, but you might guess to whom we are referring.
If you happen to remember and want to meet her, please come to our
meeting at the time and date specified on the bottom of this letter.*

*One more thing: we are an anonymous underground network that
operates through secret word exchanges, using "silver trout" as our code.
However, thanks to your outstanding fishing article, we were actually able
to try silver trout fishing this past summer. From now on we are planning
to go fishing every summer. If you were to join us in this endeavor, it would
truly be a great honor. I would like to suggest to you once again that
we are intimately linked by our pasts, even aside from this recent shared
interest in fishing.*

*The third Saturday of September (18th) 18:00, Café Telephone at the
Old Kwanghwa Gate*
P.S. *Please burn this correspondence after you've read it.*

I looked down at this strange postcard, smoking one cigarette after
another. My head slowly began to throb, the blood started coursing
faster through my veins, and the pulse in my temple beat hard against
my eardrums. I reread the postcard more closely while polishing off some
leftover beer from the fridge. Who sent this postcard that was more like
a subpoena than an invitation? The third Saturday was this week. Telephone just happened to be a café I frequent near the Old Kwanghwa
Gate, believe it or not. These people clearly knew who I am. Damn. Who

was this woman I'd supposedly dated and parted from in the past? Who remembered their exes' names anyway? I lay on the sofa and stared hard again at the postcard of Curtis's *Hopi Indians*. Billie Holiday's record was still rotating soundlessly on the turntable.

The fishing article they were referring to was one I'd serialized in the *Daily News* the previous spring and summer entitled "Following the Road, Following the Water." It was part of a weekly feature series published in the "Life and Leisure" column as a useful reference for fishermen. The press team had traveled all over the country to take pictures of the best fishing grounds, gathering information on nearby lodgings and strategies for navigating local traffic. I had to travel around the country myself for five straight months examining each of these famous fishing spots as these articles became more and more popular with readers. It had been a good opportunity that came my way through a connection at a newspaper publishing company. I'd been bored at the time working as an ad photographer after years of struggling in creative photography. This meant officially working as a pressman, and taking as many landscape photos as I wanted. By then, I had grown sick and tired of doing commercial photography for firms and ad agencies, so I jumped at the chance to do something different. Since I was a ten-year veteran of fishing, the series was almost guaranteed to be a success.

My mind descended into greater chaos as I lay in bed, restless and unable to fall asleep. The postcard image I'd left on top of the dining table refused to disappear from my eyes.

So *Hopi Indians* had been unexpectedly delivered one day by an underground group operating under the guise of "The Silver Trout Fishing Network." I could not begin to fathom the presumed "intimate" relationship between me and this group. Maybe I slept with one of them in the past. After all, they were insisting that I had.

Was it about two in the morning? Like a sleepwalker I slowly climbed out of bed and picked up the postcard.

I *did* remember in the deepest recesses of my heart. Moments from a time so dark that they had been transformed into transparencies and discarded. I had given the Curtis photography collection to "her" long ago as a present.

She was the one who'd called me, … that's right. As part of some anonymous group. Who could have guessed that she still existed somewhere in Seoul?

❋

That was three years before. Enough time for someone like me to have gone through countless relationships. Anyhow, she was the one who in the fall of that year had simply vanished like the closing scene in a movie. Speaking of movies, she had been an actress and commercial model. She studied acting in college and had some B-movie roles but never got much exposure. When I first met her, she had been shooting a TV commercial for some clothing company. We were both twenty-seven at the time, and both coincidently had July birthdays. She was already too old to make it as an actress. Knowing this, she continued working as a commercial model just to eke out a living. She'd started out as an underwear model but by the time we were going out, she was modeling for small business catalogues. An opportunity had just opened up for her to be in a swimsuit commercial for a larger corporation. I had been working as a photographer for an ad agency at the time, and had gone to Cheju Island to shoot the swimsuit commercial. That was where we met.

Ch'ongmi Kim. I'd always wondered if her name meant fresh rice or fresh beauty. But I never asked. I just liked to wonder about things like that silently.

The commercial was scheduled to come out during the summer, and the early spring beach shoot was tough on the staff as well as the models. The girls had to go in and out of the icy seawater again and again during retakes, and shoot scenes four or five times including revisions and alternatives, holding the same pose no matter how exhausted they were, until the executive producer was satisfied. The TV commercial was going to air for a long time and needed to be flawless.

The sea felt dry, almost like a desert. Behind us was a field of yellow rape flowers, symbol of Cheju Island, but we did not have time to enjoy the scenery. The models had to smile like cheap dolls in the cold, enduring the abrasive language the staff hurled at them for days on end. The agency, moreover, was trying to keep within budget and had booked the cheapest inn, making the stay even more uncomfortable. Following the shoot the staff went out for drinks downtown, and on top of everything, they forced the models to serve them like hostess girls.

The very last night of the four-day stay, I left the party to rest alone at the inn for a while. Around midnight I decided to get some fresh air along the beach. Night after night of heavy drinking had left my body feeling as if it were disintegrating like grains of sand. The wind was cold but the giant full moon tacitly swayed and floated like a flying saucer over the cobalt-colored sea. It was then that I discovered her crouching in a field of blossoms. I approached thinking I would console her, thinking of all the humiliation she'd had to endure from the drunken staff every night.

"I left because I was getting nauseous. I can't drink with people like that anymore. This whole thing just makes me want to throw up. It makes me realize that people are just the same everywhere."

Her face was swollen and feverish-looking. Blowing cigarette smoke toward the sea, she coughed several times. Her sadness kept her calm despite her exhaustion. She shuddered with cold from time to time. My eyes rested for a while on a flock of birds flying over the horizon.

"Are those geese or seagulls?" she asked me, pointing at the horizon with her cigarette butt, while I regretted not bringing along a camera. There was a sparkle in her voice.

But the birds were so far away that I couldn't quite pinpoint what they were. They couldn't have been geese though.

"Geese would have left already."

"Yes, they would have, huh?"

Instead of responding I simply nodded my head. Pausing, she turned to me and asked, "Do you think they're homing birds or migratory ones?"

She was inquisitive. Her heart was as pure as a river sprite's or she would not have been asking all these questions.

"Well, they look migratory like swallows. As for homing animals, you're thinking of pigeons, honeybees, salmon, trout, and silver trout."

"Ah, I see."

"They use the sun as their compass during their mass migration, so their destination is always determined by the sun's position."

"Where did you learn all that?" she asks me again, looking up trustingly with her river sprite face. River sprite—I pictured kids in the summer frolicking naked in the water, and let out a tiny chuckle. The river sprite, an imaginary creature that looks human and sounds like a crying child.

She had asked the question while I was preoccupied with that absurd image.

"It's not as if I know that much about it, but I used to fish a bit when I was young. Silver trout always return home to their river of origin."

"Ah, silver trout."

"Yes, right about now the silver trout would be swimming against the current from the ocean back to the river. When the cherry blossoms are in bloom and the days are warmed by a southern wind. Then in the autumn they return to the river mouth where they were born and die after spawning their eggs. They're similar to marine salmon, which also swim upstream to their birthplace."

"Wow, I didn't know that."

After this pleasant exchange I began to ramble on about my experiences fishing for silver trout. She listened to my words, quietly nodding her head. The yellow blossoms behind me were rustling, busily chattering away as well.

"I started silver trout fishing with my father when I was five."

"Fascinating. So where did you go to fish?"

"You name it, the Milyang River, the Somchin, as well as Kangwondo streams like Namdaech'on, Pukch'on, Maupch'on, Chusuch'on, Nakp'ungch'on, Wangp'ich'on."

"Wangp'ich'on? Isn't that in Ulchin?"

"How did you know that?"

I asked because I really wondered. Then she responded, almost parroting me.

"It's not as if I know anything about it, but I have passed by it several times."

"What do you mean, you've passed by it?"

"I lived in Kyongju for a while when I was little, and sometimes I would get on a bus to Samch'ok going along the eastern seaboard, and then back. Not for any special occasion, but because the ocean view from Samch'ok to P'ohang was so glorious. It's the most beautiful road in our country. But I've never heard of silver trout making their homes in Ulchin's Wangp'ich'on. Anyway, in retrospect, I think I took that bus whenever I needed to get away."

Sensing the sudden awkwardness she lowered her head and cracked a shy smile. Not that it was something to smile about. After my father's death, I too had visited Kyongju a couple of times to take in the beautiful coastline, usually after one of my solitary trout fishing trips to Wangp'ich'on. Of course I also went to Kyongju to see the Sokkuram Buddhist statue.

I gazed at her warmly.

"That means we could have bumped into each other on a bus or something."

Not understanding, she raised questioning eyes at me. I tried another route.

"We must share some kind of karma or something then."

At this my heart overflowed with sorrow and yearning. I started imagining the two of us traveling the coast. She must have been thinking the same thing because when our eyes met she immediately lowered hers and played with the sand for a while. My mind was deeply immersed in thoughts of silver trout.

All of a sudden I felt myself blacking out as if I had a huge hangover. My whole body went limp, and I found myself gazing numbly into the swaying ocean moonlight, my jaw fallen practically to my knees. I could not figure out how much time had passed.

Then, she slowly ran her hand down my shoulder. Like an unexpected guest knocking on the window.

In our clumsiness and awkwardness she and I started pushing through the transparent space that had isolated us, and brought our mouths together limply. I quivered to realize at that moment how longing could produce desire. All of a sudden she was nestled in my arms like a baby. Everything happened so quickly that I had to try numbly to take deep breaths. I had no idea what to do next. She clasped my neck tightly, shaking, and said, "Hold me."

She and I became one in that sea of yellow blossoms, free of regret or promises. As the moonlight faded so did we, slowly floating away like the ebbing tide.

A week after I came back to Seoul, I saw her again at a café in Insadong. Her face was pale that day as if she'd been suffering from some emotional distress. We sat in silence as she chain-smoked and sipped beer. She seemed to be struggling with something, but I didn't know how to begin to help. When midnight drew near she rose unsteadily from her seat and asked me to let her rest. I took her to the nearest inn. We watched television in silence for a while, and without planning to, I undressed her and climbed into bed.

She closed her eyes and lay there like a mummy. It was only after we had begun to have sex that I realized this was not what she'd wanted. The "act" ended uneventfully. Then she opened her eyes slowly, and listlessly mumbled.

"Everything's become scary. Even this."

I continued to see her for a couple of months afterward. We usually had fried pork cutlets or beefsteak for dinner, drank some beer, got intoxicated and had mediocre sex. It was always the same. Fried pork cutlet, beer, sex, beefsteak, beer, sex, fried pork cutlet, beer, sex . . . we weren't that into the sex, but did it anyway like people stranded on an island with nothing else to do.

I waited for her one autumn day in front of a downtown theater.

I remember waiting for a pretty long time, not questioning why she might have asked to meet me at a theater. Dressed in a purple Burberry coat, she snuck in the back way twenty minutes after the movie had begun. She took me into the dark movie theater, just as I was getting over the unfamiliarity and discomfort of not being able to recognize her right away. We kept our eyes glued to the screen until the very end of the movie, like complete strangers. Time passed awkwardly until the bell rang and the lights came on. Bleary-eyed, the rest of the audience rose from their seats to leave. Suddenly she blurted out, "Man stranded in a desert."

I looked up at her. That was when I realized that her words were aimed at me. Her face was pale and stiff as usual.

"A man addicted to his wounds."

She repeated this as if her eyes were drilling a hole in the snowy screen. I listened to her, frozen in place.

"Pretends to be vulnerable emotionally but is inconsiderate and cold. A terminator."

"...!?"

"A scary man."

With this her head drooped as if her neck had broken and she began sobbing. She continued crying quietly until a couple came to claim their seats for the next show.

We came out of the theater, passed by Uljiro Boulevard and Paek Hospital, and crossed the walkway toward Myongdong Cathedral, all in utter silence. The longer we walked, the more acutely I felt the distance between us, as if with each step we were growing further and further apart. I approached the hill that led to the cathedral and realized I could not possibly catch up with her. But this was what she wanted. With this revelation I paused in the middle of the street in the midst of a sea of people making their descent. She never stopped to wait for me though, and soon buried herself among the throngs without bothering to look back, not even once. She became smaller and smaller, like a single letter inscribed in a book, and vanished completely from my sight.

When I returned home that night I donned my fisherman's outfit—a pair of polarized glasses, tights, yellow boots, and a landing net at my waist—and stood in front of the mirror scrutinizing myself.

After that, I would see her occasionally on TV or in magazines, but did not feel it would be possible to see her in person again. It was as if she had completely disappeared from my life. The Cheju Island commercial stopped airing after a season, and she disappeared from the media about a year after that.

I sat waiting, staring at the autumn rain streaming down the window that Saturday evening. Telephone was booming with people who'd been drinking since the early afternoon. The manager shot me dirty looks for only ordering a beer and occupying a whole window seat. He was normally gracious but today his severe glances were unwelcoming. Five minutes before six. Still smoking, I looked at my watch. I only had to wait another five minutes.

Sitting on my living room sofa that very morning I had burned, in an ashtray, the postcard they had sent. It was tucked between the pages of a book so no one would have found it, but it seemed to be calling out to me, "I told you to burn me!" The "Disappearing Tribe"—the *Hopi Indians*—disappeared quite literally in my ashtray.

Then something unexpected happened. Until that morning I had been ambivalent about going out to the Telephone Cafe, but staring at the ashes I began to miss "her." I'd developed a sudden urge to go out and meet her.

I began feeling antsy as the clock struck six. I thought I'd order another beer but instead glanced toward the window and decided to wait a bit longer. Just then I heard someone calling my name. It was the phone. I walked up to the counter and answered. It was a familiar voice.

"It's so loud where you are. Come out to the parking lot behind Sejong Cultural Center. I'll be in a red sports car, waiting for you."

It was the woman who'd called me Wednesday. After I hung up the phone, I walked out of the café, and crossed over to the parking lot across the street.

A woman with long hair and sunglasses sat smoking inside a red sports car. I paused for a moment during my approach and studied her, ignoring the raindrops starting to fall. The door swung open silently. "Get in," the woman coughed out. I got into the car as if sucked inside.

I sat awkwardly looking out at the raindrops splattering the window, until she had finished her cigarette. Outside, people were floating in the night's misty darkness. I found myself inhaling the perfume of the woman sitting next to me.

"I've never had a frozen corpse in my car before."

She initiated the conversation with a dry remark yet her tone was gracious. Or maybe her attempt at a joke created an air of friendliness. To tell the truth, I really was frozen stiff.

"This is the first time I've ridden in a red hearse," I shot right back at her.

"This hearse, . . . there are times it accelerates as if trying to escape death. Drunk with speed."

"...if it accelerates to the speed of light, time would stop and we would escape death."

"Then space itself would bend out of shape."

"If we were to go even faster than light ..."

"Then, we'd return ... to the place we must go to."

She turned on the engine. As the windshield wipers clicked on, I felt as if my brief conversation with her had been a dream. She maneuvered the car expertly past the Koreana Hotel and slid into the lane toward Grand West Gate. Jane Birkin's "Yesterday Yes a Day" played quietly on the car stereo. Was it the theme song from *Madame Claude*? It had been more than ten years since I'd heard it ... At any rate, one thing seemed certain, I seemed to be revisiting the past, maybe even spiraling into it.

"Are you usually this quiet?" she shot at me, watching the road ahead.

"I tend to be a slow and clumsy speaker. They say this is typical of men born in the Year of the Dragon."

"I already knew you were born in the Year of the Dragon. Should I take a stab at your birthday as well?"

Doubting she'd guess right, I looked at her indifferently.

"July twelfth, 1964."

I felt my blood curdle as goose bumps rose all over my body. The suspicions I'd temporarily pushed aside all resurfaced. Who were these people and why did they know so much about me? I shot her a fierce look but she remained unperturbed. Laughing casually, she said, "It was only a guess, but was I right?" Her face, framed by hair that flowed down to her chin, was actually quite beautiful, but at the moment she looked as frightful as a ghost. Those sunglasses of hers were even more mesmerizing. But I didn't want to be drawn in by her so easily.

"You must work at the local office, right? Don't you have more important things to remember than my profile?"

"We were all born in the same year. July 1964, to be precise. Are you starting to get it?"

What did she mean "we"? All born in the same year and the same month! Unable to stand any more suspense, I was about to yell at her to stop the car, but we ended up stopping anyway because of the horrific traffic jam in front of the *Donga Daily News* building. My nerves tightened, and I began to feel flushed.

"You might want to try and relax. If I were to tell you that we were all born in Seoul, I'm afraid you'd try to jump out the window."

Charcoal-colored cigarette smoke filled the air. Suddenly my head began to ache and an indescribable fatigue came over me.

"I'm getting carsick. Can you at least crack open the window a bit?"

"Sure. It's understandable that thinking about the past is making you nauseous."

I felt better when gentle raindrops cooled my face. But my heart was still racing. There was no sign of the traffic clearing on Mapo Bridge.

"Where are you taking me?" I turned and asked her, "and how about letting me see your face. I don't like being kidnapped like this. You have to give me something to go on, anything at all."

She remained quiet for a time. The sound of the rain grew louder. After rain the autumn leaves would be a deeper crimson. The car proceeded about ten more yards and then stopped again. "Tell me," I said again. She appeared to think hard about where to begin.

"Have you ever heard of the famous artist, Arnulf Rainer?"

Her voice became deep and throaty. She didn't really seem to expect a response so I didn't answer.

"Then do you know what body painting is?"

Yes, I remembered it from some art magazine. I'd seen pictures of men and women covered with paint, walking down a path or lying in a park.

"It's an elevated form of art that disregards social taboos and expresses freedom in life. I'll quiz you a bit now. If you get it right, I'll put a star up for you tonight."

The car turned left at the Kongdoktong rotary and headed toward Sogang University. The rain and fog descended so heavily it felt as if we were swimming through a black sea.

"This car contains things that were killed because they dissented, things deformed by pain, frustrated ambitions, and other things of that sort. Are you beginning to catch on?"

"So now this funeral hearse is some sort of a racing cemetery?"

"Yes, a cemetery, but one dreaming of rebirth."

"Okay."

"We have our own constitution, so to speak."

"Sure," I responded blankly.

"Article 1 Clause 1 of Eluard's poem 'Freedom,' Clause 2 in Schweiger's novel *Wake Up and Face the Sorrow*, Clause 3 from Jarmusch's film *Stranger than Paradise*, Clause 4 Mozart, Clause 5 Van Gogh and Munch, Article 2 Clause 1 marijuana, Clause 2 camera and free sex, Clause 3 spaceships, Clause 4 India and Tibet, Article 3 Clause 1 beer cans and sandy beaches, Clause 2 Maria Callas and Mike Oldfield, Clause 3 Roland Barthes and Pascal Resnais . . ."

She unemotionally rattled off a list, enunciating each word as if reading from some menu.

"You must know that some of those things are illegal," I commented in a low voice.

"Hmph, haven't you heard of the phrase 'vanished without a trace'? Look here. We won't even know when and where we'll meet again. Do you understand?"

Vanished without a trace . . . I repeated this to myself, thinking of the Hopi Indians. Wondering if these people would also vanish into the depths of an abyss.

"Okay, now let me start the questions."

Suddenly she became more animated and stepped on the accelerator. We glided swiftly down the road ignoring every traffic light. The sports car zigzagged between rows of automobiles like a beetle high on some phosphorescent drug. I wiped the cold sweat off my forehead.

"Would you ever have thought that all these articles from our constitution are on this car?"

"On this car?"

"Yes. On this very car."

For the first time, I sensed a strange anxiety come over her face. Her movements became more abrupt, and the air around us suddenly chilled. Without a word I pretended to look around inside the car. It was the kind of question that could only be answered by the questioner. So I sat there, blindly staring ahead without even bothering to come up with a response. The car stopped at a light, and she started to try to explain in that same lackluster voice.

"I . . . painted them all over the car, on this car. Then I painted everything over with red. Just as in body painting."

I stared at her blankly.

"You mean this very car?"

"Yes, so that they would no longer be suppressed or managed, yet protected from further attack or damage. It's analogous to the structure of our underground network. We are finding ways to recover within a state of unboundedness."

A state of unboundedness . . . It was within this state of unbounded consciousness that I was moving toward an unknown state. Yet there was no way to escape. I could only move forward.

Were we going in the direction of Hongik University? She muttered, "We're here," as the car disappeared into a narrow alley in the café area. It had all happened so quickly, I began to feel myself getting agitated again.

As we had near the Old Kanghwa Palace, we stayed inside the car for a while. She turned off the radio, the headlights, and the engine, and started smoking again. Her face disappeared and reappeared each time she exhaled and inhaled. Though I was tempted to say it had been an awesome drive, now wasn't the time for levity. I was trapped inside this car like a captive in a holding cell. There was one last thing I wanted to ask her. But the time never seemed right, and the waiting only grew more painful. I wasn't the first to break the silence. She took off her sunglasses and looked directly into my eyes. For a brief moment, she took my breath away. Her eyes resembled those of Monica Vitti in the film *L'Eclisse*. They were soft and luminous. Somewhere I heard a distant sound like a water jug rolling around.

"You have traveled back to July 1964 in a time machine. You will not be able to leave until tomorrow morning. You must promise no matter what happens that you will not try to leave."

"I promise. But there's something I need to know. It's the reason I came all the way here."

The sound of the rolling water jug stopped, drowned out by street noise. She nodded as if telling me to proceed.

"Tell me if she's here. This is very important to me."

"She's here," she confirmed.

"Let me explain. Our very first meeting was two springs ago. An unknown actress at the time, she began to meet with a group of magazine writers, college lecturers, and artists at a cafe in Sinch'on. This grew into what we have today. They all had different reasons for joining but all the members had been rejected by life in some way. They sought out others like themselves, and the meetings became more and more secretive. As time passed, architects, doctors, underground singers, and poets joined the group, but membership was eventually restricted to those born in July of 1964 as a way to strengthen club solidarity. Of course, to the outside world, all these people continue to lead normal lives. But all the members are unable to find any grounding in that existence. We meet in secret once or twice a month. In a way we are leading a double life, unable to accept the real world. So we live as people who've built an entirely different community underground. This is why we decided to use the coded language of silver trout among ourselves. It is here that we practice over and over again strategies for survival."

I looked through the dim window and took stock of the world we had just passed through. I was not sure whether I belonged here or there. "Okay, let's go," she said as she unfastened her seat belt. I was jolted from my numbness. Then she got out of the car.

Unfamiliar concrete roads stretching on and on. Eaves of roofs connecting in all directions, and between them, dark, cramped alleys. The rhythmic sound of her walking in front of me, blocking my way. Finally the sudden hazy silhouette of a stairway. Icy darkness pressed down on my back and chilled my heart.

I was roused out of my stupor by the heavy sound of a knock and turned to look at the wooden door of the underground shed in front of me. My rain-soaked body started to shake. I noticed that her silhouette was also trembling before me, standing a dark distance away.

I was overcome by a sudden desire to stand there all night in that exact position. Carried away by a strange excitement, I just wanted to stay with her in front of that unopened door. But I heard footsteps from within, scraping toward the door. I was overwhelmed all of a sudden by an intense urge to hug her. How could I have explained this unstemmable tide of longing sweeping over me?

I was afraid. I'd never really met people that different from myself. It was really beyond my realm of experience. But before the hand I had reached out could make contact with her I heard her talking to someone inside.

The door opened with a creak.

"It's raining," a man said in a scratchy voice. His face was occluded by a strange darkness. There was a stream of blue light along the path he had just taken. I was surprised by the warmth of his hand, which I shook. He remained silent as I followed him along a corridor. I began to feel numb again as I took in the scent of wood and another unfamiliar odor, sour and vinegary. Maybe it was the smell of burning candles, but I couldn't be sure. I was barely able to keep my balance. The hall felt so much longer than it really was.

Eventually, I heard people talking. The fading blue light revealed the texture of the wooden floor, and the smell of alcohol assaulted my nostrils along with the smell of burning plants. I saw lit candles arranged in a circle. Then my consciousness dropped away like a lizard's tail. I meant less than a single candle. I was nothing more than clothing draped over empty air. All the commotion in that airtight place stopped when I entered, and once-scattered eyes focused on the very space of my existence. There were about ten people there. Some were lying around holding cups of wine, some were half naked and holding each other in the corner, still others were strumming guitars, reading by candlelight, or drinking coffee. All these scenes were channeled into my pupils. I stood alone in a corner of the room, confused as to how I should act. When the tension dissipated, I realized that their looks were signs of approval. They only wanted to confirm that I wasn't a threat. One of them mumbled without even looking at me, "The world is divided into two groups: our side or their side. You have just crossed over to our side."

I sat uncomfortably on the corner of a cabinet that held some books. Had I really come to the other side of the world? The woman who'd brought me disappeared briefly and returned in a different outfit, carrying a green bottle of alcohol. It could have been wine, but there was no way I could even register its taste. She poured some into a cup, and I gulped down two glasses quickly.

"Stay here. Until someone comes for you."

She left me then to join the others.

From that point on, no one gave me a second glance or even tried to talk to me. They just sat around as before, occasionally clinking their glasses in the midst of incessant chatter. I found my whole existence again reduced to that of a burnt-out candle, and apprehensively tried to keep track of time. I couldn't find any traces of "her," although they said she was here. I wondered who would come for me, and when?

My mind wandered again, thinking about the Hopis, that tragic tribe standing on a windy mesa waiting for eternal oblivion. I thought of them and the woman who had left me long ago.

I waited and waited some more, until I forgot the meaning of patience. I could do nothing else. I finished the bottle of alcohol and passed the time listening to the chatter around me. Nothing happened. They turned their backs on me, engrossed in their own business. I wasn't being neglected, just excluded.

I hadn't noticed that they had all begun to gather in a circle. They had stopped chattering. I watched them closely, expecting something to happen.

They sat bent over, as if about to throw up, chuckling quietly and chanting, "Peace, peace." Even though I had never seen such a thing, I knew intuitively what they were doing. The smell of burning marijuana rose slowly and clung to my nostrils. My guard went up instinctively, but my body became lethargic as my pulse slowed.

Right then, someone tapped me on the shoulder. I was stunned and couldn't turn around at first.

…My body recognized that hand, though. Its size, shape, weight, and feeling as it touched my shoulder. It was then that I realized how much I had missed that very familiar hand. I also knew I was in no position to indulge in such a reverie.

The hand took my own silently and pulled me to an unknown place beyond a door behind the cabinet.

"I have been spiraling down ever since that time," she said.

What did she mean by "that time"? I could only see three chairs in the room where we were sitting. It felt like a small dank café. A candle burned dimly on the table, but the interior was dark, mysterious, and cold. Here I was, seeing her again after all these years, in a basement cellar that looked like a defunct bar. She sat, motionless, on a chair in the corner. Her face was pale and drawn, like a frozen face scribbled on a white sketchpad. Her skinny bare feet peeking out from underneath her skirt were the only proof she was alive. The words we exchanged seemed surreal. I was barely holding on between reality and illusion.

I had returned to that original place.

From inside the sketchpad her voice droned forth. I felt tormented by its tenacity. Her desiccated look was empty. I shook my head and stared at the cold darkness of the floor.

"You, too, are now beginning your return. Until now you have been straying far, far from here. You might have forgotten the way back forever."

I did feel as if I had drifted too far from where I belonged, as if I had existed in isolation all this time. In a desert outside existence.

"I want to return now," I said, painfully.

For a moment her face swayed like a water plant in the candlelight. I recalled the night I first met her, on Cheju Beach. Spring, the yellow blossoms, the geese, silver trout, the moon, the *river sprite*, . . . all those things. The girl I had met in that beautiful mythical place. Thinking such thoughts, I found courage and made a declaration: I would cast off all ambition, deceit, and vanity, as well as this sleepless age.

No, you need to go back further. You need to come back to the place you once were. She repeated this again and again, and I felt my heart grow sicker.

I told her I was back at the Wangp'i River in Ulchin. I knew I had to talk this way.

". . . Come, a little more," she said.

Then I sensed shaking and agitation in her once expressionless face. In the midst of it all I realized that our time together had scarred her in incurable ways.

She stood there with her mouth open, trembling like a silver trout spawning its eggs. Staring at me like this, she slid against the wall, whimpering softly.

I knew that to return to my distant origin, the place where I belonged, I would need many more days and nights.

I drew closer to her and firmly grabbed hold of her icy hand, which felt drained of human warmth.

I held her hand until morning, and threw away thirty years of my life to return upstream to that place where I belonged.

931122.

I received a second envelope from them on the first snowy night back in Seoul.

Mi-na Choi ✸ *Korea*

Mi-na Choi has been active as a writer publishing short stories and novels since 1956. However, until now she has not been widely published outside of Korea. She was born in Kwangju in 1932 and graduated from Chunnam High School in 1949. Within a few years she was submitting stories to *Yamun*, a woman's magazine. From the outset of her career as an author, she has been recognized for the depth of maternal feeling in her work. Korean literary commentators point to the consistent poignancy of her themes addressing the isolation and loneliness of traditional Korean family relationships. This is reflected in "Third Meeting," which holds up a looking glass to the deeper structure of traditional male-dominated Korean marital relationships such as the author portrays in her story.

Third Meeting

Translated by Trevor Carolan and Kwangshik Jane Kwon

KYUNG-SOOK SAT DAZED. THE STINGING TONE OF HER HUSBAND'S voice demanding answers to her delayed immigration departure still lingered.

Out of habit, Seuk-ho's face swam before her.

Her husband had spoken to her during the international call as if he'd known precisely why she was stalling—that she was desperately waiting for Seuk-ho. But it was impossible that he could know that. And anyway, why should anyone over the age of fifty be obliged to go and live so far away in a foreign country at all?

Customarily, Kyung-sook obeyed her husband without complaint, yet on this one matter she dodged him. She understood, however, that she had neither the basis nor the will to overturn the finality of his decision. She would have to emigrate to America. Seuk-ho was the one remaining problem. She couldn't leave without meeting him face to face one last time.

Kyung-sook didn't even know his address. In waiting for Seuk-ho she'd already cancelled her airline reservations several times. Now only three days remained until her irrevocable departure. With each passing moment she burned with expectation.

Suddenly, she heard the sound of a baby crying. At first it sounded like the neighbor's television. Then, certain it came from the front of her house, she flung open the bedroom door and rushed to the gate. An abandoned child. It was wrapped in a quilt. She rummaged for a light to see in the dusk. The infant looked to be three or four months old. Grimacing, the baby began to wail.

"How could this be?" Kyung-sook picked up the baby and brought it near her face. Its tender cheeks were cold. She looked around the alley. Whoever had left the child might still be watching. It was useless to stand about wondering, so closing the gate, she hurried inside.

Laying the baby on the floor, she probed in its wrapping. There was a letter. The moment she saw the handwriting her face darkened.

Hearing a knock upon the gate, Kyung-sook hesitated. She was laundering a pile of wash in the yard. "Who is it?" she called.

No answer. She returned to her laundry, soaking clothes in a tub. The gate shook again. "Who is it?" she called again, annoyed. Silence.

Ordinarily, the shabby gate squeaked on windy days, but today was exceptionally fair and sunny. Neighborhood rascals liked to rattle the gate as a game, although if that were the case she should have heard their footsteps. Kyung-sook went and opened the latch. Her house stood at the head of an alley. From there she could see as far as the main road lined with its cinder-block row houses, but there was no trace of the little ruffians.

"Oh, damn, I've no time for this...."

She returned inside. Halfway to the courtyard water-tap she shifted her steps, propped herself quietly in a corner and waited for the nuisances to reappear, relishing the thought of teaching whoever it was a stiff lesson. Carefully, she unhooked the latch and held her breath. Minutes passed. Then, with footsteps almost faint beyond hearing, the gate rattled. Kyung-sook seized it open and raced outside. A boy of eleven or twelve streaked off quickly. For a moment Kyung-sook was startled, not knowing why.

"Is it possible?"

Without time to calm her thumping heart, she ran breathlessly after the boy who disappeared down a nearby alley. Kyung-sook found him there, forehead pressed hard to the concrete wall, head closely shaven, dressed in blue jeans and T-shirt, his anguished features plainly new to town, in from peasant country. She lifted his chin.

"Just arrived?" The boy looked on blankly.

"If you came all this way, why didn't you step in?" Her voice passed dryly from her lips, trembling. It was the first time he'd come looking for her. From Chungnam village, six long years ago. He'd been five. She'd left him with her mother.

Seuk-ho stood unmoving, pressed to the fence. Unaccountably, worry began to creep up on Kyung-sook. She took the boy by his shoulder. Was there some problem? Had he done something wrong and run away? She stared at her son glumly. Seuk-ho.

It could all be discussed later. The immediate problem was where to take him. She led him to a run-down local restaurant. They sat facing each other, mother and son, the first time in a long while.

"Did you have a hard time finding the house?" No answer.

"Did you tell your grandmother you were coming?"

Nothing. Unreachable, the boy sat with clenched teeth until their food arrived. Kyung-sook placed a spoon in Seuk-ho's hand.

"Eat now, all right?" She stroked his hair, listening to her own pleading voice. The boy finally lifted his chopsticks and she breathed a heavy sigh of relief. Seuk-ho emptied his bowl in a blink. He was famished. "Should I order more?" she asked, but the boy shook his head. Kyung-sook studied her son's shirt front. It looked new. Her mother had complained that the boy chewed his undershirts to rags and she grieved at hearing such stories. The boy released his frustration this way, she believed. Always he had something in his mouth and if nothing else was around, he tugged at the front of his T-shirt and chewed it.

"A starving ghost must have gotten him." It was too much to ask of an aged, illiterate mother that she could understand Seuk-ho's emptiness. "What's the use of all this mother and daughter hardship anyway?" her mother would say, "No matter how we raise this child, in the end he'll leave and return to his father's family. Just wait and see if there's no truth to the old saying."

Her mother's grudge against Kyung-sook's in-laws never ended. When Seuk-ho's father met his death working on a tuna boat off Samoan waters, her in-laws had intercepted a large compensation settlement. Kyung-sook herself had long ago given up the quarrel but could not forgive the pain they'd caused by refusing to help raise their own grandson.

"Did you come by the night train?" Kyung-sook questioned him steadily, trying to break the boy's silence. He resisted her as best he could. She felt the stifled scream boiling up in his heart. Hadn't she sworn they would live together when there was enough money? Yet she, his own mother, had never come for him, and now Seuk-ho had arrived on his own. She grew a little afraid. She also considered if it wasn't to her own salvation that Seuk-ho wouldn't open his mouth. What might happen if he did; what terrible accusations might spill forth? Her spine chilled at the prospect.

From her workpants' pockets Kyung-sook fetched a few crumbled bills and paid for the meal. A thousand *won* was cut from tomorrow's business fund, she reflected. But it was hardly the time to worry about such things. Setting off heavily, she was forced to pause repeatedly for the boy who kept falling behind. Nearing the house her legs grew heavier and heavier, as though they'd been bound in chains. Her mind was a muddle of thoughts. As his mother, she could not simply send him back to the country, yet keeping him here was a serious problem.

"I came to attend a middle school in Seoul." It was the first he'd spoken. Hearing the rough country voice from behind, she cringed. Her heart sank as if she'd been assaulted, and her dream that the boy had run away specifically to see her was harshly rebuked, exposing her inner fears.

They stood together in front of her house, but Kyung-sook hesitated, unable to venture inside. Through the window came the sound of voices. Kang-guk and Kang-sung, her stepsons, were talking, but this was not the only reason she delayed. The problem of how she should explain them to her poor son—all the momentous changes in her life—lay heavy on her shoulders.

She turned and looked at the boy. With one hand thrust in his pocket, Seuk-ho's shadow overpowered her like a giant. She had a weighty task to accomplish and there was no way out of it. Kyung-sook pushed open the gate. Inside were the two rooms she rented with her second husband. From one came the shouts and thumps of a wrestling match.

"What are you doing?"

As Kyung-sook opened the door, Kang-guk grabbed Kang-sung's waistband and was about to throw him. He glared at her.

"What the heck! Where've you been?" he demanded. "Where's our lunch?"

It was scarcely the first time she'd experienced such talk, but today because of Seuk-ho it made her feel faint. "You must be hungry. Wait a moment..."

Seuk-ho stared at her as if saying, what's going on here? She struggled to maintain control. "Aren't you coming in?" she asked him. Hearing this, her stepsons poked out their heads out together.

"Who's *that?*"

"Where'd that hick roll in from?"

Thirteen year old Kang-guk, and Kang-sung, two years younger, flashed their eyes like cats at a bird. Seeing Seuk-ho's uncomprehending expression, Kyung-sook turned her glance away as if she'd seen something she shouldn't have.

"This is Seuk-ho. He's come up from the country. Play together nicely," she mumbled vaguely, anxiously thinking she must get Seuk-ho into the boys' room. Only by mingling with them could he stay with his mother for a few days.

"From the country, eh? Come on in!" teased Kang-guk, mocking Seuk-ho's country dialect.

The boy looked confused and seemed to think his mother was a housemaid. He turned his attention toward her. Kyung-sook understood that her son wanted to know the truth, but she was unable to open her mouth. Pointing to the next rooms she asked sheepishly, "Do you want to come in?"

Seuk-ho followed silently into the main bedroom, which was the same size as the boys' room but featured several long shabby box-drawers piled with faded bedding. He glanced at the room: men's shirts, trousers, her own stretched-out skirts and sweaters were hung about the walls. Kyung-sook could barely lift her head; it was as if the boy had discovered her living as a concubine.

"*What?* Ran away! Hey, you, hillbilly! Get back here right this minute!" Stamping his feet threateningly, Kang-guk's voice pierced the door. Sweat now soaked Kyung-sook's back. She could scarcely suppress the violent urge to silence Kang-guk's mouth herself.

"I'll be back shortly. Wait here." Leaving Seuk-ho in her room, she went to the kitchen and made lunch. But she was not herself. How was a young man to suffer such insults? As quickly as she could, she rushed into the boys room with a serving tray.

"You call this food?"

"Do you think we're some kind of dogs!" Kang-sung, the younger, glowered demonically.

"I'll make something nicer for dinner, come now, eat." She was whispering now, half begging.

"*Hmph!* You think we don't know what's going on? You're really making it for that hillbilly brat, aren't you?" Kang-guk growled as if he was about to kick the meal tray over. "Well, it's out of the question. If you go off to the markets we won't leave you alone."

Kyung-sook sighed anew. She resented her second husband, who out of endless guilt toward them let his sons behave this way. They'd lost their mother at the ages of five and three, and never had she seen him scold them sternly. Only later had she learned that on his being widowed, four different women had struggled to care for his contemptible sons. None could cope with the harassment from the pair of them. For that reason alone, her husband's love toward her was dear to Kyung-sook. Seeing her endure through repeated, unspeakable crises with his boys, her husband thought of Kyung-sook as a treasure. But there was more . . . her own stubborn pride. She would not fail the remarriage which had thus far sustained her.

"Seuk-ho has come." She hinted this to her husband on his return home from work.

"Who's Seuk-ho?"

Her husband rolled his eyeballs, then said, "Ah yes. Absent-minded me." Scratching his head, he went into their room. "So Seuk-ho has come . . ." Her husband tried to stroke the boy's head, but Seuk-ho slipped away like a mudfish. Without looking at her husband he finally kicked open the door and went outside.

"Where are you going? Don't be like that. Come back inside." Kyung-sook tried calming the boy outside by holding his arm as slowly, his anger and bewilderment gave way to realization—an opportunity not lost on his mother who urged him back inside. As mother and son re-entered, the ill-tempered stepsons glared at Seuk-ho with delight as if a curious new toy had rolled in.

Lying in bed with her husband, Kyung-sook was unable to sleep for worry. Inexplicably, she felt as though she were in bed with another man. Her husband too was uneasy, tossing repeatedly. It was plain enough to guess what must be going through his mind. As a man, he wouldn't wish to say, "Return him to his grandmother," but his sons would never entertain the thought of Seuk-ho living together with them all. Under the circumstances, even as nonsense he could not make such an offer. That would be his position.

Kyung-sook thought of leaving forever with Seuk-ho. Even so, the scars left upon her son would never heal and she hadn't the money to lease a private room anyway.

Thump! From the other room came a terrific hammering sound. Kyung-sook sharpened her hearing. Hoping perhaps she had heard it wrong, she forced herself back to sleep. *Thump!* The wall shook again. As if he had also guessed her husband held his breath. Kyung-sook opened the door to calm her pounding heart. The light was out. It fell quiet again. She stood outside the door, wondering.

In the morning when she came outside to cook breakfast she almost screamed. Seuk-ho stood against the gate. Before she could utter a word, the boy stuck his palm out abruptly. He wanted the return fare home.

"Are you leaving without breakfast?" Even as she spoke, Kyung-sook shrank back, knowing that she had exposed her own inner wish: that Seuk-ho would leave of his own accord.

Wracked with guilt, Kyung-sook could not forgive herself for feeling unburdened after sending her own precious son away. She abandoned her trade as a vendor. On the fourth day, as she lay ill in bed, a letter arrived from her mother that brought another strong blow. Her mother wrote that when she'd removed Seuk-ho's clothes to change him on his return from tramping off to Seoul, his body was battered with bruises and scratches. After this, Kyung-sook developed symptoms of a heart malaise no medicine could cure, eating away at her health. Her attitude sharpened toward her stepsons. Still, she forced herself to persevere until the pair reached maturity.

Then news came that Seuk-ho had started middle school and required financial support. Asking money of her ljack-of-all-trades husband for the upkeep of a son not his own was pointless. Rising from her sick bed, Kyung-sook resurrected the old cooking wagon she'd abandoned in back of the kitchen. Scrubbing and repairing it, she steeled herself to return to frying sweet cakes out on the streets again. She could save up funds for Seuk-ho by selling fruit in summer and fried pancakes in winter.

Back at her old trade, she worked doggedly. Now, even during lean periods at home she refused to offer up a scrap of her income. How else could she possibly assuage her guilt toward her son, her own flesh and blood? For her pains she received recriminating "two pocket" looks from her husband that widened the growing distance between them.

Seuk-ho, she learned, moved on to attend secondary school at a provincial capital near his grandmother. Never once did he attempt to contact her again. That he had advanced and become a high school student was very admirable; indeed, she could scarcely resist her desire to see him. Once, she wrote indicating that she would like to visit him during the holidays.

"I do not wish to see you. If you must come to see me, I cannot stop you, but please understand that I shall not be at home then." That was his reply. It was not unreasonable, of course: The one occasion her son had come to see his own mother, he'd been assaulted by strangers. On top of that, his own mother had slept with an unknown man in the next room. Kyung-sook sighed deeply at the intensity of the grudge now imbued in her son's very marrow.

She met him for the second time seven years later. Surprisingly, Seuk-ho came to see her after graduating high school on his way to national military service. Seeing him, Kyung-sook shivered and collapsed in her chair. He was the breathing image of his departed father, standing tall, youthful, thick-haired. A man.

"How are you?" he inquired calmly.

"Good heavens…" She was speechless. Oh, my son, she dearly wanted to cry, but the words would not come out and she swallowed them, wanting terribly to keep him even one night no matter what, if only to show him how his step-brothers had changed. Perhaps their father's endless compassion alone had guided them straight; the pair had improved remarkably as they aged.

Kyung-sook wished desperately to show she no longer lived as wretchedly and cowardly as before—and above all else, how tearfully, gratefully, she admired the young man who now stood before his mother. Preparing dishes for him, her vision was blinded by tears. Slicing her finger, even as it bled she was unaware of the pain. At dinner, her husband returned home.

"It's Seuk-ho."

Her husband looked puzzled. "What?"

"It's Seuk-ho."

Unexpectedly, he grew cold. Her own husband. How could he do this? Her heart trembled, her blood boiled. Realizing that unless she controlled her raging anger it could prove an irrecoverable blow, she demanded, "How can you be like that to him!" At that moment, Kang-guk and Kang-sung announced their return.

"You don't recognize Seuk-ho, do you?"

Seuk-ho rose from the floor. The brothers scrambled in memory, then greeted him with smiles. "Whoa, it's been a long time!" To Kyung-sook, this was comfort enough. She ran to the kitchen and cried her fill. As her anger subsided a little, she prepared a dinner table for the three boys in their room.

"Why don't you go to university instead of entering the army?" Kang-guk asked. Seuk-ho replied he would decide on further study once his national duty was complete. Her husband tried to begin conversation but Kyung-sook was in no mood to listen.

"Seeing him all grown up like that startled me. I never expected it," he murmured indifferently.

"Don't say any more."

"I must seem very narrow-minded . . ."

Kyung-sook cut him short. He had seen his wife's first husband in Seuk-ho's features. Her heart tightened again with guilt—not only toward Seuk-ho, but now toward her present husband as well. Was she undeniably such a sinner?

Only one postcard came from her son in the Army, a few lines inquiring after her health, but in them Kyung-sook sensed he had forgiven his mother. She cried uncontrollably through the day. Other changes, mainly pleasant, came while Seuk-ho was away. Whatever the reason though, Seuk-ho never wrote again. Kyung-sook waited patiently in anticipation, but even when the time came for completion of his duty, no news arrived. During this time, the foreman at the factory where her husband worked had emigrated to America and sent her husband an invitation. He left shortly thereafter. Three years later, having settled in successfully himself, he sent word that he wanted Kyung-sook to proceed with steps for emigration herself.

And so, even though these procedures were all completed, she now found herself delaying her departure with this and that flimsy excuse. It had been easier while her stepsons were still with her, but she was out of excuses and her husband rightly suspected something. He was writing and telephoning every week. Kyung-sook tore open the envelope from the baby's quilt. "Mother, please accept my child," it read. "It's been a year since my marriage. While we struggle toward a stable living, please raise this child like a mother. I cannot promise when, but I will come with my wife to get the child and will see you then. From Seuk-ho."

A milk bottle lay inside the blanket. From the way he was crying, the infant must be starving. There were tears. She lifted up the baby, giving him the bottle to suck. The more she looked at him, the more he resembled Seuk-ho. The child sucked hungrily. Soon after, pushing away the nipple with his tongue, he began breathing softly.

"Has he really left his child with me because he has a problem earning a living?" Suddenly there was this elemental question. Wouldn't it be from the assurance of his own mother's love that her grown son had trusted this baby to her? She had advertised her imminent departure in the newspapers in hope of seeing her son once last time. If not for this one reason alone, why would he come in the way of his mother's emigration?

Kyung-sook hugged the baby closer. The distance between her son and her had narrowed sharply and she felt an electricity flowing between them. No, it was as if an old indigestion had finally cleared. Her heart was opening wide. It was not simply that she'd heard Seuk-ho calling her "Mother" for the first time. It was more. For a moment, she was confused by it all. She could not properly gauge the depth of the changes occurring inside her. There could be no further delaying her one, fateful decision. She would tell her husband her departure was postponed. Lifting the receiver, she dialed international.

"Then, when *will* you be coming?"

"That ... I can't answer," she said. For in truth, she could not honestly say more.

Xu Xi ✹ *Hong Kong*

Xu Xi is one of Hong Kong's foremost contemporary English-language novelists. A native of Hong Kong from a Chinese-Indonesian family, she has been a resident of that city, intermittently, for some thirty years. Her first stories and essays appeared in the *South China Morning Post*. In 1979, her first short story written as a quasi-adult, "The Sea Islands," was published in *Imprint*, a journal from the University of Hong Kong. She came to international attention in 1996 with the publication of *The Daughters of Hui*, a fiction collection that *Asiaweek* called one of the top ten best books of the year. After some 18 years in international marketing and management, Xu Xi quit the corporate world to write full time. The author of three novels and several fiction collections, her work has been published and broadcast internationally. Xu Xi holds an MFA in fiction from the University of Massachusetts at Amherst, and has been a writer-in-residence at the Jack Kerouac Project in Orlando, Florida, and at Lingnan University in Hong Kong. Recently, she has edited, with Mike Ingram, *City Voices* (2003), a comprehensive gathering of writing from Hong Kong by more than 70 writers. In 2007, she was nominated for the inaugural Man Asian Literary Prize. Xu Xi divides her time between her home city and New York.

Until the Next Century

"QINGFU." HE HANDED HER THE CHILLED CHAMPAGNE.

She took it and kissed the tip of his nose. "Quick, close the door." Even now, she welcomed him this way, recalling the first time when, embarrassed by his presence, she wanted to pull him in, to conceal him from the neighbors.

He loosened his tie. His jacket hung untidily over his arm. "Are you well?"

"Same as usual." She hung his jacket in the closet. Long before she knew better, she would drape it on the back of a chair, thinking, there were plenty of chairs and this way, when their time was up, he could grab it and run. But he proved careless, sitting in the same chair his jacket was on, leaning against it, rumpling it further. In the end, she'd given up and put it away, out of his clumsy reach.

"It's been awhile."

How like him to be vague. "Six months."

"*Shi ma?*"

He had lapsed into Mandarin, but she held her tongue. Why argue anymore that reality was lived in Cantonese? Besides, Hong Kong's transformation was already well underway; their city would enter the new century as "China." "Things have changed a little." Seeing the flicker of disbelief in his eyes, she added, "It does, you know, with time."

"Time, what's time? We're forever 'young at heart,' aren't we?"

She winced. No imagination, ever. "You're almost seventy."

"Sixty-eight," he corrected.

"Only for one more day." That would get him. Still the pursuit of youth. A moment's jocularity passed; the familiar irritation rose, stuck in her gullet. "Why did you want to see me?"

"Don't I always want to? Besides, who else looks after you like I do?"

The presumption! "I'm fine."

"I thought we could celebrate." When she did not respond, her face hard, he added, "You like remembering. It is our anniversary after all."

"Would have been." The words leapt out, more sharply than she intended.

"Would have been," he repeated.

They had met on a New Year's Eve, about half an hour before midnight. The party was a large one, at the home of an artistic Shanghainese family who had Westerners as friends. She came along reluctantly with a girlfriend, her classmate from university. Her own upbringing was strict. Had her parents known she was consorting with such cosmopolitan types, from Shanghai to boot, she would have had hell to pay. She was nineteen.

"Remember how I kissed you?" The quaver in his voice interrupted.

"Only because I let you."

"You were my first Southern girl." Because he was originally from Beijing, having escaped, nine years earlier in '49, alone.

"But you've kissed others since."

"No, only you, my *Gwongdung* love."

They had held this conversation many times, improvising variations to amuse themselves. She insisted he make love to her in Cantonese, *Gwongdung wah*. When he wanted to tease, he would speak Mandarin all evening, and she would laugh, holding her hands over her ears, saying *mouh yahn sik teng*—"no one knows how to hear," no one comprehends—and he would pull them away and whisper Northern endearments. After all these years, her Mandarin had become proficient; her ears were attuned to his accent. However, his *Gwongdung wah* never did sound quite right.

It wasn't a game anymore, hadn't been one for a long while.

"Will you drink with me?"

She considered a moment. "All right."

"Get us some glasses?" He began unwinding the wire on the cork.

She obliged, but noted the inexpensive brand, wondering, why couldn't he at least have brought Dom or something, if he must celebrate. She would have liked the treat, and it wasn't as if he couldn't afford it.

A quiet pop, unlike the shouting bullets of old. Before, she would let the froth and foam wash over her hands and lips, wetting her clothes, laughing as they fell upon each others' hearts. He still had beautiful hands, free of the welter of veins that plagued hers. Only the slightest tremor now as he poured.

"I'd have brought it over this morning. With a big bunch of pink roses and wild hybrids from Holland, and arranged them in your mother's vase before you got home, the way I used to surprise you."

She sipped rapidly at the overflow, in time to halt the spill. "At our age, we don't surprise."

He clinked her glass lightly before he drank.

In 1984, she had asked him to return the key to her flat.

"But why?" His shock was palpable.

"It would be more . . . convenient."

He had given her a sapphire and diamond bracelet that very evening, a gift for her forty-fifth birthday. What he didn't realize was that she knew it was originally a present for his wife who hadn't liked it because she wanted a certain Qing porcelain instead. He planned at first to return it to the jeweler, Linda Chow, but changed his mind at the shop. Her discovery of that fact had been entirely circumstantial. Linda Chow had wondered aloud about his decision to Jane Ho at their weekly *mahjeuk* table. Jane, being the incurable story-teller, repeated this when they'd run into each other one day, the way she'd probably told countless others, mindlessly, without real malice. Jane, of course, didn't know about them. Nobody did.

But that wasn't the reason she wanted her key.

"Convenient? For whom?" He almost shouted.

"Me, of course. It is my home."

"I've never presumed otherwise."

"Then it isn't a problem?" She could not restrain the challenge in her voice.

He glared in cold anger, unyielding. "Tell me why."

"I think it's better if I don't, for both of us."

"I need to know," he insisted. And then, grazing her cheek with his fingers, "Please?"

She refused to look at him. Since their life together began, she felt he adopted too Western a face, practically staring at people, and asking the same of her, insisting always that she "look at me." She complied out of consideration but found it alien. Right now, however, she looked away because she wanted to be honest. "It would be preferable to avoid unnecessary surprises."

When he left that afternoon, he did so in a fury, and refused to return for over a year. His absences saddened her a little, but did not cause heartache. She only wanted parity, but by then she had lowered all expectations of him to virtually nil. It sufficed to embrace the memory of love. A pity, though, that she could never wear the bracelet publicly since Linda would be bound to recognize it, something that simply didn't occur to him. Discretion was her burden, not his.

Yet he did return, tortured by their time apart, unable to sever the connection. There isn't any reason to be angry, she reassured, as he undressed her, tore at her garments, drew her in greedily, desperately, reviving his soul.

He refilled his empty glass. "Do you still see ...?"

She tried not to smile, but failed. He couldn't, had never been able to ask the question outright, despite all his demands of others to be straightforward, railing against business associates, staff, friends, even family. His lack of diplomacy bled ink on the social pages.

"Not since the year before last."

"He was only the ... second, right?"

"I believe in longevity."

Amusement lit his eyes, despite the jealous flash. He was youthful yet, and handsome; black strands lingered among the gray. He stood straight, conscious of his stoop. At nineteen, she had pledged passion to his image—hair like coal and eyes as warm as the sky on a summer's night. This afternoon he appeared tired; he allowed his shoulders to slump.

"I believed too, once."

Such maudlin tendencies! How she hated them. "You've had a good life."

"It's far from over. I still can, you know." He stretched an arm around her waist.

She pushed it away, exasperated. "Enough."

"Please."

"Don't make me pity you."

"I don't need pity. Just you."

"You don't need me. No one needs anyone."

His arm retreated and he sat down. "More champagne?"

She shook her head. When he had showed her the Viagra last year, gleefully, like a child, she almost lost her temper. That was when she told him not to visit again. He did, of course, because life could not keep them apart. "I'm tired," she declared.

"You don't eat enough." His voice rich with concern. "Let me order you some Hainan chicken rice. You like that. The broth will do you good."

Chicken rice again. Did he think she ate nothing else? "No. It'll spoil my appetite."

"Oh, are you going out tonight?"

"Why ask? You know I do every year."

"I'm sorry."

"Stop apologizing."

He took hold of both her hands. "*Qingfu*," he said. Love-wife.

"Don't call me that. It's not what I am."

"I'm sorry."

And what she could recall of the night he first kissed her was that he said, afterward, "I can't take you home."

She had been startled by the sensation of his proximity. Her whole body swayed dreamily, encouraged by the champagne. Everything about that almost midnight moment had been new, delicious, swaddling her legs, hips, waist, breasts, arms in a heavenly wrap. She hadn't quite heard what he said. "I'm sorry?"

"I can't take you home."

"Oh, that's all right." She supposed it was, because from the moment they met, a mere twenty minutes ago, reality disappeared, flushed away into nothingness.

"In fact, I have to find my partner. Before midnight."

She stared at him quizzically.

"I came with someone tonight. A woman."

She giggled. "Then you better not let her find us."

He scribbled her number in his notebook and promised to call. During the year that followed, she went often to meet him at cinemas, in parks, at bus stops. As long as her parents didn't know. They wouldn't have approved of this older man, this entrepreneur who rented out property for a living. Shameful, they would have called it. Exploiting your own kind. His later wealth and social standing would have justified nothing in their eyes.

All that year, he had begged her to surrender. Such nonsense, she'd say. You men make too much of all that. Then it shouldn't matter, he argued. Privately, she agreed, although she wouldn't say so to him. What she wanted was to know the certainty of her love. He persisted. She found she needed to see no one else. He would wait, he said, until forever.

There was a moment she finally knew.

It was summer. Her mother had been coughing, and she was making soup for her as prescribed by their herbalist. As she hovered over the bitter aroma, she heard the faint cough. It brought her back to the day when she was four, holding onto her mother's hand as they left their home in Guang-zhou. "We'll stay with uncle until we find our own place," her mother said, between coughs. "Will I like it over there?" she wanted to know. "Oh yes, your father has set up a nice shop for his antiques. On Hollywood Road, imagine, what a name for a street! We'll have a good life, you'll see." "How long will we live in Hong Kong?" "As long as you want. Until ..." Her mother searched for words to make her laugh. "Until the next century. How would you like that?"

Later that day, after her mother had fallen asleep, she went out to meet him. He reached for the tip of her nose in greeting. "Where to, today?"

She grabbed hold of his hand, cool and comforting in its closeness, and kissed him below the ear. "Forever," she replied.

He gripped her so tightly she could scarcely breathe. "You've made me the happiest man in the world."

Two days later, he told her that Janet Ogilvy had accepted his marriage proposal, and that they could no longer meet. The following year, her mother died. Her mother was fifty-two.

✵

"So why did you want to meet?" It was almost five-thirty. She had to get ready soon. Tonight was exceptional. She was going to dinner and the Philharmonic's concert with Linda Chow, whose children were all in Canada, and who was alone since her husband's death three years ago. They were both expected at Jane Ho's party for the millennium moment. Linda was the punctual type; besides, there was no explaining him, especially not now.

"You haven't drunk yours."

"I don't drink much anymore." She did not hide her impatience.

He swiveled his champagne flute on its base. "I have to go soon too."

Then stop wasting time, she wanted to say. Out with it. Instead she waited, thinking, he had become, not exactly annoying or boring, but something she didn't recognize.

"Janna's getting divorced. She called from London." He meant his third child, the daughter after Janet's first miscarriage.

"That's a shame. I hope she knows she can come home if she wants." Because Janna didn't get along with her mother.

"My children, they're all so ... English."

She almost shouted—well what did you expect? Hadn't she warned him, urged him to be a father, to show his children his love. They can't read your heart, she'd told him over and over again. You have to show them you care by the things you do, not by what you say. He had been at home so little, and Janet was an Anglophile. It was useless repeating herself. Things were hard on all five kids since Janet floated off into her own "spiritual" space after the cancer. Yet as she looked into his troubled eyes, she failed to connect, failed to feel anything more than a polite sympathy. Neither he, nor anyone, deserved the sorrows of life.

Yet surely their paths forked and always had? Unlike her, he had no family and tried to create his own. Janet Ogilvy was beautiful once, and Eurasian, with privileged access into colonial English society. It was what he chose in marrying ... no, it was more than mere choice. He desired, lusted after, craved all that Janet represented so desperately that it became something else, something stronger. A feeling like love.

"I don't have anyone to talk to," he complained.

"You have family, friends, your club, the world. You've been knighted by the Queen and shaken hands with Deng. All of Hong Kong knows who you are."

"I need you."

"No you don't."

"You're still angry."

"No."

"Forgive me?"

"I am not angry at you. I've never really been angry."

"Then why won't you love me anymore?"

He had drunk too quickly and too much. She had to get him out before he made a fool of himself. Taking hold of his glass, she tried to wrest it gently away, expecting his fingers to loosen. He surprised her by gripping the stem.

"Don't patronize me."

She pulled up her hands as if he'd pointed a pistol at her.

"Done."

"Marriage is the beginning of death," he told her when they met again, seven years after his wedding. She had not attended. Her presence would have upset Janet, who suspected but did not know of their little affair. At twenty, she had had no great expectations after her virginal sacrifice. He had been fun, a break from life's routine, a passion tornado.

By now, he was rising in society and reasonably wealthy.

They had run into each other on Hillwood Road near her home. He was driving past when he spotted her.

"And what about you? Why haven't you married?"

"No one wants me," she smiled.

"Still the joker."

"Life isn't so serious."

"That's easy for you to say, with no family responsibilities."

She wanted to say, parenthood can be planned, but refrained. Her father taught that incivility did not become a lady. "So how many now?"

"Three. Another girl. Janet wants at least two more."

"How nice. Well, pleased to see you again. Give Janet my regards." Her father wasn't well and she wanted to get back to him.

But he dallied. "You're still very beautiful."

"We spinsters keep well."

"Can I come see you?"

"And 'be the number three?'"

He laughed. "Why not? It's quite 'expected,' as you Cantonese say."

Afterwards, she regretted it. She hadn't meant at all to suggest . . . she had no desire for an affair. No reason either to tell him about Joseph Chan, the civil servant who wanted to marry her and would have made a fine husband. She couldn't explain her reluctance. Love was deaf to mere declarations, and marriage, at least to Joseph, seemed unnecessary.

Perhaps if her father had lived, she would never have quit teaching or gone abroad for her Ph.D., and their lives could have progressed as friendly, if distant, acquaintances. She did not regret starting what they called their "silly people's secret thing" when they became lovers and continued during her time in the U.S. Wonderful memories, sweetened by age. He looked so tired now, so burdened by life. What did his ambitions matter anymore?

He poured himself more champagne and sipped, wistfully perturbed.

"What do you want from me?" she asked.

"I don't know."

"Things aren't the same."

"But why not? Why won't you tell me? We've been together so long you've become a part of me. Don't take that away. It's pointless to separate now. Let me see you. We belong to each other." His voice trembled. "Besides, you owe me just a little, don't you think?"

"I don't owe you. You told me yourself the very day we met." The day, she knew, he gave the gift of love, without expectations or demands.

"It isn't about that. I love you."

"Don't confuse yourself."

"Then what? Because you think I can't?"

She grimaced. "Don't be ridiculous. It was never just about sex."

"Then why won't you love me?" When she gazed at the ceiling and did not reply, he repeated, "It's because you think I can't, isn't it? Isn't it?"

Always, always. It would always be about him. She refused to break her gaze.

Thirty, she mused, had been her year to take a stand. It was the year she quit teaching and attended, reluctantly, a New Year's Eve party. He was there alone. Janet was ill.

That night, he took her home and made her feel nineteen again.

His visits were sporadic at first. Her father was already dead and she owned the family flat where she lived alone. He came more often; it became like his second home, but without his contribution. Had he offered money, pride would have insisted she refuse it.

She wanted more of him, but did not demand, knowing it wouldn't be fair. Two years later, she left for graduate school in Massachusetts. Away from home, their relationship became real.

He declared love a lot, and most of the time, she ignored him. He needed to brag; the rest of his life did not allow such space. After each visit he paid her abroad, he would report back greater successes, in business and social affairs. That's excellent, she'd tell him, now don't talk too long or your telephone bill will clear out your bank account. Olden days. Easy hours peering at art slides and researching her thesis. Days to dream about going home, to take over the modest business her father left behind. Daughter, we're proud of you, she could hear her parents say. Their voice softened her loss, making it possible to go on.

Only once did she believe his declaration.

It happened when May flowers bloomed. After four years, he was impatient for her return. "I hate leaving you," he said. "Why don't you come home?" He said that often now, which she usually dismissed with a joke. But this time, something stirred. Perhaps it was the darling buds.

"Why should I hurry back? It's more awkward for us there." He kissed the tip of her nose.

"We can change that." For a moment, life burst open in magnificent radiance, although she remained cautious.

"What is it you intend to do?"

That was when he declared, "I love you. I'll leave Janet."

For once, she was silent. A promise of life demanded real attention. "You're not serious."

"I am."

"Why?"

"She doesn't make me happy the way you can. She doesn't understand me."

"What would we do?"

"I'd buy us a new home and I'll begin again. It would have to be a bigger place than yours, so that my children can visit. I won't be cruel to Janet. I know you wouldn't want me to do that. Everything will be fair."

Forget!

"What's the matter?" He had come out of himself and the champagne. "You look upset."

"It's nothing. I haven't been well."

"You see, I knew it. You haven't been eating enough, have you?" He stood and gripped her shoulders. "You need me."

Dirty dishes and stained sheets marched past the years. Her friends marveled that she never kept a domestic helper. How could she, if she didn't want word to get out, if she didn't want people to know? No, it was impossible. People in America do their own housework so why shouldn't I? She faced their world, defiant.

On the table, a puddle of spilled champagne.

"Stop it." She said. "Leave me alone."

He attempted an embrace, pinning her firmly against him. "One more time, please?" He licked her neck.

How could she tell him she felt nothing, that she had stopped feeling years ago?

"I'm not angry at you anymore," he reassured her. "Not even about your young men, when you made a fool of yourself. It was some mid-life thing. Tougher for a woman. I've forgiven you."

She shoved him away. "You're the fool."

"*Gwongdung* dragon." His voice was teasing. "My only love."

"Leave, please. Or I'll tell Janet." It burst out, escaping her lips. The words whirled chains before his eyes. She had never threatened. Not once.

He gazed at her in silent horror. "After all this time? Why?"

Because, exploded the silent scream, because you were unfair. To me, to all your children, to Janet. You perpetuated what you had no business doing. You made a mockery of truth and a fool of me. You promised without the intent to fulfill and worse, expected forgiveness. Life isn't about forgiveness and the wasting of our energies. Life is about love, not just the feeling of love.

The silence gripped her. She was sixty and still she hadn't spoken.

"You don't mean it," he said.

"I do."

He froze. His whole body seemed to shrink. And then his eyes searched round the flat. She removed his jacket from the closet.

"Oh," he began.

She knew what would follow—you hung it up, how kind of you—uttered in obtuse surprise. His words would have unleashed the scream completely, and then there would be no going back. She spoke before he could. "I'll be your *qingfu*."

❀

The day she first said that was two years after her return from the US. They had not seen each other in months, not since he admitted he could not leave Janet and his family, and begged to end their relationship.

"I shouldn't be here," he said when he arrived, his arms filled with roses.

The petals were too open, she thought, as she placed them in water. "What do you want from me?"

"I can't let you go."

"Why not? I did." Only lightness and air, no betrayal of hurt. When her mother was dying and she knew it, she hadn't been able to stop her tears. *Don't,* her mother told her. *Live for love, not pain. Only fools carry pain as if their hearts depend on it. Look after your father. That's all I ask.*

"It destroys me to think of you with someone else."

Joseph Chan had taken her to the last New Year's ball, and she knew he'd seen her. "That's ridiculous. You ended it."

He became curt. "We've been through all that."

"Then there's nothing more to say."

He reached for her waist. "I love you."

She held herself away from him. "I know that."

"But it wouldn't be fair to make you my ..."

"What?" Her eyes glimmered with laughter and tears. "Your *qingfu*?"

"No! I wouldn't waste your life like that."

"It isn't yours to waste."

"What do you mean? Don't you want someone to look after you?"

That was the first moment her burden of shame lightened. If she kept him, the power would be hers. She had looked after her father and because of it the pain of his death hadn't cut as deep. If she cared for him too— he brought laughter, after all, and at least the feeling of love—her life might be a little less empty.

"*Qingfu*. It's just a word," she told him.

His eyes lit up with the exhilaration of success. "Then you don't mind? You'll take me back?"

Very well, she decided. There wasn't really anyone else she wanted. Had she become his wife, marriage might have been the beginning of death. But to be his *qingfu*, the "wife" who gives the feeling of love ... even if she would never forgive him, she could at least forgive herself for indulging in sorrow over his betrayal, and absolve herself of that intense, unbearable, private shame, more painful because she couldn't shout it to the world. Their "silly people's secret thing." Like the secret of the king's donkey ears, the words floated away with the winds, freeing her.

"You will?" Hope returned to his eyes.

"In memory."

His face fell. "But we've been together ... over forty years."

"My parents didn't even have that many," she replied. "Besides, it was really thirty. I count us only from after your marriage. Thirty good years, though."

"But what will you do?"

"It's not like I depend on anyone. I'll do what I've always done. Look after the store, travel, see people, celebrate each New Year's Eve because my friends throw the best parties. These days, I may even meet another Beijing man." She giggled like a nineteen year old.

He frowned. "But what will I do?"

You, she wanted to ask. Do you really think this is still about you? His voice betrayed such worry that she had to choke back her laughter.

"Well, I'm glad you're amused." He put on his jacket, miffed but resigned.

Kissing his cheek, she was struck by its papery texture. "You, my love," she whispered to the air, "are a freed man." The door closed behind him.

Six o'clock. Heavens, how late. She really must make a move. She needed to get ready for the night ahead, for the pleasures that were yet to come.

Gilda Cordero-Fernando ❋ *Philippines*

An acclaimed fiction writer and essayist, Gilda Cordero-Fernando wrote short fiction between 1952 and 1970 before turning to nonfiction and publishing. Her works include *Story Collection* (1994) and *Ningning* (1997), a children's story that also introduced her work as an artist. As a publisher, she has produced large illustrated Filipiniana volumes such as *Turn of the Century, Culinary Culture of the Philippines*, and *History of the Burgis*. In 1993 she received the Patnubay ng Sining award for literature, followed by the Cultural Center of the Philippines award for literature and publishing in 1994. In her recent work *Pinoy Pop Culture* (2001), she targets the identity crisis of contemporary Filipino youth enthralled with the West who barely notice what their own country and people have to offer. "Bushouse," a revised version of a story Cordero-Fernando wrote earlier in her career, is a searching look at Manila's underclass; readers will note its archetypal "no exit" images drawn from daily life in developing world shantytowns.

Bushouse

DAY BEGINS EARLY IN OUR WORLD OF BUSHOUSES, IN THE twenty dwellings like ours which are the shells of old buses, without seats or engines. The wheels, too, are gone and each bus rests on four steel drums. Each has been repainted, some neatly enclosed by low milk-box fences, with curtains at the windows and pots of purple bachelor buttons blooming at the door.

Our buses are partitioned into *sala* and bedroom. I sit on the ruined sofa where my mother dreams upon an embroidered pillow with the smell of *morus* about her, and with my crippled brother Jaime tucked up in a crocheted coverlet at her feet. An old clock ticks loudly over a sewing machine fixed up as a dresser. Below, a kettle of ginger sings on the wood-stove in the worm hollow of the engine cavity.

Our bus still proudly carries its "Naic" destination board like a lawyer's shingle, for it is one of the Cavite buses which are not half as old as the Baguio fleet, and retired only because they've gone of style. The bus company supplies these dwellings free of charge to its drivers and mechanics so that they are within reach twenty-four hours a day. A week after they picked up the limbs of my father down a ravine on Kennon Road, my mother was awarded this bus of ours along with a pension.

All over the compound, people splash in corrugated-tin bathrooms attached to the backs of the buses. Open water pipes serve as showers. That woman, Chedang, with a towel wrapped around her head, she has what you call executive ability. Soon she'll be off to her job washing clothes for an American family at six pesos a day, leaving her infant in care of a neighbor to whom she pays fifty centavos.

And see old Mang Camilo going down his two adobe steps with a green towel about his waist. A retired mailman and father-in-law of one of the mechanics, every morning he makes his grandchildren gather dead flies and cockroaches, the wings and legs of which he detaches and puts in a matchbox. Each week he eats at a different restaurant, and just before the end of the meal, he drops a dead fly or a cockroach leg into the soup or the fish. It is just the thing to frighten five or ten pesos out of the Chinese manager, or at the worst a free meal, and that is how an old man without visible means like Mang Camilo can live.

Water and electricity are no problem in the bushouses. Each family is allowed its own connection to the company house, and somewhere in the middle of the compound one comes upon a snarl of wires and pipes. For a fixed minimum rate we use as much water as we wish, and electricity too—if we promise to use only one bulb. When the inspector comes, alarm spreads through the grapevine and we hide all the radios, flatirons, and electric fans we have around.

Jaime, my brother, likes to be propped up with cushions in front of the steering wheel, propelling the grounded dinosaur a million miles an hour with noises he makes with his mouth. In his dreams he enters a parking lot filled with mirror-shiny cars and into the door of a Club where it is forever night. Stars blink eternally on the ceiling, blue with fat painted clouds. He waits, and soon, soon, a red-cloaked magician comes and envelopes Jaime in his arms.

Living in the bushouse, we always feel like we're going somewhere, though it's just an illusion: We never get any place at all. The company is going broke; there are layoffs; salaries are fifteen days late, yet no one dares strike lest the company close down altogether. We've learned to make the blanket fit, and we develop small business schemes on the side.

The most envied man in the compound is one-legged Arsenio Bito, who runs the company *carinderia*. That's because he was once run over by a train and lived to collect the insurance. Since then, our laid-off men try to get run over by a vehicle—just slightly: a sprained ankle, a twisted knee, enough for bit of payoff money during a hopeless month, or a few days in hospital with clean sheets and three meals a day. Of course, not everyone's so lucky—one young man, dead drunk, decided to lie down on the railway tracks and get his feet broken. Cloudily, he lay down at an intersection where two tracks meet. Only it was not the expected local that passed, but the raging Ilocos Express that came and you can imagine the rest.

The bus drivers like to hold drinking bouts at Arsenio Bito's, where the specialty is dog meat. The drivers themselves supply the dogs, which are never run down deliberately, but if one is run over accidentally, well, then there's no help for it: The quivering animal is hauled aboard. Arsenio is a specialist at preparing dog. Black ones are the best and Arsenio lops off the head, hanging it upside down to let the blood drain. Late in the afternoon he cleans the intestines and singes off the hair by swinging the carcass over a fire. Then he quarters the flesh, cooking it in a pot with a handful of tiny red peppers and a thick red sauce.

In happier days, my mother would beg a dog from some faraway relative and bring it home for Arsenio Bito to cook, and for my father and his friends to eat. Animals are not allowed on Manila buses, but even then my mother would put the dog in a sack and board a bus until the conductor put her down at the nearest corner. Eventually she'd get home for nightfall and my father, happy at the gift, would dance my mother in the bedroom.

Anything left of a dog roast, my mother carefully salts and dries on the roof, for it is better than the locusts, crickets, frogs, and rats that the poor must eat in time of need. My mother's hair is long and white, her skin gleams, and her eyes, when they are not swollen with sleep or worry, are luminous. Even when she nags she is lovely—the way she nagged my father to bathe himself of the doggy odor that comes of eating canine flesh. Jaime and I close our eyes and listen: It is like a lullaby.

Now the mist lifts and it is six o'clock. My mother begins to stir, and, watching her, I stiffen. Jaime wakes and my morning begins. I carry him to the floor matting for his exercises, encasing his twisted legs in tubes of stiff cardboard and raising them up in the air six dozen times. I massage his knees, which are crooked, and loosen the fingers of his hands, which are balled up tightly into fists. An Igorot fortune teller once predicted that Jaime would walk at seven, but my brother will be nine in September and hasn't walked a step. Every day he must be carried, washed, fed, bathed and massaged, nor can he sit up by himself. The only way he can move is by rolling around and around. Wherever I go, my brother goes, wearing his white shoes with their soles that are never soiled. We may as well be Siamese twins. He is the reason I've stopped going to school, the reason I do not study Hair Culture or Dressmaking like other young girls in the compound.

Each year, Jaime gets heavier and longer. His thin legs dangle almost to my knees and carrying him around will soon look obscene. Who will care for him then? I tie him to the high chair and put him outside in a spot of sun. There he watches the boys fly their kites from the roof of the company house that is their playground. Up on the roofs they also chase each other, in mortal danger of falling to the concrete below. Occasionally, a mother looks up from fighting with other wives over scrap metal and screeches out her lungs for the boys to come down. Plunge from a roof, or get squashed by a bus—what is the difference?

With breakfast ready, I carry Jaime inside and give him a spoon. My mother wakes, and from the way she sits staring at the frazzled tips of her slippers, I am afraid it will be a difficult day. I fetch her a cup of ginger brew, kneeling on the bed, and combing her long hair with a buffalo horn comb—plaiting its soft loose tresses, reassuring her that she is my most beautiful and necessary mother; that she is wise and exceptional, lovely and loved. With a glazed look she walks to the window to touch a grasshopper on the glass.

Jaime finishes his breakfast. I bathe him outside in a sawn-off drum of water, letting his legs thrash to strengthen them, and taking care to hold his armpits firmly lest he drown. Mother sobs inside the bus as she sweeps up the food Jaime has scattered on the floor. She thinks of my dead father, and soon, I hope, she will curl on the sagging sofa and escape into sleep. Sometimes she sleeps for days on end. When at last she wakes, mother is sweet and refreshed, smothers Jaime with kisses, and does not need reassurance she is lovely and cherished.

How my parents loved each other! At night, they went arm in arm to the movies, leaving Jaime and me alone on the mat in the dark. Perhaps it is from being left alone nights my brother and I are not afraid of supernatural beings. Often, father and mother commended us to the care of the ghosts who love us. We even caught glimpses of their diaphanous faces watching through the window to see that we were not cold, or that animals did not come to harm us.

Sometimes, it is the magician, Simon Plaza, my father's best friend, who comes down the hills and the valleys of our slumber, to see that we are well. Tonight it storms terribly. For safety, the power is cut off at the company house: It is completely dark. Simon lights a candle and stands there, his face and arms radiant in the glow. He performs in a nightclub and says he bathes in phosphorescent water, but Jaime and I smile secretly, for we know better. Simon is a magician and intimate with the ghosts who love us. Soon he will invite them in, one and all.

Our bushouse rocks in the storm and we are restless and cannot sleep. Simon sits on the floor cutting dolls out of newspaper. With a gesture of his hands the paper dolls rise and dance by themselves, casting weird shadows on the darkened wails. Simon whistles and moves his fingers; the dolls step and twirl in a waltz. Before long we are asleep.

After father died, Simon took us to Los Baños hot springs. My mother laughed happily in a loose flowered dress, as the four of us bathed in the warm sulfur waters. Los Baños is a queer kind of pool; most of the bathers are paralytic, palsied, or lame. Picking up my crippled brother, my mother laughed delightedly and carried him deeper and deeper into the pool. As the water began lapping at his chin, Jaime grew terrified and screamed.

"Don't be afraid," my mother said, hugging him tightly. Can't you see how much I love you? Why should you drown when I love you?"

Jaime screamed louder and clutched her neck in a stranglehold. They thrashed savagely until, realizing what was happening, Simon swam to fetch them back to safety. So much for medicinal pools.

Thinking of father overwhelms my mother. She grows depressed and runs sobbing to the street outside, throwing herself in the middle of the road, arms spread-eagled, waiting for the merciful wheels of a six-by-six to end her misery. Anxiously, I follow, darting between rushing cars that swerve to avoid her. On my knees I beg her come home but she will not move: I don't know that she even hears me.

The local policeman saunters by to scold us. I'm unable to lift my mother and he is too lazy to help, so we harangue in the traffic. Once, when some of our chickens came home pierced with darts to die bleeding at our doorstep, we complained to the officer. He said, "I'll keep an eye peeled for the culprit, but in the meantime, I need that dead fowl as evidence." Now he berates us noisily in the road, threatening to arrest the pair of us for obstruction—to have us picked up by the van and thrown in jail with murderers and prostitutes. But after a time, he simply gives up and saunters off. He's seen it all before.

I return home just long enough to rinse the clothes I've soaked in the tub, and to cook rice and a little fish. Then with this lunch I haul Jaime side-saddle along with a kettle, an umbrella, and a small mat. We brave the onslaught of traffic and I unroll the mat in the whirlpool of whizzing cars and buses. My mother lies motionless, the noon sun beating ferociously upon her. Her skin has darkened and I fear she has perished of sunstroke, or has already died: I lay an ear on her breast and feel a reassuring sob. Planting the umbrella firmly on the mat, I unwrap our bit of lunch with vehicles rushing past. There, in the midst of the traffic, we sit picnic style.

At sundown my mother consents to be led home, still sobbing softly, and I must reassure her a hundred times that she is beautiful and extraordinary, wanted, lovely and loved. I am near exhaustion. The bushouse is a mess. In my hurry I've forgotten to lock the door and the wire mesh cupboard is empty: Neighbors have helped themselves to our sugar, our dog meat, and rice. We are without a grain or a leaf left to cook. Jaime whimpers on the mat for his dinner. I threaten to pull down the stingray whip from the wall and still his hunger forever. Mother curls up and goes to sleep, hopefully until Judgment Day.

The sun streams in through the windows of the bus next morning and I am still cross.

Surprisingly, mother has woken early and washed herself with pumice. Her eyes are dewy; her skin glows again with cleanliness, and to atone for yesterday she has borrowed rice and chocolate from a neighbor: She stirs a fragrant porridge in the pot.

Mother, of course, would never dream of cleaning Jaime, who lies in a pool of waste. Lips blue with hunger, he cowers at my feet, not daring to make a sound. I catch an image of myself in the jagged mirror—face gray with weariness, mouth drooping, hair a tangled viper's nest. Every day, it seems, I grow thinner and uglier while my mother grows yet more lovely— her cheeks rosy, her mouth voluptuous, petulant—her smooth white body ready for love.

I slop porridge on a tin plate and place it beside Jaime, this child who is a scab on my heart. I need a bath. Searching for a towel, I see him on all fours, face buried ravenously in porridge, mush on his ears, on his nose, shit on his limbs: How ugly are the children our heedless parents spawn on this earth!

I run out in a wind that cuts like a knife against my cheeks; out into the starless night in search of Simon the magician. In the nightclub where he works I stand inside the kitchen door. The bray of a saxophone hits my ear and drums dissipate in low rumbles. Then the bandleader announces The Leopard Prince—our Simon.

My prince strides from the gloom, dressed not in his flaming cloak, but in ridiculous costume complete with ears and tail. Smoke floats from the tables amid a wave of titters. Simon slips the jacket off his shoulders; his eyes roam the room; he stands, bare-chested in the stage-lights, animal skin glistening with oil or sweat, with a silly tail dangling between the pillars of his legs.

Producing a shiny safety pin, he presents it for inspection under the lights. Throwing back his head, he introduces its glinting point, inch by inch, into the softness of his throat. A wave of uneasy laughter ripples over the tables. His throat swells and contracts with the effort. I close my eyes in pain. At last, the point makes its appearance on the other side. Now it is done. He locks the safety pin triumphantly over the thick pinch of flesh.

"It's a fake!" someone yells, but in one corner a woman's voice cries in distress. A waiter moves forward with an empty whisky bottle; the Leopard Prince breaks it on the lip of a smoking brazier. Scattering the fragments on the floor with the sole of his shoes, he lies full length on the broken shards, rolling over them, then stands up quickly, exhibiting to all the unmarked skin of his back.

Now he gathers a handful of glass. With tremendous effort, he crushes it bare-handed. "A glass of water!" he calls. Then, handful of glass in his mouth, he chews it meditatively, gurgling it down with water.

Now this Leopard Prince produces feathered darts from a wooden chest. "Throw one at my back," he orders the bandleader. The bandleader retreats, then throws the dart with all his might at Simon. But his aim is unsure and the dart hangs gingerly from Simon's shoulder by a snip of skin.

Waiters pass out darts on silver platters among the crowd. Then from all directions of the room darts fly at the Leopard Prince, his back now a tattoo of pink, orange and purple feathered darts. As the audience applauds, Simon's mouth tapers tautly to a bitter smile.

In the dressing area I run to his arms—Simon's arms. His costume smells of cockroaches and he laughs to see me there, muddy cheeks and all, and he hugs me against his breast like a child, rocking me there for a long moment.

There is a doughnut on a blue dish. Simon gives me a fork and I shake my head, for the brightness is in my eyes and I cannot eat when my throat is full. The band leads in a song about bluebirds, but who might ever see a bluebird in the bushouse compound where they are stoned by the boys?

"You don't want to eat?" he asks. "It's really quite good, you know, once you get used to it."

My tears are falling; he turns his back. I see where the darts have been, gaping like pale pink mouths on his back, and he says, his head hanging tiredly between his shoulders, "If you will yourself not to bleed, you will not bleed." Slowly, I begin to eat.

In summer, Simon Plaza walks into our lives and sets up shop in an abandoned bus. Now he's a witch doctor performing "operations." The air is electric with his presence. Children descend from their games on the roof and the bus dwellers gaze at him in awe. He carries many bags with live things fighting inside but will not let anyone touch either bags or baskets. We stand at the doorway, drinking in the wonder that is Simon: He sloughs off his load at the stair, opens his arms and we come into them, to the warmth of this father-image with whom I am half in love.

He looks at my mother without speaking. She sits piecing together the news from the *Chronicle,* unaware he has come: teenagers have stoned a duck-egg vendor to death; a newborn baby is found in a garbage can; a despondent octogenarian hangs himself from the rafters of his hut. She looks up and sees Simon unable to reconcile such news with his presence.

My mother pats her hair in place, and scolds the magician for his attentions. Suddenly, she is the soul of efficiency, striding to the front of the bus and feeling for the live eel in the water drum that serves as our refrigerator. She must prepare a good meal! Now my brother and I scramble among Simon's bags and baskets, full of chickens, dozens of them, tied by their legs. And meat—kilos of it: yellow-fatted beef, strings of flesh, bloody pork. My mother ties on an apron and goes to work on them: salting, boiling, marinating, sausage-making. All must be cooked before nightfall lest it spoil.

By midnight, tired, we are done and sit by the light of the candles in our musty bus. My mother's laughter trembles like a leaf in night air, like old times, as if my father were alive again.

The evening is touched with Simon's magic.

Other young people my age go off to the rites of summer, but all morning I slaughter chickens in secret, looking like the Quezon City Killer.

Who should peek over the fence but Rogel, my suitor, carrying home a bundle of kindling.

"Your magician's a fake," he says without preliminary. "I bought a love potion he said was mixed by an *encanto*. Well, that's it: I put it in your flowers yesterday and you still don't love me a crumb."

"He probably guessed whom you were giving it to. That's why."

"What are you killing so many chickens for?" he asks. "Are you so rich?"

"I'm sick of chickens," I say. "Couldn't stand to eat them after this."

"Then why buy them at all?"

"Because we need the blood for Simon's operations."

"For what?"

"Today Simon is performing his healing. I put the blood in small capsules like this, see? Simon pretends to cut up the patient with his bare hands and one of these capsules is between his fingers, see? He squeezes it quickly—he is quick with his hands, you know. It spurts like human blood. The rest I serve up to him in cotton balls."

"And still you say he is not a fake?"

"No," I say. "He resorts to this thing because he doesn't want to use his power. You don't waste your gift on every little man with a lump on his face and a couple of pesos. It's got to be used sparingly or you lose it."

"What about Jaime, your little brother?" Rogel asks sarcastically. "If Simon Plaza is so good, why hasn't he made Jaime walk?"

Rogel has chipped at my idol. Now I am sore. Penitently he comes round the gate and drops beside me to help pluck the chickens. His hair creeps like poison ivy down his cheeks; his lavender pants are so tight in the crotch they must surely must have come off somebody's wash-line. For a moment, we are very close among the entrails and the feathers, the blood all around us in lard cans.

"If you tell anybody about this," I say, "I will slit you open myself. And I mean it."

At three o'clock the bus is ready. The floor has been waxed with candle drippings, and there is a table in the center with a clean coverlet over it. From behind the blinds I see drivers, mechanics, their wives, and others from outside the compound. There is Chayoung, who stands in line all day for rice that she immediately resells for profit; there is Mang Cardo, the *Magpapa-Jesus* who closes the eyes of the dead. And in the center stands Piciong Putla with his needle-marked arm. Every week Piciong sells his blood to a different Red Cross. Blanched as a soup bone he waits while his vampire children, who imbibe their father's blood in the form of *camotes* and porkbones and shellfish and tripe, fly their kites unconcernedly on the roofs. In the compound we pay for everything we get, with a bit of our skin, or our heart, our sanity, or our blood.

Simon Plaza emerges. There is a hush. Then the patients, who have heard of and believe in his operations of faith, crowd eagerly to the door.

Simon selects a woman, saying he will remove the tumor from her uterus that causes her asthma. Meekly, nervously, she stretches out on the table. I cover her legs and expose her belly. Simon looks steadfastly into her eyes. She swoons. With his hand, he makes a cutting gesture on her stomach, spurting out blood. One of her relatives is splashed and they are much impressed. Simon massages the woman's flesh vigorously with his fingers and blood flows gorily down either side of her tummy.

Then Simon parts "the wound" triumphantly, coming up with a large tumor. A spectator faints. The tumor is the size of a goose egg in his hand. Carefully, I save it in a bottle, for it is the only plastic tumor we have, then pass it around for examination. Simon blows on the wound, removing his hand, and there is no scar, no pain, only traces of blood. The patient wakes and proclaims to the world that she is cured.

That day there are thirty-two operations of various types—eye, nose, lung, stomach, uterus, tonsil, spine. By nightfall, my mother's apron over-flows with bills and coins.

Simon announces to us that he is joining a troupe of magicians leaving for Hong Kong. He may never return. We are inconsolable. He refuses the money my mother hands over: Keep it for a rainy day, he says. Buying bottles of rum, he sits in the rusty bus getting drunk.

Come morning, Jaime astride my back, we visit the pig-roasting place nearby the pit of the fighting cocks. Twenty or twenty-five *lechons* turn on spits: great, disenchanted sows with sagging udders and paralyzed tongues, with eyes so rheumy they must have died in their sleep or been knocked down by a bus; young roasters with slit bellies and stab wounds; sucklings, plucked in the pink of infancy. Sold, cut up, and weighed on crooked scales at the stalls near the Church of Santo Domingo, they turn on the spits, losing the marks of their agony, and become burnished repasts fit for kings. One sweaty man in soot-covered pants shovels coal to feed the crackling embers. In the bushouses, if you cannot afford the price of a movie, you watch instead the *lechon*.

A cookboy promises Jaime a pig tail and I leave him to sit near the pit. Back at the compound, by the hill where they are clearing land for a stadium, bushouses are being shifted by forklift. Our homes are an eyesore for future stadium crowds. Already, half of the bus company land has been sold. It is only a matter of time before the owner sells the rest—and us.

Under a *sampaloc* tree, I sit on a hill where lately there must have stopped a pair of lovers: wrecked flowers, two straws, and shredded kleenex tissues are scattered about. I place some of the flowers in my hair, in my ears, between my toes. Soon, soon, someone may discover me lying in this abandoned place of love, flower bedecked, bereft, desirable.

Deciding to see if Simon has gotten over his drunk, I follow a trail beaten through the grass by those who've brought their aches and pains to his door. I also ache with an unfathomable disease. My feet make no noise in the weeds.

Hair pomaded, one long brown arm dangling to the floor, Simon sleeps, snoring softly. Like an ant my fingers crawl up the secret road of his arm, moist with blossoms. Amulets rest on the brown plain of his torso, and as he sighs and stirs, I finger each one as if I have held his heart.

It is as warm as an oven. My blouse sticks to my back. I push my head and shoulders out of the window; even so, there is not a breath of air to catch. Restlessly, I walk bare foot on the dirty floor and I see myself in his large, cracked mirror: seventeen, cropped hair, eyes black as ripened *lomboy*. My reflection shows fine, even teeth and the dimple at the corner of my mouth I have deepened for years with my finger, until now it is a well of destruction ensnaring all men.

My love stirs and wakes. I feel his eyes. He is leaving. I must be sure he will remember me. I remove my blouse, every button, and my virginal breasts come forth. I purse my lips and regard my image critically in the mirror; then just as casually slough my skirt. My half slip has a tear; I pass a finger gently on its tattered lace.

Unclothed, defiantly I walk upon the radiant floor of the bus—not a sound in the heat save my breathing and that of Simon, eyes glowing in the shadow of his arm. I sigh and pause by the window. Why does Simon not pluck me? Why not reach out a gentle hand even if he perish with desire? A man is not his thoughts or his desires, but what he does.

Simon looks at me from beneath a shielding arm; a world of pain in his eyes. I have loved him from the day I was born. He rises on the bench like a creaky old man, wipes the sweat from his forehead, and stares at me steadily with steely eyes. A blur of tears. *Someday,* he says gravely, staring at his clasped and quiet hands: *Someday I shall have you.* Another time. Another place.

I wait at the end of the bench, crumpled with defeat. What is the use—loving a man all your life when after eternities of waiting, he says, "Someday"?

Your days of magic are numbered, Simon Plaza. I will have you also: your hair washed gray, your skin sere, your eyes cracked and dim, your limbs in plaster casts. Tenderly, I shall wrap you in cerements and lie with you in the womb of the grave.

Simon stands helpless, hugging himself as if unbearably cold. He gathers the different pieces of myself from the floor and hands them to me one by one: underthings, torn half-slip, printed skirt, the cotton blouse.

Outside, the wind moans in the kapok trees and I hear the screech of children flying their kites on the roof. I walk past Rogel sitting idly on a stack of tires at the back of the repair depot. He sees the sadness in my face and runs past axles and fenders and broken radiators, to stand in my way and tell me he loves me infinitely. Look, he says; another love charm, guaranteed genuine: the organs of a crocodile sewn in plastic. He holds my hand and I let him kiss me in the grass. Ah, with Simon, I shall die of hunger and thirst.

Protected by the Midnight Boys. No one will touch this Stand, reads the legend on the empty stall in this, our jungle world. Rogel and I sit on a narrow plank, tracing hearts on a mist of rain on the glass. I am careful to ball up the back of my skirt, which is stained with blood. Out on the street, two blind beggars lead each other home in the rain.

With a start, remembering Jaime, I begin to run. Surely, someone has had the sense to carry him under a roof? I motion Rogel not to follow and pick my way quickly through the houses. Near the curb of a tumbledown house, I swerve: Two men carry in a stolen television out of the rain.

The roasting place is deserted, the whole place an ashy swamp. Searching for Jaime among the wreckage of coal baskets and stones I hear a small cry and find him, this child nobody wants, half-buried in mud, lips blue with cold, raging with fever, a frightful rattle in his throat.

I carry him home in fitful rain. The door is locked and I knock with all my might and shout and rattle, but mother has slid the bolt. She sits without speaking in darkness. I plead through the windows, wondering if she guesses my secret: She will not come to the door.

We shall stay forever, it seems, in this drizzle, this child and I. Then through the mist I make out a familiar figure with an umbrella, approaching from the distance. Invulnerable to death, deceit, illness, love, and all the sores that plague a man, he walks in the drizzle toward us. Simon Plaza, come to save us again. I turn bitterly away. He walks toward us, puts his sheltering umbrella wordlessly over our shivering forms and leads us to the door. There, relieving me of my burden, searching my pale and weary face, his eyes slide down my blouse, relentlessly downward to the dark stain on my skirt, which all the rain in the world cannot wash out. Anger flickers in his eyes. His palm comes down in a cold, stinging slap. I reel against the flowerpots. He attacks the door with his fists.

Through the splintered door, I can barely make out my mother, huddled in the gloom, staring at a spot on the wall. Torn blankets and clothes are all over the floor. Simon deposits Jaime on the sofa without speaking and stoops out the door. I survey our impermanent kingdom with gentleness at last—my mother wrapped in her world of dreams, the cripple shivering on the bed, the three of us. Taking up the torn blankets from the floor, I set to right the ravished chairs and turn on the lights above our bushouse windows.

Marianne Villanueva ✳ *Philippines*

Born in 1958, Villanueva published her first collection of short fiction, *Ginseng and Other Tales of Manila*, in 1991; it was a finalist for the Philippines' National Book Award. Her story "Silence" was shortlisted for the 1999 O. Henry Award. She co-edited, with poet Virginia Cerenio, the anthology *Going Home to a Landscape* (2003), which gathers together the writings of Filipina women from around the world. More recently, Villanueva's book *Mayor of the Roses* was the inaugural publication of the Miami University Press Fiction Series in 2005. Villanueva received a B.A. from Ateneo University, Manila, and earned a master's degree in Creative Writing and East Asian Studies at Stanford.

Lizard

WHEN WITO WAS LITTLE, STRANGERS HAD A WAY OF COMING up to her and saying, "I knew your mother when you were not even a twinkle in her eye." Then they would tell her stories of how, when her mother was only thirteen or fourteen, they had seen her in a concert, or how they had taken the ferry with her once from Bacolod to Iloilo. Sometimes, returning home from school in the late afternoon, Wito would see a stranger sitting on the *lanai* with her mother, having a late afternoon meal. At her entrance, the stranger would look startled and say something like, "Is this...? I had no idea how big she was! How long has it been since...?"

Listening to all these strangers, Wito learned that her mother had been quite famous—that once she had played the piano and traveled from town to town, giving concerts. Her mother didn't seem to want to talk about those days, though other people reminded her. Then she would tell Wito that she had led a very hard life, and that she got paid very little for her concerts, perhaps only a few dozen *pesos* for hours of practice, that often she played for people who didn't understand the music and talked and ate while she played. She said she did it only because she was poor, and because her own mother needed things like a refrigerator, a stove. She said she never saw any of the money she made; she gave it all to her mother.

As Wito's mother talked, Wito would watch her face—the large, dark eyes growing alternately bitter and sad. Her mother was very dark. Growing up, she said, the neighborhood children called her *balut*—"duck egg." Wito's grandmother tried all sorts of things to make her more *mestiza*—rubbing *kalamansi* juice on her skin twice a day, applying a paste made from menstrual blood—but none of it seemed to work.

Because she had been playing the piano since she was four, her hands were not like those of the other girls—the palms were hard and stiff, and large blue veins leaped out between the bones. She kept them folded up in her skirt, or resting, palms upward, on her lap. After many years, it began to hurt to straighten the fingers, and so she kept them curled up all the time, like the fingers of a paralytic.

Whenever Wito heard her mother speak and looked at her twisted hands, she felt very sorry for her. She herself was always so full of complaints. She hated, for instance, to eat okra, which the cook served nearly every day because it was her father's favorite vegetable, and she hated the nuns at the convent school who were always scolding her for talking too loudly or for not sitting with her knees together. But what were all these difficulties in comparison to being made to sit at the piano for four hours straight, playing the same piece over and over, as her grandmother had made her mother do?

When Wito was the new girl at school, the nuns were very excited and were always asking her to play something. Wito knew only "Chopsticks" and some tunes she could play by ear. When it finally came out that she could not play, Mother Remedios, the music teacher, could not conceal her disappointment. "What a shame!" she said. "What a shame!" Wito had to squeeze her hands hard between her knees to keep from saying something. If anyone had asked her for an explanation, she would have said that there was a piano in their home, which stood in a corner of the living room. It was not at all like the piano at school, which was small and badly scratched, and where Mother Remedios sat day after day banging out "Assumpta est Maria" for the congregation. The piano at home was black and enormous: a Steinway, the only one of its kind in the town. Every day a maid ran a soft cloth over the yellowing ivory keys, and now and then Wito would see a man come to strike the chords and, listening, nod his head, like a doctor satisfied with a patient's heartbeat. But whereas the piano at school was homely and seemed expressly made for Mother Remedios's flailing attacks on it, the piano at home had at some point, and

Wito could not explain how, acquired an aura of evil, so that its being in the house at all came to seem like something of a curse. Wito knew very well that her mother cared nothing for it and would have had it taken away if not for the protests of her grandmother.

Because there were always others in school who behaved like Mother Remedios and assumed Wito was musically accomplished, Wito learned that there were certain things people expected of her mother and, by extension, of herself. These people would loom before her, smiling and loud, saying, "Play something for us! Play!" But when they discovered Wito could not play, they would become very disappointed, and then they would turn their backs and forget about her.

Wito had seen the pictures of her mother in the photo albums: the black and white pictures of her mother dressed in flowing gowns, holding bouquets of roses, and smiling at the camera. In the pictures her mother's face was very round, and her eyebrows very dark and pointed and she smiled as though she were afraid of something. But the dresses hanging in Wito's mother's closet now were different. They were ordinary dresses for going to the market or for visiting with relatives.

Sometimes, late at night, Wito would be awakened by an unfamiliar sound. She would lie on her back, staring at the big gray lizard who lived on her ceiling. Sometimes she thought she could make out the lizard's heartbeat in its throat, which went up and down, up and down, in time to some music. It always took her some time to realize that the music was coming from downstairs, from the piano. The sound was wild and sorrowful, and Wito did not like listening to it. She would put her pillows over her ears, and curl up tightly in her blanket, trying to shut out the noise. It always seemed a long, long time before the sound stopped and she could fall asleep again. That was how Wito came to think of the piano and the night as belonging together.

But these were not things she could tell anyone in her school, not even her best friend Veronica, who lived just around the corner and who often came over to play. Veronica's mother had said to Wito once: "I read something about your mother in the *Manila Chronicle*. Is she still playing?" Wito could only shake her head dumbly. Veronica's mother had gone on to say what a shame that was; Wito's mother had been a famous pianist before she had gotten married.

Wito's grandmother had said once that Wito's hands were like her mother's. She could never forget that day. Wito had been digging for earthworms in the garden, not for any particular reason but because it was something she liked to do, when her grandmother came up unexpectedly behind her and said, "You have your mother's hands." At that time, it had frightened Wito very much. She hadn't known what it meant, to have such hands. Only it seemed to her that her mother was often sad, and that perhaps if her hands were not that way she would be happier. At first, looking at her hands, Wito saw only that they were white and smooth. She could not see anything in them that even closely resembled her mother's. After a while she thought she could just make out the faint, blue tracery of veins beneath the skin, and at one point in particular, just between her right thumb and forefinger, the vein was unusually prominent. When she wrote something, the vein bulged with the effort, and sometimes, it writhed and even seemed to jump. Then Wito worried very much, and tried massaging that particular place or letting her hand dangle in cold running water until she saw the vein begin to subside a little.

Whenever her grandmother visited, Wito remained up in her room. Everything about the old woman seemed hard—the way her cheek felt when Wito greeted her, the way she held her back when she was supposed to be reclining on the sofa. Even her hair was hard and springy. It rose straight up from her forehead with two white streaks on either side, making her look, to Wito, like a witch. Her eyes were small—two bright black points—and her lips were thin and always tightly pressed together.

Wito noticed that her grandmother came more often during the milling season, when Wito's father had to stay late on the farm. At such times, her grandmother would spend nearly an entire day at the house. She would be at the breakfast table when Wito came down in the morning, and she would still be there at dinnertime, sitting in her father's accustomed place, helping herself to the dishes the maid passed around the table.

Then her grandmother would take it into her head that Wito must learn how to play the piano. Her hard fingers on Wito's shoulder would propel the girl to the piano stool, and sitting there, Wito would be forced to look at the piano pieces her grandmother had brought with her—pieces that seemed like ciphers, with odd little symbols that Wito could never understand, no matter how often her grandmother explained them. Her grandmother would sigh, and in that sigh was some deep and buried anger Wito could feel. It frightened her. Her grandmother would take Wito's fingers and spread them open over the keys. "This way, this way," she would say.

The summer Wito was eight, there was a drought and her father was often away for days at a time. He was worried about the farm, and about whether the *sakadas* were getting enough water for themselves.

Wito expected her grandmother to come over more often, but for a long time she stayed away. Finally, when she did come, she seemed to bring with her a great bitterness. Wito saw her one day when she had just come home from school, sitting with her mother on the flowered sofa on the *lanai*.

They must have been sitting there a long time. Her grandmother was leaning forward, saying something in a low insistent voice, while Wito's mother listened with bent head. Wito saw how intently her grandmother gazed at her mother, how there seemed to be something about her mother that kept drawing the older woman forward, so that it seemed she might reach out any moment and touch or, perhaps, hit her. Wito saw how her mother hung her head, and knew that she was crying. The back of her neck, covered with fine, black hair, looked narrow and exposed.

Wito thought she caught the words "shameful" and "waste," but then her grandmother saw her and broke off abruptly.

When Wito went up to greet her grandmother, the old woman's cheek felt dry, like parchment, whereas her mother's cheek was soft and moist, and when Wito turned to leave, her mother pulled her close. Her mother's arms encircled her, forcing her to face her grandmother. The old woman looked down at Wito, and in her eyes there was nothing of love or sympathy, or even recognition.

Her mother remained holding Wito like that for a long time, not looking again at Wito's grandmother. Finally the old woman said, "Pah!" impatiently and got up to go. She walked slowly and stiffly down the length of the *lanai* and Wito could hear her jabbing angrily with her cane at the plants in the garden. It seemed a long time before she heard the gate shut.

That night Wito's mother was very quiet. When Wito went to her to ask to be held, she said, "Not now, it is time for your bath," and when Wito came back a little later, "I am tired. See what Zenaida is cooking for supper." Wito's father returned earlier than expected, and Wito saw her mother sigh, as though her father's coming only added to her trouble.

Wito's father had just come from the farm, yet his white shoes were immaculate. His polished fingernails gleamed in the light of the dining room chandelier.

Wito's mother had told her that when Wito's father was growing up, he had a boy follow after him to tie his shoelaces whenever they came undone. This boy, an old man now, still came around now and then and told Wito's mother stories of when her husband was a young boy, and how he had rescued him from this and that scrape. Wito, too, would listen, and it seemed to her that her father and her mother's childhoods were very different, and that the difference was so great it seemed a miracle her father and her mother had ever found each other.

Wito's mother asked all the usual questions—how the *enkargados* were getting along, whether Pacing, the wife of one of the *sakadas*, had her baby yet, and whether much damage had been inflicted by the drought. Her father answered distractedly. The cook served cabbage rolls, fish stew, and the inevitable okra. Her father ate with great appetite, hunched over his plate.

As he ate, Wito found herself looking carefully at her father's face. Before, she had considered him ugly. Her father had a large, squashed-looking nose that was somehow always red, and he had the square face and heavy jowls of a bulldog. His hair began halfway back from his head, and there was not much of it. Moreover, it was always greasy and smelled of a pungent, green gel that Wito's mother called *"pomada."*

Wito knew almost everything that had happened between her father and her mother before she was born. Her mother liked to say how her father had camped out on her doorstep for days, and although she didn't like him at first, she finally began to pity him. Wito's grandmother had been against her father. She had made disparaging remarks about him wherever he came to visit. Wito's mother said she began to love Wito's father because of the patient way he would sit in the living room, waiting for her and pretending not to hear the harangues of Wito's grandmother. When things became very bad between Wito's mother and her grandmother, her parents eloped. Her mother left her family a note, explaining what she had done and why, and asked them to please keep all her concert gowns because she didn't want to see them any longer. Wito's grandmother had been so angry that even after Wito was born, it was some months before she could bring herself to visit her daughter's house. Then, when she finally did have a look at Wito, she noted that the baby had her father's small, wide-set eyes, and pronounced her ugly. Wito's mother had immediately snatched her up and fled from the room, but it was too late. Some of her grandmother's sentiment had already been communicated to Wito. That was why she was always ashamed when visitors to the house would look at her and say, "She takes after her father." After that, she would stick a clothespin on her nose when she thought no one was looking.

Her father was always silent. Her mother was usually gay and full of stories, while her father sat stolidly behind his newspaper, and did not seem interested in the things Wito had to tell him. The only time he held her was when she kissed him goodnight. Wito was afraid that if her father found out what she thought of his looks, he would be very angry. He might even begin to dislike her.

But this evening, it seemed that her father's arrival dispelled the bad feeling her grandmother had left in the house. This bad feeling had seemed to hover over everything, so that she took no pleasure in playing in the garden as she usually did in the late afternoon, nor even in the bowl of yams boiled in coconut milk that Zenaida had made especially for her. Now that her father was home, everything was all right once more. She was glad to watch him eat, glad to watch him enjoying his food. For this reason, she could not understand why her mother said suddenly, in the middle of the meal, "*Mamang* was here today."

After speaking, a stubborn look came over her mother's face, and it seemed she didn't want to talk anymore. Wito's father continued sucking on a fish bone for a few moments. Then, without raising his head, he said quietly, "What did she want?"

"Oh!" her mother said, making a gesture of exasperation. "She was in one of her moods again. She went on and on about how I was wasting my talent, that I should start giving concerts again. I told her I wasn't interested in that kind of life any longer, and it led to her saying other things. She was angry, so angry!"

Her mother went on in this vein for a few more moments. Her father only grunted now and then in reply, while scooping some last bits of rice into his mouth. After a while he noticed Wito staring and said, "If you've finished eating, you can leave the table."

Wito got up at once. Almost as soon as she stepped out of the dining room; she heard her mother's voice resume its complaints. The sound was like a river, the way it flowed and twisted about, but always rushing, rushing forward, and her father's occasional grunts were like the rocks that stood in that river, stoic and indifferent. Wito herself could not withstand the force of this river. It was so hard, so petulant, so full of bitterness and suffering. She went up to her room, feeling tired and a little sad.

When Zenaida came up as usual to undress Wito and put her to bed, she found her already curled up in her blanket, her head buried in her pillow.

"What's the matter?" Zenaida asked. "Aren't you feeling well?" Wito shook her head.

Zenaida had been her *yaya* since Wito was a baby. The woman used to sleep on a mat at the foot of Wito's bed, but just this year her father had ordered Zenaida to sleep downstairs with the other help, saying that Wito was "getting too big for that." Wito had not complained before, but now she wanted her *yaya* to stay and put her arms around her.

Zenaida knelt by the bed and felt Wito's forehead. Her hands felt cool, the roughened palms strangely comforting. Wito looked up at the woman's face. It was a homely face, broad and flat with small, black eyes set close together on either side of a bridgeless nose. There was a scar running from the bottom of her nose through her upper lip that, Wito's mother had explained once, had been the result of an operation. Because of this disfigurement, Wito had never thought of Zenaida as being the same as other people. She had often made fun of her behind her back, and imitated her slow, stolid walk. But now, looking at that face, she did not find it ugly. She remained looking at Zenaida for a long time, until she fell asleep.

The next day was Saturday. Since there was no school, Wito could stay in bed late. She lay on her stomach, listening to her own breathing, to the bird sounds in the garden. As she tried to recall the events of the previous evening, she was overcome by a form of nausea, strange and unexplained. It made her feel as though she were standing on the rolling deck of a great ship. She remembered Zenaida coming in, and Zenaida's cool hand pressed against her forehead, and she remembered watching to see if Zenaida would pull her hand away in fright because Wito felt sure that she was indeed very, very hot inside. But Zenaida had said only, "It is nothing," and then turned off the light—wasn't that what she had done?—and then for a long time Wito had remained awake in the darkness, trying to puzzle out the meaning of her mother's bitterness.

It seemed to her that in one way or another, in all her parents' conversations, they always came up against this "thing," like an obstacle that one is careful to walk around. It was shadowy now, but sometimes, like last night, it would assume unexpected shape and significance. It would emerge, startling and huge, as out of a mist, and then even ordinary, everyday things—this cup Wito was holding in her hand, the saucer for it to rest on, this bowl with the chipped edge, this slant of light, this leaf, oh, everything!—became twisted out of shape, not themselves. Perhaps this explained the nausea that Wito felt whenever the horizon, which should stay still, would not. She had felt it standing on the deck of the great ship (which was in actuality only the ferry; she had taken it dozens of times, back and forth between the islands). At that time the clouds had looked like whorls—spinning, spinning.

Perhaps this was why Wito could not bear to see her mother crying or looking even a little sad. When she saw her mother was in one of her moods, she would sing and dance and clap her hands, as though the sound of her voice and her clapping were all the cure her mother needed. She would pat her mother's hair, her arms, her lips, in a sudden excess of anxiety, as though her mother were a thing in danger of breaking apart like the eggs Zenaida cracked in the kitchen, and only the pressure of Wito's hands could hold all the pieces together.

Now she heard her mother's voice below, speaking to the gardener. It was a cheerful, even voice, not the one of last night. It was nearly noon. The trees at the far edge of the garden looked strangely flat—like paper cutouts. Her mother, in a bright pink sundress, a golf umbrella balanced over her right shoulder to shield her from the sun, was bending over some bushes. When she moved, she seemed to blur a little.

Wito lay back on her bed and closed her eyes. Through her eyelids she could feel the sun in hot pulses of light. Was she only imagining it or had she really seen the *gumamela*, the *santan*, all in bloom at once, all along the garden wall? Even now that she had her eyes closed and was lying back on the bed, she could still see the reds and oranges of the flowers seeming to blaze among the cool green of the leaves. She imagined she could smell the newly cut grass and the fresh-dug earth where her mother was getting ready to plant a new tree. A strange thought came to her: Perhaps, if she went to the garden at this moment, she would find her mother as she had been, restored and whole. Then she would will her to remain that way forever. The longing to see her mother whole again became so over-whelming that Wito immediately got up and dressed.

Once outside, Wito paused. The heat was intense. It clung to her face and arms, to the back of her neck. The grass was dry—so dry it seemed to have bleached out and faded. The earth was hard and packed, and. Wito thought how, even if it were to rain now, there could not be much water that could penetrate that sealed surface.

She saw her mother leaning against a corner of the house, waving a palm-leaf fan slowly back and forth across her face. Her mother had not seen her. She was looking down at the ground and seemed to be thinking. Just at the moment when Wito would have called out to her, she caught sight of something reflected against the white wall of the house. An unexpected shadow had appeared in profile to her mother's body. There was a head, or what Wito assumed was a head, though it looked nothing like her mother's, and had long, pointed teeth. When her mother turned her head a little, the shadow moved, too. Only when Wito had come a little closer did she finally make out what it was—there, growing out of her mother's back, was a huge, scaly lizard.

Wito did not scream, did not cry out. Even when the thing actually raised its head and looked straight at her, she did not think to run away. She saw how her mother continued to walk by the wall, bending down every now and then to inspect the flower beds, and how easily she carried the creature on her back, as though it had no weight at all. When her mother straightened abruptly, the creature did not fall, did not even slip, but remained looking blandly at Wito over her mother's shoulder, its long red tongue just brushing her mother's right ear. When her mother raised a hand to tuck a loose strand of hair behind her ear, the creature adroitly moved its head to avoid touching her.

Just then her mother saw Wito and smiled. When she smiled, her cheeks jumped up, nearly covering her eyes. Her hair was in a bun at the back of her head, but a few strands had escaped near the bottom and clung in little damp circles to her neck. Her neck, Wito noticed for the first time, was thick, with little grooves running all around it.

"Come, Wito!" her mother called. "Shall we have breakfast?" Wito merely nodded and trailed slowly behind her mother, from a distance.

Her father was reclining on the sofa on the *lanai*, reading the paper. When her mother called to him, he quickly put down his paper and joined them at the dining room table. Wito saw that he was preoccupied. He hardly touched the mangoes, dried fish, and fried sweet sausage that her mother placed before him. After a long silence he said, "I must get back to the farm. There's a lot of work to be done." Her mother made no comment but calmly continued passing the dishes and pouring the coffee.

"Would you like some of this, Wito?" she would ask from time to time, and took no notice when Wito failed to answer her. Finally she turned to her husband and said, "When will you be back?"

"Late," Wito's father replied. "We have to find more spring water—there's no telling how much longer this drought will last."

Wito kept looking at her father, but he was eating just the way he always did: hunched over his plate, fingers holding a dried fish to his mouth. He didn't seem to notice anything different about his wife. But then, Wito thought, perhaps he had grown used to the thing growing out of her back, and no longed thought about it.

Wito wondered how it was when her mother slept. Did she sleep peacefully or did the thing torment her, making it difficult, for example, for her to lie on her back or to breathe properly? She wondered if her father, reaching for her mother in the middle of the night, did not brush against the thing by accident, and think perhaps it was his wife's face that he had touched.

When the maid came to clear away the dishes, Wito's mother went back into the garden, but Wito excused herself and went up to her room. There, she ran to the window and looked at her mother in the garden. From this distance, she couldn't make out the creature, and her mother was just a woman in a pink sundress bending over a bougainvillea bush.

Now it seemed to Wito that the mother she had known was another person, different from this one who had just been revealed. When Wito thought of that mother now, it was as though she existed only in the past, as though all the things they had done together were remembered, like pictures in an album. She began to go over some of their favorite activities in her mind. In the evening, her mother had sometimes called Wito to come and brush her hair. Then, handing Wito the ivory-handled brush, she would sit on a low stool in front of her, with her back turned. Wito remembered how heavy her mother's long, black hair had felt in her hands, how difficult it had always been to brush, like brushing the matted fur of some animal, and how it always smelled faintly of coconut oil. Her mother would turn her head now and then to look at Wito and smile, and in smiling looked so beautiful that Wito was reminded of the statue of the Virgin in the Santuario de San Antonio.

Then there had been the times at the farm when Wito had watched her mother talking to the *sakadas*. How they had looked at her, those people without any shoes—with shining, grateful eyes, as though she were a Maria Makiling just come down from the mountain. "Ah, Impeng," her mother would say to one, "you seem to have lost your teeth," and the poor soul could only giggle in sudden embarrassment, covering her toothless mouth with one hand.

At other times, her mother asked her to sit on her lap and they would play silly games. Her favorite was the one where her mother would ask, "Who is my *kamatis*? Who is my *sibuyas*?" How happy it made her to shout "me" to each of her mother's questions, and to be rewarded with one of her mother's kisses.

At such times, she could almost believe that her mother was another person, a person who laughed and whose laugh had truth and substance, whose laugh chased away poisons and evil spirits and made things whole when they were broken. This mother, Wito could easily believe, lived in light and air, and moved about easily in brightly lit rooms, singing.

Now Wito heard her father's voice in the garden, and she ran to the window to see him. Her father was taking his leave of her mother. He turned to go but something her mother said made him turn, made him come back and rest a large, clumsy hand on the back of her neck. Wito's mother bent her head, and the shadow on the grass opened its mouth and showed its long, pointed teeth.

Alfian Bin Sa'at ✻ *Singapore*

An ethnic Javanese, Alfian Bin Sa'at was born in Singapore in 1977. He attended the National University of Singapore, where he established a reputation writing for the theatre. His English-language plays include *Fighting* (1994), *Don't Say I Say* (2001), and *Happy Endings: Asian Boys Vol. 3* (2007). His Malay-language plays include *Dongeng (Myth)* (1997), *Causeway* (1998), and *Minah & Monyet (Minah & Monkey)* (2003). A controversial writer who does not shy away from gay or political issues, his published works include the poetry volume *One Fierce Hour* (1998), and the short story collection *Corridor* (1999), for which he received the Singapore Literature Prize Commendation Award.

Pillow

I SAW HIS EYES FLASH FOR A MOMENT, AND THE NEXT MINUTE I saw tears.

"Haven't I been good to you?" he asked, looking around. There was only another couple in the teahouse, and they were hidden behind a cabinet of tea sets.

"You're crying," I sighed. "You're crying again."

"Yes I know I am! Why do you keep doing this to me?"

I looked away, looked at steam rising from the spout of a small clay teapot, looked at clear water bubbling in a Pyrex pot over a stove, looked at the blue flame.

"Is this what you like to see? A fifty-year-old man? Looking like this?"

"No."

"Then why?" He reached out to touch my forearm, which was resting on the table. He had well-manicured nails, and rings on his fingers. I shrunk away, but not forcefully, in disgust. Mechanically, like it was a reflex.

He blinked, and knitted his brow. I looked at a rice-paper scroll of Chinese calligraphy and imagined his tears smearing it, forming runny streaks. I imagined myself swallowing the tea although it tasted like seawater. I remembered those tears when I kissed his face and he told me how happy he was, in a voice so soft it was like a girlish whisper.

"I paged you at least ten times, but you never returned any of them." His voice was low, the way people's voices were when they want to convince themselves that they are talking with reason and not emotion.

"I was busy."

"Busy with what? Busy with whom?"

"I can't."

"Can't what? What is wrong?"

"Stop asking me these questions," I finally said. I said it softer the second time, although it wasn't too harsh the first time round. "Just stop asking me these questions. I'm tired."

"You're eighteen! What is there to be tired about? I'll take care of you. What are you tired of?"

"You," I told him, looking away, to the window where drops of rain had gathered. "You're making me tired." There should have been a certain sense of triumph in the way I said it, as if it were something I had been meaning to say for a long time. But when it came out it sounded so truthful that there was no way I could have intended it to hurt.

I remembered the first time it happened. He was my father's friend. He came over to our house one day and he caught me looking out from my room. The next week he told me to stop calling him "uncle." The week after he touched my thigh while we were driving down Changi Road in his Mercedes. He had picked me up from school earlier in the evening. I had closed my eyes and let him.

"What is this music playing now?" I had asked him.

"You like it? It's Mahler. Gustav Mahler." He inched his hand to the inside of my thighs. I didn't move.

"I don't listen to classical."

"You should," he said, his voice a little unsteady. "You should because," his hand was working on my zip now, "you should, because classical music is good."

My eyes were still shut and in my mind I could see the street lamps that stretched and sloped ahead, a million birthday candles I could puff out the moment I lifted my eyelids. When I did just that, we were in a car park under a rain tree, and he was crying.

"I didn't mean to," he sobbed. "I'll drive you home."

"No, it's all right," I told him.

"I'm an old man," he said, looking at me only from his rearview mirror. "Most of my friends, they're married, they have kids. One of them is seeing his son graduate next week. I eat out a lot. I don't have holiday photographs, I don't have cards done in crayons, I've got this king-size bed, cost me a lot, but you know what? It's got only one pillow."

"Why didn't you get married?"

He turned on the headlamps and illuminated the tree that stood in front of us. Then, he turned it on brighter and I could almost see the ants scurrying on the forlorn bark of the tree. Finally he turned them off and the tree fell back into shadows. He frowned, as if wondering what that show of light was all about.

"Some things just don't happen. Some things don't work out like they should. When you get to my age you'll know."

"I think I already know." I ran a finger against the edge of the dashboard and wiped it from side to side, as if I were erasing a name.

"I have a lot of money," he said, his eyes glued to the mirror. "But nobody to spend it on. I open my bank book and I see so many zeros. You know, sometimes I watch those commercials and I actually dial in. I think it's what happens when you think you have too much money. I've bought myself an Abdomenizer, a kitchen helper that's supposed to turn cucumber slices into flowers, a treadmill, a tube of white stuff that gets rid of every stain. It's amazing, the things you can buy. And last week I bought this tray, you can put frozen food on it and it melts fast. I tried it, I put an ice cube on it and it turned to water in three minutes flat."

"That's nice," I said, not really knowing what to say. "It really does that?"

"Yeah. But you know, spending on yourself isn't the same as spending on someone else. I'd love to go buy things for people, things they'd appreciate." He paused for a while. "I'm an old man."

"You keep saying that."

"It doesn't matter to you?"

His apartment was well-kept, clean uncluttered. If he wanted to move, I guess he could have packed everything into five boxes. He was right about his bed; there was only one pillow on it. At least he wasn't a liar, I thought, before I let him melt in my arms, his face gently nudging, his fingers moving around the trunk of my body, like someone clawing at shadows. I kept thinking of the tree in the car park, and the ants, and whether the tree knew anything when the ants chewed off crumbs of bark. I wondered if plants were capable of pain. I let his tears fall on my shoulder, his lips planting wet ovals on my skin. With my eyes closed I pictured his mouth opening and closing like the sphincter of a sea anemone. When I was about to fall asleep he lifted my head and eased the one pillow under my head.

"I love you," he had said then, too pleadingly to have meant anything.

I looked at the clay tea cup in front of me and turned it round and round with my thumb and forefinger. Tea drinking was an ancient tradition, dating back to the time when men had long goatees and wispy eyebrows. I looked at my own hands and imagined mottles forming. I imagined the bones wrapping skin tighter around them like old men huddling in from the cold. I realized that the harder I tried to keep my hand still, the more it trembled.

He started, "I know a lot of your friends are going out with all the young . . . studs." I wanted to laugh at how he kept using the word. "And I know sometimes you don't like being seen with me."

"We've gone through this already."

"Tell me you won't leave me."

"I can't make those kinds of promises." I finally looked up to meet his face, and I gazed boldly, at the onslaught of lines around his eyes, his thinning, black-dyed hair, the hinged lines at the sides of his lips. "I'm too young."

He frowned again, and then turned the stove off. I was startled, as if all this time everything I had said needed the hissing sound of the flame.

"How can you say this to me?"

"I'm sorry. I'm just tired. Of Mahler. And teahouses. And sitting in your car. I'm tired."

"I could pay for your driving lessons."

"I don't want to drive. I want to start walking. On my own."

He scrunched up his eyes and shook his head slowly as if assembling his words before he would release them. But what came out was a scramble of phrases, a blathering, and for a moment I remembered how in brief stolen moments I had allowed him to smudge the line between pity and love.

"I always think of you, at the office. I think of how lucky I am, to have you—I look out at the sky—and I'm not afraid of it turning gray. The night starts smelling like you, on my answering machine there is only your voice, and when I have dreams they're the color of your skin. You know? When I'm with you I gain back my old rhythms, I start to forget. At my age the last thing you want is to remember. When I'm with you I forget that I'm supposed to be fifty."

I turned away when I caught sight of another teardrop falling against the bark of the tabletop. I called out for the bill and leafed through my own wallet for the money I had saved up all week for this one tea session. I placed the money on a tray and looked at the man who removed the tea set, the tea leaves dark and soggy. I looked at him longer than a boy should, and let my eyes trail the way his legs took tentative strides away from our table, away from the mess he had cleared, all the way until he was out of sight.

"I knew this would happen one day. I knew it wouldn't last." He was trying his best to keep his voice from trembling.

He was about to drive me home when I told him to take a detour back to his place. I wanted to take back my things, books and magazines, underwear. I wanted to start all over again.

When I walked into his room I started collecting my things, from under the desk, from the shelves, the rattling drawers. I found an Economics assignment I thought I had lost, and a fantasy novel that I didn't finish. It was placed between two of his books, *The Seven Habits of Highly Effective People* and *How to Win Friends and Influence People*, a corner still carefully dog-eared. I wondered if he had picked up my book to read one day, in an effort to find out what "boys my age" were reading. The spine was wrinkled and I knew he had; I was much more careful with my books. I went to the window to look out at the car park below, and tried to see if I could recognize which tree it was that I saw on the day my life took a turning. But I couldn't. Rows of rain trees, their leaflets folded as if to protect them from the night. Ants trickling like red sap down their trunks. The street lamps bulbous with their amber glow and the burnt husks of winged ants.

I removed my clothes and sat on his bed, with his pillow propped between my thighs. Then I folded my clothes neatly because they seemed to look so out of place in the well-kept room. It was cold but I stayed that way for a while, trying not to shiver. He came in five minutes later, his eyes raw.

"Hey," I said. "You've never showed me that thing you said you bought. The one that makes things melt fast."

He crawled onto the bed and tried to fix me in the eyes. He placed his palms on my knees. They were as cold as ice.

"I want you to promise that you'll never do that to me again. Did you know how I felt driving you all the way back? I could have just turned the steering wheel and we wouldn't have ended up here."

I just kept silent and smiled at him. It was a smile to show him how tired I was, how late it was, a well-worn smile excavated from a time when I was still young. He reached out his hand and took away the pillow. My hand rested on his chest as if to both push him away and support him as he leaned forward, first into my neck, as I rolled on my back, then my ears, my hair, his lips grazing over all the places his tears couldn't reach. When we finally kissed, he could only reach the corner of my lips because half my face was buried in his pillow. When we made love he mentioned my name several times, as if it were the only name he knew. "Oh," he called. "Oh Simon, please! Please!"

That night, and I promised myself that night only, I decided to let him have the pillow. But I didn't say anything. Just held his head on my lap between my hands, trying to remember a song whose tune was at the tip of my tongue but whose words I couldn't recall. After he fell asleep and started snoring I changed my mind and pulled the pillow away from under his head. I started thinking of all the friends I had lost, and the boys whose favors I had tried so hard to win back in secondary school, mentioning their full names one by one. And then for those whose names I had forgotten I mentioned what I most recalled about them: The one with the flapping shirt. The one with the dark nipples. The one with the flying shoelaces. I even tried to remember silly things like how my mother looked like when I was four years old. I cradled the pillow tightly and pressed my nose into it. I had a feeling that if I were to come up for air my face would crack into hundreds of wrinkles.

K. S. Maniam ✸ *Malaysia*

K. S. Maniam was born in 1942 and educated in both Tamil and English. He studied to become a teacher at Wolverhampton from 1963–64, and taught for several years in Kedah before going to the University of Malaya, from which he graduated in 1973. Recognized as one of Asia's foremost writers, Maniam has published plays, novels, and short fiction that have won a number of literary awards. In 1987, he won first prize in The New Straits Times–McDonald Short Story Competition for "The Loved Flaw," and in 1990, he was awarded first prize in The New Straits Times–Shell Short Story Competition for "Haunting the Tiger." His short fiction has been published in a number of collections, including *Haunting the Tiger: Contemporary Stories from Malaysia* (1996), and *The Colors of Heaven: Short Stories from the Pacific Rim* (1992). For ten years, Maniam served as an associate professor in the English department at the University of Malaya. He is now a full-time writer and lives with his wife and children in Subang Jaya, Selangor, Malaysia.

Arriving

WHEN KRISHNAN LEFT THE COFFEESHOP, WHERE HE HAD BEEN drinking Chinese tea with his friends, he was unsteady on his feet. The familiar buildings he walked past came tilting at him. A crow, scavenging at a pile of garbage, squawked and flew to shelter in a nearby rain tree.

He didn't mean that, he told himself. We've known each other for too long. *Pendatang!* Only politicians campaigning for votes used that word. Not always. Some minister had gone up to the platform to discourage its use. These people are not *pendatangs*. Their great-grandfathers were *pendatangs*. Some of their grandfathers were *pendatangs*. Their fathers were not *pendatangs*. They're not *pendatangs*. The minister had spoken angrily, heatedly. Krishnan remembered. Newspapers hardly used the word after that. Or only in special cases. Krishnan remembered that.

As he neared his house, he hesitated. He looked at the corner terrace house he had bought thirty years ago, drawing out his meager savings for its down payment. You'll become bankrupt *lah*, his friends had told him. Twenty thousand dollars! Lot of money, man! But he had managed. The house stood as he had bought it; no extensions or renovations jutted out and distorted the kitchen or the porch.

He pushed open the outer gate—always unlocked—and went up the short, cemented driveway. His wife appeared at the grille-doors and let him into the house. (She had insisted that the iron grilles be fitted, saying, "I'm the one who's always at home!")

"Something the matter?" she said.

"No," he said, lying down on the sofa.

"Sure? Any palpitations?" she asked.

She had picked up the word palpitations from a pamphlet on stress and heart diseases, hearing that men in their forties onwards had to be careful.

"Any pain?"

"Maybe," he said. "I don't want to talk about it."

"Who's going to talk? We've to do something," she said.

"Not that kind of pain," he said.

His wife let him be. The occasions he withdrew into himself, to be alone, were rare, and he always came out of these spells refreshed and cheerful. And he always ate with renewed appetite. But not that evening. He still lay, not stirring, on the sofa at dinner time.

"The food's ready," his wife said.

"I'm not hungry," he said.

"Too much Chinese tea?"

"I just don't feel like eating," he said, surprised by this anger at his wife.

"Something's really wrong," she said, sitting down in an armchair, watching him.

He turned his head—something he had never done—away from his wife, towards the clutch of darkness in the corner. Mat's face crowded in on him, large, cynical, angry. What had he said to make him so furious? he wondered.

"If you get hungry, the food's on the table," his wife said and went to fold and put away the day's laundry.

Krishnan hardly heard her. Had they been talking about imports and exports? Computer technology? The breaking up of the East European block? He couldn't decide. He only remembered Mat's many faces: Mat puffing up his cheeks, Mat blinking and yawning, Mat pursing his lips in indignation. Then the shattering accusation: "You *pendatang*!" And Mat had walked away.

What did it mean, *pendatang*? Arrivals? Illegals?

Pendatang. He had heard the word used on the Vietnamese people coming to the east coast of the country by the boatloads. Soon they became the boat people. The courage of these people had astonished Krishnan. He thought of the long, cramped, hazardous voyage. He read in the newspapers of their being attacked by pirates; the young women raped and the men flung overboard to drown and the flesh on their bodies sucked away by horny fish lips. They belonged nowhere; their feet could never touch firm land. He was horrified at the defacing done to a people by violence and ideology. In his dreams he was haunted by a face floating in the sea, ravaged beyond recognition by the greed for power and possessions.

Pendatang. He had seen these other people, the Indonesians, at construction sites. Building the Tudor-Spanish-Moorish houses in the suburbs. They themselves camped in makeshift shacks and bathed in the open, at the common tap. The women's sarongs, knotted at their breasts, clung to their bodies like dried, brown blood. The children's skins were covered with the soil their parents had dug up to lay the foundations for the houses. In the evenings, having nowhere to go, they sat under dim bulbs, and quarreled. Men fought over women, over the soft touch of love on the labor-calloused flesh. Or had something gone wrong in the conversion of the ringgit into the rupiah and the relatives back home forced to starve?

Krishnan stiffened against the sudden, engulfing darkness that threatened to blank out everything he had known about himself. He was the vagrant, blotted-out face bobbing to the hidden currents in the sea of dissolution. He clutched at memory, he clawed at familiarity.

But he only floated, set adrift by this new uncertainty, towards an unfamiliar landfall.

"The ship stank of human dung," his father's words came to him, "and we, the human cattle, floated above that odor, towards our new land."

He tried hard to recall his father's memories of his voyage out to Malaysia, but his mind was choked with some strange obstruction. Krishnan lay in that region between water and land trying to putt away from the matted, dark intrusion, but his determination seemed to fail. Yes, it had been his determination that had kept him innocent of his father's experiences. He had decided, when he became aware of his budding consciousness, not to be influenced by other people's memories and nostalgia.

His wife shook him by the shoulder, startling away the thin, forming lines of submerged recollections.

"At least come to bed," she said and stood, waiting.

He followed her to their bedroom and changed into a sarong and T-shirt, his arms flailing as if against some wave of the unknown, and lay down beside her. In the dark he saw her shoulder rise and fall like the faint outline of a land he had never known. His son and daughter—expecting her first child—were out there, absorbed by the land rocking on its own, unfathomable center.

He struggled against the dark waters of uncertainty for a long time. Many times he was sucked into a fathomless fear but, finally, he rose to the surface, strengthened. He lay watching the rest of the night crumble away into a new torment.

The morning, when he sat near the door with his cup of tea, did not come up at him with its dew-and-soil-soaked grass, did not come with its soft and unimposing light. Instead he caught a whiff of rotten sewage being carried down the monsoon drain from across the road. The light falling across the doorway ran points of harshness into his awakened flesh.

Pendatang. One who arrives. One who goes through different experiences to reach the most enlightening knowledge, he thought. How like my father's thinking! How foolishly I thought I didn't come from his loins!

In the evening he bathed, the water slapping against a new grittiness on his skin, and put on the pants he had worn to work. He felt he was getting into another struggle, different from the one Mat and he had gone through with Mr. Cuthbert, their British boss, before Independence.

As he passed, on his way to the coffeeshop, the houses he had accepted as solid and unshakable for more than thirty years, he thought he detected cracks here and there. No, they were not just splits in the concrete work. They were more than that: the Chinese sundry shop at the corner seemed to wobble on its isolation. He had heard a lot about that shop when he came to live in the neighborhood. But, at that time, they had only been stories for him. A string of words from different mouths, adding color to the place. Now these stories became sinister episodes in a life that had remained inaccessible to him.

They smacked of the agony of a private history: They all spoke of the attempt of a man to shape himself after his own dreams. Ah Ho, he no good, they had said. Running away, hiding from things he done before. Now thinking he only shopkeeper. But he bring the money from bad deeds he done before. Now dress simple, looking like he never cut people up or kill them maybe. Didn't run far. Can't hide from past too long. These things catch up, you know. One day a gang come, beat him up, smash up his shop. But the man still stubborn. Next day he pretend nothing happen. Build up his shop again. Another time the gang come again. Do bad things to his daughter. Still the man pretend nothing happen. If me, my spirit will rise. Will smash up the faces of those thugs!

But when Krishnan passed the old man, Ah Ho, standing behind the counter, the old man smiled at him as if his life had been, so far, an untroubled one.

The street beyond Ah Ho's shop curved into a beckoning distance as each shop thrust its own past at Krishnan. Getting to the coffeeshop was like traveling against a slope. Each patch of the road intruded upon him, wanting to be known.

At last he sighted, in the interior of the coffeeshop, the people he had no difficulty in remembering. They were connected, web-like, to a round marble table that reflected the turning fan and the still glaze of the teapot. Even as he approached them, he saw their hands weave into hair-thin fragility their solidarity.

"Here at last!" Wong said.

"What happened to you, man?" Teng said. "Not yet retired from your wife?"

Their laughter brightened the table like the shine of unreal gold.

"You can't retire from anything," Krishnan said.

"Wah, how the man change!" Teng said.

Wong, the more serious among them, looked at Krishnan as if seeing him for the first time. "All words. Nothing comes from that," he said.

"Only when you're innocent," Krishnan said. "To be innocent is to be stupid."

"You've known Mat for a long time," Wong said. "You should know better."

"I don't know anything." Krishnan said, "But it isn't too late."

"Not late!" Teng said. "Look who's talking! We're all late. One foot already in grave."

"We must go in peace, man," Francis Lim, a Christian but who had not abandoned his Chinese habits, said.

"As if we were never awake," Krishnan said, almost to himself. "But where's he?"

"He come once or twice," Wong said. "Maybe won't come again."

"Something there deep inside..." Krishnan said.

"Nothing deep there, man," Francis Lim said. "Just jetsam, flotsam words."

Listening to them, Krishnan felt he was cut adrift again and was floating away to those grasping lips that would tear him to shreds.

He sat there, not listening, waiting, recollecting. He had once seen Wong strike, with lightning fury, at the waiter who had not come with his pot of tea on time. Wong had lashed out with an energy that, though lying hidden beneath the surface, came exploding through with instinct-charged aggression. His hand went for the bread knife with practiced sureness. The proprietor had stepped in, pacified him by reviling the worker, and led Wong, who still trembled with the uncompleted assault, back to the table.

Beneath Francis Lim's Christian sense of charity, Krishnan remembered seeing a violent self-possessiveness. They had been talking about the individual rights of the citizens in the country.

"What individual rights?" he had almost thundered. "You take what you can and don't let go. Those are the only rights you have."

"Chop-chop," Teng had said. "You fist, you knife, you gun. That give you what you want. You stand up, somebody kick you down some more."

And he had laughed, saying, "You know who that somebody." He was looking at Mat. But they had all laughed, including Mat, as if they all accepted the deceptions they practiced on each other.

"This not like you, man," Teng now said. "Think. Think. What for think?"

Krishnan came out of his musings; he stared, disoriented, at Teng. The man's humor-jowled face was also laced with a trace of viciousness. His jokes seemed to bite, cling and make vulnerable Krishnan's distress. Their rugged edges sawed and dismembered the fragile reassurances he floated upon.

"For you, all right," Krishnan said, "no need to think. I have to. Didn't think all my life."

But no one said anything. They sat drinking their Chinese tea and ruminating on the fading evening light that made the tables and chairs shadows, and the men ghosts.

The treacherous gloom of the dying day was thick with the betrayal of his friends. He staggered through the labyrinthine deceit, his earlier determination deserting him as some fickle frailty. He saw no struggle ahead of him, only surrender. But the thought came to him, in the light of his new knowledge, that he had always been turning away from circumstances and people. To give in to himself. How right Mat was! he thought. He was always coming into himself. Yes, he was a *pendatang*!

His wife received him again, her face reflecting the bitter strain on his own: They had lived close together without really knowing what went on inside each other. She glowed when he glowed; he was pleased when she was pleased. Had anything happened behind that glow and that pleasure?

He hugged this doubt to himself throughout the simple meal she had prepared and throughout the night as he lay beside the unquestioning heave of known and unknown flesh. He sweated and strange sounds caught in his throat as he waited for the man of the night before to reach out to him.

Instead somebody else came. At first Krishnan could not recognize him. The flesh was so young, firm and unlined; the face was so rounded, placid and untouched. Could he have come from all that confidence? he wondered. Then he stilled his mind and watched as this young man moved, worked, talked and fell into the snares of friendship.

There he was moving with Mat. They are in the office and Mat has just come out from Mr. Cuthbert's office, after a dressing down. There is an expression on Mat's face Krishnan does not understand.

"Upstart!" Mat says. "Who does he think he is? Coming here to teach me. To teach me!"

Krishnan is reminded of a freshwater fish taken out and put into a bucket of sea water. The scaly thing bucks and rebuffs, striking out, indignantly, at some substance in the water that threatens it with domination. Mat's face is all bathed in a fine sweat of rejection. Then it changes, breaks out into playfulness.

"A time will come," Mat says. "Let's go eat!" The stairs leading into the sunshine and to the food stalls is covered with their daily stepping out. The ascent on their return—energies restored—is caked with relief and camaraderie. But Krishnan sees a shadow following them, in and out of the building, and sinking out of sight when they are at their desks, working.

As he watches, the shadow goes underground: it divides and submerges itself in Mat and in himself. Whenever they talk about Mr. Cuthbert, Krishnan can feel it straining against the tide of words. He watches Mat, he watches himself: the faces are flushed by a common sympathy, by a common fear. Now the door to Mr. Cuthbert's room does not remain shut on some impenetrable world of authority. It swings outward, beckoning, and draws Mat and Krishnan past its fearsome threshold.

Getting accustomed to its darkness, they see that there is no furniture in the room. The walls are maps; the floor is time moving without pause. When they try to steady themselves their bodies shiver. Mat and Krishnan look at each other, their skins sweating fear. Only their minds are alive, preparing to ward off the shadows detaching themselves from the maps, from the time-floor.

Then, suddenly, their minds cannot repel anything, not the shadows, not the countries that come hurtling at them through time. The fear they have held onto leaves them. The boundary of their self-centered consciousness, breaks, and releases them into the continuum of a new awareness. And the people come through the centuries, their clothes patchy with history but their faces aglow with abstraction, aglow with enigmatic wholeness. Krishnan and Mat are specks of fascination in the tide of wholeness.

And as specks of unenclosed awareness they flow along the banks of time, recognizing here a primeval adventurer, there an Alexander outdistancing their native lands; there is Buddha in his bubble of meditation and further down the Greek sages wrapped up in their own wisdom. Riding the time cells, they go past the cataclysm of nations at war, cultures in conflict, and come to their own histories and see the conquistadors bringing their ships and their ways of living to the country's shores. There is no stopping time and soon Mr. Cuthbert comes into their vision, puny and defeated, his personal history in tatters but his spirit shining through to the future. Then Mat and Krishnan come face-to-face with the figure of a man, historyless, moving on the current of discovery, and when they look behind him there is nothing; when they look where he is looking there is a swirling mist of everything.

Then Krishnan stepped out and awakened into his own consciousness. His fear was gone, banished by a wide-ranging bewilderment. In the dark he sensed the contours of his wife's body, enclosing emptiness. Their lives had been a mere accumulation of days, the shell of a house, the husks of practical tasks. He had turned away and reduced to a comfortable dot all that he did not want to understand. That had been his reaction on being summoned to Mr. Cuthbert's office: to shun that which made one man dominate another and turn inwards into his cocoon of assurances.

"The loins of my father, the loins of history," he thought, wonderingly, as he got up quietly from the bed and went to the living room. He switched on the dim wall light and, opening the front door, looked out on the quiet street.

"*Pendatang*," he told himself as he observed the shadows of the trees, telephone and electric poles trail off into a deeper, richer blackness. He had the feeling that he was looking at what had happened before and what lay before him without dismay, without fear.

"*Pendatang*," he said softly, gratefully. "*Pendatang. Pendatang. Pendatang.*"

The word went inside him, into something other than self-consciousness. It went beyond the fish-sucked bodies of the boat people, beyond the clay-covered skins of the construction workers. It went beyond the pursed indignation of Mat's lips, the puffed-up smugness of his cheeks. It did not take Krishnan into himself; it took him into the beyond.

Daylight and his wife found Krishnan seated beside the door, gazing soberly on the street that ran past the house.

"You didn't sleep at all?" his wife asked.

"Sometimes you must be more awake than asleep," he said, turning to look at her.

The smile that had been absent for a while resumed to her lips. She went to the kitchen to make his coffee, wondering if he would have the ravenous appetite that marked his emergence from the occasional and self-imposed isolation.

When she served lunch, he ate like someone about to begin an endless journey, relishing every morsel and yet not overfilling himself. She thought she saw in his eyes a light that she had not seen before—a light that gathered whatever happened around him to the pinpoint of a large purpose. In the evening she watched him go out to meet his friends and though she barely understood what he had gone through in recent weeks, she could not help noticing a new dignity that carried the figure of her husband over puddle and drain, past hut and bungalow, round the comer to the unfamiliar.

Krishnan walked towards the coffeeshop, the calm unsteadiness inside him absorbing whatever he saw and heard along the way. As he approached the garbage can he saw the crow that had squawked away before now foraging among the offal of fowl and fish, unperturbed.

Its glossy, folded wings landscaped a darkness that reached into the one inside him. He thought it looked like a conquistador pecking away at the wastes of history, trying to salvage. "As Ah Ho did," Krishnan thought as he passed the sundry shop.

When he entered the coffeeshop he saw Wong, Francis Lim, and Teng seated at the usual table as if they had not left it since the last time he had been with them. The table still held in its glaze their gesticulating shadows, given, he thought, to surrender.

"Look who here!" Teng said. "So fresh! So wife service you good, ah?"

"Your wife given up already?" Krishnan said.

Wong and Francis Lim looked at him, coming out from their self-absorbed stillness.

"Your friend here *lah*, looking for you," Teng said.

"That Mat," Wong said. "Strange man."

"We should try to understand him," Krishnan said.

"You wasted a lifetime doing that," Francis Lim said.

"Maybe I looked from the wrong side," Krishnan said.

"You can change your position as many times as you want," Wong said, "but he won't."

"The change will be good for us," Krishnan said.

Teng laughed and the others sniggered; Krishnan listened to the ripples of skepticism, undiscouraged. He saw before him many evenings, filled with light and filled with shadows. Unchanging, between light and shadow, Mat would say, "*Pendatang*!"

Krishnan would say, "Yes, I'm always arriving, arriving. I'll never reach. Reaching is dying. Reaching is not arriving. Arriving at what? I don't know. Only arriving. Never getting there. Arriving."

Mulaika Hijjas ✳ *Malaysia*

Mulaika Hijjas is from Kuala Lumpur, Malaysia, but now lives in London. After leaving university, she spent two years working full time on a collection of short stories before earning a Ph.D. at the School of Oriental and African Studies on nineteenth-century Malay poetry by women. She has published short fiction in literary journals in the United States, Malaysia, and Hong Kong, and in 2006 was the David T. K. Wong Fellow in creative writing at the University of East Anglia. Her work addresses the disjunctures of Malaysia's swiftly transforming society.

Confinement

THE FIRST DAY THEY CAME, I WAS SWEEPING THE GROUND AROUND the house. I did this every day, scratching circular patterns in the dirt with the broom, even though I knew that by the evening there would be more leaves and chicken shit and the ground would be scuffed with footprints. I did not want the neighbors to be able to say, on top of everything else, that we were dirty. They would have to admit, no matter what they said about my mother, that at least her eldest daughter kept the house neat. Not that they ever said such things to my face; they were very polite and took care to voice other people's opinions rather than their own. "Pak Soud said such-and-such a thing to me the other day about your mother, Ria, and I was so shocked I hardly knew what to say!" "That Mak Teh with her stinking mouth said a dreadful thing to me about your family—" The rasp of the broom did not drown out those voices.

I was outside sweeping the ground in the late afternoon—the sky blue and harsh as metal and the fish eagles screaming overhead—when their car came over the rise in the road. Big and shiny like a battleship, it reflected the sun so it hurt my eyes to look. It turned onto our land, leaving tire tracks on the ground I had just swept. Nobody we knew owned such a car—no car had stopped in front of our house since the funeral, when Pak Abas had loaned his van to take the body to the *surau*. All I could think was that these people had got lost and needed directions back to the main road, or that they wanted to buy the land, and our luck had changed.

161

"People here, Nek!" I yelled, gripping the broom in both hands and squinting at the car.

The passenger door opened, and a woman stepped out, the hem of her *kain* trailing on the ground for an instant while she swung her legs out of the car. Small and slim, she had hair cut short to the chin, and just from looking at her gray-and-black batik *baju kurung*, I could tell it had cost even more than the *baju* Pak Abas's daughter Su had worn at her wedding. The woman wore sunglasses and I couldn't see her eyes, but I felt them flicker over me. Then a man got out of the driver's side: a white man, not really white but pale and speckled red, the color of a chicken's egg, and as tall and lanky as the pole ghost. He smiled, a little, and nodded at me jerkily, perhaps embarrassed at being so tall and pale.

Without waiting for the man to speak, the woman asked, "This is the house of Puan Timah Ayub, isn't it?"

"Ria, go and make tea for the guests," my grandmother said. She was standing at the top of the verandah stairs. "Go."

I went to the back of the house, to the kitchen, and began to heat the water for the tea. I thought about going to stand by the door of the room where they sat so I could hear what these people wanted, but my grandmother would not have liked that. She might have to go down the steps one at a time, but she could still handle a *rotan* and, as she had told me many times, she didn't think I was too old for a beating. Even though I was old enough to stop school and go to work and old enough for the boys at the bus stop to click their tongues at me, I was not too old to be beaten. My grandmother had been expecting these people—she had kept this a secret cuddled to her breasts—and hadn't said a word to me. In those days she used to talk to me from morning to night, her complaints and grudges and worries spilling out of her mouth in an endless stream until I wanted to take the scissors and sever her tongue. But she had no one else to talk to—the other children were too young to understand, and my mother had made herself deaf to what anyone said—so I kept my hands busy washing the rice or pounding the chili and nodded, Yes, yes, it's terrible, Nek, so many terrible things to happen in Nek's old age, in Nek's old age when Nek should be resting after a life bathed in sweat, when Nek's children and grandchildren should kneel and kiss Nek's hands every day.

At last the water boiled and I steeped the tea, too quickly, so that it probably tasted of nothing but condensed milk, and brought the pot in on a tray with our best cups and saucers. I set a cup down in front of my grandmother, and then one in front of the man, and then the woman, and poured slowly. None of them said anything. My grandmother stared at me; the man picked up his tea and immediately began to drink, even though it was still too hot; the woman smoothed her hair back with her hands. Each hand had a ring and nails shaped into perfect ovals. She had pushed the sunglasses back on her head, and I could see that her eyes were beautiful, brown like tea that has been steeped to bitterness.

"Ria, go and take care of your mother."

In my mother's room it was dark and hot. She didn't like the light—it made her restless—so we had to keep the curtains closed all day, even though that meant no breeze could get in. The leaves of the calendar on the wall hung limp and still. The top page of the calendar had a picture of women in traditional dress, white teeth against red lips, for the month of April. Now it was November. My mother was asleep, lying on her side with her back to the wall and her mouth slightly open. When she was asleep, she looked like a child, like my little sister Eton, only her belly was huge with the seventh month of pregnancy. Her body seemed brittle and tiny, as though all her energy had been sucked into that great belly. Her chest rose and fell, rose and fell, and over the sound of her breathing I could make out the conversation in the next room.

"Your daughter is not well?"

"Well enough. A sickness of the heart, but her body is healthy. You need not worry about the child—already my daughter has had six children, and they are all strong and healthy. The one you saw just now is the eldest."

"How long has she been sick?"

"Since her husband died. Seven months."

"They say that if a woman is too unhappy with the child in the womb, the child will have bad luck."

"The *kampung* people say that. I would not have thought you would believe such things."

"I don't. But my husband and I want to take your daughter to the doctor, to make sure she is healthy, as you say. If she goes often to the doctor, we can make sure that the birth will be easy for her."

Only the woman spoke. Perhaps her husband did not speak Malay. After a while they left, the car drove off down the road, and I got up and left the hot, airless room where my mother's chest rose and fell. My grandmother was sitting and looking out through the doorway. I put the cups and saucers on a tray to take back to the kitchen. The woman's cup was still full, still warm against my fingers.

"They are going to give us five thousand ringgit, Ria. You know, you could go to school again." I could almost see the calculations swarming around her head like mosquitoes: five thousand, enough for Ria to go back to school, for the others to stay in school, to get the gold bracelets back from the pawnshop, to get us all new clothes, to start a shop by the roadside, enough for everything.

"I don't like school," I said, and took the tray into the kitchen.

Since my father died, we had been living off my grandmother's savings. First we used my parents' savings, but that didn't last long; and for a while the people at the mosque gave us some money, until the story got out that the father of the baby was not my father. Pak Abas sometimes gave us a bit of money, twenty ringgit a month, to soothe his guilt. When the rambutans were in season, we sold almost a truckload to a Chinese man from town, and that brought in some money. But now there was no more fruit and no more money either. So I suppose I should have felt grateful for five thousand ringgit.

I took the dirty clothes to the well where I had to wash them every day. We didn't have piped water, so I had to keep drawing up the bucket until my back felt as though it would split and my hands were rubbed red by the rope. I washed Mak Teh's dirty clothes also, in exchange for her looking after my brothers. She got the better end of the bargain. All she did was watch Amin and Husin rolling in the dirt with her children and shout at them if they wandered too far from the house or went into her kitchen. I washed her clothes: I scrubbed them against the concrete slab by the well, rubbed the sweat stains and blood with the blue plastic brush, pulled up buckets of water to rinse out the suds and filth, wrung each garment into a tight corkscrew to get the water out, hung them up on the line, ran to get them if it began to rain, took them down when they were dry, and folded them, tied them in a neat bundle, and carried them over to her house. But Mak Teh also gave my brothers lunch every day, which was two less stomachs at a meal to worry about, my grandmother said, and so I washed her clothes.

The well was behind our house and had been built by my father and Pak Abas eight years ago, when our family first moved to the village. Then, I was just a little girl; Eton, Melor, Husin, and Amin had not been born yet. Pak Abas had arranged for a bulldozer to come and dig the well for us because my father was his friend. After the bulldozer had dug a round, deep hole in the earth, half as deep as it had to be, my father jumped down into it with the tape measure. My mother and I stood at the edge of the hole watching him, his head almost a meter beneath our feet, orange clay up to his knees. He looked up at us, and frowned a bit because the sun was in his eyes. When he finished taking the measurements, he couldn't get a foothold on the slippery walls of the well. "Hey, Abas, come and help me get out!" he yelled. "I've got myself stuck." Pak Abas came and leant over the side, extending his hand. My father grasped it, and the next thing any of us knew, both of them were at the bottom, a tangle of limbs in the sticky mud. My mother shrieked with laughter, and every time she told the story, she would say that the two of them were just like a pair of wallowing buffaloes. My father had laughed as soon as he had disentangled himself from Pak Abas, but Pak Abas was angry because his clothes were dirtied.

My father died of dengue. Dengue is carried by mosquitoes, which breed in still water. At the hospital in the town where my father died, the doctor asked us why we hadn't put medicine in the well to kill the mosquito larvae. My father told us not to, I said, he told us it made the water taste bad. So we didn't do it, or we forgot—I don't know which. Anyway, the mosquitoes could have come from anywhere: from the neighbor's well, from the rubbish tip where water collected in plastic bags and rusting cans.

Looking down into the well now, I saw my face floating on the surface of the water. A frog had fallen in somehow, and the rhythmic kick, kick of its legs sent shimmers through my reflection. I dropped the bucket down to try and scoop it out—even frogs cannot swim forever. But the bucket frightened it, and it dove under. I watched for it to come up again, and when it did, I tried to catch it in the bucket but it swam out of my reach. At last, I gave up: I had the clothes to wash, and when I was finished, I looked into the well and saw my reflection upon the water, perfect and still.

In the evening I went over to Mak Teh's house to fetch my brothers home. Mak Teh was sitting on the steps in front of her house, fanning herself with a tin plate.

"You had some visitors, Ria?"

"Yes. Do you have the clothes for me to wash?"

"The visitors were relatives?"

"Oh no, Mak Teh, friends of my grandmother."

"From when she worked in Kuala Lumpur?"

"Yes."

"Your grandmother's friends are rich!"

I returned to the house, carrying Amin on my hip as Husin kicked a stone in front of him as he walked. Pak Abas was there. Pak Abas visited us when he pleased, propping his bicycle against one of the stilts of our house and taking his place in the rattan chair as if the twenty ringgit and the baby gave him that right. He liked to tell us that now that my father was dead and we had no one else to depend on, we should think of him as an uncle. Behind his back, my grandmother snorted and said that we had her, and even if she was an old woman, she was better than a man who was only clever at chasing other people's wives. In Pak Abas's hearing she was much more complimentary because he had a van, a television, and contacts in the government and he gave us twenty ringgit a month. Every day he would ask to see my mother, and every day my grandmother would put excuses in his way: she is praying, ill, in confinement. He never pressed the matter, asking once and then leaning back in his chair with a contented sigh, as if an obligation had been lifted off his back.

But now his face bore the shocked expression of one who has, having gone down to the river a thousand times to bathe, on the thousand-and-first time been knifed in the back.

"You want to give the child away just like that?!" he roared, oblivious to my brothers and me coming up the stairs.

My grandmother sighed the way she did when speaking to the man who came to collect the installments for the sewing machine. Usually he'd relent and tell us to be sure to have the money by the following week. "What can we do?" she said to Pak Abas. "We are poor people. God gives and God takes away."

"But don't you know that Allah will provide? There's no need to throw away the child!"

"This is Allah's providence, isn't it? The woman has no child of her own, and we have no money to look after it. We can barely put rice in our stomachs as it is. You know that."

"I forbid it!"

My grandmother gazed at him calmly. "Who are you to forbid anything? Only the father has that right. If you were the father, we would of course follow your wishes. And if you were the father, you would support the child, and us too."

"I say I won't allow it! I'll tell the people in the religious department, and they will stop it. I hear the man is a heathen, the child will not be Muslim—I'll see to it that you are punished!"

"And I'll see to it that your friends the officials get the full story. Anyone in this *kampung* will be happy to tell them. And they will see to it that you are punished—with a crazy wife and seven more mouths to feed."

Pak Abas shut *his* mouth, thundered down the stairs, rushing past my brothers and me, got on his bicycle, and set off down the road so fast that he went straight through a pothole and almost met with an accident.

My grandmother stood up and retied her *sarung*. "Some people," she said, "born to make trouble."

After that, there were no more visits from Pak Abas, and certainly none from the religious department. A week later, the couple came again, in a different car, also big and shiny, and the woman wore a different *baju*, of green and yellow floral batik. They wanted to take my mother to the doctor. By this time all my brothers and sisters knew what was happening, and all were in a fever to see the rich woman from Kuala Lumpur and her white husband. My grandmother made them bathe and put on their nice clothes so that the couple could see what a handsome family we were. My little sister Wati and I washed and dressed my mother, and as usual she did not make a sound, even when we sluiced the cold well water over her head. I soaped her balloon-tight belly and felt the child kick. Wati talked to her the whole time: "Mak, today, you know, there are visitors, come to see us all the way from Kuala Lumpur, come to see you because they have heard how pretty you are . . ." She was still pretty: smooth skin and straight, thick hair. The nights she spent screaming and throwing herself against the locked door of her room, while I sat in the dark in the other room trying to stop the children's crying, did not show on her face. The little ones were afraid of her now, but that didn't matter because she didn't notice. "And then they will take the baby away to the big house where they have air-con and TV and *nasi lemak* for breakfast every day . . ." Wati prattled on. "And on Hari Raya we will visit them, *salam-salam*, and they'll give us Raya money and we'll eat lots of cakes and *satay* . . ." After a while I told her to be quiet.

My mother also did not make a sound while I dragged the comb through her hair and then twisted it into a bun. When she was ready, I gripped her by the arm and guided her toward the car, which squatted, huge and menacing like a beached shark, in front of our house. My mother could walk perfectly well, but she stumbled now and then, as if she couldn't see the unevenness of the ground. The man and the woman stood by, watching our progress out of the house. I didn't know how to open the car door at first, and the man lunged forward and opened it for me. Wati giggled at that, but when my grandmother told her that she had to stay home and look after the others, she began to sulk instead. As the car pulled onto the road, I looked back and saw Wati still standing there, staring after us.

My mother sat in the back between my grandmother and me. The woman kept eyeing us in the rear-vision mirror. I watched the houses rushing by and hoped that people would not come over to our house to interrogate Wati about the big car, the couple from Kuala Lumpur, and the baby, but I knew they would. Driving down the highway, I felt we were going too fast, too fast, and I had to grip the seat to stop from crying out. My grandmother was perfectly calm, answering the woman's questions about my parents and our family and concocting the story we would tell the doctors at the hospital. My mother would be the woman's cousin and we poor relatives being helped by our kind, rich relative. I didn't think anyone would believe this, but I supposed the doctors didn't need to believe.

In the hospital, my grandmother and the woman went in to see the doctor with my mother, but I had to wait outside with the man. We sat on plastic chairs in the hall, and the nurses strode past us, pushing trolleys or carrying folders, their shoes clicking across the tiles. I asked the man if he spoke Malay. "A little only," he said, and I had to bite my cheeks to stop from laughing at his accent. So the child would grow up speaking English, and if it was ever to meet Wati, Eton, Melor, Husin, Amin, and me, all we would be able to say to each other would be *hello, good morning, good afternoon, good evening, my name is, what's your name, where are you going*. It was a good thing that we would never meet.

They were taking a long time in the doctor's office. The man went away and came back with a Coca-Cola and a rose syrup. I took the Coca-Cola, so I could watch him drink the sweet pink stuff.

"Nice!" he said, and I almost choked on my drink. "New Zealand," he said, "me."

"Kampung Air Keruh," I said, "me."

"Pretty. Nice. I like." And I couldn't tell if he was talking about our *kampung*, my mother, me, or the rose syrup, and I burst out laughing. He laughed too, but I don't think it was about the same thing.

When we reached home, it was dark. The road to our house seemed more pitted and uneven, and the bushes by the side of the road dragged against the car. My grandmother, my mother, and I got out and the car drove away again, leaving us with only the light of the paraffin lamp that Wati brought out to us. That night my mother had a bad spell. My grandmother sat outside her door reading the Quran aloud, on and on, her voice a steady drone, and my mother screamed, on and on.

The couple came every week. We only ever saw two cars, but the woman had so many dresses that she never wore the same one twice. My grandmother allowed Wati to go with them when they took my mother to the hospital because I didn't want to, and she came back with long stories about the man buying her snacks and cakes, and all the nurses flirting with him. The visits to the doctor always made my grandmother nervous. "The doctor, he asked a lot of questions, Ria, about why she was not talking, and all I could say is that it is her fate, how do I know why? And I said, But isn't it true that her body is healthy, the baby will be healthy, and he had to admit yes, but he kept asking so many questions. And he spoke to Puan Aishah in English a long time." We all knew that the woman and her husband had tried at first to follow the rules and adopt from the government agencies, but a woman with a white husband would never be given a Malay child. We all knew that she needed us. But my grandmother was afraid that they might think again of the bad luck that was bred into the blood and bones of my mother's child and change their minds. We could not afford that.

When my mother's labor pains began, I ran over to Mak Teh's and telephoned the number in Kuala Lumpur. The man answered, and I told him that it was time and they should come now. Only after I had hung up did it occur to me that perhaps he hadn't understood. But they were there in half an hour, with the two cars, the woman wearing a Western suit. We got my mother into a car; I was afraid that she was going to start screaming, but she only whimpered a little. She looked at me once, and I thought she saw me and was about to speak, but then her gaze slid past me. Wati didn't want to go with us; she stood at the top of the stairs leading up to the house, holding Amin in one hand and Melor in the other, just watching us leave. Melor waved her little flapping wave, and then we were gone.

It was an easy birth. My grandmother was right: my mother was strong and the baby was healthy. My grandmother walked out of the delivery room holding the baby in her arms to show her to me: another girl, her head as bald and smooth as an egg, face crumpled in a howl, and tiny fists clenched in anger at being so rudely dropped into the world. My grandmother was crying—out of happiness from holding five thousand ringgit in her arms or out of sorrow, I don't know. She wanted me to hold the baby, but I dug my fingernails into my palms and did not move. My grandmother turned instead to the woman, who took the baby awkwardly, as if she had never held one before. The baby scrabbled at her, eyes shut but mouth agape, and I wondered where they would get milk from. They would have to hire a wet nurse. My mother was exhausted or sedated in the delivery room, her breasts useless. We were all—the man, the woman, my grandmother, and I—staring at the baby, looking at her as if she were the only baby in the world. I thought then that we could have got more than five thousand ringgit for her. I thought then how the child would never have too little food to quiet her stomach, would never be laughed at in school for being stupid, would never stand knee deep in the mud, would never look down into a well and see her face floating on the water, would never have a mother like mine, and I wished she had never been born.

Putu Oka Sukanta ✹ *Indonesia*

Putu Oka Sukanta was born in Singaraja, northern Bali, in 1939, and he has been active as a writer since he was 16. From 1966 until 1976, he was a political prisoner following the military coup d'état that brought General Suharto to power. He has since been invited overseas for theater performances, poetry readings, and literary conferences in Sri Lanka, Bangladesh, Australia, Malaysia, Germany, and France. His works include children's books, three collections of poetry, and two volumes of short stories. He works as an acupuncturist and has also written on alternative medicine. His story reflects the depth of animist and Hindu traditions in Balinese culture, which continue to thrive alongside this fabled island's increasing modernity.

Storm Clouds over the Island of Paradise

Translated by Vern Cork

WAITING ON THE SHORE AT THE PORT OF KETAPANG, TINI GAZED far into the distance, trying to penetrate the black curtain of night obscuring her view. The shimmering of the lights on the opposite shore indicated that life was going on over there, but she wasn't sure exactly where the ship was going to take her. The lamps to her left twinkled like a group of fireflies against the dark of the earth. So too did the lamps on her right, reaching into the distance in silence. Which side were the beaches of Bali on now, she wondered.

Even if the deep blue sky had been clear and filled with stars, she wouldn't have known which end Gilimanuk was. There was nothing visible to her except the vague outline of a row of hills resembling a fort restricting her view. And there at the foot of these hills the lights twinkled. Whether they were the lamps of fishing boats or of houses near the beach, she didn't know. The opaque blue sea lay spread out like a carpet.

Reluctant to leave the shores of Java, she hesitated before heading for the ship ready waiting to take her across the straits. The bus that had brought her from Jakarta was queued up with others to go on board the ferry. And on the bus was her mother.

She felt very isolated amongst the crowds of passengers as her feet took her unwillingly but inevitably to the upper deck of the ship. Most of the other passengers, too drowsy to stir, had remained in the buses, but there were still quite a few who climbed up to the waiting lounge on the upper deck, many of them eager to enjoy the sea breeze.

Tini felt so alone. Alone in her loneliness. Estranged. She found a seat at the end of an empty bench and sank into the quietness of the night with the shadows of the calm and peaceful hills.

When at last the ship moved off, she watched as the beach of Ketapang drew further and further away. She wrapped her arms around herself, feeling her hair tousled by the wind, her eyes misting over and filling with tears. She tried hard to contain her emotions, but her heart whispered brokenly: "Farewell freedom!" She glanced at her watch. It was five minutes past midnight ...

When she looked at the time again, it was twelve thirty. The ship had berthed at the port of Gilimanuk, and the passengers stared out at a Balinese split gate.

"Are these the gates to a Temple of the Dead?" Tini asked herself. For a *Pura Dalem* temple was the last resting place for the bodies of those whom God had called home.

"No, it can't be so," she thought. "Though I'm lying here with no strength on this earth, yet fresh blood pulses through my veins. I'm a living corpse. My spirit is being murdered. Oh my heart!" And at the moment when her feet touched the ground of the Island of Paradise, her heart screamed out in rebellion: "Why did I have to be born as the high caste Brahmana Ida Ayu Ketut Sumartini? Why not just plain ordinary Ketut Sumartini? Why must I bear the noble title Ida Ayu? Why?"

She stepped up into her bus as it slowed down, and sat next to her mother, sinking back in the seat. She closed her eyes, but found it impossible to sleep. Warm tears seeped from beneath her lids, and with her eyes tightly shut, she felt as if there was a firm arm around her shoulders. She heard a voice filled with love whispering to her.

"Whatever your mother does to us is an obstacle we must overcome. It all depends on the two of us. What power on earth can separate two hearts joined as one?"

Tini swallowed her tears. Loving fingers brushed her cheeks, her hand was held in the warmth of his. She rested her head on his shoulder. Feelings of anger and love rose in her heart. She felt the intimacy of gentle kisses on the crown of her head.

"Until now we've been winning this struggle. The *dukun* they consulted hasn't succeeded in separating us. They'll never succeed as long as we remain firmly united. And we've overcome the last magic token. No tricks of evil black magic will ever defeat the purity of our feelings."

The voice, full of confidence, echoed in her ears. She opened her eyes, wishing to see the man she loved, but he wasn't there. All that remained was a beautiful memory giving her the strength to continue to love.

She smiled a little, remembering the experiences she'd had. Ever since her family had learned that she was in a relationship with a man of a lower caste, almost all her relatives had shown hostility toward her; particularly her mother, and the aunt in whose house she was living. She received letter after letter from Bali, all of them filled with the same advice: Don't do what you know is wrong. In other words, have nothing more to do with that low-caste man: Find someone else of your own caste. Then when she had shown no signs she was going to change, strange things began to happen.

On returning home from university, she often found little offerings under her bed. At other times, she noticed her pillow had a strange smell, and on investigating she found something scented under her mattress. She knew what was happening. They had asked a *dukun*—a medicine man—to try to influence her feelings.

All these incidents she recounted to Nyoman Astawa, her boyfriend.

"If we believe, it can affect us," Nyoman said. "But if we pay no attention, and if our hearts don't waver when we find these things, then they can do us no harm."

"But I'm frightened, darling. Even though we don't believe in all this, we're still Balinese."

"True, Tini, we're Balinese. But you must realize that the Godhead, Ida Sang Hyang Widi Wasa, is higher and more powerful than any black magic. We must pray to strengthen our beliefs. There's no other way. We can oppose evil in our own hearts. And our heart's strength will come as a blessing from God. Ida Sang Hyang Widi Wasa will help us."

As the days went by Tini was more and more aware that all her relatives had turned against her. She was all on her own except for Nyoman Astawa, and he came less frequently to her house once her aunt had warned him directly not to pester Ida Ayu Ketut Sumartini. Since then they'd had to meet elsewhere.

The house where she boarded now turned into a kind of frightening cage, where she always felt anxious and suspicious. She never felt at peace there. Sometimes she was afraid even to go into her own room. It seemed as if evil spirits lay in wait for her there. Once that sort of feeling took hold of her, the hairs on the back of her neck would stand on end, and she'd finish by not going inside even though she'd been standing in the doorway. She would quickly back away, then go to the kitchen and drink a glass of sugar water, as Nyoman had told her to do. Then she'd spend a few minutes calming herself by reading in the lounge room. Or she'd keep busy playing cassettes. Only when she'd calmed down would she go to her room. Once, she'd lifted up her mattress, and found nothing. She'd checked underneath it, and opened the cupboard. There was nothing out of the ordinary. Then as her eyes scoured the room, she'd seen a small wrapped object hanging by the door-frame. Her heart beat fast, she broke into a sweat. She could see that the package was made of plain cloth, and as she gazed at it, her aunt had suddenly appeared.

"That just came from Bali. Don't touch it. For safety's sake," her aunt warned her, immediately on the defensive.

"And look," she went on, "They've sent these two silver bracelets. They're pretty, aren't they? Just right for your wrist. One's for you and the other's for me. Such lovely gifts are meant to be worn."

Pretending to do it lovingly, her aunt fastened the bracelet on her right wrist, and wore the other one herself. She noticed her aunt's lips murmuring a prayer.

"I don't like wearing bracelets," Tini muttered.

"Oh, but you must. See how pretty it makes your hand look. You really should wear it. All the family wish for your well-being."

Tini hated it. Somehow she controlled the anger which welled up and was consuming her heart. But she couldn't hold back her tears. She broke down sobbing. Her breath came in gasps, her hands trembled.

"I feel so weak." She moved and lay down, her mind full of confusion.

"Ah, that's a sign that you've been put under a spell. That fellow has had magic worked on you," her aunt said and went away in disgust, leaving her alone in her room. Tini broke into tears. She covered her mouth and put her pillow over her head. She felt full of bitterness. As though her wounds had been splashed with vinegar.

News of what had happened that day soon reached Bali. And from Bali another package was sent a few days later.

"You must keep this in your bra. Have it with you all the time," her aunt said. Tini took the white package and held it close to her breast. Then she left the house to go to the University. Her thoughts had been troubled since the night before, when she'd been aware that her aunt had cautiously entered her room and fanned a cloth, as though she were getting rid of mosquitoes. A few drops of water had fallen on Tini's face, but she kept her eyes closed as though she were asleep. After that, she lay awake the whole night long. Feelings of fear, irritation, insult, a desire to rebel, and all sorts of other emotions were mixed together so that her mind was unable to rest.

That day, she didn't attend lectures. From a public telephone booth she arranged a meeting with her boyfriend, and at two o'clock she went to his house. There they agreed to open the packet that had just arrived. Stitch by stitch they undid it, and found it contained several needles, five grains of rice, herbs, thread, cotton and some other objects with something scribbled on them.

"So this stuff is what you're so afraid of, Tini," Nyoman Astawa said. "In the olden days of Majapahit or Jayaprana it would have been natural for us to be frightened. But not now. Why should we be afraid? Objects like these have no power or meaning so long as we don't give them any. This is just trash. Don't you think we should just burn it?" Nyoman Astawa made an effort to restrain his anger, but he couldn't succeed in disguising it. His eyes grew bigger, and the tiny red veins in his eyeballs inflamed as he held his breath. Tini was acutely conscious of all this.

"What do you think, Nyoman?"

"Let's burn it."

"But I'm still afraid," Tini said. She held onto Nyoman's hand as he went to light a match.

"Why?" The glint in his eyes shone into Tini's eyes and she felt his courage ignite her own.

"The *dukun* will find out."

"How could he? He's far away in Bali. Only God will know." He struck the match and this time Tini's hand didn't restrain him. The contents of the package in the ashtray were soon consumed by flames. Nyoman Astawa watched them burning and glanced occasionally at his girlfriend's face. In her eyes he could see a shadow of fear and tension reflected.

"Look, Tini—it's all turned to ashes now. Except for the needles." They held hands tightly, then hugged each other lovingly. Presently they refilled the pouch with cotton from a drawer.

But in spite of all this, the couple were finally forced to split up. The whole of Tini's extended family agreed that she must be moved to Bali. This was the only way they could hope to save the family's reputation. And with no chance of negotiating, Tini was forced to go with her mother, who had come to fetch her.

Before they were separated, the two lovers were able to go to the temple to pray together and make vows to each other before the gods. They took a bundle of flowers and incense and prayed to Ida Sang Hyang Widi Wasa that a way might be opened to them to express their love for one another.

"God is far more powerful than the *dukun*, Tini," Nyoman said. "A pure heart can never be overcome by evil. Make your heart strong until our time comes..."

Now all that was behind her, and in the bus, Tini finally fell asleep. And in the half light of dawn, her mother woke and looked long at the face of her daughter.

At five o'clock, just as the eastern sky was turning a glorious red, the bus arrived at their house. The mother woke her daughter; they got down and found several people waiting for them. But Tini was shocked when she was forbidden to enter the house compound because the person preparing the offerings for their arrival wasn't quite ready. She couldn't get over this. She had never imagined that such a disaster could befall her. She was overcome with feelings of hatred, and wept bitter tears.

"Be patient, Dayu Tut. We are all praying for your safety." Tini didn't know whose voice had spoken from among the crowd. She could only weep, as she covered her face with her hands. In the meantime, the offerings had been finalized, and she followed the instructions of her grandmother, who was the person in charge of the proceedings.

What her family was doing she could never forgive. She felt deeply humiliated. Her boyfriend had been equated with a danger to overcome. The ceremony greeting her was one used specially for someone who had just escaped from some danger, such as recovering after a period in hospital, or having been involved in a near-fatal accident. A ceremony, in fact, for people saved from the jaws of death.

Her heart screamed out a protest, but she could do nothing to oppose all this. Nothing but weep. And at the height of her grief, she hadn't any idea what was happening. She collapsed, overwhelmed, and lost consciousness.

Her relatives were making more and more commotion. The *dukun* was called, and Tini regained consciousness to hear him muttering at her side. She swore and she cursed, yet not a word escaped her lips.

During those first days in Bali, she argued incessantly with her mother, Dayu Biang. It didn't make sense to her that her older brother had been able to marry a girl of lower caste, while she, as a woman of high Brahmana caste, found her desire to marry a man of lower caste constantly thwarted. And for what reason? Especially in these more progressive times.

"A man can raise the status of his wife if she's from a lower caste," her mother said. "The woman becomes our caste. But with you, it would be the opposite. You'd lose your status with a low-caste man! You'd be dragged down. Down! Wouldn't you feel ashamed? We would."

"But that isn't fair," Tini protested. "God created us equal at birth."

"Remember you're a Balinese. Not a Muslim or Christian."

"Oh, it's all so old-fashioned!" She tried to walk away. But her mother was persistent.

"What?"

"These traditional fashions passed down by my caste. They're too restrictive for me now I've grown up. If they're forced on me they'll tear apart and my naked self will be revealed."

"So this is the result of you doing your schooling far away from home?" her mother said angrily.

Wounds to the heart never heal. After spending several months with her family, Tini still didn't feel at peace. She'd had no chance of writing to Nyoman Astawa yet, but she constantly kept in her mind the promises they'd made at the temple in Jakarta. Although she was far from content, she tried to hide this by taking part in all the family's activities. And so her family came to believe, as the *dukun* said, that Tini had broken up with Nyoman Astawa. She was never prevented from going to the movies or other shows. In fact, all her wishes were fulfilled by her family, and finally, she came to be well liked by all her relatives.

Then one day at the hairdresser's, by chance, she ran into an old friend from her school days in Bali. Mery took her home to her house near the market. And afterwards Tini often visited her, and thanks to Mery's protections she began communicating with Nyoman Astawa again.

The festival of Galungan kept all Balinese Hindus busy, and Ida Ayu Ketut Sumartini was no exception. She was occupied just like any other Balinese woman. In the early morning she was ready to go to the temple, carrying offerings on her head. She prayed in all truth and sincerity. The family watched her happily, although they couldn't be certain exactly what she was murmuring. They didn't realize that she was making use of this opportunity to pray not only for the protection of the gods and her ancestors, but also to say a silent farewell and to ask for forgiveness. Feelings of sadness made her blood run hot for a moment as she realized that she was leaving behind what she'd loved since she was a little girl. She looked around her at the building in the family temple, the environment in which she had been born and raised, and which she must now leave behind her. Happy memories haunted her mind, the crowds in the temple at her tooth filing ceremony, the day when her father had died and his cremation.

"Oh my gods and ancestors, forgive your servant," she prayed. "I will continue to worship you from afar. I am leaving soon, and will be despised if I come back here to worship you. Oh gods and ancestors, I know you will hear when I call you no matter where I am ..."

In the evening there was an *arja* drama performance in the community hall. She only watched for a short time, and then went back to her bedroom. She began to feel uncertain.

"Am I strong enough to leave this house behind? Do I have the strength to drag myself even further away from the love of my family? Is it true that happiness awaits me when I arrive there?" She tossed and turned, unable to sleep, listening to the vague sounds of the gamelan and the laughter of the audience. Toward morning she drifted into a brief uneasy sleep.

She told her mother merely that she was off to Mery's. And so she left.

But when her mother heard a visitor calling from the doorway after sunset, Ida Ayu Ketut Sumartini still had not returned home. Her mother had begun to inquire about her daughter from the neighbors during the afternoon. But it never passed through her mind that that evening, the day after Galungan, she would receive visitors like this.

"Is anyone at home?" the visitors called again, and she hurried to open the door. Three men dressed in traditional costume were waiting there and Dayu Biang's heart almost burst at the sight of these unexpected guests. It took all her determination to face them, but once their purpose was made clear to her, she fainted away. The men had been sent by Nyoman Astawa's family to inform her that Ida Ayu Ketut Sumartini had run off with her boyfriend and they were going to get married. The family were thrown into a state of shock. One member went off to find the *dukun* who had been involved. However, unfortunately, he had not returned home since Galungan, and was still at a gambling place.

At the moment when the great orb of the sun slipped down to the foot of the mountains, a plane was taking off at Ngurah Rai airport. The red rays were becoming fainter, leaving remnants of gold at the edges of the black clouds hanging over the island of Bali.

"Look, Tini, we are going straight through those black rain clouds in this plane. Look down there at paradise laid out in all its beauty." The two of them contemplated the view from the plane's window.

The Garuda Airlines plane soared up into the sky, passing through the banks of black clouds that sullied the Balinese sky, and the clouds parted like a black cloth split by some sharp, foreign object.

Once the plane was above them, the clouds, like cotton wool, closed over again and prevented the couple looking down from seeing, below them, the island known as paradise.

Ketut Sumartini whispered in her heart, "I will love you from afar."

She nestled her head on her boyfriend's shoulder.

Martin Aleida ✻ *Indonesia*

Martin Aleida was born in Tanjung Balai, North Sumatra, in 1943. He studied at the Literary Academy "Multatuli" Jakarta in the early 1960s, and later in the Language and Linguistics program at Georgetown University in Washington, DC. He has had a distinguished career as a journalist and editor, including working for the cultural magazine *Zaman Baru*, the newspaper *Harian Rakyat*, the well-known journal *Tempo*, and Nippon Hoso Kyokai, Jakarta. From 1986–2001, he worked as an Information Officer for the United Nations Information Center in Jakarta. A full-time freelance writer, he has published the novel *Jamangilak Tak Pernah Menangis*, as well as the story collections *Malam Kelabu, Ilyana dan Aku*, and *Leontin Dewangga*.

Dewangga's Pendant

FIGHTING AGAINST THE STABBING PAIN, THE WOMAN IN THE BED furrowed her brow. Her eyebrows were sparse, gnawed by chemotherapy. Twisting her face into a grimace, withstanding the pain, her nose looked sharper. Then she closed her eyes behind drooping eyelids. No traces were left to show that once curling eyelashes had grown there. These eyelashes had been the subject of never-ending praise from her husband, Abdullah Peureulak, who now sat speechless at the side of the bed.

Wanting to share her pain, Abdullah gently placed his hand under his wife's, taking up her fingers and threading them between his. In her husband's grip, the woman's fingers became warm. It was only the warmth brought by her husband's blood that flowed through her fingers. Abdullah knew that his grip was nothing more than an expression of sympathy. How painful the disease was, only his wife knew. At the edge of the bed Abdullah was no more than a husband slowly losing his mind. He didn't know how to share this pain with his wife.

The smell of chloroform and the glare of the sun caught in the opaque windowpane surrounded Abdullah, who leaned forward and kissed his wife's cheeks and lips for the hundredth time.

Those eyes. His wife's eyes . . . ah, he still remembered the first time he embraced his wife and beheld her eyes, closed, hiding her bright round irises, thirty years ago. Those eyes had their own contribution to their life together. Those eyes had never ceased to be a source of amazement, to the point that Dewangga Suiciate, the woman who became his wife, became awkward before her husband, not knowing how to respond to the shackles of praise and flattery that, whispered, fell in a torrent from her husband's lips, even later, when both their children had grown to adulthood. But now her eyelids, her eyebrows, the round irises that stirred his soul were the only remainder of her struggle against the disease that had tortured her for the past two years.

Suddenly the woman lying flat on the bed stirred. She glanced to the side as if to assure herself that her husband was still waiting at her bedside. That glance made Abdullah strengthen his grip, warming her hand in his. With a quavering, weak voice that could still persuade with its tone, the woman spoke: "I am still strong enough to listen. I will never regret. Tell me, darling. Now would be better."

The request made her husband's neck droop. For two weeks Dewangga, lying in bed and deathly pale, had waited for her husband's throat to unclamp, to stop hesitating, to say what he needed to say. In Abdullah's heart there was a wish to regret those words that had irrevocably jumped from his mouth two weeks before: that he, with his wife's permission, wanted to say something that throughout their marriage he had kept hidden. Two weeks ago Abdullah had made the promise at the side of her bed, when his wife was at the peak of her resistance against the cutting blade of her disease. But the words remained stuck in Abdullah's throat. His desire had not been achieved. The words were frozen on his tongue. Abdullah felt like he was sinning to say what was in his heart, because he knew the buried words, if uncovered, would worsen his wife's suffering as she lay stretched out and fading before him.

But seeing how hard his wife was struggling against the disease, and how narrow her hopes of survival were, as the cancer brought her closer to death, Abdullah made the decision to swallow his doubts, and be honest with his wife, who had been his companion for the past thirty years. "Now! I must say it now!" his heart screamed out. Whatever would happen, Dewangga, his beloved wife, could not die carrying a betrayed promise. If she had to go, it would be with a clear blue sky trailed by wisps of clouds as white as cotton.

So Abdullah slid his chair closer, bringing his lips to his wife's ear. He spoke in a slow voice, like one who was unpacking an old secret, swearing a new confession that even the walls of the hospital, white and damp, were not allowed to hear. Because of his gentleness, from the ceiling it seemed as if Abdullah were offering praise, spilling out all of his longing for a lover he had not met for years, whom, upon meeting, he finds stretched out and alone, fighting against a disease in a hospital bed. The tremble in Abdullah's voice could be heard as he whispered, linking word with word to tell his story . . .

1965–1966

The political enmity between the army and the Left resolved itself after a group of soldiers captured and killed several generals who were accused of treason and harassing women. But, for reasons unknown, the leader of the kidnapping lost his decisiveness and did not know what to do after the battle had started. This hesitancy that he could not shake opened an opportunity for the allies of the generals to hit back, which they did bloodily. They extinguished their enemies, and communists and leftists were accused of being behind the attempted coup d'état. What followed was a battle against thousands of citizens, including children and nursing mothers, mostly in villages and small cities. If saved from death, they were forced into concentration camps or jails, or exiled to small wasteland islands for crimes that required no evidence. This is the abuse of humanity in this country that will never be forgotten, with random victims and indiscriminate cruelty of incomparable baseness in the history of this people.

Abdullah, who was born and raised in Peureulak, had good fortune. He was only held for a year at an army base in Jakarta. When he was captured, there were no signs that he was still in touch with friends who were deemed to be involved in "the red's efforts to regain their strength and rise again." Two sheets of paper ripped from a schoolboy's notebook were saved in his wallet. His father had written in his unique scrawl, learned as a schoolboy under the Dutch. The flow of his letters indicated simplicity but tenacity. The pull of the lines didn't change from the first letter to the closing salutation.

The letter explained that his father, along with his mother, was going on pilgrimage to Mecca by boat, and that it would take the same amount of time as it would for three full moons to rise from behind the coconut fronds. As all pilgrims had done before them, they were going on this trip fully prepared for death. Holy death. They might be buried at sea, sunk with a heavy stone, or buried in the barren Arab land with no grave-stone, no name. The letter also explained how their possessions were to be divided among Abdullah and his siblings.

The divine intention of his parents was already in action before the ink on their last will and testament was dry. By the time the two pilgrims set out, ready for death on God's road upon leaving Uleleu harbor, the letter had already become a lifesaver for their son, Abdullah Peureulak, roving far away on the island of Java.

Abdullah was confused. He couldn't understand the relationship between the political beliefs that had had him thrown into military prison and religion. Though the long debate with his parents still rang in his ears, he had been determined to establish an organization of film workers. On this path, he had been sure that he would easily be able to enter the world of the silver screen. His parents had given in, accepting his will, with only one message that to his ears sounded like an order: "All right, but don't forget to pray."

The interrogators took his father's last will and testament as proof of their assessment: This was a young man of average height, wavy hair, eyes that protruded a bit from his skull with a sharp gaze, thin lips, and slightly pointed nose, who made no attempt to hide that he had been a part of a film organization under the influence of Communists. There was no need to keep him in prison. He would just be a waste of sandy rice, the daily provision of nutrition to maintain prisoners so they could still suffer torture as punishment for the "political evil" that they had committed.

"Dul . . . you can go. We don't want to know where you go. Go home to Aceh, to your mother's lap, or to the house where we first caught you. We don't care. Just remember, you have to report to us once a week. You don't need to ask until when. We're the army, and this is the decision. Don't try anything again. Shiftless bastard. You're lucky we're letting you go. Got it?!" With that, he was led out of the camp.

The decision was so unexpected that his heart leapt and pounded upon hearing it. He had been nervous facing the unsuspected decision. Of course he could not refuse it. Would he rather be accused as an enemy and be tortured?! His heart was torn. He would have to leave his friends who were facing the same political misfortune. The decision of the military authorities was part of their tactic to crush his spirit. He was deliberately separated from his friends. He had to go out into the open world, with no friends and no possessions. Everyone he knew had been taken into camps or prisons, and if they weren't dead he had no idea where they were. His heart ached to think of his friends still cooped up in prison, while he was released, sauntering about free. Many among those he left faced torture and disease. Two days earlier he had heard that at least ten prisoners had died of cholera in Tangerang prison, and the epidemic was still raging. The guards didn't care. He heard also that they weren't given medicine. The prison families had to take care of their own, trapped within those walls, husbands, wives, children or close friends, smuggling in medicine for each other.

A hundred steps after leaving the camp, Abdullah Peureulak wanted to turn, to look back. But no. Now he had to struggle to find an answer to the one question that dogged the new life in the free world that had just been handed to him: Where should he go? Like a newly released bird flapping its wings, where should he perch after being let out of the oppressive concentration camp? Going to the house where he was originally arrested was not possible. Because it was the organization's office, all of his possessions would certainly have been taken by the military. The same would be true for the other possessions of the organization; they would have been stolen by those who considered themselves the winners of the crisis that enveloped this country. His relatives were all too far away, across the sea. All his friends were hanging in suspense, waiting in jail with no end to the darkness in sight. Where will you go, unlucky man?

Finally he summoned up his courage and dragged his anxious steps toward the house where he had once rented a room, called Cikini. There he found that the only one left in the large house was the landlady. According to her story, one night all the residents were picked up by a few thugs and a fully armed military team. They were taken in a military truck to who knows where. Then, falling as if to kiss Abdullah's knees, his former landlady begged him never to come back. Don't tempt the military to return, to confiscate this house. For the safety of the owner, for the safety of the neighbors, for everyone, don't come back again.

Abdullah was silent for a moment. He no longer felt like a young man in his prime, carrying a bundle of two sets of clothes, his only possessions in the world. He felt like an old depraved leper who must be kept out of sight. With a shriveled heart, he left the landlady.

He started this unimaginable adventure when he resolved to leave Peureulak to try his luck in Jakarta, to be a film actor. If he couldn't be as good as Orson Welles from Hollywood, he could at least be like Zainal Abidin in *Si'Anak Mdan*. But the life that he found was not full of parties. He spent his nights in broken-down freight cars left unrepaired in Manggarai, Jatinegara, or Beos, or next to the shacks rented to hookers in Galur, Planet Senen, or Kota Paris. For months he lived by a canal near the National Monument. A few times he was arrested in police operations against vagrants and prostitutes, only to be dumped out again at Serpong. Abdullah and twenty or thirty other humans were treated like ten-cent coins, left to crawl back and trace the edges of asphalt or graveled roads, giving themselves back up to the streets of the capital city, where else? This was their only choice.

His brain was not yet petrified; he was still looking for a way out so that he would not die of starvation. Applying to a film company was impossible. He could be reported as a PKI infiltrator, an accusation that would get him tossed back into jail or get his throat cut. He had already decided to say that by the age of twenty-five, he had acted in only one film, and that one just a black-and-white. The door was closed tightly on those dreams. The talent that was given to him, in the form of a handsome face with clear eyes and a captivating stare, and enough intelligence for an actor, would have to give in to the situation handed him by the march of time.

Daydreaming, watching the commotion of people entering and exiting Senen Market, he offered to carry bags for overloaded shoppers. Scared, hesitant, his heart raced the first time he offered help to a middle-aged woman carrying two bags full of vegetables. Maybe because his eyes were honest, the woman received him with a friendly smile and allowed him to carry her shopping bags. He followed behind the woman's steps. Crossing the railroad tracks, turning in and out of small alleys, they reached the neighborhood of Bungur. The woman lived in a small house located on a busy street. She supported herself with a small café in the front of her house. There were only two people living there, the woman and her daughter.

The good fortune of that one shopping trip was incalculable for the unlucky actor washed up in the corner of the market. The woman from Bungur was not like most. Besides giving him some money for his services, she also served Abdullah a plate of food. Not ten times had he helped the woman carry her shopping bags from the market, and his heart was already tethered to that small café. Quietly, he stole glances at the mirror to enjoy the reflected image of her daughter's eyes as she offered him a plate of rice and a glass of hot sweet tea. There were no flies buzzing, no grit on the tabletop. One morning, the girl's bright eyes shone at him from the mirror with a calm, piercing look. She looked as if she were offering more than rice. Glancing sideways, persuasively, she whispered, "What you feel I also feel. If you wish, take me wherever you are going . . ."

Holding those eyes with his own, the saliva dried up in the young actor-turned-vagrant's mouth. As if to hold back his shame, he dropped his gaze to the floor. He didn't believe life was as easy as the girl in the mirror said. Love always offered a forked road, faithfulness or betrayal. Which one would triumph in the end? His heart fell in confusion. But don't misunderstand. This did not mean he would refuse her. The eyes of the serving girl were too good to neglect, her gaze too charming not to return, impossible to ignore. He had beheld thousands of eyes when he was still in school and while shooting films. But those eyes, connected to the arms, covered in soft delicate hair, that offered him breakfast, were round and challenging, bright and perfect, like a fragment of divine inspiration reflected in the mirror.

His eyes were still nailed to the floor. His heart beat. He was made so awkward by the look in those eyes that he left suddenly, without a thank-you, without a goodbye. He must now start the second part of his struggle after being let out of jail. Would he answer those awe-inspiring eyes, or forget them? Or give in to being a coolie, every day carrying packages for the woman from Bungur? For a sailor who for months had been bobbing up and down with no hope, there was nothing more promising than a mirage of dry land, somewhere he could sink his anchor. So, on the forty-first day, the man from Peureulak was seen sitting together with the girl, the couple leaning against each other, when the last customers left the café.

On the sixtieth day the couple, drunk with love and romance, flew in a pedicab toward Situ Lembang Park. There the girl's eyes could not escape his gaze, his praise, his embrace, while their two pairs of feet splashed in a lake that whispered to the leaves of the bamboo stands, bent by the wind. Dewangga let herself be swept away in the current of his adoration. When she closed her eyes, as if to give herself up, the longing in the heart of that young man from Peureulak reverberated inside him even more. He wanted to fly her away, lift up that girl who was sprawled on his lap, take her anywhere . . . Love should be limited to this, gentlemen. But yet, the young couple was not able to resist. On the seventieth night, as her mother traveled home to Muncar, East Java, they were kept so far out in loving and answering each other's love that the boundaries collapsed. They let themselves burn with passion, while love was left behind. Afterwards, drops of bridal blood, that village myth, were nowhere to be found on the even blue sheet. But, Abdullah didn't think anything of it. Where, and who, had already thrust through that delicate membrane never fostered any suspicion in his mind. For Abdullah, that was Dewangga's personal right, his lover who had given her heart as his safe harbor. There was no authority anywhere that could claim that right from her. Abdullah instead gave her the warmest, longest kisses and whispered words of love as they lay exhausted, falling from the peak of pleasure. No woman will ever find this from a man who simply uses her for his own release.

When for two months Dewangga had no need for sanitary napkins to keep the dark red flow from staining her underwear, and early in the morning was taken ill and suddenly vomited, her mother was beyond happiness. She was so pleased she hugged Abdullah Peureulak long and hard. Abdullah interpreted this as a sign of welcome to this small family. He felt that embrace was not a demand that he be responsible for what had happened to Dewangga. He considered it a decree that must be followed and love that must be returned.

Dewangga's mother called a painter. The whole house was repainted, including the front café. A few members of her family came from Muncar. The café was closed for a whole day and used for the simple wedding ceremony between Abdullah, son of Peureulak, and Dewangga, daughter of Muncar. When his mother-in-law offered to buy him a coat for the ceremony, Abdullah gently refused. He wanted to wear a light blue long-sleeved shirt and black trousers, which he bought himself. By then, besides helping Dewangga's mother, he had also started selling used books and other goods on Kramat Raya Street, about two kilometers from Bungur.

The café, the mother, and Dewangga, her daughter, were a blessing for Abdullah. Hunger had become a thing of the past. The house that doubled as a café became his safe haven. His life was slowly crawling upward. It continued as such until the day when Abdullah ran into a film actor on the street who invited him back into the world of movies. After thinking long and hard about his safety, he accepted the invitation. In the beginning, he worked as a script boy. A few years later, he was trusted to write scenarios for movies or television shows. His confidence seemed slowly to restore itself, even though he still had to report to the military base once a month. This obligation he fulfilled without his wife's or his mother-in-law's knowledge. He was able to buy, on credit, a simple house in East Jakarta. Abdullah, his wife, their two daughters, and his mother-in-law, now old and frail, lived there together. The café had been rented out. Abdullah was able to take full responsibility for these four human lives.

The change in their standard of living blew in a fresh breeze that occasionally raised questions. Dewangga, his wife, often encountered things that raised her suspicion. After the collapse of the regime that had ruled for thirty-two years, Abdullah was frequently visited by guests, and from their conversations it seemed that they were old friends. Once he received a visit from a close friend by the name of Sibarani, a music conductor who had studied in a conservatory in Germany. Another day a man named Agam Wispi, a poet, came to call, a man who had been abroad during the political crisis of 1965, and had been forced to remain in the Netherlands. Once there was a telephone call from a man named Sobron Aidit. At least three people called to give news of the death of the actor Zainal Abidin. Many other visitors made Dewangga doubt who exactly her husband Abdullah Peureulak was, the young man adopted by her mother from Senen Market, the handsome tramp with a good heart. Not once but twice, when Dewangga was offering snacks and drinks to her husband's guests, she noticed Abdullah communicating something with his eyes to his guest, a request not to continue talk of certain politics, looking out of the corner of his eyes at Dewangga, an order not to let his wife hear that kind of talk. Because she was someone else, from a different group, he didn't know.

But Dewangga never aired her concerns to Abdullah. For her as a wife, there was nothing more that he needed to prove: Her husband provided for her and showed his love every day, even when their children were grown. Starting the first time their eyes met in the mirror in the café in Bungur thirty years ago, Abdullah was always honest and affectionate to Dewangga, with her eyes that never failed to enchant him.

The series of strange visitors reminded Dewangga of one episode in their life as a family. Once, because of a school assignment, one of their daughters asked to be taken to Lobang Buaya Museum. After walking through the exhibits, looking at the dioramas of the battle of the generals in 1965, their daughter concluded, "The PKI was so cruel!" Dewangga nodded her head calmly. Abdullah, however, seemed to answer in a cold, small voice, as if he wanted to correct his daughter. A stutter could be heard in his voice, "Yes, yes ... cr ... cruel."

It didn't occur to Dewangga to investigate what was in her husband's heart. She didn't want Abdullah's love and faithfulness to waver because of that kind of suspicion.

The dim neon bulb, the stark white walls, the opaque windowpane, and the smell of chloroform in the hospital room pressed down upon them. Coming to the end of his story, still at his wife's side, Abdullah Peureulak stroked Dewangga's hand and kissed her eyes, which had been closed the whole time he spoke.

"I've said what I wanted to say. Forgive me if I have deceived you. Forgive me if you feel tricked. I had just gotten out of prison for being part of the September 30th Movement when I met you, 'Ewa." Abdullah seemed to struggle to pull breath into his chest. For a few moments he was as still as stone, waiting for his wife's response, as she lay stretched out on the hospital bed.

Dewangga cocked her head a bit and raised her eyelids to look at Abdullah. There was no sadness in those eyes. She looked at him firmly, with resolve. With a smile, she said, "As long as I have known you, you have always been preoccupied with my eyes. Thank you." Weakly she removed her hand from Abdullah's grip, and slipped her fingers to her deflated, flat chest. "Take this pendant. I never showed you before, there is a clasp here. Open it and look," she said.

Abdullah was surprised. His hands shook as he held the ornament. When he opened the clasp, there appeared a kind of green crescent moon. But it looked as if there was a kind of handle at one end of it, the whole design nicely placed on a red metal face. That symbol seemed to have its own charm, forcing Abdullah to bow his head. He remembered that this was the symbol of a farmers' movement that was launched to demand basic agrarian rights, to limit landholdings to five hectares per person. Landholdings any larger than that were to be seized by landless farmers. The farmers' movement had banners with this kind of crescent symbol. The movement had led to violent village battles between those with vast expanses of land and the suffering poor.

"I felt my father's kind and loving fingers fasten this necklace with its silver pendant on my neck when I was seventeen. My father never came home again. It was 1965, and an executioner sent from the landlord came to rip him away from us. After that, my mother and I also were arrested. Our freedom was given in return for my body, after the camp commandant forced himself upon me."

The words themselves made Dewangga's narrow, emaciated chest tremble, her heart racing when she remembered that most painful time in her life. She wanted to bite her lip until she tasted blood when the memory returned of the figure of the camp commandant who suddenly tossed his green uniform into the corner of the interrogation room and grabbed her, stripping her with the devil in his heart. Dewangga, who had only just become a woman, muffled her scream when the evil authority drove his hard flesh, the same thickness as his big toe, into her groin. He left her, humiliated, sobbing in the corner, when he was finished. She held back drops of blood, a stinging pain between her thighs and a stabbing pain behind both her black eyes, the result of refusing the uniformed man's angry invitation. Tears streamed down her cheeks, strengthening the truth of what her father had once said: how dark the world is, constantly under the threat of violence. Dewangga closed her eyes. And when she looked at Abdullah, waiting like a stone at her side, she knew that the cruelty of that uniformed man could never be compared to the sincere tenderness she had always felt from her husband. In the hands of her husband she had truly been adored as a woman. How honorable Abdullah had been, every time he approached Dewangga with love. He would give himself to her, holding himself back so that they could reach climax together, not allowing either one of them to be disappointed . . . Uncountable times her husband had kissed her toes, bathing her with kisses until dawn, stroking her whole body after their far travels through love when night fell. Dewangga's body became flushed remembering all that, comparing this most essential love with the cruelest heartlessness.

The smell of chloroform and the weak neon glow sunk their hearts even further in that small hospital room.

Dewangga looked deeply into her husband's eyes. She brought his hands, prayer-like, to her chest. "Forgive me, my husband. Forgive my mother as well. And believe me, I am proud to be your wife. I have never regretted it. Never. Not even as much as a strand of hair, split into a thousand."

Outside, the slowly falling dusk began to spy on them. Dewangga closed her eyes.

Nyi Pu Lay ✸ *Burma*

Nyi Pu Lay is a satirical writer and artist. He was born in 1952, the son of two prominent Burmese left-wing writers and intellectuals from Mandalay, Ludu U Hla and Ludu Daw Amar. Nyi Pu Lay began writing satirically in journals in 1985 and soon became a popular figure. In 1990, he was arrested with six others and later sentenced to ten years' imprisonment on charges of being in contact with illegal organizations. It is believed, however, that he was arrested for his writing and family background. He was initially held in Insein Prison in Rangoon, and then moved to Thayet Prison in Central Burma, which made it harder for his family to visit him. As its translator has noted, "The Python," published in 1988, reflects Burmese discontent with the expansion into historic cities like Mandalay by Sino-Burmese and Chinese businessmen, some of whom have flourished within Burma's thuggish military dictatorship through their involvement in the drug and "blood jades" trades. In the story that follows, U Myo Khin is the unspoken poster child for such property dealings; readers may note the various offhand cultural references pointing to his origin and sketchy background.

The Python

Translated by Vicky J. Bowman

THE FRONT DOOR, WHICH WAS ALWAYS KEPT CLOSED, HAD BEEN opened.

Sitting in the front room, U Taw Daw was gazing vacantly out onto the road. The armchair in which he was reclining had once belonged to his father. Rather than cover it in nylon or cloth, his father had upholstered it in leather so that it would endure years of use. In the days when the cover had been new, the leather had been stiff and strong-smelling. His father had sat there throughout his many discussions concerning all shapes and sizes of beans and pulses with his broker friends. Here, his father had read his way through the newspapers of the day: *Ludu, Baho-si, Man-khit*. And here, he had riffled his way through the piles of banknotes bearing the signature of the then treasury secretary, Maung Kaung. In those days, they had lived in a big wooden house on stilts, painted with creosote. When he had grown up, his father had pulled down the old house and built a new two-story brick building, and it was in this home that U Taw Daw had learned all he knew about chickpeas and pigeon peas and every variety of bean.

Nowadays, the armchair's leather cover had been worn as soft as velvet, and although the leather was not burnished or polished, the color shone out of its smooth surface, and the seams had all but sunk into the material. Contact with years of *longyis* had frayed some of the stitching, and the padding at the head of the chair was stained brown with coconut hair oil. The embroidery on the headrest was his father's own handiwork and the stitches were so regular that one might have thought they had been sewn by machine.

The clock that his father had used to teach him how to tell the time was still attached to the east wall. To this day, a piece of paper was attached to the base with the red letters *SUN* in his father's hand, boxed off in blue pencil—it was a note to remind him to rewind the clock once a week. Although the face of the clock had begun to yellow, the black roman numerals still stood out clearly. Second by second, it still kept good time. Two of its hands told the hour, and a third pointed to the date: All three still rotated correctly and today the third hand was pointing to the fifth day of the month.

U Taw Daw sat gazing around him at the house, the compound, the furniture, all the household goods and kitchen utensils, down to the thermos flask and betel box—everything he saw had been left to him by his parents.

His thoughts then turned to his younger half brother, U Aung Toe, and his nephew, Maung Thant Zin. U Taw Daw's business had been sliding downhill for some time. Despite the fact that none of the three had any weakness for gambling or drinking or other forms of entertainment, they still had to dip into their savings from time to time, and, while dipping in on the one hand, they were still trying to earn on the other, but little by little, like an evaporating mothball, their bundle of savings was diminishing. Nowadays, they had to work hard just to repay the money that they had borrowed.

Business was not booming. He bought when the price was high but then all went awry and the price of his stockpiled beans didn't rise as it should have, so that when he sold his beans, he failed to make a profit.

In fact, business was a disaster. Although he could bear one bad year, or even two, after three or four bad years on the run, he was in deep trouble. Just as a boat cast adrift must be chased by another boat, so the sums of money that had drained away had to be chased by more money. And once he discovered he was no longer able to send good money after bad, what was to be done? He and his wife had often discussed this very question. The first person to come up with advice had been Ko Nyi Aung, one of their relatives, who was a property broker. "Uncle," he had said, "I could easily get you eight hundred thousand kyats for this place of yours."

When U Taw Daw had heard this, he had flown into a rage and came close to beating him. "Get out! Get out!" he had sputtered, his face bright red with fury. But it had only been a little misunderstanding between age and youth. Ko Nyi Aung had not taken offense, and had apologized to his uncle, saying that he had no idea that he was so attached to the place. Soon after, he was to be found coming and going in his regular manner, and he never missed coming with gifts for his elders on festival days.

Outside in the road, the bicycles steamed past. U Taw Daw's house was close to the petrol pump used by the buses plying the routes all around town, so that buses from all lines rumbled by outside. This was the business quarter of Mandalay, full of brokers and merchants, and full of warehouses, bean-processing factories, oil mills, wheat mills, car-maintenance workshops, and video parlors. As he gazed out onto the road, U Taw Daw shivered and put on his jacket. The workers from the bean factory across the road had started to lay out a tarpaulin to spread out the beans. On the roof of the building, he noticed a row of pigeons sitting, gazing expectantly at the tarpaulin, waiting for their supper.

Through the fence-posts of the compound, U Taw Daw caught sight of his wife returning from the market, twenty minutes earlier than usual. From afar, Daw Daw Thwin tried to gauge her husband's expression. He had been gloomy for many days, but in the last two or three, his despondency had become more obvious.

Carrying her basket by her side, Daw Daw Thwin went straight in through the house to the kitchen at the back. Neither said a word to the other. Sitting in his armchair, U Taw Daw continued to stare out at the road. Usually, when Daw Daw Thwin returned from the markets, he would get up to open the gate of the compound for her, and help her with her shopping basket. "What are you going to cook for me today, Ma Thwin?" he would ask, and she would perhaps reply, "Shall I cook us up some fish with some nice sour soup?" Or, if it had been a day when she bought pork: "I thought I'd cook you a bit of that pork curry that you like, dear." Whatever dish Daw Daw Thwin suggested, U Taw Daw invariably responded, "Mmm, that'd be just fine." But today, they behaved as if they were hardly on speaking terms, like a couple on the verge of divorce.

Suddenly his reverie was interrupted by the appearance of his young brother, U Aung Toe, smiling broadly and asking him how he was. "Uh, well enough—where's young Maung Thant Zin?" he replied.

"He's coming along later, he went off to buy a quid of betel." U Aung Toe took a look around the house. U Taw Daw inclined his head toward the brass betel box and said, "There's plenty in there." Then he resumed his gazing at the road.

When he heard two honks of a car horn, his heart skipped a beat and he turned his head to look. But the car sped on past, without stopping in front of the house. Every time he heard a car horn, his stomach gave a lurch, and he would turn to look and check his watch.

Maung Thant Zin arrived, his quid of betel making his cheek bulge. "Uncle, what curry is Aunty Thwin cooking for us today?" he asked, his words rendered virtually unintelligible by the betel quid. "I'm sure you're going to give us something delicious today, aren't you?"

U Taw Daw tried to smile. "Of course, we're planning to," he said.

The conversation stopped. No one uttered a word. The two older men just stared glumly into space, while young Maung Thant Zin silently studied the house. The photographs were still on the walls. The bed, the furniture—all were where they had always been. The room was as silent as a morgue, the most recent arrival having been infected by the miserable thoughts of the two older men. He stopped chewing his betel quid, and didn't even get up to spit out the juice.

A car pulled up in front of the house, the latest model, in bright red. The sound of the engine running could scarcely be heard. U Taw Daw's jaw sagged and he murmured, "I think this must be them." The other two turned to look. The driver of the car glanced up at U Taw Daw and another face appeared next to his. From the moment the car pulled up at the doorstep, U Taw Daw felt like a patient who had just been told that his cancer was confirmed. Ko Nyi Aung climbed out of the car first, while the other man raised the windows and gently closed the door on his side, quite unlike the slam Ko Nyi Aung had given on his side.

"Uncle! Uncle, I'm so sorry we're a little late," Ko Nyi Aung was calling. U Taw Daw said nothing, forcing a smile. In fact, they had arrived on the dot.

"It's my fault we're late, I'm afraid. I had some business to finish concerning a building in the Chan Aye Tha Zan Quarter." Ko Nyi Aung's voice echoed around the silent room and his booming tones seemed at odds with the surroundings.

Ko Nyi Aung quickly took stock of the situation, realizing everyone was putting on a brave face. Daw Daw Thwin came bustling out of the kitchen, asking "Maung Nyi Aung, did you eat before you came?" The others knew she was simply looking for words to fill the silence. Disconcerted, Ko Nyi Aung replied that he had just eaten. Thant Zin handed him a betel quid. The other man had brought in a holdall made of a rough, scaly fabric, the kind that some termed a snakeskin bag, others a Penang bag. As he watched the newcomer, U Taw Daw felt his breathing become even more constricted, as if a weight were bearing down on his chest. Again he forced a smile.

The men placed the bag on the bench and Nyi Aung carried out the introductions: "Uncle, Aunty, this is Ko Myo Khin." As U Taw Daw was wondering what to do next, the newcomer stretched out his hand toward him. Caught off guard by the unexpected gesture, U Taw Daw rose hastily from his armchair and grasped the proffered hand. When he touched it, he noticed how cold and clammy the palm was, as soft and supple as a girl's. U Aung Toe broke in, "Sit down, please, sit down in this chair here." "Yes, sit down, do sit down, Ko Myo Khin," urged U Taw Daw.

The room again fell silent. Each smiled at the other, although they had not a thing to smile about. "It's all wrong that we should be silent like this," thought U Taw Daw, and he blurted out, "Ko Myo Khin, are you from these parts? Were you born in Mandalay?"

No sooner had he asked the question than he realized he had made a mistake. He felt embarrassed at the thought of appearing unduly nosy.

"He says he hasn't been in this city long, Uncle," interrupted Ko Nyi Aung. After a while, Daw Daw Thwin went back out into the kitchen again. The newcomer simply smiled.

From the moment Ko Myo Khin had stepped through the doorway, they had all been sizing him up. Quite young; in the prime of his life; maybe about forty or so. On his wrist he wore a gold watch, which was set off well by his yellow-toned skin. On his left ring finger was a bright green ring. He was smartly dressed, and U Taw Daw guessed that his clothes must be quite expensive.

Bundles of bank notes were plainly visible, protruding from the snake-skin bag, and U Taw Daw was thinking that once he took this money, the house and land would no longer be his. He and his wife would be forced to move out to the so-called new pastures in the suburbs that were more in keeping with their financial means.

Ko Myo Khin started to undo the string tying up the bag containing the money. U Taw Daw wondered if Ko Nyi Aung had mentioned that they wanted to stay on in the house for another two weeks. He had assumed that the buyer would not pay up in full until they actually moved out, so would he hold some back? He took the handkerchief from his pocket and wiped the beads of sweat from his brow.

U Myo Khin tipped out the contents of the snakeskin bag onto the long table on which U Taw Daw's father had once displayed samples of his beans and pulses to the other brokers. Holding up the two corners of the bag, he shook it out until the last bits of dust came tumbling out with bundles of money. Three or four bundles fell off the edge of the table. Of all of the bundles of green, turquoise, crimson, and brown notes, the crimson notes predominated. If anyone asked, U Taw Daw would have had to admit that he had never handled so much money in his life.

His eyes glazed over and he stared straight ahead without seeing a thing. He was remembering the people to whom he owed everything, his parents, and was only brought back to earth by the voice of U Myo Khin. What was that the man had just said? U Taw Daw started and stared about him wildly.

Ko Nyi Aung repeated what the buyer had said. "Ko Myo Khin says he brought the money along without counting it properly first. He just bundled it up. So Uncle Aung Toe and Thant Zin should check it carefully. Whatever's missing, you're just to say. He'll make up the shortfall."

U Aung Toe put a little water in a teacup and put it down next to him so that he could wet his thumb and index finger as he counted the money. Thant Zin spat the betel juice into the spittoon. They started to count the money and Ko Nyi Aung made a move to close the front door so that people outside would not be able to see them counting. But Ko Myo Khin indicated with a wave of his hand that it should be left open.

Ko Myo Khin was apparently suffering none of the agonies being endured by U Taw Daw; he was sitting calmly on the wooden chair, and far from inspecting the rear of the house, he did not even bother to inspect the immediate interior. This was the first time he had stepped across the threshold; yet here he was, behaving more like a man who had just come home to his own hearth than someone buying a house.

U Aung Toe and his son were counting the money deliberately, placing the bundles of money to one side after each had been counted. U Taw Daw sat wondering if it would help any if he took part in the counting of the money rather than just looking on. He knew that in his present state of mind it would be easy to make a mistake. But he felt a need to assuage his misery by some methodical counting. He brooded over the merits of joining in and finally lifted his eyes, which had been glued to the floor. He had come to a decision.

He would count the money. That way, the whole business would be over more quickly. Ko Myo Khin and Ko Aung Toe and everyone else would leave the sooner, and he would be left in peace.

The first thing he did was to search for a bundle of notes stapled together by the bank. But he failed to find a single one. As he reached for a bundle, Ko Nyi Aung immediately glanced across at his uncle in surprise, as if to say that this was no way for his uncle to behave. U Taw Daw, who could not bear to be on the receiving end of such a look, pretended not to notice. His hands were trembling so much that it was only with concentrated effort that he succeeded in untying the bundle and started to count ten-kyat notes. Holding down the bundle with the heel of his left hand, he turned the notes over one by one with his right index finger as if his fingers were climbing stairs step by step. This was the method that his father had taught him. Carefully he counted the thousand notes and found neither a note short nor a note too many. U Taw Daw picked out another bundle, and as he counted, he could feel Ko Nyi Aung's eyes upon him. Ko Myo Khin stood up and wandered out to the car, as if the counting of the money had nothing to do with him whatsoever, as if he knew without a shadow of doubt that the counters were not going to try and pull a fast one. He did not even look back over his shoulder. U Taw Daw wanted to call across to his brother and nephew to make sure that they counted correctly, but in Ko Myo Khin's absence, perhaps it was better to say nothing so that any misunderstanding could be avoided.

Ko Myo Khin walked back to the house carrying a gold cigarette case that he had left in the car. U Taw Daw realized with embarrassment that he had neglected to offer his guests anything to smoke—although, on reflection, Ko Myo Khin did not strike him as the sort who would accept the offer of a cheroot. Meanwhile, the bundle he was counting only seemed to contain ninety-eight notes. He scratched his head and then began counting again very slowly from the beginning. As he counted, he was praying that there would not be any missing after all. If there really was a shortfall, what was he to do? Should he mention it? U Aung Toe and his son had been counting for some time, but he hadn't heard *them* say that they had found any shortfall. U Taw Daw had previously been wetting his fingers from U Aung Toe's teacup; but now he counted this bundle again, using his own spit.

He stopped at nine and heaved a huge sigh of relief, not bothering to recount the last note which remained under his finger. He fished out his handkerchief from his pocket and took off his jacket. Ko Nyi Aung looked the other way and lit up a cigarette offered to him by Ko Myo Khin.

As they counted the money, the seconds ticked by and started to mount up. By now they had counted about a quarter of Ko Myo Khin's pile of money and so far not one of them had said that a bundle was short.

Next, U Taw Daw picked up a bundle of forty-five–kyat notes, while Ko Myo Khin picked up the newspaper and started to read. Ko Nyi Aung inhaled his cigarette with a long, drawn out breath.

U Taw Daw had counted the bundle carefully. One forty-five–kyat note was missing. This time there was no mistake. One forty-five–kyat note, out of a pile of over a million. It would be embarrassing to mention it. He held the bundle in his hand and wondered what he should do. "It had to be my bundle, didn't it?" he thought to himself and looked over to Thant Zin, who was counting his bundle. "There's one short," he whispered and held up a single finger as he passed over the bundle. The finger shook imperceptibly. Ko Myo Khin lowered his newspaper and looked up.

Almost unable to contain himself, U Taw Daw followed Thant Zin's every movement and counted along with him under his breath. Thant Zin was clearly a faster and more accurate counter than himself. The bundle under his fingers passed from thick to thin. U Taw Daw was on the edge of his seat asking "How many? How many?" like an accused man waiting for the sentence to be passed down. He and Thant Zin arrived simultaneously at the final figure. Thant Zin pushed the incomplete bundle across to Ko Myo Khin saying, "Here, you count it too," but the latter simply smiled and slowly shook his head. Reaching into a bundle of money he was keeping separate, he pulled out a forty-five–kyat note and handed it to Thant Zin.

As the pile of counted notes grew, so did U Taw Daw feel his strength ebbing away. U Aung Toe said that his bundle was two notes short. Thant Zin made as if to count it again to be sure, but Ko Myo Khin again just smiled, and, saying something which U Aung Toe could not understand, gestured with the palm of his hand that it would not be necessary to recount it and took out two fifteen-kyat notes. He appeared not to want to waste any time. He lit up a cigarette and returned to reading the newspaper, looking like a man without a care in the world, quite unruffled, more like an automaton then a human being.

All that could be heard was the sound of the old clock ticking and the quiet rustle of notes. U Taw Daw finished a bundle and decided that he could not count another note. Leaning back in the armchair he looked long and hard at this man, Ko Myo Khin, who had come to buy his house for eleven *lakhs* when four months ago it had only been valued at eight. Ko Myo Khin was still perusing the newspaper, his lips moving as he read as if he was spelling out each line word by word.

"Did Maung Nyi Aung mention that we would like to stay on here another two weeks?" asked U Taw Daw.

The money counters stopped with their fingers in midair. Speaking in the same slow manner as he had been perusing the newspaper, Ko Myo Khin said something that none of them understood except Ko Nyi Aung, who repeated it for their benefit: "If you want to stay on another two weeks, you can stay. I will still give you the money now in full. But please make sure that you move out on the day you say you will."

Samruan Singh ✽ *Thailand*

Samruan Singh is the pen name of Surasinghsamruam Shimbhanao. Born in 1949 at Thonburi, his village upbringing was lean. From an early age he worked as a hawker in local markets, but was able to gain an education based on his exceptional learning abilities. Trained as a teacher, he never forgot the disadvantages faced by poor students from the countryside. After working near Chiang Mai and around Nakhon Sri Thammarat in the deep south, he returned north and researched peasant life—folklore, religion, children's games, communal rituals, and folksongs. Singh began publishing in these areas for Bangkok journals such as *Jaturat*, writing under pseudonyms to avoid harsh military censorship. Influenced by the social-activist writers Sulak Sivaraksa and Khamsingh Srinawak, as well as by the New Journalism from the U.S., he adopted the short story with its safer "fictional" grounding as a means of portraying the grinding struggle of Thailand's poor. Dating from 1979, Singh's final story, "The Necklace," is the oldest selection in this anthology, yet it remains a bleak emblem of the darker aspects of globalization. Its insight into an unlettered opium farmer's fight to stay "legit" echoes uneasily America's own earlier Mississippi delta blues.

The Necklace

Translated by Katherine A. Bowie

THIS YEAR'S APRIL SUN WAS HOTTER THAN ANY BEFORE. IT appeared to be scorching everything, desiccating all in view. Leaves, if not parched to a red-brown color, had wilted to faded green and looked like they would soon die. The breeze blew intermittently, but only to sweep the burning heat against one's skin. The land in the vicinity of this village still had no trees tall enough to help block the sun's rays or the hot wind. By the time they moved down to these mountain foothills less than three years ago, all the big trees in the forest had already been uprooted by gigantic machinery.

Lao Jong walked over to the waterstand. He took the water dipper made from a half-gourd and, scooping up some cloudy white water from the clay jar, drank it thirstily. The tea he had boiled earlier had already vanished from the jar. Today he was drinking more water than any other day. He gazed absently at the public well far in the distance. Its water was also almost gone. The sun's rays danced and shimmered, keeping time with the noisy chirping of the cicadas that were all about. Everything was so dry. The only exception was the mountain range on the horizon, its blue-green majestically peaceful and coolly refreshing.

This year was exceptionally arid. Two or three days ago his friends who had just come down from Mount Intanon told him that it was also dry in the mountains. It was especially bad where the military superhighway was starting to erode. Most of the trees in that area were pitifully desiccated. The famous Delavayi rhododendron trees and sphagnum mosses that the city folk like to come up to admire already looked dead. And it wasn't at all clear if they would revive enough in the upcoming rainy season to bloom, as they usually did, in the cold season.

He had also heard that lowlanders both near and far away were complaining that there was not enough water for them to plant in the dry season. The irrigation canals weren't carrying as much water as in previous years. But Lao Jong was neither happy nor sad about this news because neither he nor his fellow villagers planted or planned to plant in the dry season anyway.

"Let's go. Are you ready to go yet?" Ee Moi, his wife, reproached him. He returned the gourd water dipper to its rest. He turned and grabbed his machete lying nearby.

"Okay. Let's go. We should try to hurry. There are only two of us to do the work. Otherwise we will be behind everyone else, just like last year," he replied gently as he opened the door and walked out in front. Extending him a banana-leaf cigar, Ee Moi followed him.

Their black clothes really absorbed the heat. After just moments in the sun, their clothes pressing against their skin felt as if they would catch fire any minute, were it not for their pouring sweat to douse it. The trees and branches that the two of them had cut and stacked on a previous day were now dry and brittle in the middle of the sunshine. Lao Jong inhaled the cigar smoke before he spoke, without turning around to look at his wife.

"Look, with such strong sunshine, everything really dried quickly. I'm worried that the people around us will burn their fields before us. Once they start burning, their fire will spill over to our fields, just like last year.

It will burn what we have cut before we have a chance to collect the firewood. And we'll have problems with the trees we haven't felled yet because the fire will burn the surrounding kindling. If we burn after everyone, there won't be enough kindling left to finish burning off the weeds. Lowlanders don't know how to do upland agriculture properly. When they decide they want to burn, they just do so. Once they've started their fires, they don't pay much attention to the other uses the fields could have. They don't want to ask us how to do it properly because they are afraid of losing face to mountain people."

"Of course. We've been so slow," Ee Moi replied to her husband's lament. "You lost so much time waiting to hire a tractor. When that wasn't possible, that left just the two of us to do all the work by ourselves. So how could we possibly keep up with them?"

Lao Jong felt a flash of anger. He glanced briefly at his wife's face. As he turned away, he teased her gently, "Precisely, how much can two people do? I'd like to find another wife or two, so there would be three or four of us to do the work."

"If you have the money to marry more, go ahead. Then things will be easier for me. I'll have someone to help me work in the fields," Ee Moi retorted instantly.

Soon the two reached the area where they had left off in the morning. Diverse scents from the trees and branches that had been cut and stacked into piles wafted to their noses. The leaves had curled into gray-green tubes from the heat of the sun.

Husband and wife extinguished their banana-leaf cigars and put them away for later. They began to cut the remaining trees with expert skill. Soon the patch of forest would be flattened to the ground. From nearby fields, the sound of the tractors roared up from time to time. Each time the roars completely drowned the sound of their two machetes hitting the trees.

"With only five *rai* of land, if we leave the tree stumps in the ground as we did when we farmed in the mountains, what can we plant to support us? Especially these days, when the prices for crops are so low," Lao Jong complained as he raised his shirtsleeve to wipe off the sweat dripping into his eyes. He looked over toward his wife, who was absorbed in slashing the trees. She stopped abruptly and looked at her husband quizzically before answering.

"If we don't leave the stumps, we would have to bend way over low to the ground to fell them. Why would we do that? The lowlanders don't know how to cut trees efficiently at all. They cut low down to the ground. That way really hurts the back. Even leaving stumps one or two feet off the ground hurts badly enough as it is."

"No, no. I don't mean that. Of course leaving taller stumps is better. Not only is it easier on the back, but it has the advantage that next year it will have branches and leaves that we can use to burn off the weeds again. But here is not like in the mountains, where we can clear as much land as we want. On a small plot of land like this, planting just between the stumps like we did in the mountains means we won't be able to plant enough to eat." Lao Jong stopped speaking briefly and glanced at his wife. Seeing she was still listening intently, he continued speaking as he cut the trees before him.

"That's why I wanted to hire a tractor to dig out the tree stumps. We'd just have to hire it one time and we would be fine. But we have no money."

Ee Moi appeared angry. "When will you quit talking about the tractor for once and for all? Last year you were obsessed with waiting for the tractor and so we fell behind everyone else. Why are you so focused on it? Each of our two hands are still strong. Once we have burned off the fields, we can help each other dig and pull out the tree stumps. Soon it will be done. Do you want to sell another necklace?"

Lao Jong was speechless. He tried to swallow the pain deep in his breast. His left hand unconsciously reached up and touched the silver necklace at the base of his throat. His largest and most beautiful necklace was no longer there.

He thought back to when he had first come down from the mountains. He didn't blame himself for moving because he had been taken in by the radio advertisement broadcast in his language. Things had come to the point that he and his friends had to resettle because there was no viable land left near their old village for cutting and clearing upland fields. The land was all degraded. The good land near their village for planting upland crops throughout their lifetimes had become private property. Some of his friends resettled higher on the mountains not far from their old places, but he, Ee Moi and a few friends chose to settle in the lowlands both out of curiosity and the dream that maybe it would be as good as the radio claimed.

When they first came down from the mountains, he felt excited and proud that everyone welcomed him and his friends so warmly. The district officer thanked them all for cooperating with the government by not planting opium and cutting down the forest. He and his friends received prepared house plots without any of the complications that many lowlanders faced. When Ee Moi told the doctor that she didn't want to have any children yet because she still had to help her husband farming, the doctor gave her a free injection and told her at the same time that if after one year she still didn't want to have any children, she should come again for another injection. And if she developed any abnormalities of her uterus, the doctor would treat her for free. A group of well-dressed Caucasians and Thais came to their homes and introduced them to a new religion. This religion had only one spirit, who was very powerful. Any given year one only had to host one or two ceremonies. It didn't require any elaborate ritual offerings. It didn't have to be fed often or given very much, unlike the mountain spirits. And those who worshipped this single spirit helped each other out all the time. Eventually, Lao Jong and his group decided to convert and worship this single spirit.

"These thorny bushes don't need to be cut. They're already dry and there is a lot of cogon grass around here. Once we start the burn, they will catch fire easily," Ee Moi said, interrupting his thoughts.

In the end the trees in the area were all felled. Only scattered stumps and thorny bushes remained. The neighboring plots of land had long been cleared by the power of labor and the ever-transcendent power of money. The sun was setting behind the mountaintops, spreading its golden glow over the landscape.

"Moi, why don't you go back to the housework. I can collect the fire-wood by myself," he said to his wife. She was resting, smoking a cigar on a nearby hillock. With no further ado, she got up and started to walk off. She turned around to tell Lao Jong.

"Don't come back too late, okay? Don't worry if you can't get it all done. Tomorrow we will help each other collect fire wood all day and it will be fine. The day after that we can help each other prepare the fire-trails. And then all that is left is the burning itself."

Lao Jong nodded his head in agreement, but he continued sitting smoking his cigar. He let his thoughts wander. After the burning, they would still have to hoe and loosen the soil. They couldn't afford to wait for rain to soften the earth first. They probably didn't have enough time to dig out the tree stumps. Otherwise it would be like last year all over again. If they planted after everyone else, they might as well not plant at all. He vividly recalled last year's painful lesson.

Last year he planted sweet corn for a foreign-owned canning factory just like the majority of the other villagers in his village. Corn is easily planted; its roots are like those of opium poppies and he had planted it before. Villagers who encouraged him to plant it told him that it was easier than other crops because one didn't have to invest capital and didn't have to take much risk. The factory would loan them the seeds, fertilizer, and pesticides. At harvest, the company would buy the whole crop at a guaranteed price of one baht per kilo. Furthermore, if they had a good crop, the company wouldn't charge for the seeds they borrowed.

Lao Jong thought scornfully of those who had encouraged him to join and spoken as if the factory's system were the best way in the world to help the farmers. In fact, if those villagers knew about the way opium was planted in the mountains, they would be ashamed of themselves. In the mountains, people who plant opium can even ask their buyers for cash advances equal to the value of their entire opium crop. In addition, they don't have to bother with signing any confusing papers. Furthermore, the harvest price per *rai* was much higher. And what's more, if one borrowed money and had a bad harvest, one could postpone the loan and pay it back in the following year without even having to pay interest.

Thinking about investment capital upset him even more since it was the reason that everything went wrong last year. He had waited and waited for the loan he thought he could get from the cooperative to hire a tractor. By the time he was certain that he wouldn't get any money, it was almost too late to plant. He and his wife had only been able to do a superficial job of felling the trees as they rushed to get the fields planted. Even though his friends who had already finished their fields came to help, he still finished planting his fields a week later than everyone else. So of course his sweet corn matured later than everyone else's. When the company's truck came to buy the crops, he was not ready to sell. He had to plead for the factory's truck to come back for his on a different day. Perhaps because his corn crop was small, they weren't very interested in it, but the company didn't come until several days after the appointed time. By that point, most of his corn crop was too ripe for canning standards. He almost had to beg the company people to buy his crop, even though they offered a price lower than originally guaranteed. The company representatives kindly agreed to help him out by buying just enough of his crop so that he could pay back the cost of the seed, fertilizer and insecticide. For months, he and his wife had to eat boiled corn instead of rice.

He threw away the banana leaf cigar stub that had gone out by itself in his hand. He got up, chose wood that was big enough to use as firewood and collected it into piles. As he bent and stooped gathering the wood, the two silver necklaces around his throat knocked against each other making a clinking sound. The sound reminded him of their presence and of the loss of his largest and most beautiful necklace, the one which had the most meaning for him and which never should have escaped him.

It had happened because he had been open to new experiences. With everyone singing the praises of cooperatives, Lao Jong had been thoroughly convinced and asked to join the subdistrict cooperative immediately. When he needed 70 baht as the initial registration fee, he didn't hesitate to remove his necklace and pawn it with a merchant in the town market. Once he received the loan from the cooperative, he planned to redeem it.

He couldn't remember how many times he had walked to ask about the loan from the cooperative. Each time took at least half a day. The answer he would get was "we don't have the money yet," "the money hasn't come yet," and finally "the money came, but it was not enough." The last answer made him despair. The government didn't have enough money, but without sufficient funds how was it supposed to help anyone? After that, his necklace fell into the hands of the pawnbroker, but not until after he walked back and forth to pay the interest of 14 baht per month for almost 10 months. And it was a thousand times more painful when he finally realized that the "credit" of hill-tribe people like him was not considered good enough for them to be able to borrow money easily. Even if the cooperative had money, they didn't want to lend it to him. He had no assets to use as collateral. Although he had land, that was meaningless since it had no legal title. It was as if lowlanders only trusted what was on "paper."

Ee Moi had cried when she learned about it. It would have been better to have lost his two smaller necklaces than to have forfeited the big one. But how could anyone have known that he would have to lose it? That large necklace was the reason that he and Ee Moi met and eventually married.

Five years ago, at the *nohbaejo* festival celebrated in the mountain village, the boys and girls had had a good time playing *bohkohnnaa* with each other. The boys always lost this ball game. Then the girls were able to confiscate their necklaces. According to custom, they forced the youth to ransom them back, some with songs, some by dancing, and others by blowing the *tamyia* and *kaeng* musical instruments until the girls were satisfied. His large necklace was confiscated by Ee Moi. She wouldn't return it until he won it back playing *bohkohnnaa*. She felt that the boys had lost too easily and she acted as if she were going to quit playing.

He lifted the pile of firewood onto his shoulders and prepared to return. These five *rai* of land stretched far enough to make him feel alone and separate from other villagers who were working their own plots. But the fact that he was a hilltribesman, a mountain person, already made him feel like a stranger in this village. As a result of the land lottery, he received a plot next to lowlanders who were not very friendly toward him.

The rays of the sun had long disappeared, but it was not yet completely dark. He threw the pile of firewood that he had been carrying in the yard by his house. He stopped for a moment and stood with his head bowed looking intently at the ground. If only the farming plots had been plowed like the land around his house, it would be wonderful. Sighing as he thought about it, he opened the door to his hut and went inside. Ee Moi greeted him the moment she saw him.

"You're home earlier than other days. Is something wrong? You look worried."

"Never mind. I've just been doing too much thinking. Is there something you want me to help you with?"

"No, nothing. Everything's ready. We could eat right away, but if you want to rest first, that's fine too."

Lao Jong didn't say anything. He collapsed and sat down on the ground in his house near the hearth. Ee Moi handed him a stool, but he didn't take it. He preferred to sit on the ground. In his house only the sleeping platform and kitchen shelf were not flush on the ground. Old memories returned. The song that Ee Moi sang after he ransomed the necklace when he won the *bohkohnnaa* game echoed in his mind.

Jyy lang to dae yyy juu, tyyn tuu tae yaakaa mua tuu mua trong.
Jae sea tyy trong plaaj jia wong kuu mua jao jia tia kua am plaa.

Just as creeks flow in their beds,
so brides pass through the doors of their homes
to live with their husbands like penned pets.
The girls' tears flow with the suffering welling in their hearts.

He took the teacup from his wife that she had poured for him, and his thoughts became even more disquieted. He didn't want to think that he was the cause that his beloved wife must suffer. As a husband he tried to help his wife far more than other men in the mountains. Hill tribe men assumed the responsibilities for hosting visitors and engaging in business trade, but they left their wives and children to do the farming. Those with money took on several wives to help with the farm work. But Lao Jong tried to work the fields even more than his wife. And no matter how much money he had, he didn't think about taking other women as wives.

Lao Jong picked up a cigar and lit it. He inhaled several times in succession. Ee Moi looked at him with strange look in her eyes and smiled at him slightly before speaking.

"Don't worry so much. I have thought it through. I will give you my necklace and bracelet to sell and we will have enough money to hire a tractor. Even if we can't plow it all, it will still help a lot. If we get a good price for our crops this year, you can buy me new ones. Otherwise, it's alright if you can't. I will wear just one necklace to make sure that the spirit *tuchengtuchii* in our old village will recognize me, that's enough."

Lao Jong looked at his wife. When he saw how earnest her eyes were, he was shocked. "What are you saying? There is no way I will do that. I have already lost one and that pains me greatly. Are you sure that if we sell yours, we will have enough money to buy it back? I have already been hurt enough by the cooperative. Don't let yourself be hurt by the company too. I won't do that. I certainly won't let you suffer like that."

Ee Moi avoided his eyes and asked as casually as possible, "And so what will you do?"

Lao Jong clenched his teeth so hard his cheeks bulged for a time, before he answered tensely, "We will do as much as we can. Let's see how things go this year. If nothing improves, I will take you back home to the mountains."

As he was speaking, he poured the tea into the ashes of the fireplace. The smell of the charcoal ash as the water hit it rose up and filled his nostrils.

It was like the smell of the fields as they soaked up the first rain after they were burned. It was a smell that was buried in his blood since the days of his ancestors. It was a smell that gave new hope of a new prosperity taking root. When he lived in the mountains, this was the smell that permeated the air throughout the whole village at the beginning of the rainy season. It was the sign that everyone had aged another crop, another year.

"Water belongs to the fish.

"The sky belongs to the birds.

"The mountains belong to the Meo."

Ee Moi murmured the saying disconsolately in the language of the central Thai. The husband and wife fell silent. Tears welled in their eyes.

Kong Bunchhoeun ✸ *Cambodia*

Kong Bunchhoeun was born in 1939 under French colonial rule in Battambang province. He survived the Japanese occupation and in 1957 moved to Phnom Penh, where he published his first book, *The River of Death*. In 1963 he was imprisoned for six months for publishing a novel that criticized a high official in the then royal government. Later, during Pol Pot's murderous post-Liberation regime, he escaped execution thanks to a Khmer Rouge cadre who had read his novels and testified that Kong had "a profound sense of social justice." With the fall of the Khmer Rouge, he returned to the capital in 1981 and worked for the Ministry of Culture. Kong's work includes scores of books, including poetry, popular songs, plays, and novels. However, as a result of publishing *The Destiny of Marina* in 2000—a critique against what he termed "the culture of arrogance" that he believed had become institutionalized—he was compelled to flee the country. "A Mysterious Passenger" harks both to the enduring Cambodian folk belief in supernatural powers and spirits, and to the lingering shadow of Pol Pot's "Killing Fields," the communist holocaust that led to the deaths of millions.

A Mysterious Passenger

*Translated from Khmer to French by Christophe Macquet
and from French to English by Marie-Christine Garneau and Theo Garneau*

IT IS LATE AFTERNOON, NEARLY FOUR O'CLOCK. RETURNING TO the capital, a Toyota Corona disappears into the shadow of Pech Nil Mountain, halfway between Phnom Penh and Kompong Som. At the wheel is a thirty-year-old man: close-cropped hair, dark skin, hatchet-faced features with slightly protruding eyes, and deeply furrowed brow, which gives him an expression of constant worry.

Next to him, a man with a light complexion but features that are typically Khmer: handsome, Eurasian, about thirty-five years old. A vague smile floats on his lips. He has an intelligent face. His large, dark eyes gaze languidly at the passing countryside. He is holding a small video camera. From time to time, he asks his driver to slow down so that he can film something in the landscape.

213

Abruptly, the driver turns to the man in the seat beside him and, using the deferential form of address, asks softly, "Elder Brother Veasna, when do you think you'll be going back to America?"

The handsome Veasna lowers the camera and manages a slight smile. It's evident he's not interested in chatting. "That must be the tenth time you've asked me that question, Chan! Don't you want me to stay here in Cambodia?"

"Me? You must be kidding!" the driver responds. But the furrows in his brow grow even deeper. "Before you arrived, every day was dull. But now that you're here, I'm never bored!" He sighs. "I'm sorry to insist, Elder Brother. It's just that every time I ask, you either say nothing or you change the subject."

Veasna turns slowly to his driver. The sincere melancholy in the driver's tone has surprised him.

"Well, I can see you aren't going to give up easily. Okay, stop worrying about it. I'll answer your question. But while I do, be sure to concentrate on your driving. This winding road is especially dangerous, and I don't want to end up at the bottom of the ravine."

"Don't worry, Elder Brother. I'm not like other drivers. I talk a lot while I'm driving, but I always keep my eyes on the road, and both hands on the wheel."

"Your driving doesn't usually worry me," the Cambodian American says, lifting his eyebrows slightly. "But last night when you were dancing at Snake Island, you looked pretty frisky. I wouldn't be surprised if your eyesight is a little blurry today ..."

Chan bursts out laughing. Easing the car expertly into a sharp curve, he smiles broadly, the ends of his mouth turned up like a gondola.

"Oh, yeah! Ha ha! You've got bags under your eyes, too, Elder Brother! Last night it looked to me like you weren't feeling any pain either. Ah, yes. With all those gorgeous girls ... Were you able to film some of them?"

"Film them? What for?"

"What do you mean, 'What for?' I thought that was the purpose of your trip this time: to crisscross Cambodia and film all the beautiful Khmer women! Isn't that why we borrowed your parents' car?"

"That's partly true," Veasna concedes, slowly nodding. "But I'm not here to film bargirls!"

"Well, I'll be damned!" Chan replies, not daring to take his eyes off the road. "What more do you want? Didn't you see those curves, those glowing faces? They were all as gorgeous as the celestial *apsaras* on the walls of Angkor Wat!"

The car reaches a small wooden bridge that's badly decaying and in need of repair. Veasna holds his breath until they have crossed the hazard.

"What I'm looking for," he says finally, casting a glance behind him at the bridge, "is a young country girl ... a girl from the rice fields."

"A girl from the rice fields?!" squawks the driver. "You mean to tell me you're filming peasant girls? Forgive me for saying so, but they're not at all to my taste. They're far—very far—below the beauty of my little flowers at Snake Island."

The passenger's expression stiffens slightly. "Maybe so," he says, trying to smile, "but those nocturnal beauties of yours are nothing without powder, lipstick, and the pulsing of the neon lights. What I'm interested in are peasant girls—like the girls from Veal Renh or Prey Nup, for example. They have such natural grace, beauty—and without any makeup or false lighting. And then there's the exquisite reserve in their manner: a blend of sweetness and shyness ..."

Chan scratches his head. He doesn't really understand, but he doesn't want to contradict his companion. All the same, with a forced smile he continues. "There can't be too many people who think like that, you know. But after all, why not? You can film such girls if you want. The most important thing, though, is that you answer my question."

Veasna once again raises his camera to his eye. "What were you asking, Chan?"

The driver lets out a groan. "As if you didn't know! Well, this time you won't get off so easily, Elder Brother! If you don't answer me right now, I am going to stop the car!"

Veasna abruptly puts down the camera, takes a breath, and says gently, "My friend, don't get so worked up. Okay then, here's your answer: I'm going back to the U.S. in one month."

"Are you telling me the truth, Elder Brother?" asks the driver, a curious tone in his voice.

"That's the honest truth," Veasna responds with a faraway gaze. "It's printed in black and white on my plane ticket."

Chan sighs deeply. His despondency seems absolute.

"What's the matter?" Veasna asks, concerned now. "What's the long face for?"

"Nothing, Elder Brother," says the driver faintly. "It's just that I would have liked for you to go sooner, that's all."

Veasna's expression darkens. "But why? Are you expecting trouble to break out in Cambodia?"

"Oh no, not at all. It's something to do with me."

"To do with you? Well then, come on, Chan, tell me. Out with it!" In answer, Chan presses the brakes and brings the car to a stop under a tree.

"Now what?" Veasna protests, dumbfounded. "What are you doing? Why are you stopping the car like this? We're in the middle of a forest, there's not a soul around, the sky is clouding over, and it's about to storm any minute. We'll never make it back on time."

Chan gets out of the car.

"This won't take long," he says, taking a deep breath. "I just need to calm down a bit before explaining this to you. Don't worry. Besides, we wouldn't have made it back before nightfall anyway."

"Then speak!" Veasna says through the open window of the car. "Why the hell must I leave Cambodia when I haven't even finished my work?"

Chan's face takes on an expression of infinite sadness. "It's because," he says in a trembling voice, "I'm in love. On top of that, the dates have been set. I only have a few days to get an engagement present, and the marriage is two weeks later. You just have to leave, Veasna, as soon as possible. Tomorrow or the day after . . . You really must go and tell my older sister."

Veasna is stunned. "What? That's all? But can't you just send your sister a fax?"

"A fax . . . but I don't have her address or her telephone number . . ."

At this point, Veasna begins to lose his composure. He gets out of the car and walks over to Chan. "You don't have her telephone number? Your sister has never sent her number to you in her letters?" Above them, the sky is darkening. In the distance, storm clouds are gathering in a black, foreboding mass above the mountain peaks.

"Well, actually I've never received any letters from her."

"Then how do you know she's in America? Give it to me straight, Chan. I can't make heads or tails of what you're telling me!"

The driver bends down, plucks a small flower out of the grass, and places it between his lips. "My sister and I," he continues, his voice fading, "were separated in 1975, when the Khmer Rouge took Phnom Penh. I thought she was lost to me forever. But just a week ago, I found out she's alive and residing in America."

Veasna covers his face with his hands. "Okay. So how did you find out?" The driver hesitates.

"Well, Chan, someone must have told you, yes?" Veasna is becoming impatient. He brings his face close to Chan's. "This someone must certainly know her address and telephone number!"

Chan spits the flower out of his mouth. "No, Elder Brother," he says, finally blurting it out. "A fortuneteller told me ..."

Veasna jumps back as if suddenly bitten by an ant in a tender part of his anatomy. "A fortuneteller?!" he exclaims.

"Yes," stammers the driver, bobbing his head from side to side like an iguana. "The other day, you know ... The other day when I took you for a visit to the Wat Phnom ... well, I took the opportunity to consult a famous psychic ... This master psychic told me everything ... that my sister was still alive ... that she is living in America ... So now do you understand, Veasna? You simply must help me! You have to go back and find her for me!"

Veasna looks skyward as if for help. High in a tree, two or three, birds take flight effortlessly on slow wings.

"Of all things ... How could you, Younger Brother? You who are so practical minded, who drive heavy equipment for a living. How could you believe in the predictions of fortunetellers?!"

Chan takes Veasna's arm and tugs on it gently. "I assure you, Elder Brother, this person is amazing! Two weeks before you came to Cambodia, he told a friend of mine who had his motorbike stolen that it would reappear in three days. And guess what—unbelievable! On exactly the third day, my friend found his motorbike! Trust me, Veasna. My sister is alive. Since the fortuneteller gave me this news, I've dreamed of her almost every night."

Veasna stops looking at the sky. "I don't want to interfere with your beliefs, Chan ... but come on, this is the computer age we're living in!"

"What can I say?" answers the driver. "Computer age or not, people here have absolute faith in these things. Help me, Veasna, please! Don't abandon me!"

"Okay," says the Cambodian American man gravely. "Let me see if I understand what you're really saying: You want me to find your sister and tell her to send you money for your engagement present. Is that it?"

Chan joyfully circles Veasna on tiptoe. "Yes! Yes!" he cries, his eyes full of tears. "That's exactly it. Oh, you know how to heal my wounded heart, Elder Brother! It's true that I am poor and if my sister doesn't help me, I will have lost a priceless jewel for a wife."

Veasna gets in the backseat of the car and smiles magnanimously. "All right. Okay, you can count on me. All right. But let's get going. It'll be dark soon."

Chan glances quickly at the road and starts the car. Behind him, he hears Veasna's resonant voice.

"I feel sorry for you, Younger Brother. There are so many Khmers in America, hundreds of thousands of them. How in the world will I be able to find your sister if you don't even have her address?"

"Ah, but my sister is special. She used to be the lead dancer in the Royal Ballet! A star!"

"A ballet star?!" exclaims Veasna, his curiosity piqued now. "What's her name?"

Chan savors his triumph. "You see," he says, brimming over with pride, "you haven't heard anything yet and you are already on the edge of your seat. How will you handle it when you know her name?! Trust me, Veasna, you will find her!"

An enormous clap of thunder interrupts the driver. The sky turns black. Explosive gusts of wind cover the narrow road with clouds of dust. Visibility is nearly zero. And then the terrifying, deafening storm strikes with full force. Sheets of angry rain crash on the car so violently that they threaten to shatter the windshield. Chan stomps on the accelerator, trying to escape this dark storm as quickly as possible.

"How strange," he mutters. "One would think the sky was angry about something . . ."

"Stop, Chan!" Veasna shouts. "I think I see someone waving at us. Slow down! Slow down!"

Chan takes his foot off the gas and turns on his high beams. "Where? I can't see a thing."

"There. That figure on the side of the road, under the tamarind tree. It looks like a woman. Hey, she's trying to signal to us."

The car swerves slightly to the shoulder of the road.

"Oh, yes. Now I can see her. Hmmm . . . But what's a woman doing in such a desolate place at this hour of the night? What's going on, Elder Brother? This doesn't look good . . ."

"Someone is signaling for help," interrupts Veasna sternly. "We must stop! What are you afraid of? Come on, pull over quick. Hey, look. She's coming toward us!"

Chan would have preferred to drive on by, but this isn't his car. He does what Veasna tells him to do and pulls off the road to stop next to the tamarind tree. A woman dressed in black, her head covered with a white *krama*, approaches them.

By this time, Veasna has rolled down his window. In spite of the darkness and the pouring rain, he can make out a form. It is indeed a young woman. She appears to be twenty-two or twenty-three years old at most.

And suddenly her face is close enough for him to see: a face arrestingly beautiful and overpowering . . . Veasna feels himself stirred to the depths of his being.

I have been going around this country for almost two weeks, he thinks to himself, *and I have never seen a girl so beautiful.*

"Is anything wrong, young lady?" asks Chan.

But before the beautiful young woman can answer, Veasna takes over the conversation. "Please, get in," he says, quickly opening the back door. "You're going to be soaked. We can talk afterwards."

"Thank you, gentlemen. Thank you so very much."

Her voice . . . is like music, like the celestial music that comes down from Mount Kailash's fabled summit; melodious and so marvelously beautiful with the strange power to make one's blood well up inside the heart, to transform one's heart into a volcano about to erupt. Chan dares not speak. He lets Veasna do the talking.

"What are you doing out here alone, miss?"

The young woman unties her white *krama* and pats her wet forehead. "I came to visit my aunt," she says with the smile of an innocent child. "She lives in the woods, close to here. I was on my way back home when the storm caught me by surprise."

Every word that falls from her lips is like the offering of flowers at a shrine. Veasna inhales with growing ecstasy the fateful scent of ambrosia. He cannot take his eyes from her. She appears more and more beautiful to him with each passing moment.

"I see, I see," he answers, feeling never more alive than at that instant. "And where do you live, miss?"

She lowers her eyes shyly. "At the foot of Mount Kirirom."

Chan, who until then had been content to observe the young woman in the rearview mirror brusquely interrupts, as if he were waking from a dream. "Perfect! That's perfect! That's not far from here! Ten kilometers at the most!"

"Then it's no problem, miss," Veasna says, nodding and smiling, "to drop you off at your home. Come on, Chan, let's go!"

After a brief sidelong glance in the rearview mirror, Chan starts the car and begins driving, this time more cautiously.

The winds and rain have redoubled their violence. In an effort to dispel the malevolent atmosphere created by the storm, Veasna decides to strike up a conversation. "So...what is the name of this place?" he asks.

The beautiful young woman beside him seems to be making an effort to remember. "I think ...I think that the old folks call it the Hill of the Three Skulls," she says, lifting her eyes.

Chan turns slightly toward her. Her words seem to have awakened something in him. "The Hill of the Three Skulls ... Yes, I do remember. Something horrible happened there under Pol Pot."

"Do you know the story, Chan?"

"Vaguely," the driver answers, keeping his attention on the road. "I was deported to this region."

The eyes of the beautiful woman light up. "Then you must know the Plain of the Dead Jackal," she says in a clear voice.

Chan's lips begin to tremble. "Yes, I worked there. I was part of the mobile brigade. Brrr...just hearing the name gives me goose flesh! And you, miss?"

The car has begun to accelerate. In the dim glow of its interior lights, the young woman's voice seems even more beautiful.

"Yes, I worked down there, too. But I don't know much about its story."

A bolt of lightning explodes nearby with a terrifying roar. Its blue-white flash illuminates the car's interior and reflects in the eyes of the young woman, who is visibly frightened.

"And ...and what if you told us a little more of the story, Chan?" Veasna says softly.

"Oh no, not now," answers the driver, who is trembling like a leaf. "I don't like to talk about ghosts when I'm driving."

Veasna holds his nose. "So are you saying that this is a story about ghosts?"

"Yes. It's about three young sisters. People say that they were murdered in a most terrible manner."

With a startled cry, Veasna interrupts. He has noticed that the young woman is on the verge of tears. "That's enough, Chan! Our passenger does not feel very well."

Chan stops speaking immediately. "Excuse me, miss. Maybe this story touches you personally?"

The beautiful young woman is making an effort not to cry. "No," she says in a barely audible voice, "it's just that I can't bear sad stories. I cry, cry . . . every time . . . I don't know why . . ."

Another bolt of lightning illuminates the interior of the car.

"I understand," says Veasna, settling deeper into his seat. "Let's not talk about it anymore."

Then, after a moment of silence, he grumbles, "Damn it! Don't you smell anything? It's like the smell of something rotten . . . Can't you smell it, Chan?"

Holding his nose too, the driver says, "Yes, you're right. Could there be a dead buffalo on the side of the road?"

"No. I have the air conditioner turned on, and the windows are tightly closed."

"Maybe there's a dead rat in the car."

"A dead rat? In my car? Why would there be a dead rat in my car?"

Veasna continues to hold his nose tightly. "Maybe you stepped in something, Chan?"

At this point, the young woman speaks up, smiling sweetly. "You're not imagining things, gentlemen," she says in her serene voice. "I helped my aunt to fill up several jars of fish paste today. The smell of the *prahoc* must still be with me. I'm very sorry that it bothers you so much."

"*Prahoc*!" Veasna exclaims, delighted. "Right! That's it! That's the smell of *prahoc*!"

Chan loudly joins in. "Veasna may have lived a long time in America, but he's not grossed out by our *prahoc*! At restaurants he always asks for more!"

The beautiful woman lifts her eyes. "Very well then," she says in her silky voice, "if we're lucky enough to see each other again, I'll offer both of you a little jar of *prahoc* as a token of gratitude."

"Thank you in advance, miss. Prepared by you, I am certain it will be delicious."

The rain has lessened slightly, but Chan, who does not feel reassured, maintains the same speed. Suddenly he yells, "Oh no!" Looking right and left, he says, "I think we might have gone past your house. Can you look out and see if we have, miss?"

The young woman looks through the window, and now it is she who is alarmed. "A bit, yes, a little bit. But it's okay. I can jump out right here. This is fine."

Veasna sighs. "Over here? But we're deep in the woods. Where is your house?"

"Over there," she says, pointing. "Beyond the first row of trees..."

Veasna rolls down his window and squints. "But it's still raining and you don't have anything to cover yourself with..."

"Don't worry," says the young woman as she opens the door. "I'll change my clothes when I get home. Well ... thank you, gentlemen. Goodbye."

"Goodbye, miss," says Veasna, slightly dispirited. "If you had not lived so far, I would have accompanied you home."

The mysterious young woman presses her palms together in a gesture of farewell. In a low voice, nearly whispering, she says, "Don't worry yourself. You have shown enough proof of the goodness of your heart..."

The sky growls again, but now the sound is deeper, occurring in long tympanic rumbles. The storm seems to be moving away, though the winds still blow and the shadows still flicker ominously.

The young woman wraps the white *krama* around her head, then slowly and delicately steps off the road and disappears into the shadows of the massive trees. Veasna's heart has stopped beating. His gaze is arrested by the beauty of her bare foot and the charm, grace, and suppleness with which she walks.

"What are you looking at now, Elder Brother?" says Chan, tapping nervously on the wheel. "She's gone, there's nothing more to see."

He starts the engine, and Veasna comes out of his trance. "She was right. The smell disappeared when she did. Chan, tell me: What do you think of this girl?"

"Not much," answers the driver with a forced air of nonchalance. "She was a peasant girl, just a peasant girl. In principle, we should have had her pay us for the ride."

"What are you talking about?" Veasna replies indignantly. "Giving her a ride didn't cost us anything." Then he adds with sudden joy, "She was beautiful! Beautiful! I think she could have asked me to take her all the way to Phnom Penh!"

Chan cannot pretend any longer. "Yes, she was indeed really beautiful. Marvelously beautiful. My eyes didn't leave the rearview mirror. It's hard to believe. A girl like her, in such a desolate place, so far away from everything..."

"I've got to tell you, Chan. Never, never have I seen such beauty. The face of an angel, framed by long hair gleaming like jade. Eyes like beautiful black diamonds under such delicately curved eyebrows. A small nose, lightly curved, lips full and velvety. The delicious dimples on her cheeks..."

"And then all the rest!" blurts out the driver, who is keen to continue this inventory. "That walk of a cat...that supernatural grace...The humble blouse and modest sarong—you can just imagine what's underneath..."

"Stop, Chan!" Veasna shouts suddenly.

Chan is so startled he nearly lets go of the wheel.

"What now, Elder Brother?"

Veasna has had the wind knocked out of him. His heart is pounding in his chest. "There, just for an instant, while you were talking, I turned around and saw her behind the glass, her eyes fixed on mine. I was about to speak to her, but she vanished into thin air. My God! My hair is standing on end!"

Chan bursts out laughing. "You are hallucinating, my friend. You're thinking too much about her."

"But just now I saw her as clearly as I see you, Chan. I saw her. She had a white rose behind her ear."

"Forget all about that, Elder Brother. We are arriving in Kompong Speu Province."

Outhine Bounyavong ❋ *Laos*

Outhine Bounyavong was born in 1942. One of the most prominent contemporary writers in Laos, he has enjoyed a long career as a journalist, editor, and translator. His work is customarily animated with Laotian virtues of simplicity, compassion, respect for age, and other village social mores. From 1975 to 1990 he worked at the State Publishing House in Vientiane as a book editor, translating foreign literature from Thai, English, and French. After 1990, he worked with the Ministry of Information and Culture, with responsibility for children's books and contemporary literature. He has visited the United States on two occasions: once with a delegation of Southeast Asian journalists in 1973, and again twenty years later with his wife, the textile and literary scholar Duangdeuan, when she received a research fellowship at the University of Washington. He has also taught the Lao language in Seattle, and *Mother's Beloved*, a collection from which this story is selected, began as a translation project during his Seattle residency. He lives in Vientiane.

Wrapped-Ash Delight

Translated by Bounheng Inversin and Daniel Duffy

WHEN NANG PIEW FINISHED WASHING, THE SUN HAD NOT YET set behind the mountain. Its yellow rays shone over the treetops beside the river, glittering on the rippled water flowing softly down below. She draped the well-wrung cloth over her forearm and prepared to climb back up the riverbank. Then a shiny object on the ground caught her eye. She picked it up to look at it more closely. It was heavy ... valuable—it was a silver belt!

She looked around. A few steps away, down by the river, two or three people were bathing. They weren't paying any attention to her, so she hid her find under the wet cloth and continued her walk up the slope toward home, her heart thumping unsteadily. She hadn't decided yet whether she should go looking for the rightful owner of the belt or keep it for herself. However, her first reaction was to get away from that area by the river as quickly as possible before anybody saw her there.

As soon as she was over the bank, she bumped into Nang Oie, who was half running and half walking to the river with a worried look.

"Have you seen my silver belt?" asked Nang Oie.

"Oh, no!" Nang Piew answered automatically, trying to keep her voice as calm as possible.

Nang Oie continued on her way to the river without any more questions, for she was in a hurry to find her lost possession.

When she arrived home, Nang Piew caressed the belt with shaky hands. She was not used to stealing or finding lost valuables. After wrapping the belt around her waist, she turned left and right in front of the mirror. She looked at her reflection in the mirror and saw an unhappy face full of worries, suspicion . . . full of questions.

"Maybe people will find out I have it," she thought first.

"There's no way they can know, because a lot of people use that place by the river for bathing. In fact, almost everybody in the village uses that spot," she assured herself, trying to regain control of her thoughts.

"Should I tell Father and Mother about it?" she wondered.

"Well, if I do, they'll probably make me return it. But I've already told Nang Oie I haven't seen it. It's not a good idea to turn my words around now."

Nang Piew racked her brain but could not come up with the right answer. On the one hand, she wanted to return the silver belt, but on the other, she wanted very much to keep it for herself. She was the daughter of a peasant couple whose life lacked a good many luxuries. If she kept the belt, she would have to wait a long time before she could wear it, as she lived in a small rural village where everybody knew everybody else. When a person borrowed something from another person, everyone in the village knew about it right away. It would take a while for everyone in the village to forget about this missing object. And when that time came, how would she explain the belt to her parents? "Where did you get that belt?" they would ask. The problem seemed to get bigger and bigger. What lies would she have to tell her parents in order to convince them?

She thought about Nang Oie, who lived farther up the street at the other end of the village. She was a young teenager and began wearing her silver belt little more than a year ago. Before that, she'd worn an ordinary belt. She had not been allowed to use the silver one for fear that she might lose it. Nang Oie's mother died when she was only ten years old. Four years later, her father remarried. It was now two years since the new wife had moved in. Nang Piew remembered well the passing of Pa Soi, Nang

Oie's mother. She died after hemorrhaging in childbirth, leaving six small children as orphans. It had been a sad time for the whole community.

As she remembered this period of sorrow, Nang Piew wanted to return the belt. But another thought prevented her from doing so: Nobody knew. Nobody had seen her with the belt, so it didn't matter if she decided to keep it. If there was a problem later, she could always sell the belt at a jewelry store in town. However, her conscience kept reminding her that failing to return other people's belongings isn't right. It is a sin. She hid the belt in a secure place and left the room. She looked left and right with the worried thought that Nang Oie might have followed her home.

On that same evening, the *kuan bahn*, the village headman, called a meeting at his house. Those who had gone bathing before sunset at that particular area by the river were asked to attend. Loong Pong's family, whose house was located by the riverbank, had witnessed a number of people bathing at the time. Among them were Nang Piew and four or five elders of the village. The *kuan bahn* and the senior members explained the situation, then admonished whoever had found the belt to return it to its rightful owner. There was a heated discussion. When it was over, nobody had admitted to the crime.

The *kuan bahn* was compelled to come up with another strategy. He told everyone involved to wrap ashes in a package of banana leaves. Everyone should bring his or her package the following evening to the *kuan bahn*'s house. This would give the culprit time to reconsider his or her mistake.

On the way home, Nang Piew tried to keep her behavior as normal as possible, but the harder she tried, the more abnormal she became. It seemed to her that many eyes followed her wherever she went. If she coughed, the cough sounded unusual. When she smiled, the expression seemed dry and empty. When she spoke, her speech seemed insincere.

Her heart was heavy. She was not very happy. She was constantly afraid that people were going to come and search her house for the belt. The following day, while she was sitting inside, deep in thought about the silver belt and wondering what to do with it, she heard Nang Oie's voice at the gate.

"Hello! Anybody home?" Nang Oie called.

Nang Piew was startled. She moved closer to the wall and, peeping through a hole, saw Nang Oie enter the yard. Suddenly Nang Piew's mother, who was busy dyeing cloth in the back, called out to Nang Oie, "I'm over here!"

"Oh, I thought nobody was home because it was so quiet. My mother asked me to come and borrow a ladder from you, Auntie, to collect betel leaves. She plans to visit relatives and would like to take some betel as a gift."

"Go right ahead. The ladder is stored on the side of the barn. By the way, Oie, has your belt been found yet?"

"No, Auntie. I'm afraid it's lost forever. Mother is very cross with me. She thinks that I'm irresponsible."

Up in the house, Nang Piew listened quietly. When she was sure that Nang Oie was not there to inquire about the belt, she felt a little relieved and went down to meet her in the yard.

"Where's your mother going, Oie?" asked Nang Piew, trying to keep her voice as calm and friendly as possible.

"She said she was going to Bahn Lak Sao to ask a relative for some help in finding a soothsayer who can tell us the whereabouts of my belt. She may leave tomorrow or the day after."

Upon hearing this, Nang Piew felt more worried and, in quite a hurry, guided Nang Oie to the barn where the ladder was kept. She helped Nang Oie by carrying the other end of the ladder and walking behind her.

"So you haven't found the belt yet?" asked Nang Piew.

"No, Piew. I've looked everywhere. Oh, I miss it so much."

"Maybe it fell in the river." Nang Piew tried to deflect Nang Oie's belief that someone had really taken it.

"No, I don't think so. I searched through the water all over that area and I haven't found it."

The two arrived at the front gate. Nang Piew released her end of the ladder and let Nang Oie carry it home by herself, as it was not very heavy.

After dinner that evening, there was another gathering at the *kuan bahn*'s house. The crowd that gathered this time was bigger than usual. People came to watch, to witness the event. The people who were supposed to bring ashes each walked to an empty room with his or her package inside a covered basket. This way, nobody knew which package belonged to whom. Each person left his or her package in the room, then came out to sit and wait with the rest of the crowd. Nang Piew put her ash package among the others. Each package, wrapped in banana leaves, contained ashes and chili, symbols of fiery pain for those who steal. After the last package had been carried in, the *kuan bahn* brought them all outside and placed them in front of the crowd. This was the very moment everyone had been waiting for: the opening of the packages.

An elder had the honor of opening the packages. He unwrapped each one carefully and calmly. First, he pulled out the stick that held the package together, then he opened the banana wrapper, and at last he stirred the ash slowly with a stick. The crowd held its breath in mingled anxiety and anticipation. The first package contained only ash and chili, and the second was exactly the same. Starting with the third one, the elder stirred the ashes only two or three times. He didn't need to poke through it too much because the belt was a big object. As soon as the package was opened, one could easily see whether or not it was there, unlike a ring or an earring, which would require a thorough search.

The unwrapping of the packages captured the interest of the crowd. Everybody watched attentively. No one spoke, or even blinked an eye. It was like uncovering a pot of gold that had just been dug out of the earth. The opening of packages continued steadily through fifteen packages but the object in question did not appear. Many people thought this all might indeed prove to be a waste of time. The sixteenth, seventeenth, and eighteenth packages were the same. The elder felt a little discouraged, but he was obliged to go on with the job. When he pulled out the stick that held the nineteenth package and opened the leaves, a big pile of ash came tumbling down to reveal a shiny object. Everyone cheered with delight. There were screams of happiness from those who had come to witness the event as well as from those who had brought the ash, including the one who had returned the belt, whom no one could name. The loudest scream of all was from Nang Oie, the owner of the belt, who was choked with happiness. The noisy commotion symbolized the love, solidarity, sincerity, and brotherhood that had been shared by all in this village from many generations.

The opening of the packages ended with the nineteenth. Although five remained, no one felt it was necessary to continue.

Niaz Zaman ❁ *Bangladesh*

Niaz Zaman is professor of English at the University of Dhaka. She has also taught at George Washington University, where she earned her PhD, and from 1981–1983 served as Educational Attaché at the Bangladesh Embassy in Washington, D.C. She has also published articles and books on women's folk art. Among her major publications are *The Art of Kantha Embroidery*, the first book-length study of the *kantha*; *The Confessional Art of Tennessee Williams*; and *A Divided Legacy: The Partition in Selected Novels of India, Pakistan and Bangladesh*, which won a National Archives Award. As a creative writer, she has published an autobiographical novel, *The Crooked Neem Tree*; *The Dance and Other Stories*, the titular story of which won an *Asiaweek* Short Story Award; and *Didima's Necklace and Other Stories*.

The Dance

Last year had been a bad one for Padmapukur, as it was for the rest of the country. The rains had neither fallen in time nor in plenty and the grain fields had only produced half their normal yield. The mango crop had been bad, the fish catch poor. This year foreboded even worse. There had been no rains at the end of Magh. The first of the Bengali new year had not been ushered in by the usual thunderstorm. It was Ashar now. The days should have been one long gray drizzle, but the sky was a brilliant azure instead. And when the wind blew, it whirled up a hot, dry dust. The fields were parched, brown stubble on rock-hard soil. The shallow ponds had long since dried up and the lotus blossoms, after which the village had been named, had withered and forgotten to bloom.

People had forgotten their God, the bearded *maulanas* said. They had stopped praying and fasting. They were allowing their daughters to go to school, delay marriage till long after puberty. They were encouraging them to go without veils, permitting them to sing and dance. Even now, when God's wrath was upon them, they were encouraging them to sing and dance in Barshabaran festivities. Unless people reformed, the drought would not be over. People must pray for forgiveness if Padmapukur were to be saved from this manifestation of God's anger. There must be special prayers for rain, for God's mercy.

A rickshaw was hired and for several days it went around with a loud-speaker. The time and date of the special prayers were announced. But Padmapukur also had its share of other religions and, not to be outdone in case rain actually fell after prayers led by the white-bearded *imam*, the shaven priests with caste marks on their foreheads also declared special prayers for rain. Coincidentally or otherwise, the prayers took place almost simultaneously. But no rain fell.

Then someone suggested—no one was sure who made the suggestion—that perhaps a frog marriage would help bring rain clouds. No frogs were, however, to be seen, and the exporters of frog legs were blamed for the drought. Unless there are frogs, someone said, there will be no rain. There were a few halfhearted attempts at taking out processions, at marching to the capital to demand a ban on the export of frogs. But it was very hot under the cloudless sky and the idea was soon dropped.

Children were let out from school to hunt for frogs. Several days later, two frogs were found and preparations were made for the frog marriage. The children went around chanting songs and collecting *chanda* for the marriage feast. The frog wedding was celebrated with due ceremony, with children dancing to rain songs. But despite everything, the skies remained as brilliantly blue and cloudless as before.

Nazimuddin was worried. He remembered the great famine, when people had fallen by the roadside and only dogs and crows had fattened. If the rains did not come soon, people would start to die. But when Habib Miah told him about Kakima's idea, he laughed scornfully. Weren't all the village girls singing and dancing "*Allah megh de, pani de, chhaya du tui...?*" God, give us the rain clouds, give us the rain, give us the coolness of shade.

Habib Miah was silent for some time but he was desperate. Last year's paddy would not see him through another year. Kakima was old, he muttered, perhaps she was mad, but suppose a girl dancing in the field truly did bring rain?

When Karim Moral heard the idea from Rashid Miah, he wondered what the *moulvis* would say. It smacked of a paganism they had converted from centuries ago.

There would be no harm to try, Rashid Miah mumbled. All the men would remain indoors. The girl would disrobe in the field. If it worked,

Padmapukur would be saved from drought and famine. Perhaps the whole country would be saved.

"It is foolish," Karim whispered to Rashid Miah, "it is sacrilege."

That night Karim could not sleep. The village depended on him. The villagers came to him with their disputes, with their problems. Sometimes they grumbled, but he was fair and just, and they respected him and obeyed his advice. Suppose the rains did come after such a dance—would anyone criticize him for allowing it to take place? And if the rains did not come, would anyone laugh? They would be too busy dying to care. He groaned. His wife sat up. "What is the matter," she asked him. Karim told her.

"We have also been discussing it," Karim's wife whispered in the dark.

"Should we allow such a dance to take place, Mother of Salim?" Karim asked.

"It may come to nothing," his wife said "but suppose it works . . ."

"It is a special dance," Karim said. "It is said few know it."

"Kakima would know it," the woman muttered. "But you must see to it that no man ventures forth the night of the dance."

"I shall announce it by drum," Karim told her, "and no man shall venture forth that night."

"It must be a dark night when the moon rises late," Karim's wife said. "Next Thursday will be the full moon."

"It shall be done then," Karim muttered. "But who will dance such a dance?"

"Many girls in the village dance nowadays. It can be any one of them who is willing," the woman said.

But Kakima told them that the girl with the longest, blackest hair must be chosen. The rain clouds must dance on earth before the rain clouds will dance in the sky. She must be young, and her skin must be smooth and unblemished. Her breasts must be ripe and her hips ready. Not a virgin, she said, and not a mother. And her hair must be like the rain clouds in the sky.

Bela's hair was the longest and darkest. Married two months only, she was not a virgin and not a mother. But Karim did not want his daughter dancing in the fields under the night sky.

"She is as much my daughter as yours," Bela's mother told him. "No one shall see her. Every woman will keep her man at home, every mother her son. For the sake of Padmapukur you must agree. For the sake of Tota, your first grandson who will die if his mother's milk fails."

Bela's husband was angry. A graduate from the university, he scorned the whole idea. It was folly, he said.

Bela laughed and tossed her head. The thought of dancing excited her. She had been the best dancer at school and her feet twitched when she heard music. But married women did not dance, at least decent Muslim women did not.

"How can you even think of dancing?" Shamsuddin asked her. "Everyone will know you are dancing there without anything on."

Bela cast her eyes down. Even her husband had not seen her without some covering on her body. At night it had always been dark. She had only felt him, as he had her. Neither of them had seen the body of the other.

"One hears of Hindu temples and the prostitutes dancing there. To think that an educated girl like you, one who has done her Matric, should even think of performing such a dance! If only I could get a job in the city, I should leave my job in this school and go away from all these foolish, superstitious people."

"But you have not got a job in the city and if the rains don't come soon, it will not matter whether you get a job in town or not," Bela retorted.

"Do you believe that your dancing will bring rain?" the husband asked.

"No," Bela said, "I do not believe. But suppose it does work. Would it not be foolish not to try?"

The bearded elders shook their heads when they heard, but they looked at their parched fields and withering cows and were silent.

Bela went to Manik Babu, who had taught her dancing when she was at school. She had not danced for a long time, but when Manik Babu touched the *tabla*, Bela felt the rhythm flow through her body and become part of her. Her feet glided in and out of the intricate patterns, her arms swayed. It was as if Bela had never stopped dancing.

Then Bela went to Kakima. She did not always understand what the old woman said. Her mind wandered, as that of old people often did, and she talked of people Bela did not know, of things Bela did not understand.

"Does such a dance really work, Kakima?" Bela asked. "Have you ever known anyone performing such a dance and bringing rain?"

"When I was young," Kakima told her, "my hair was long and dark but not as long and dark as yours. Lakshmi's was longer and darker but they would not let her dance. But you must dance, my child, until the music stops."

"But there will be no music, Kakima. No one will be out there in the fields when I go to dance."

"There is always music," Kakima said, "for those who hear." And the old woman fell asleep where she sat.

It would be difficult to keep the young men at home, so Habib Miah suggested a *jatra* with the elders of the village sitting on the outside edge of the crowd.

The young men were disappointed. It would have been fun to watch Bela dance. Even through the sari they had seen the movement of her limbs and felt a fire in their veins. But Bela was also Karim's daughter and they all belonged to the village. So though they were disappointed, they all knew that they would stay till early morning watching the story of Rupban, which they knew almost by heart.

On the night of the full moon, the people gathered at the school yard where the *jatra* stage was set up. Karim moved around, and everyone knew that he was seeing to it that no man was missing.

The women were not in the school yard. They would escort Bela to the fields, then come back to await the return of their men from the *jatra*.

It was dark when the women set forth from their huts. As they walked down the narrow path leading to the fields, they sang and the hurricane lanterns in their hands swayed and bobbed in time to their steps. In the dark Bela's red sari appeared black and her loose hair, flung out behind her, looked like gathering rain clouds.

The stars shone in the night sky as pitilessly as the sun had shone by day. Except for the lights the women carried, there were no other lights twinkling as far as the eye could see. Tonight, no villager would stray on to the fields.

"Are you afraid, Bela?" the woman next to her whispered. Bela shook her head. "No. Strangely enough, I am not afraid tonight."

"*Jinns* attack women with open hair at night," Runu said.

"No," Bela said "*Jinns* do not frighten me tonight."

"We shall be far away," Putul said. "If anything should happen, we would not hear you."

"All the men are at the *jatra*. And it will go on long after I return. Baba will see to it that no one leaves until the moon rises. There is plenty of time for me to dance and wear my clothes before that happens. Why should I be afraid?"

When the women left her at the edge of the field, Bela put down her *kalsi* of water carefully. She watched the line of lights bobbing slowly away from her. When the last light disappeared amid the trees and the huts, Bela unwrapped her sari in the dark. Slowly she folded it and laid it carefully on the dried grass. She slipped out of her blouse and petticoat and placed them one by one on the sari.

Then, picking up the *kalsi*, she stepped on to the field. The ground was hard stone that hurt her feet, the stubble were thorns that pierced them. Bela dipped her fingers into the *kalsi* and scattered the precious drops on to the parched earth. Again and again she dipped her fingers into the water and the reluctant water drops soaked into the thirsty earth. When the water was finished, Bela set the *kalsi* down and took a few tentative dance steps.

How can I dance to no music? she thought. She tried to remember the rhythm Manik Babu had played and it was easier to dance then, listening to the hidden music in her mind. As her steps quickened, the music seemed to grow until her ears told her that she could hear it.

It appeared to spring from the dark, star-spattered sky, from the dry stubble below her feet, from the black trees beyond the horizon.

It was a music she had never heard before, yet it was all the music that had ever played. It grew louder and Bela's feet moved faster, keeping pace with it. Her body whirled as the dust whirls before an April storm. Her black hair flung out behind like swift rain clouds driving before a hurricane. Her body glistened as she danced and the drops soaked into the parched earth. Her heart beat in a frenzy she had never known.

Then Bela heard the drums roll. There was a crash, as of thunder. She put her hands to her ears, afraid. The music stopped and her steps faltered.

At first she thought that it was the moon rising, but as her eyes focused in the dark, she saw that it was not a light at all. She gave a cry and tried to hide behind the veil of her hair.

The man stood on the edge of the field. A light seemed to play on his limbs, golden on his gold. A white garment was flung carelessly across his body.

Bela knew him to be a stranger, because Padmapukur was a small village and everyone knew everyone else. Gradually the trembling of her limbs stopped, her hands dropped to the side.

"Who are you?" she asked. "Where do you come from that you stray on to the fields tonight? "

The stranger smiled and in his smile she saw her husband. But when she looked again, she realized that he did not resemble Shamsuddin in the least.

"I come from far away," the stranger replied. "Why were you dancing alone in the fields?"

She was shamed before him. "We are fools in the village," she said. "But the lands are dry, the people desperate. Someone said that if a girl dances in the fields for rain...."

"The Rain God answers," the stranger said. He held out his hand to her. "Come."

Her shame left her. He was not mocking her. He was not laughing. She went to him and wondered why she did so. Everything was strange tonight, she thought, like a dream. She thought of her husband and remembered how he felt against her.

The stranger's garment fell from him and she cried out for wonder. He was so beautiful. More beautiful than any man she had seen. His face was the color of the warming sun, his limbs the color of ripening padi.

He was all the strength and vitality she had known, all the vibrant pulsations she had felt in her husband's arms. She opened unto him as the lotus opens unto the sun, and his heat and life were consumed in the soft moistness of her being. It was a consummation such as she had never known.

Her eyes were limpid pools in the dark softness of her face; his were blazing lights.

"What is your name?" she asked. "At least tell me that."

"I have many names," he said. "Some call me Prem. Some Suraj."

Much later she slept, and when she awoke he was gone. She felt a strange emptiness that he should have left. She felt no guilt, only fullness and fulfillment that made her limbs sweetly heavy. She lay on the earth, smooth and soft now, ripe for tilling, for sowing the tender seeds.

As she lay there a gentle breeze uplifted one strand of hair and blew it across her face. Bela opened her eyes and looked up at the sky. She gave a cry—the stars could no longer be seen. A flash of lightning lit up the landscape and she saw the first raindrop splash into her *kalsi*.

About the Editor

TREVOR CAROLAN WAS BORN IN YORKSHIRE, ENGLAND. His family emigrated to British Columbia and he was educated there and in California. His publications have been translated into five languages and include *Return to Stillness: Twenty Years with a Tai Chi Master*, *The Pillow Book of Dr. Jazz*, the acclaimed anthology *The Colors of Heaven: Stories from the Pacific Rim*, and co-translations of several modern Taoist classics. He holds an interdisciplinary Ph.D. from Bond University in Queensland, Australia. A longtime activist on behalf of human rights and Pacific coast watershed issues, he has also served as an elected municipal councilor and political columnist in North Vancouver, Canada. He teaches English at the University of the Fraser Valley.

About the Translators

JOHN BALCOM lives and works in Monterey, California. He received his Ph.D. in Chinese and comparative literature at Washington University in St. Louis.

YINGTSIH BALCOM received her B.A. in English and American literature from Cheng Kung University in 1976.

ALLAN H. BARR was born in Montreal and grew up in Britain, visiting China for the first time as a British Council exchange student in 1977-78. His translation of Yu Hua's debut novel *Cries in the Drizzle* was published by Anchor in 2007, and he has also translated a collection of short stories by Yu Hua, from which "Their Son" is drawn. He is Professor of Chinese at Pomona College in Claremont, California.

KATHERINE A. BOWIE is Professor of Anthropology at the University of Wisconsin–Madison, where she is affiliated with the Center for Southeast Asian Studies. She first traveled to Thailand in 1974 and received her Ph.D. in Anthropology from the University of Chicago in 1988. In 1996 she was a Fulbright Visiting Scholar at Khon Kaen University, Thailand.

VICKY J. BOWMAN served as the British ambassador to the Union of Burma. She lives in London.

VERN CORK was born in Sydney, Australia, in 1946 and trained as a teacher and librarian. He began visiting Bali in the early 1970s and has since published *Stories from the Morning of the World*, a collection of Balinese folktales, and translated *The Bali Arts Festival Album*.

TREVOR CAROLAN is co-translator from the Chinese of *The Book of the Heart* and *The Supreme Way*. On behalf of PEN International and the Buddhist Peace Fellowship, he has co-translated such writers of conscience as Thich Tue Sy from Vietnam and Kim Chi-ha from Korea.

241

DANIEL DUFFY was born in New Haven, Connecticut, in 1960. He has been an avid promoter of Vietnamese literature in the United States for two decades. He worked as a literary editor under critic Harold Bloom, and later, with the distinguished scholar Huynh Sanh Thong, helped revive the *Viet Nam Forum* at the Yale Council on Southeast Asia Studies. In the mid-1990s he worked at Thế Giới Publishing House in Hanoi. For his labors of conscience on behalf of Vietnamese writers he was banned for life from Vietnam.

MARIE-CHRISTINE GARNEAU is a professor of French language and literature at the University of Hawai'i, Mānoa.

THEO GARNEAU has a master's degree in French literature from the University of Hawai'i at Mānoa and is a master's degree candidate in English.

BOUNHENG INVERSIN has served as President of the Lao American Women Association (LAWA) in Maryland, and as Board Member with the International Buddhist Committee in Washington, D.C.

KWANGSHIK JANE KWON was born in Korea's Kyungsang-namdo province in 1957. After completing her initial education in Seoul, she emigrated to Vancouver in 1976. She has worked as a legal translator and diplomatic interpreter, and served with visiting delegations of Asian Government officials concerned with environmental exchange research. She is married to Canadian author Trevor Carolan; their translations of Korean poet Kim Chi-ha have been widely published.

YOUNG-JUN LEE received a B.A. from Yonsei University, as well as an M.A. and Ph.D. from Harvard University in modern Korean literature. He has taught at the University of California, Berkeley, and Harvard University.

KATE MCCANDLESS was born in New Jersey and emigrated to Nova Scotia in the 1970s. She studied Japanese in Tokyo and for several years worked as an editor/translator with the distinguished publishing firm Kodansha. An ordained Zen priest in the Soto Zen tradition, she is married and lives in Mission, British Columbia.

RALPH MCCARTHY is the translator of novelists Dazai Osamu and Murakami Ryu, among others. He lives in Southern California.

CHRISTOPHE MACQUET is a translator, teacher, and researcher. He was born in 1968 in Boulogne-sur-Mer, France. He received an M.A. in literature and taught French for two years in the Philippines. He has taught literature and translation at the Royal University of Phnom Penh, where he served as head of the French translation program. Currently he lives in Argentina.

JENNY PUTIN is a professor of Chinese language and literature in Britain. She has served as Secretary for the British Association of Chinese Studies. Her translations of Hong Ying have appeared in *A Lipstick Called Red Pepper: Fiction about Gay and Lesbian Love in China.*

PETER ZINOMAN teaches Southeast Asian history at the University of California, Berkeley. He is a former Resident Director of the Council on International Educational Exchange's Study Center in Hanoi. His translations have been published in *Grand Street*, *Vietnam Generation*, *Vietnam Forum*, and the anthologies *Night Again*, *The Other Side of Heaven*, and *Vietnam, A Traveler's Literary Companion.*

Credits

(continued from p. iv)

Gilda Cordero-Fernando, "Bushouse," copyright Gilda Cordero-Fernando. Revised edition copyright 2003, Trevor Carolan. Reprinted by permission of Gilda Cordero-Fernando, 2008.

Mulaika Hijjas, "Confinement," copyright 1999 by Mulaika Hijjas. Originally published in *Mānoa* 11:1, Honolulu, 1999. Reprinted by permission of the author.

Pham Thi Hoai, "Nine Down Makes Ten," copyright 1993 by Pham Thi Hoai. Translation copyright 1994 by Peter Zinoman. Reprinted from *Grand Street* 43, *in Night, Again* by permission of Seven Stories Press, 2008.

Nyi Pu Lay, "The Python," copyright 1988. Translation copyright 1993 by Vicky J. Bowman. Originally published in *Tha-ya*, Rangoon. Reprinted by permission of the author and translator, 2008, from *Inked Over, Ripped Out*, ed. Anna J. Allot. PEN America Center, 1993.

Ku Ling, "Lord Beile," copyright 1991. Translation copyright 1999 by John and Yingtsih Balcom. First published in *Renditions* Nos 35 & 36 (1991), pp. 121–129. Reprinted by permission of the Research Centre for Translation, The Chinese University of Hong Kong.

K. S. Maniam, "Arriving," copyright 1995. Originally published in *Arriving and Other Stories*, Times Publishing, Singapore. Reprinted by permission of the author, 2008.

Yun Dae Nyeong, "The Silver Trout Fishing Network." Translation copyright by Young-Jun Lee, 2007. Originally published in *Azalea* Vol. One, 2008. Reprinted by permission of the Korea Institute, Harvard University, 2008.

Shogo Oketani, "A Day and A Half of Freedom," copyright 2008 by Shogo Oketani. Translation copyright 2008 by Ralph McCarthy. Reprinted by permission of *Kyoto Journal* and the translator.

Alfian Bin Sa'at, "Pillow," copyright 1998, Alfian Bin Sa'at. Originally published in *Corridors and Other Stories*. Raffles SNP, Singapore, 1999. Reprinted by permission of Alfian Bin Sa'at, 2008.

Samruan Singh, "The Necklace," copyright 1978. Reprinted from *Voices from the Thai Countryside*, by Samruan Singh (translated by Katherine Bowie) by permission of the Center for Southeast Asian Studies, University of Wisconsin–Madison, 2008.

Putu Oka Sukanta, "Storm Clouds over the Island of Paradise," copyright 1978. Translation copyright 1996, by Vern Cork. Originally published in *Bali Behind the Screen*, Daruma Press, Darlington, NSW, 1996. Reprinted by permission of the author.

Seiko Tanabe, "The Innocent," copyright Seiko Tanabe. Translation copyright by Kate McCandless, 2003. Originally published in *Sekenshirazu*, Kodansha, Tokyo, 1982. Reprinted by permission of Seiko Tanabe, 2008.

Marianne Villanueva, "Lizard," copyright 1991. Originally published in *Ginseng and Other Tales from Manila*, Ateneo de Manila University. Reprinted by permission of the author.

Xu Xi, "Until the Next Century," copyright 2001 by Xu Xi, a.k.a. S. Komala. Originally published in *Carve* journal, 2000; and in *History's Fiction*, Chameleon Press Ltd., Hong Kong. Reprinted by permission of Xu Xi, a.k.a. S. Komala, 2008.

Hong Ying, "The Snuff Bottle," copyright 1999 by Hong Ying. Translation copyright 1999, Jenny Putin. Originally published in *A Lipstick Called Red Pepper*: *Fiction about Gay and Lesbian Love in China*, Bochum: Ruhr-University Press, Germany, 1999. Reprinted by permission of Hong Ying, 2008.